# PHOENIX GREY AND THE BLOOD FARM

GREY SISTERS SAGA

BOOK TWO

## CRISTINE COURCY

SMASHED HOUSE PUBLISHING LLC

*For Scarlette, who gave me courage.*
*For Brianna, who gave me faith.*
*And for Grace, who gave me everything else.*

# CONTENTS

# BASKET CASE

He was screaming.

My eyes flew open.

I ripped off my sheets and nearly toppled out of bed as I scrambled to get to him.

"Cole! COLE!"

I grabbed his shoulders and shook him free from the nightmare.

Cole St. Claire's dark eyes popped open, wild and terrified. He sat up. My hands gripped his arms. His breathing was labored as he blinked several times.

"You're okay." I panted. My heart knocked against my chest. "It was just a dream."

Cole stared at the door of the motel room, refusing to look at me.

"You want to talk about it?" I studied his face as it settled into the stony, stoic expression he'd developed ever since we'd left home. I hated that face. My hands fell away from him.

"I need to get some air," Cole mumbled.

"That's it then?" I frowned. "You're leaving, just like that?"

Cole got out of bed and was halfway to the door before I grabbed him and held him fast.

"You've been having nightmares since we left Nile. You need to talk to me, Cole...I can help you."

Cole looked at me coolly. "No, you can't."

And then he was gone.

I forced myself to stand, rooted to the spot on the old, moldy carpet. I wouldn't go chasing after him. If he wanted to leave, let him. Everybody left eventually...I was used to it. My eyes burned. I shoved the heel of my hand into my eyes and pushed the tears back where they came from. With a shaky scoff, I glanced around the room. I might as well start packing.

We'd been on the road looking for signs of the demon that'd killed Logan DeVarney's older brother, Traven, for weeks. That's where he was now, with my twin sister, Seraphina...out looking for demon signs. So far, we'd come up with nothing. Logan had assumed as much. Before his brother was murdered, they'd been hunting this demon for the better part of a decade. It was apparently impossible to find...unless it wanted to be found. After all this disappointment and dealing with Cole, I was getting restless and depressed, two things that didn't suit my personality at all. I stuffed a few shirts into my duffel bag as Mama's familiar, a black cat named Icarus, rubbed against my legs.

The door lock clicked open. I turned, ready to start arguing with Cole, but it was only Logan.

"You lose my sister?" I shoved more clothes in the bag.

Logan dropped his ruck onto the tiny motel table and moved to the coffee machine and fired it up. "A bit early for packing, isn't it? You should get some sleep."

I grunted and continued to fill my bag.

"Wouldn't magic make that easier?"

I glared at him. "Right. The last thing I need is Phin to come in here and get all bent out of shape about *that*."

Logan shrugged, conceding my point. "She's a witch without magic. It's hard for her."

Duh. I nodded sarcastically, as though he hadn't just stated the obvious. "Which is why I avoid using my magic in front of her."

He leaned against the kitchenette counter with his mug in his hand. He sipped slowly as he watched me. "Phoenix...it's four in the morning...you really should get some sleep."

"I'll be fine."

"If you say so—coffee, then?"

"Sure."

Logan poured me a cup and passed it to me. "You want to talk about it?"

"Nope." I took a deep drink from the mug. It burned my throat all the way down, but the taste was worse than the pain. I made a face.

Logan laughed. "Seraphina likes it black...I take it you prefer—"

"Sugar." I stuck out my tongue like a cat with a hairball. "Lots of sugar."

I went to the kitchenette and ripped open sugar packet after sugar packet, dumping them all into the coffee, one by one. "Where are we headed next?"

Logan sighed heavily, as though the question had been weighing on his mind. "I was thinking we could head to Syracuse. It's toward the middle of the state...there have been a few possible signs in the area."

I glanced over my mug at Logan.

"What?" He furrowed his brow, and his mouth formed an apprehensive line.

"Do you think we should try to find a case to solve instead? Hunt a monster—save somebody? I mean, the demon is so powerful, it isn't going to be found unless it wants us to find it...you said as much yourself when we left Nile..."

Logan sighed again. He rubbed the back of his neck and

scowled at the dirty carpet. "I'll think about it, Phoenix. I just—can't *stop* thinking about it. You know? I mean...if you were in my position, wouldn't you feel obligated to keep going?"

I chewed the inside of my cheek. No question. "Yes. I would. But then I'd think about all the people who still needed help. My sister wouldn't want me to ignore them all just to get her some payback. And from what I know of Traven, he wouldn't want you to, either."

Logan glanced sideways (and down) at me. I barely came up to his chin. After a moment, he gave me a curt nod. "Fine. Give me Syracuse and then we'll get you out on your first—well, your first *official* hunt."

My face split into a wide grin. I clapped him hard on the back. His coffee sloshed.

"You're all right, DeVarney. You're all right."

The drive down to Upstate New York was a long one. It was similar to Vermont in the wide-open spaces and rolling mountains...but everything seemed bigger and wider and longer in New York. By lunch time, our stomachs were growling, and I convinced Logan we should stop for food.

Cole turned his van into the first diner we found, which was a cute little place right off the highway called Fat Kat's. I got out, followed by Icarus, who bounded off into the woods behind the diner in search of mice. Logan and Seraphina pulled up beside us in his truck.

We all headed inside and grabbed a booth. The place was relatively packed for its remote location. It must've been a local favorite, like the ferry dock diner back home. I snatched up the nearest menu and began to scan the breakfast entrees.

Seraphina sat quietly. Probably because she was just going to order toast or something equally depressing. I, on the other hand, saw no reason not to fill up while we had the chance. I smiled as I read the description of the "Green Mountain Boys' Breakfast Platter."

I felt Logan's eyes on me and glared across the table at him. "Yes?"

Logan snickered. "Nothing...it's just—" He licked his lips as he struggled to contain his grin. "You're going to get the Mountain Boy thing, aren't you?"

My cheeks burned. "*No.*" Not anymore...

Logan grinned.

I hated his stupid face sometimes. Of course, I had to be nice to him, considering his brother was murdered by a demon and all... but sometimes...I wanted nothing more than to hex his—

"What can I get for you?" The waitress held her notepad out at the ready as her eyes moved over us.

I smiled sweetly at her, but Logan spoke up before I could. He pointed at Seraphina, who was absentmindedly running her fingers through her long, blonde hair. "Black coffee and toast for the blonde and myself, and—" Logan nodded toward me with a smirk. "A Mountain Boys' Breakfast for the box-dyed redhead."

I stuck my tongue out at him. He'd been making fun of my hair since I went from black with orange tips to black with chunky, cherry-red streaks.

"Cole?" Logan prompted, still smirking at me.

I gritted my teeth and began to shred a napkin in my lap as Cole asked for water. The waitress nodded and left the table.

"That's all you want?" I demanded, the napkin crushed in my hand.

Cole shrugged. Then he stared pointedly out the window. I scoffed and opened my mouth to argue, but Seraphina pinched my arm underneath the table.

I let out a yelp. I turned to snap at her, but before I could, she grabbed my arm and tugged me out of the booth. "We'll be right back." She smiled sweetly at the boys. "Bathroom."

She shoved me in front of her, and we headed toward the back of the diner, me stomping all the way. Then she pulled me to a stop in front of the bathroom door, just out of sight.

"What?" I hissed.

Seraphina's face was kind and patient as I scowled up at her. Out of all the differences between us, our height difference was the most irritating. Having her tower over me during every emotional argument and heated discussion made everything more maddening.

She gave me a rueful smile. "You need to give Cole his space."

I blinked, my amber eyes incredulous. "His *space*? All he's had since Bird Island is space! He needs to—"

"He *will*, Phoenix." Phin placed her hands gingerly on my shoulders, her silver eyes sharp and serious. "He will. You just need to give him time—and space. Okay?"

I scowled and looked away. My eyes landed on the bulletin board beside the bathroom. My expression softened at the sight of a homemade missing child poster. I nudged out from under Phin's hands and nodded toward the picture.

Seraphina glanced at the poster. She let out a small gasp.

I stood so close to the poster I was almost nose to nose with the photo.

"For a second, I could've sworn it was—"

"Fawn," we murmured together.

It wasn't.

But with the little girl's mischievous smile, her light hair, warm like swirling honey, and the golden-brown hue in her round, hooded eyes, it was just familiar enough to cause a jolt to the heart.

My eyes moved over the description.

"Come on." Seraphina tapped her hand on my shoulder. Her eyes still lingered on the poster. "Your mountain of food thing just came out."

I nodded absently, making a mental note to light a candle for the little girl tonight.

·  ·  ·

Syracuse was a bust. The potential demonic possession Logan had read about was just a mentally unstable man with domestic issues. Logan was disappointed, but he hid it well. One thing to be said about Logan: He didn't brood like some people. I glared at Cole as he pulled the van into the mall parking garage. Nope. Logan was stoic, keeping his emotions in check, unlike *some people* who continued to mope around despite having every reason in the world to be happy. I eyed Cole as he shut off the van and pocketed his keys.

Cole sighed. Then he glanced at me out of the corner of his eye. "Say it."

I shrugged. "Say what?"

Cole leaned on the steering wheel and turned in his seat to face me. "Nix, I can *feel* the frustration radiating off you. It's like you've got Cyclops's laser eyes and they're burning into the side of my head. So, why don't you just spit it out?"

I pursed my lips in a disapproving pout. Fine. "You've got to stop feeling sorry for yourself. It's annoying the hex out of me."

Cole ran a hand through his thick black hair. "I'm not feeling sorry for myself." He looked at me with his dark, soulful eyes. "I'm just feeling *sorry*. I can't forget what I did to you in that church—"

"You didn't do anything—" I snapped, my amber eyes flashing. "We've been over this a billion times now. It wasn't *you*. It was the demon."

Cole scoffed. He shook his head and rolled his eyes. "God, Nix, can't you ever just listen for once? It's not that simple to me."

"So—what? You're just going to be mopey and depressed for the rest of your life?"

"Phoenix—"

"No, Cole. God." I scrunched up my face. "You gotta get over it."

Cole recoiled as though I'd slapped him. "Get over it?"

I shrugged. "Yeah. It happened. It's done. It's over. You can't do anything about it. All you can do now is look forward. But you're not. You're wallowing in the worst moment of our lives. Do you *like* being there?"

Cole's eyes narrowed. "Do I like—"

"No?" I demanded sharply. "Okay...great. Then pull yourself the hex out of there!" I kicked open the van door and slammed it shut.

Logan and Phin had parked the truck beside us. As soon as they saw me get out of the van, they followed suit, jumping down from the truck. I marched past and kept walking along the line of cars.

"Phoenix!" Seraphina called from behind.

I held up a hand. "I need a minute!"

I stalked all the way to the edge of the parking garage and leaned over the railing. The cold November wind ruffled my hair and pushed against my hoodie. I shivered.

After a moment, Seraphina's warm hand rested on my shoulder. "Hey—"

"I know, I know." My eyes burned. "He needs space."

Her hand tightened in a reassuring squeeze. "It's hard. I get it. But it'll get better. You just need to dig deep for some patience, Phoenix. I promise you, it'll get better."

I blinked. A tear slid down my cheek. Angrily, I rubbed my face into my arm. I sniffed in the cold. "Right...but what if it doesn't?"

Seraphina wrapped me in a one-armed hug. She didn't have an answer. There was no answer.

"Hey—" Seraphina nudged me with a small smile. "Logan said this place has the best mac and cheese bacon burgers ever. He stopped here with Traven a few years ago. You wanna check it out?"

I frowned and shrugged.

Seraphina's silver eyes sparkled. "Okay—well, he *also* said that they have a specialty cupcake shop..."

I cocked an eyebrow.

She grinned. "Uh huh, see?" Seraphina squeezed me tighter as I found a smile. "Come on...cupcakes, and then burgers."

Reluctantly, I allowed her to lead me away from the edge and walk me back toward the boys. Her arm still wrapped around me, she leaned her head on mine. "I knew you'd perk up. You can't ever stay gloomy. It's one of your best qualities."

I frowned as I glanced sideways (and up) at her suspiciously. "You hate that about me."

Seraphina scoffed and shook her head. Her cheeks pinched pink.

I pursed my lips on a smirk. "You say it makes me more Labrador than witch."

Seraphina groaned and shoved off me. "Oh, whatever."

I laughed and looped my arm through hers, pulling her back into me. "I appreciate the lies. It's nice to know you care so much."

Seraphina glanced down at me from the corner of her eye. A shy smile played at the corner of her mouth. "I do, Nix. A lot."

I tried to find another smile, but all I could think about was how just a few weeks ago...she hadn't. She'd done everything she could to get away from me. I'd forgiven her. In a heartbeat. But there was still a twist in the pit of my stomach when I thought of it.

Maybe everything wasn't as okay as I wanted it to be.


Once we'd had our fill of cupcakes—or rather, *I* had had our fill of cupcakes—Seraphina jumped up, gripping the backpack strap at her shoulder. "You guys ready?"

Logan leaned back in his chair with his hands threaded behind his head. He smiled up at Seraphina, amused by her childish enthusiasm.

I had to hide my smirk behind what remained of my cheesecake cupcake. I took a big bite and spoke through my mouthful of sugar. "You know what? I spotted a cookie stand on the second floor of this place...and it was right by that vintage record store..."

Seraphina's shoulders slumped. "Okay...well, can we go after the—?"

"No, no." I shook my head, licked the sugar off my thumb, and waved a hand. "I mean, you and Logan go on ahead."

Seraphina glanced at Logan. She nibbled nervously on her lower lip. "I don't know...I thought it'd be good for us *all* to go...like team building..."

I scoffed. "We had enough team building back on Bird Island. We're good, Phin."

Logan stood quickly. He clapped a hand on Cole's back. "See you guys later."

"You two have fun..." I smiled wickedly, mischief sparkling in my eyes. "We'll meet you outside the food court in an hour?" I cocked an eyebrow at Logan. "How long does it last, Logan?"

Seraphina looked at Logan, whose tan cheeks burned burgundy. He scowled at me as he tossed his backpack over his shoulder. "Let's go, Sam."

Seraphina hesitated. "Are you sure, Phoenix?"

I grinned like a Cheshire cat. "Yup."

Seraphina gave me a small smile and bent to give Cole a hug where he sat hunched over the table. She whispered something to him just before she pulled away. He gave her a weak smile. Then, with a wave and a bounce of her blonde hair, she was gone, Logan following close by her side.

I wiggled my fingers in a cheeky wave. But my grin faded when I looked back at Cole, who stared moodily after them.

I opened my mouth to argue some more, but Cole spoke first. "Why does he call her 'Sam?'"

A sly smirk slid on my face. I glanced back at them. They were both so tall. I could still see the tops of their heads as they disappeared into the crowd. I looked back at Cole. His dark eyes found mine. A small smile teased at the corner of his mouth. My heart lightened with hope. My smirk smoothed into a bright grin. Cole hardly met my eyes anymore. Much less smiled—or sort of smiled —at me.

I leaned toward him over the table and waved him close. Cole bent his head near mine. "You can't tell Seraphina, okay? She doesn't know why, either..."

Cole's smile pressed into his left dimple. "Okay..."

"Promise?" I prompted.

Cole's smile almost crinkled his eyes. "Promise, Nix."

I swallowed thickly. My heart ached slightly at the sight of his smile. I'd missed it. So much. I cleared my throat. "I caught Logan watching this old TV show one night—I think we were back in Plattsburgh...it's about a *witch* named *Samantha*..."

Cole grinned, his forehead creased as he cocked an eyebrow. "*Bewitched*? Why would he watch—"

I snickered and shrugged, sitting back in my seat. "No idea." But I had an idea.

Cole glanced at his watch. "Okay, so we have an hour for cookies..."

I gathered my trash. "We aren't getting cookies, Cole." I stood quickly and tossed the cupcake wrappers in the garbage. Then I went back for my bag and slung it over my shoulder. The dozens of keychains smacked my sides. I looked down at Cole with a sly glint in my eyes. "There's a reason why I made you bring Jean." I nodded to his guitar.

I tugged him up by the arm and pulled him away from the table. Cole barely had time to grab his guitar case before I dragged him into the crowd. We headed to the first floor, and I pushed him down onto a bench near all the foot traffic.

"Seriously, Nix?" Cole crinkled his forehead, looking up at me from underneath his thick, dark lashes.

I crossed my arms over my chest and nodded curtly. "Listen— Logan may not feel guilty about his credit card scams, and Seraphina might be okay with burning through our trust funds to back this new 'business' of ours, but come on, Cole...I know you. You aren't." I bent, flipped open the guitar case, and handed Jean to Cole. She was a beautiful black acoustic, and aside from the van, Cole's favorite thing in the world. He had a few other guitars—more expensive and fancier, even...some he'd saved for years to buy—but she was forever his favorite.

Hesitantly, he took the guitar in his hands.

"Cole, your blue collar is showing. And you want to contribute." I spoke the words exactly as I'd rehearsed them in my head over and over throughout the entire trip to Syracuse. "To earn money honestly, so we can spend it honorably...or whatever." I gestured to Jean. "This is how."

Cole frowned thoughtfully. His broody mood had returned. It was like he'd sunk into a cloud. His whole being was tinted damp, cold, and gray. His hands gripped the guitar.

It was all nonsense. The stuff I'd said. In my opinion, anyway. Logan knew exactly how to play the system to get us anything we needed. And Phin and I had buckets in our bank accounts. Nobody cared whether Cole paid for anything. But I knew Cole would, if I brought it up. And another thing I knew: Cole needed to play. He hadn't held Jean since Bird Island—probably longer. Not since the demon had possessed him. He was a musician. He needed to play. And I thought, just maybe, it'd help him find his way back to himself.

Cole sighed and rolled his shoulders. He shook his dark hair out of his eyes. He wouldn't look at me. "Any requests?"

I scowled, my hands at my hips. "Bright Eyes," I snapped.

Cole looked up at me sharply.

I didn't flinch. He knew what song. "*Bright Eyes*," I repeated coolly.

"Fine."

Then his fingers moved.

The music started, the steady rhythm of his six string like the beat of my heart. I smiled and stepped back. I took a seat at the opposite side of the court, giving him all the space in the world.

And it was just Cole.

He played the entire forty-five minutes, everything from Bright Eyes to Johnny Cash. By the time I tapped him on the shoulder, he'd drawn a crowd, and his case was filled with crumpled dollar bills, change, and lollipops. He looked up at me with that simple smile that warmed my heart.

But then the spell was broken.

It was like the sight of me brought him peace...for a second. Then it made him remember. And his face fell, settling into that somber, sullen expression I'd come to hate. And my heart broke all over again.

"Ready?" He stood quickly, not waiting for my answer.

The crowd groaned and clapped and cheered. Cole held up a hand in modest humility, then he settled Jean into the case, among the offerings he had amassed. He clicked and zipped the case shut and slung it over his shoulders like an oddly shaped backpack.

We walked in silence. I was too grumpy to talk. Instead, I glared around us at all the people we passed, hating everyone. As we approached the escalators, my expression softened slightly at the sight of a girl with sad eyes, standing off to the side, passing out flyers to everyone who passed her.

Without a word to Cole, I made my way over to her through the mass of people. She had to be my age, but she dressed—old. Like a grandma or something. Slacks with a blazer, like she was getting ready for church. Her shiny, black hair was pulled back in a high ponytail with a scrunchy. A small tendril fell into her face as she handed me a flyer. My breath caught as I stared down at it.

She'd moved on to the next person, repeating her chant: "My sister, Mary, is missing. Have you seen this girl? My sister, Mary, is missing. Have you seen this girl?"

It was the same girl from the diner poster several towns away. A different flyer. Same girl. I cleared my throat, gripping the paper tightly as I watched the girl with the ponytail move from person to person. I wanted to say something. Offer her some kind of comfort. But there were no words. I folded the paper carefully and tucked it into my pocket.

When we got back to the motel, it was late, and I was uncharacteristically quiet. Seraphina went for the shower. Logan took Cole to grab some snacks from the vending machine.

I dropped down at the mini table and pulled out the flyer. Chin in my hand, I scanned the poster with a moody pout. I drummed my fingers against my cheek.

Icarus jumped up onto the table and rubbed his side against my arm, flicking his tail in my face.

I scowled. "You could just ask, you know..." I sat up straight and slapped at the cat's head.

His ears flattened underneath the rough petting. He mewed and leapt back down. Then he hopped onto the bed and blinked at me with reproachful eyes from a safe distance.

I shrugged angrily. "Have Seraphina pet you, then." My eyes went to Cole's laptop on the edge of the bed. I glanced at the poster and then back at the laptop, then at the door. Without a second thought, I hurried over to the bed, snatched the laptop, and fired it up at the table.

Eyes on the poster, I pulled up the search engine and started to type. I was so engrossed in my search, I barely noticed when the boys came back. Cole didn't say anything about his laptop. Without a word, he dropped onto the bed and clicked on the TV.

Logan switched on the coffee machine. He brewed himself a cup and then a second one, which he set in front of me, along with a pile of sugar packets.

Eyes still on the screen, I ripped open packet after packet, shaking them all into my mug. Logan took the seat across from me. I could feel his eyes on me as I poured out my last packet.

"What you got there?" Logan swiped the flyer before I could grab it back. His eyes scanned the paper despite my protests. "Missing kid?"

I nodded slowly. "I think it's a case."

He shot me a skeptical smirk as he passed the paper back. "One random missing kid and you think you have a case?" Logan cocked his eyebrow.

I shook my head. "One missing girl...and a mauled babysitter."

# ABOUT A GIRL

That got his attention. He nodded toward the computer. "What you got?"

I pulled my chair over to him and angled the computer so he could see the screen. "Mary Tran, eight years old, went missing last weekend. Her babysitter was found dead, along with the babysitter's boyfriend. The same night Mary went missing, both teenagers were mauled by an animal—best guess is a dog...one that they didn't have and wasn't ever found—inside a locked house."

Logan leaned in toward the computer. "Watertown?" He reached for the mouse pad, but I smacked his hand away.

"Did you say Watertown?" Cole called from the bed.

I glanced at him.

He'd sat up a bit on the pillows, his brow furrowed.

I frowned. So, now he wanted to talk to me?

"Yup." I turned back to the screen and scrolled for Logan. "Apparently, Mary was picked up right before the attack...by her sister's boyfriend. He says he brought her home, made sure she got inside safe, and left." I tapped her photo on the flyer. "Her foster mom and her sister both say they didn't see her in the house. Her sister was at the mall today."

"Hence the flyer..." Logan muttered, his eyes on the screen as I flipped from tab to tab.

"Exactly."

Cole's hands rested on the back of my chair. He bent in between Logan and me, so he could see the article. "Did you say a girl from Watertown?"

Logan looked at me. "Any other similar maulings in the area?"

"Actually—" I moved the mouse to click a new tab.

The bathroom door opened, and Logan turned almost instinctively. I followed his gaze and hid a smirk in the palm of my hand.

Seraphina emerged, fresh and flowery from the shower. She had snagged one of Logan's Lynyrd Skynyrd T-shirts and paired it with her pajama bottoms. She blushed prettily as all of us stared. She ran a hand through her wet hair.

"Nice shirt," I quipped, my eyes on Logan. His jaw tightened. His face burned scarlet. I could've sworn I saw him gulp. My eyes slid to Phin. She tugged on the shirt and flipped her hair over her shoulder.

"Yeah, sorry—I forgot a shirt, and this was the only thing in there..." She bit her lip and pointed her thumb back at the bathroom, her eyes on Logan. "I can change if—"

"No, no! That's—" Logan sat up a bit in the chair as though he meant to get up. Like a gentleman caller in an Austen novel.

I barely suppressed a snicker.

He cleared his throat and waved her words away. "You're good—"

"You *look* good," I chirped happily.

Logan kicked me from underneath the table. I winced at the pain. My nose crinkled as I smiled. He gave Phin a curt nod. "Keep it."

I grinned wickedly as we both turned back to the computer.

He shot me a death glare. "Let's go, Grey," he snapped gruffly.

I cleared my throat, struggling to straighten my face. "Well—"

"Uhm, I'm going to go grab a water..." Seraphina mumbled awkwardly as she headed for the door. "Anybody want anything?"

"Salt and vinegar chips!" I bounced a little in the seat.

Logan smacked Cole. "Dude, go with her. Grab me a soda."

Phin hesitated as Cole snatched up his wallet and made his way to the door. "Uh, I can get it—you can stay here, Cole."

"He could use the walk..." I muttered.

Cole yanked the door open and stalked outside without a word.

Seraphina bit her lip and raked a hand through her hair again.

I inclined my head. "What's wrong?"

Phin shook her head and forced a smile. "Nothing. See you guys." She gave a little wave and ducked out of the room.

Logan looked at me sharply as the door clicked. "When are you going to give the guy a break, huh?"

I blinked in disbelief. "*Me*?" I made a face. "When is *he* going to—"

Logan shook his head. "You have no idea what he's going through. And the last thing he needs is you angry at him while he's trying to work through it."

I rolled my eyes. "Can we get back to work, please? Or do you need a moment to fantasize about my sister and Lynyrd Skynyrd?"

Logan's eyes narrowed. Then, without another word, he nodded toward the computer.

I scooted closer to the table. "Okay...so, the interesting thing is...no. I haven't found any kind of similar maulings anywhere in the town records—"

Logan scowled. "Why is *that* interesting?"

"If you'd let me finish—" I eyed him coolly.

He waved impatiently at the screen.

I cleared my throat. "I didn't find any more maulings...but I found missing kids. A pattern of missing kids. Every sixteen years, seven kids go missing between September and November. All disappear from school without a trace. The parents swear they dropped them off, and a few people see them at the school, but then they just vanish, and by the end of the day, no one remembers seeing them anywhere."

"Kind of like the boyfriend and the little girl...he drops her off, sees her inside, and no one remembers her being there..." Logan nodded, his eyes narrowing at the screen. "Weird."

"See?" I bit down on my lips and shook my head, my eyes scanning the article. "The maulings broke the pattern."

Logan nodded thoughtfully. "Not just the mauled couple...the girl." Logan looked at me. "She wasn't taken from the school. She was taken from her house."

"If the boyfriend's not lying—" I muttered darkly.

Logan scoffed. "Right—and it could always be ordinary, everyday evil...trafficking or something sick like that...but—"

"The mauled babysitter?"

"Yeah...hard to find an ordinary explanation for that..."

I waved him away, clicking up some more tabs to illustrate my point. "But it's more than that—I checked further back. Whatever is going on, it goes back all the way to the 1930s. Every sixteen years. Like clockwork. All gone from the school without a trace."

"So, seven kids have gone missing since September?" His finger went for the mouse pad.

I smacked him away. "No." I clicked up a new tab. "Only one. And it's almost Thanksgiving. Which means—"

Logan massaged his forehead. "We could be on a time hack. A hard one." He sat up and reached for the mouse pad again.

I smacked him again.

He scowled and waved his hand at the computer. "What about the school—anything mysterious about the school itself?"

"Nothing." I frowned and shook my head. "No violent deaths. No accidents. Nothing to indicate a ghost."

"Nothing that you found, so far—" Logan corrected. He glanced at me sideways, unflinching beneath the weight of my glare. "This is a good start, Grey, but hunts take time...research. Sometimes months...it's important to do a thorough investigation before charging in with machete swinging."

I cocked an eyebrow. "You want more research?" I cleared my throat. "Gloria Godwin School was built in the late 1800s by the Godwin family. The same family who founded Watertown. It began as Gloria Godwin Academy for Girls. A boarding school where the rich people of New York would send the girls they didn't want. Then, in the 1960s, they changed the name, knocked down the dormitories, and let in the boys. Throughout the years, the school—"

Logan groaned and slapped his hand over his eyes. "All right, all right!"

"The headmistresses and principals all check out, too." I smirked in sweet satisfaction. "No weirdness, or abnormally long lifespan. As I said: nothing mysterious about the school."

"Heard." Logan's hand slid down the length of his face. "So, we've got seven kids vanishing from the school...every sixteen years?"

I nodded, my eyes scanning the article on Gloria Godwin Academy, searching for anything I missed.

"But right now, we've only got *one* missing kid. Not from the school. And a random monster attack on a babysitter and boyfriend." Logan sighed. "Not much to go on." Logan leaned forward and massaged his forehead. He winced at the screen. "So, we could be looking at a number of things..."

I clicked on a new tab, with the article from 1996. "There is one other anomaly...in 1996, one of the missing children was found. Eight-year-old Justine Kilpatrick. She and her sixteen-year-old sister, Jillian, both disappeared several weeks prior."

Logan reached for the mouse. "Where'd they find her body?"

I swatted him and scrolled down to the bottom of the article. "She was found alive. Passed out in the snow on Adelaide Road."

"Was she hurt?" Logan demanded. He tapped his fingers impatiently on the table.

"She had bruises from what the authorities suspected looked like needle marks. And she had significant blood loss...which is why she'd passed out. It was a miracle she survived. A teenage boy was driving home and found her. He rushed her to the hospital."

"Did she—"

"She refused to speak about what happened to her. The doctors called it a 'post-traumatic stress response.'"

Logan scrunched up his face, his brow furrowed into thick wrinkles. "So, we have seven missing kids...every sixteen years...one survivor with puncture wounds and blood loss...and now one missing kid, with two mauled teens..."

I looked at him, studying the hard lines of his face. "Weird, right? I mean, I've been studying monster profiles since we got on the road...nothing comes to mind..."

Logan nodded at the computer. "Pull up the page on the mauled kids."

I clicked the tab. I winced at the tacky headline: *Mauling on Movie Night.*

Logan sat back in his seat. His eyes bored into the grisly black-and-white article on the screen. He turned to me. "I guess we're heading up to Watertown in the morning."

I grinned.

I couldn't sleep. I was up all night, eyes glued to the computer, making notes on the motel notepad, and cursing the fact that we didn't have a printer.

Logan chucked a pillow at me from the bed. "Go to bed, Grey."

I chucked it back. "I'm fine—"

"I don't care about you—" Logan grumbled. "All that tapping and clicking is driving me crazy." He slapped at the nightstand, looking for the remote. He squinted down at the buttons and clicked it on. The volume was so low, it was just a soft murmur in the background.

I glanced at the TV. The black-and-white witch show flashed on the screen. My eyes slid sideways to look at Logan.

He hugged his pillow and turned on his side, his eyes on the episode.

I smiled slightly. Then I glanced at the clock. Okay. Enough for one night. I yawned and powered down the laptop. Before I climbed into bed, I checked on Cole. When we couldn't get adjoining rooms, only double beds, the boys took turns sleeping on a pull-out cot. It was Cole's turn. And he was stirring. Restless. Like he was every night. His brow was furrowed, and his mouth moved slightly. Nightmares.

Without thinking, I went to my duffel. I slapped around the potion bottles, squinting in the glow of the TV, until my thumb smoothed over the somnum label. My hand closed over the bottle, and I glanced across the room at Cole. He thrashed slightly in his sleep. Three drops of somnum, and he'd have a dreamless sleep. Finally. After weeks of tortured sleep.

But he'd always refused. Phin suspected it was some kind of atonement. Like he thought he deserved them. Masochist. I scowled as I pushed off the floor and stomped over to him. I poked him hard in the arm.

Cole gasped. His eyes flew open, his breathing labored. He grabbed me, his hand crushing my wrist.

I wrestled myself free. "Cole! You were thrashing again." I slapped the bottle into his chest. "You need to take this. Three drops. Just take it."

Cole blinked and licked his lips. He struggled to catch his breath. He swallowed, and then he nodded. His eyes closed. He nodded again. "Okay."

He sat up in the cot. I popped the bottle and dripped three careful drops onto his tongue. Then he slid back down, his chest still heaving. I stuck the stopper back in place and gripped the bottle in my palm. I made to get up, but Cole grabbed my hand. He squeezed it. Hard. He didn't open his eyes. "Thank you, Nix," he murmured.

I smiled. His hold grew slack, and his hand fell. He was asleep. I tucked his hand back onto the cot and pulled the covers up to his chin. I smoothed his hair from his forehead, still damp with cold sweat.

Maybe we'd be okay.

I glanced back at the double beds. Icarus was asleep on ours. On my pillow. Curled up like a little king. Seraphina was asleep beside him, snuggled up toward the nightstand, her hand opened limply at the edge of the bed. On the opposite side of the nightstand, Logan still hugged the pillow, curled toward her.

The sight warmed my heart.

Yup. We'd all definitely be okay.

"So, why are we heading back Upstate?" Cole squinted at the big green highway sign as he drove us underneath it. "I thought—"

I checked the map. I hit the paper as I directed Cole. "It's a straight shot. Exit 45." I tossed the map aside. Then I shoved my hand into my bag of chips and grabbed a handful.

"But what's—"

"I found us a case—"

"A case?" Cole cocked an eyebrow and glanced at me sideways.

I munched my potato chips, crunching them obnoxiously. "Yes, Cole. A case to solve. Like a monster thing? To save people? The whole reason we went on the road?" I screwed up my face and pointed my fistful of chips at him. "By the way, you never told me what you said to your dad to convince him to let you come on this little road trip. Hard to believe old man St. Claire would let you ditch school after only a few months in..."

Cole ignored my question. "And you said Watertown?"

I rolled my eyes. "Yes, Cole. *Watertown*. Why do you keep asking that?"

Cole didn't answer. Instead, he turned up the radio.

I frowned. I crumpled up my chip bag and wiped my hands on my jeans. "No...nuh uh. Cole, spill. Now."

Cole tightened his grip on the wheel. He jutted his jaw to the side and gritted his teeth.

I frowned at him. "You look like a caveman."

He rolled his eyes and shook his head. "Just forget it, Phoenix. Okay?"

"No." I kicked my feet up onto the glove box. "Why do you keep asking about Watertown?"

Cole scoffed as he shoved a hand through his thick, dark hair.

"You know me, Cole, I'm not going to stop—" I checked the radio clock. "And we've got an hour until we get even *close* to Exit 45..."

Cole closed his eyes briefly. He glanced at me. His annoyance hardened the soft features of his face.

I grinned, sugary sweet, and fluttered my eyelashes. "You know you love me."

Cole rolled his eyes and turned his attention back to the road. "I've been having nightmares, okay?"

"Everyone knows that." I scrunched up my face. "What does that have to—"

"Not about—" Cole interrupted angrily. Then he sighed heavily. His shoulders rolled forward, as though he were releasing a heavy weight off his back. "For the past week—I've been having nightmares...about a flooded town...flooded with..." He gritted his teeth. His jaw clenched as he closed his eyes again. He adjusted his hold on the wheel. Then he blinked rapidly. "Floating kids...dead kids, floating through the streets."

I stared at him. "Like a town of water...why didn't you—"

"Because it's messed up, Phoenix! *It's not freaking normal!*"

Cole shouted as he squeezed the steering wheel so tight his knuckles went white.

I flinched and looked away. Cole didn't raise his voice. Ever. But I'd heard the sound before. The sound of him yelling. Bellowing. Screaming. That night in the church. When the demon had possessed Cole. I clenched my hands into fists, my nails digging into my palms. I didn't want to think about it. I couldn't think about it. The demon cutting into me. Tiny slice after slice. Each one burning like a paper cut. A hundred paper cuts.

"Nix." Cole reached over to touch me.

Instinctively, I flinched away.

His hand flew back to the wheel. "Sorry."

Mortified, I turned in my seat, my hand on his shoulder. "No, no, Cole! It's not—"

Cole shrugged me off. "It's okay, Nix. I get it." He nodded curtly. He squinted at the road ahead of us, his face hard and stony. "I'm so sorry, Phoenix," he muttered with a stiff shake of his head.

He shouldn't be sorry. I didn't *want* him to be sorry. I crossed my arms over my chest and tried to resist the urge to sniff. My eyes burned. All the progress from yesterday, from last night—gone. All gone.

I pulled the sleeve of my hoodie up and dabbed discreetly at my nose as my eyes blurred. I cleared my throat. "So, these dreams...do they feel like premonitions or something?"

Cole gave a curt nod.

"Well, that doesn't make sense." I pinched my nose. "You aren't a psychic."

Cole shrugged.

I glanced at him sideways. He'd shut down again. I closed my eyes, my jaw clenched tight to keep my mouth shut. I wanted to yell at him. To scream at him. Anything to get him to just...be normal. But nothing I could do would help. I'd already tried everything. I punched the CD button, blasting us with the Offspring, and we drove the rest of the ride in a loud, gritty silence.

.  .  .

Watertown was small and hugged the highway on both sides. Not as small as Nile, of course...but small enough that there seemed to be a heart of the town with lots of businesses and shops and things, but outside that it was all farms and mountains for miles. We pulled into a dinky motel even shabbier than the last one, and I couldn't hide my disgust.

Icarus perched on Seraphina's shoulder like a furry, black parrot. His eyes narrowed at the state of the motel, his tail flicking with irritation.

Cole slung his bag over his shoulder. "I'm going to go check us in..."

Seraphina hurried forward. "I'll come too...they need our card information..."

I bent in the back of the van for our duffel and my backpack, muttering to myself about lice and bedbugs.

Logan leaned over my shoulder. "You can run home to your grammy anytime, Grey."

I elbowed him in the gut and slammed him in the side with my bag. He snickered and tousled my hair, giving my head a shove. I teetered off-balance. I gritted my teeth. My fingers itched to snatch my wand from my topknot. I wanted to hex him. I wanted to hex him so bad...

Logan grinned and jutted his chin toward me. "You want to hex me, don't you?"

"*No!*" I snapped angrily, pushing past him toward the lobby.

Our room was even smaller than the last one. I chucked the duffel on the bed and slammed my backpack onto the pillow. The whole bed sagged and creaked beneath the weight. I raised an eyebrow at Seraphina. She poked me with her finger and shot me a warning look.

I rolled my eyes. "Just because you're an obsessive people pleaser who'd rather suffer miserably in silence than voice your actual opinion doesn't mean *I* have to act like this doesn't stink," I muttered.

"Nix," Phin snapped, tilting her head toward the boys unpacking just feet away.

"Literally." I crinkled my nose. "Literally stinks. Ugh, what is that?"

"I think it's Phoenix," Logan said loudly.

I glanced over my shoulder.

Logan had his arm around Cole's shoulders. The height difference between them was staggering. Logan looked down at Cole, his brow furrowed and his mouth downturned. "The smell, right?" He nodded briskly. "Yup. It's gotta be Phoenix."

I went for him. Seraphina grabbed my arm and forced me down onto the bed. Logan laughed loudly, leaning into Cole for support as he nearly doubled over. I wrestled my arm from Phin and smacked at her hands. She put her hand on my forehead and shoved me backward.

"Knock it off, Nix." She pushed a hand through her silky, blonde hair. "Yeah, okay—this place is freaking gross—" She waved her arm around the room.

Logan frowned thoughtfully as he looked around.

"But we are here for a reason, aren't we?" Seraphina turned back to me, her hands on her hips. "You said there was something going on here. Something snatching little kids? Shouldn't we be getting to work instead of complaining about—"

"You're right." I jumped up off the bed and started to sort through our stuff. "But next time, we're getting a hotel," I mumbled moodily.

"You have fun with that." Logan scoffed. "Maybe hit a beauty parlor while you're at it...they can fix your head."

. . .

We set up each of the guys' laptops on the tiny table. Seraphina went through everyone's clothes and tucked them neatly into the dresser, while I went through the potions, pouches, and other witchy things and set them out on top of it. Then we both went through the books.

We'd snagged a few from our grandmother at Blackwell Manor, but most books were from Logan's personal hoard. He lugged a trunk full of them in the truck. But it was just a small sample of the DeVarney library. His dad had kept an old storage locker full of lore somewhere up in Maine. The ones in the trunk were just the most universally useful ones. When Logan had first told us, Seraphina's eyes had lit up at the thought of all those books hidden away. She was a nerd for magic study. Couldn't help it. Even after having proved to have no magical ability, old habits died hard. And although I could *do* the magic, Seraphina knew and understood more about it than I ever would.

But magic was one thing. Monsters were another. Both of us were practically clueless about hunting evil, be it creature or spirit. So as soon as we'd hit the road, Logan had put the two of us, and Cole as well, to work.

We'd all taken turns reading and rereading Logan's books; we'd even flipped through his and Traven's journals detailing the different cases they'd dealt with in the past. Logan had a lifetime of monster knowledge and experience. Cole, Phin, and I were at a huge disadvantage. Up until a month ago, none of us had known about anything other than witches and magic. If we were going to be helpful on hunts, we needed to learn—quickly.

Together, the two of us shoved Logan's book trunk up against the wall, beside the old motel TV. Then we gathered all our books and lined them neatly along the top like a shelf. Then Phin and I stuck all my notes on the wall, along with Mary Tran's missing flyer. Once we'd finished, we stepped back, our eyes on Mary's sweet smiling face.

Seraphina hugged herself. "I'm going to go call Fawn..." Cole was at her side in an instant. She waved him off. "Cole, can I—" She smiled appreciatively as he pressed his phone into her palm. "Thank you."

He nodded with a stiff twitch of a smile. Then she walked over to the bed to make the call in whatever privacy the corner of the room offered in this matchbox motel room.

"You both need phones," Logan muttered.

I scoffed. "Mama says phones interfere with magic. That's the last thing I need."

Cole stood beside me, his eyes on the flyer. I glanced at him sideways. He was staring at Mary with such intensity, it made me uneasy. I bit my lip. I looked from Mary to Cole and back again. "You look like you've seen a ghost..."

Cole looked at me sharply.

I didn't flinch. I met his dark eyes. "Did you see her? Floating in your—"

"Stop," Cole muttered under his breath. His eyes darted to Logan, who was alternating between tapping away on his laptop and flipping through an old, stained phonebook. Cole cleared his throat. "Just...forget I said anything, Phoenix. Okay?"

I scoffed. "Uhm. No. I'm not going to forget anything. You had a—"

Cole rolled his eyes and marched for the door. "I'll be back. Snack run."

"Wait! Cole, you don't have your—"

He slammed the door.

Eyes wide, mouth open, I stared at the door in shock.

"Good job, Grey." Logan smirked, his eyes on the screen. "You sure have a talent for scaring guys away. If this monster's a dude, it could really come in handy."

My eyes burned. I rolled them up to the ceiling. I glanced at Phin. She was facing the wall, cradling Cole's phone to her ear and giggling softly. I glared at Logan. "I'll be back."

Logan held up his phone for me without looking up. I snatched it, shoved it in my pocket, and stalked out the door.

I caught up with Cole outside in the parking lot. He was pacing the length of the van. The fiery phoenix mural I'd painted across the side door stood out in stark contrast to the bleak gray of the November afternoon. I hesitated on the curb before I approached him. I'd never seen him like that. Steeling myself, I gritted my teeth and charged forward.

When he noticed me, his scowl deepened. "Oh, come on, Nix —" He raked his hand through his hair as he paced. "I just need—"

I grabbed him by the shoulders, pulling him to a stop. I shoved him against the van. Cole was only a few inches taller than me. We nearly met eye to eye, amber clashing with tiger's eye. "No, Cole! No. We're going to talk about this!"

His eyes slid to the side. I shoved him hard. His head knocked against the van. He groaned through gritted teeth, and his eyes found mine.

I nodded. "Good. Get angry at me." I gave him another shove. "At least I know you can still feel things."

"You know what, Phoenix—" Cole's voice was low, trembling slightly with buried rage. "Not everybody's as perfect as you are, okay?"

"And that means what?"

His dark eyes were cold. "Not everybody can go through hell one day and be sunny and cheerful the next."

I made a face. "You think it doesn't bother me? You think I don't wake up at night terrified that I'm back on that dirty floor, his hands all over me, flaying me apart like a fish?"

"My hands." Cole shook his head, his eyes staring off to the side. "This was a mistake. I shouldn't be around you. Not anymore."

I recoiled, my lip curled in disgust. "Excuse me—you shouldn't *be around me*? What—"

"After what I did to you, I shouldn't—"

"For Fay's sake, Cole!" I rolled my eyes and backhanded his chest. "It wasn't you!"

"Like hell!" Cole bellowed.

I flinched at the sound.

"See!" Cole held up his hands and smacked them together. "It was my hands, my—I did it. And you know it! You felt it in the van..." His voice broke and his shoulders dropped in defeat. I searched his dark eyes, shining in the afternoon sunlight. He licked his lips, his voice thick with emotion. "You were scared of me. And you should be."

My eyes blurred. I struggled to swallow the lump in my throat. "Why?" I blinked. A few tears spilled down my cheeks. "Why should I be scared of you?"

Cole shook his head.

I shoved him again. My lip trembled. "No, you tell me, Cole. Why should I be scared of you? You gonna hurt me?" I taunted. My voice dripped with emotion, sharp with sarcasm. I inclined my head. "You gonna grab a knife and start carving?"

Cole scrunched up his face, his brow furrowed, his eyes pained. "I'm going back to Nile."

I flinched and fell away from him, stumbling several steps back. I gave an ironic smile through the tears. There was a ringing in my ears. I couldn't process what he'd just said.

Cole was leaving me.

Like everyone else.

I held out my arms and then dropped them to my sides. I opened my mouth, but no words came. I studied him, shoulders hunched, still flush against the van, closed off and brooding. Acting like he was some kind of martyr...protecting me...

My amber eyes flashed. My jaw tightened. How dare he? My

anger burned like fire in my veins, igniting every nerve. I shook my head, lip curled in disgust. *How dare he?*

I turned on my heel and went for Logan's truck. I snapped my fingers and the doors unlocked. Orange magic dust shimmered on the handle as I ripped it open. I slapped a hand to the ignition, and the truck roared to life. The whole time, Cole was calling for me to wait, to come back...I wasn't listening.

I wouldn't listen to him ever again.

And this time, *I* was leaving.

Cole was at the door.

The doors locked.

He banged on the window.

I revved the engine and peeled out of the parking lot, and I didn't look back.

3

# SHE'S A LADY

Normally, I would go to the Tracks. A secret path in Nile that cut through the woods and led to the lake. But I wasn't in Nile. And I had no idea where to go. But anywhere was better than standing in the parking lot with Cole St. Claire.

I sniffed and blinked through the tears as they blurred my vision. I squinted down at the radio as I jabbed at the buttons, trying to find a decent song. Logan had garbage taste in music. I cut through side streets and through blocks of thick trees and old Victorian townhouses, weaving around and around all through the heart of Watertown, trying to calm down.

Logan's phone buzzed in my pocket.

And again, and again.

I rubbed the back of my sleeve into my cheeks, groaning in frustration as the tears continued to run down my face. I squeezed the steering wheel, trying desperately to get a grip.

We were here for a reason.

I nodded stiffly. I needed to focus.

One hand on the wheel, I grabbed Logan's phone out of my pocket, pulling the antenna up with my teeth. I keyed in 411.

"Hello, this is 411," chirped the operator. "How can I help you today?"

I sniffed loudly and cleared my throat. "Hi, I'm looking for the location of the Watertown Public Library..."

It didn't take long to find. Turns out, I'd been circling it for the past ten minutes. It was nestled in the thick of town, amid all the trees and Victorian townhouses. I parked the truck and tapped the ignition. The truck purred, shuddered, and then the engine stopped. I bit my lip on my smile. Logan would be so mad. I hopped out of the truck and nearly skipped to the library. The idea of an angry Logan instantly boosted my mood.

I found a computer and started to print. Once I had a hard copy of the town map and printouts of all the articles of the missing kids, I marked their homes on the map. I scanned the spread. There wasn't any kind of pattern to the house locations. I thought maybe there was a creature that stalked them at home first before targeting them at school...but there wasn't anything similar about the homes. I traced a line through all the dots, connecting them in a lumpy shape. I scrunched up my face. Maybe Logan would be able to make sense of it...get something from it. I flipped through the articles. I needed to go back further. Use the past to predict the pattern...I printed several pages from 1996, a few from 1980, and what little they had of all the others. Everything from the abductions to anything notable about the kids.

The librarian—a tall woman with hair like swirling chocolate —gave me a funny look. She squinted up at me from her seat. "You doing some kind of research paper, hon?"

I gave a cheesy smile. "Something like that."

"Okay, well, that'll be ten dollars..."

"Oh, uh..."

Her smile started to fade as mine grew.

I rubbed my forehead as I stared down at my stack of papers

clutched tight in her hands. "Oh, okay…" I shoved my hands in my pockets. Like there'd be money.

"Here."

I flinched as Cole popped up beside me and slapped two crumpled fives on the counter. The librarian smiled at Cole and passed him the papers, all while shooting me a rude stare. I chuckled guiltily as I thanked her and pulled Cole away from the counter, back toward my workstation.

"What are you doing here, Cole?" I tugged the papers from his hands and smacked them onto the computer table. My heart pumped hot anger through my blood. "No, better yet, how the hex did you find me?"

"Logan." Cole smiled weakly. "He has a tracker on his truck."

I scoffed and rolled my eyes. My arms folded over my chest. "Okay, well, thanks for the papers. Tell Rachel I said 'Hey' when you make it back home." I dropped into the chair and started to rifle through the pages.

Cole sighed. "Phoenix, I don't know what you want from me—"

I snorted. Ignoring the question, I scanned the papers. I pulled the cap off a highlighter with my teeth and started to mark things that stood out.

Cole hesitated and then sank into the seat beside me. "How can I help?"

I wasn't listening. There was something here…in that there *wasn't* anything here. Every sixteen years…the kids were just gone. As though they'd never existed. I highlighted things about each of the victims. In the beginning, they were all girls…until they opened the school up to boys. Then the pool of victims shifted. I marked up the first boy to change the pattern. A kindergartener named Matthew Riley. Six years old. Had just signed up for fall soccer. His daddy had recently been drafted into the Vietnam War. He'd gotten his whole class to make cards for his father's platoon. There was a long article about his outreach.

I nibbled my lip as I studied his class picture that accompanied the article. I shuffled through the papers for the rest of the kids taken that year. The gender was no longer specific, but that wasn't all that was different. The victim age dropped. Before the school had shifted to co-ed, the kidnapped girls had ranged from preschool all the way up to graduating senior. Matthew Riley's year, only elementary-aged kids were taken.

My brow furrowed. I slapped around the papers scattered about on the table.

"What is it?" Cole leaned in close. His dark eyes followed my hands as they moved over the pages.

"They're all little. So little." I looked up at Cole, slightly breathless. "When the boys started to go missing with the girls, the age range lowered. Why?" I demanded, my voice sharp. I glared at him as though he should know. "Why?"

Cole blinked. His mouth opened, but nothing came out.

I looked back at the papers, shuffling them between my hands so fast orange magic dust shimmered.

Cole put a gentle hand on mine. "Hey, slow down…"

The guitar string calluses on his finger pads scratched the tops of my knuckles. I inhaled deeply and the magic burning bright in my blood simmered. I let out a grumbling exhale as I stared down at the articles.

Cole scooted his chair closer. "Well…" He cleared his throat. "If you'll excuse me for being a bit chauvinistic, the first thing I'm noticing is…innocence."

I scrunched up my face and gave him a genuinely puzzled look.

Cole crinkled his brow and flashed a sheepish grin. He pointed to the paper. "Look at him. What do you think this little guy had in common with…" He shifted through the papers and tapped a senior photo from the 1940s. A pretty girl, with a soft smile and pigtails, stared up at us. "Dottie Reed?"

I chewed on my cheek as I considered this. I looked from Matthew to Dottie. The first thing that came to mind was goodness. Sweetness. Innocence. My heart ached slightly. I swallowed, emotion swelling like a lump in my throat.

"Okay..." I moved my hands over the pages, fanning them out in a rainbow.

"Now what?" Cole prompted gently.

"Well...whatever it is...started in the '30s..."

"And you think that because..."

I glanced at him sideways. "Because that's when the first kids went missing from the school."

"Right..." Cole nodded slowly. "From the school..." He pushed off the chair and went for a nearby computer. They were big, boxy, and extremely outdated. As Cole fired it up, I half expected him to have to smack it to life. He started to type on the plastic-coated keys as I watched him from the table.

I jutted my chin at his backpack. "You should just use your laptop."

He rolled his eyes and shook the hair out of his face. After a moment (several), he finally waved me over. "Here."

I bent down over his shoulder. Cole had so many tabs up, the computer was going irritatingly slow. He could barely pull up the first one. I cocked an eyebrow at him and nodded at the blank screen.

Cole frowned, his pale cheeks pink. "Just give it a minute..."

"Should've used your laptop..." I muttered under my breath.

After a moment (several), the article finally popped on the screen. The headline read "Thirteenth Young Woman Vanished." Cole gestured to the computer. "There."

I scoffed in disbelief. I scooped up my papers. Stack hugged to my chest, I hurried to the librarian's desk. "Where do you keep the old newspapers?"

The librarian eyed me suspiciously for a moment. I shifted my feet underneath the weight of her stare. Bathed in the yellowy library lights, her eyes seemed to shine, giving her an almost feline appearance. Then she relaxed and smiled sweetly.

She gestured down the hall. "First room on the left, hon."

Cole thanked her for me as I hurried down the hallway, Converse squeaking on the waxed hardwood floor.

It didn't take long to find them. The library had several microfilm machines that displayed copies of newspapers, old records, everything. Cole and I each picked one and started clicking through it. Then I found them. The articles before the '30s. Before the school disappearances. The black-and-white articles flashed across my vision. My heart sank lower with each article.

Every year...

*Every year* people went missing.

Regularly. Dozens and dozens of people. As far back as the newspapers went—1822. Mostly young women and girls. In all the articles, they never found a kidnapper or a cause. Some suspected mountain lions...which spurred hunting parties that wiped the cats out of the area. Others suspected bears, but they never found any because bears didn't travel far east.

It would take hours to catalogue every single victim spanning a hundred years. I slapped my stack of printed papers down on the circular table in the center of the room and spread them out. I bit the cap off the highlighter, holding it in my teeth as I marched back over to the microfilm machine. Notepad and highlighter in hand like a waitress, I scribbled furiously as I read.

No pattern. There was no pattern in the pattern. Before the school disappearances started in 1932, people were taken at random from anywhere. Some stolen from their beds as though they'd run away. Some snatched on their way home from work or school. Some taken from town as they ran errands. But in every instance, every person simply vanished.

I spat out the highlighter cap and slapped the notepad on the table. I glared at Cole sideways. "This doesn't make any sense," I snapped angrily.

Cole shifted closer to study the screen. Without taking his eyes off the article glowing on the microfilm screen, he put a lollipop on the table in front of me.

I snatched it up and ripped off the wrapper. I pointed the pop at my notepad. "Do you see? It's all different!"

Cole frowned and picked up the pad. He flipped through my pages of notes. "So, if it wasn't tied to the school in the beginning...what changed?"

"Right." I shook my head and stuck the lollipop in the pocket of my cheek. "First it grabs anybody it can get, whenever it wants—then it decides to go on a diet and only grab seven kids from the school every sixteen years. Then, in the 1960s, there's boys available, so it snacks on them, too..." I scoffed and tossed up my hands in frustration. "It's like a rabbit deciding to eat carrots, and then switching to worms, and then cats." I sucked hard on the lollipop, feeling completely defeated. I gathered up all the printed papers, maps, and articles. "And then what about Mary Tran...? And the babysitter and her boyfriend..." I paused to check my notes for their names and read aloud, "Drew Graham and Nathan Campbell...mauled to death in a locked house?"

"Well, we have to look at what changed in the '30s..."

I inclined my head as I stuck the pop in my cheek. "We should look through all the papers from that year for anything odd."

A lopsided smile slid across Cole's face, his dimple deepening in his left cheek. "Should I get the coffee?"

I groaned, shoulders deflating. "This feels like a waste of time."

"Logan doesn't think so." Cole gave me a soft smile. "You know how he goes on and on about how research is the backbone of any hunt...he said the library is a great place to start."

I frowned moodily. Scrolling through dozens and dozens of microfilms was not my idea of saving the day. "What else did he say?"

Cole shrugged. "He said the two of us should stick to the missing kids, while he and Phin check out the crime scene."

I blinked. "Wait, what?" I lowered the lollipop, licking the sticky sweetness off my lips.

"He said we should look at it like two cases, until they connect...you know, the missing kids and—"

"No. No." I shook my head, shifting from one foot to the other, my hand on my hip. "Cole, did I just hear you say that Logan and Phin are going to check out the crime scene? Without us?"

Cole shrugged. "Yeah. We all drove here in the van. They took the truck. Logan was really glad your magic hadn't messed up the wiring." Cole gave me a small smile.

I didn't smile back. "They went to the crime scene without me?"

"Yeah, he said we should research the missing kids..." Cole's brow furrowed. "I told him to go ahead."

"Why?" I demanded, my temper flaring up again.

Cole's pale face flushed pink. He tossed his hair out of his eyes. "I—Nix, I wanted to talk to you—"

"Oh, now you want to—" I snorted in disbelief. I held up a hand. "So, I'm missing out on investigating the crime scene on *my* case, because you finally wanted to talk? About what, Cole?"

Cole opened his mouth and then shut it, abashed.

"Excellent." I chucked the lollipop into the waste bin. Then I swiped a hand over the mess of papers. A sprinkle of orange magic sparkled over the pages, and they slid themselves into a neat stack in my hands. I crushed them to my chest. "Let's go."

"Nix, wait—"

"No!" I snapped over my shoulder. I marched down the hall and straight out of the library.

I yanked open the van door as I hopped in the driver's seat. But before I could slam it shut, Cole caught the door.

"I wanted to talk to you because I wanted to explain..." Cole waited a minute for me to fire a retort.

But I didn't. Teeth clenched, I glared straight ahead. My eyes bored into the brick of the library.

Cole bowed his head and tried again. "Nix, I'm not leaving you. I didn't want to leave you. It's not like that. I just—" He raked a hand through his hair as he struggled to find words. "I don't want you to have to be stuck with me. Reminding you of what happened...making you feel...unsafe."

My jaw pulsed. I grabbed the steering wheel to give my hands something to do other than grab his throat.

Cole leaned on the door, his head bent to the side as he looked at me. "I don't want you to ever feel like I'm leaving you. Because I'm not. I'd never. It's just better for you if I'm not around."

I gritted my teeth together. Hard.

Cole shook his hair from his eyes. "Nix, please—"

I bit my lip and shook my head. "No."

I jumped out of the van and paced around the length of it.

"No." I stopped short and pointed a finger at him. "You're not doing anything for *me*. You're leaving for *you*. And how *dare* you try to tell me differently!"

Cole winced. "I'm not—"

"You're not being honest! With me or with yourself," I spat. "You leaving—going back to Nile? That's you running away. Running from what happened to you. It has nothing to do with how *I'm* feeling! Does it?"

Cole flinched, recoiling at my words. He shut the van door and walked toward the back of the van. He turned his back on me, his fingers threaded through his hair, his hands on the back of his head.

I sighed and crossed the distance between us. I stood behind him, hesitant to touch him. "You've been so worried about me. How I'm doing. How I'm handling things. How I'm healing—" I exhaled deeply, my shoulders rolling forward. "You're burying what happened to you. And Cole, you're not dealing with it."

I touched his arm. My lip trembled as I spoke in words thick and watery. "You were possessed by evil. Cole, it used you. It took over your body and used you in nasty, unspeakable ways. That's abhorrent. And what you're refusing to acknowledge—" My teeth came down on my lip. "Cole, what happened to you—" I closed my eyes briefly. Tears spilled down my cheeks. I took a shaky breath. "*What happened to you is just as horrific as what happened to me.*"

Cole turned slowly. I dried my damp cheeks with the back of my hoodie and met his gaze, strong and steady. His jaw was tight, and his eyes shined with his pain, but he didn't shed a single tear. He inhaled deeply through his nose, his nostrils flaring. He nodded curtly.

I let out the breath I'd been holding in a deep sigh of relief.

Then he threw his arms around me and crushed me to him. He pressed his face into my hair and breathed, "I'm so sorry, Phoenix."

I squeezed him back just as tight. "Just knock it off, will you?" I grumbled as his hug crushed my ribs.

He shoved me away from him and tousled my hair. "Whatever you say." He cleared his throat. "Babysitter's house?"

I grinned and rubbed my forehead. All the emotion had given me a headache. I pinched my temples and squinted. "Hex yes."

Drew Graham's house was deep in the heart of a neighborhood stuffed inside a forest slapped on the side of a rolling mountain... just a few blocks away from the police station and the hospital. The whole layout of the town was strange. But I kind of liked it.

The house was halfway up the mountain at the corner of a crossroad that sloped up and down so sharply it was like a teeter-totter. The driveway was at the back of the house, lower on the hill. But there was no room for the van with Logan's truck shoved in the tiny drive, so Cole had to park against the curb on the mountainside. Everything in the back—the guitar case, an old CD binder, various sports equipment, and a handful of books—all slid to the back of the van as Cole shoved it in park and cranked the emergency brake.

I glanced back at the mess. "Glad I'm in the cockpit. Much safer than the cargo area."

Cole cracked a smirk. "Let's go, nerd."

We headed out, falling into step along the sidewalk as we hiked up toward the other side of the house. It was a big, beautiful brick colonial with ivy blanketing the sides. The white picket fence around the front yard contained the wild tangle of plants. It wasn't overgrown, just out of season, but in the cold, gray afternoon of dying November, the garden looked neglected and dead. Or maybe it was just because I knew what awaited me inside. We hesitated at the gate and exchanged uneasy glances.

The black iron railing leading up the tiny brick steps to the front door was crisscrossed with bright-yellow caution tape. The stark yellow against the rail was jarring. And it made it all too real. Two kids died in the house. Horrifically. I'd been so pumped about rescuing Mary Tran and solving the mystery, I hadn't truly felt the impact of it all.

Cole cleared his throat as a car passed us. He opened the gate of the white picket fence. "Come on...we don't want to draw too much attention."

I inhaled sharply, the icy air biting my nostrils, and hugged myself against the cold. Then we crossed into the yard, hurrying down the stone walkway and up the steps, slipping underneath the yellow tape and huddling at the door. I tried the knob. It was locked. Magic warmed in my palm, glittering orange around the handle. Then the lock clicked, and the door opened underneath my hand.

The two of us slid inside the crack of the door and shut it behind us with a sharp snap.

"Phin?" I called into the quiet of the quaint little entryway. Cole elbowed me in the ribs. My eyes narrowed. "What?"

He nodded toward the floor.

I gasped. My heart lodged into my throat, along with my breath. There were deep gashes in the hardwood floor. Like some creature had ripped up the boards as it raced inside the house. I dropped down to the ground, crouched low, so my finger could trace the scratches. The wood was splintered and peeling back in small curls.

I glanced up at Cole from the floor. "Well, now we know it had wicked long claws."

"Sam called it..."

I flinched at the sound of Logan's voice at the top of the staircase. He was leaning over the banister that bordered the upstairs hallway. He shook his head, an amused twitch in the corner of his mouth.

I stood slowly. "Called what?"

"She said you wouldn't last long stuck on research detail."

I rolled my eyes. "Yeah, yeah." I slapped a hand against the railing and tugged myself up the stairs. "Maybe next time *she* should hit the books, and I'll do the grunt work."

Cole followed behind me. The weight of our steps sent the stairs groaning. When we reached the top, Logan straightened off the rail, towering over both of us, his eyebrow arched and his cheekbones sharp.

"Well?" I waved an impatient hand, my skin itching underneath his hard eyes. "Catch us up."

He jutted his head toward the hall. "Come on. We're searching Drew's room."

Cole and I followed him down the narrow hall. The hardwood creaked underneath our shoes. I frowned and eyed the floorboards. There weren't any scratches up here. "Her bedroom? Is that where they were attacked?"

"No..." Logan scoffed. "Didn't you see the marks all over the floor downstairs?" He glanced back at me as he pushed open a cracked door. "I thought you'd be a bit more observant than that..."

"Obviously we saw the scratches!" I snapped, my nose scrunching in annoyance. "Which is why I don't understand why we're up here—"

"You're with Sam." Logan put a hand at my back and guided me into the room. "Cole and I are going to check out the basement. Holler if you need anything." Logan ignored my sputtered protests and had eyes only for my sister. "You good up here?"

Seraphina sat on Drew's rose-gold, satin bed, her legs criss-crossed, and her nose pressed inside the pages of a pink flowery journal. She lowered the book, a soft, sad smile on her face. She nodded.

Cole backed out of the room without complaint. When I headed after them to argue, Logan held up his hand to stop me. "Help her. We'll be back."

My jaw slacked. My eyes blazed hot with my anger. Magic simmered warm in my hands. "But—"

Logan rolled his eyes. "I'll walk you through the attack site after."

Unbelievable. I stood, defeated, in the doorway, staring after them with wide eyes. The boys hurried down the hall and disappeared down the stairs. I looked back at Phin in outraged disbelief. I waved a hand out the door. "What just happened?"

Seraphina gave a weak, downturned smile. "I think all the pink was getting to him..."

I glanced around the room as I crossed my arms. The bedroom looked as if someone had puked up a bottle of Pepto Bismol and then tried to clean up with a bunch of doilies and lace. It was flowery and princessy and so sweet it gave me a toothache. No wonder DeVarney ran for it. I was itchy to head out the door myself. I scrunched up my nose and eyed the ruffles skirting around the bed and the mountain of stuffed animals neatly organized in the corner of the room.

"I think it's cute," Seraphina murmured, her voice with a slight edge of defense. "She was clearly a very sweet girl."

Guilt soured my stomach. I nodded begrudgingly with an apologetic wince. Yes. Much sweeter than me. I crossed the fluffy white rug stretched across the hardwood and stopped beside the bedside table. There was a picture of a girl and a guy framed in silver. His baseball cap twisted backward, he had his arm around her, pressing a kiss into her left dimple as she grinned so big her eyes crinkled closed, her short, blonde hair blowing in the beachy air. The joy radiating off them was tangible. A small smile tickled the corner of my lips.

Drew and Nathan.

"They were happy people," Seraphina said softly.

"They look it." I plopped the picture back down and turned to face Phin. "What are we doing in here, exactly?"

Seraphina held up the journal in her hands. "Research."

I groaned and rolled my eyes to the ceiling. "Seriously? What in the world could we hope to find in her bedroom?" I waved a hand back at the picture frame. "Other than the fact that she and her boyfriend looked happy in a photo one time?"

Seraphina pursed her lips into a tight, patient frown. "We need to find out as much about Drew as we can."

"Why?"

"Because that will help us figure out if she had any enemies, or—"

"Right." I nodded sarcastically. "Because it only makes sense that she'd write in her diary about a werewolf she met on her way to visit Grandma's house," I quipped dryly. I rolled my eyes. Of course, Phin was right; the journal could prove really helpful, but I didn't care. They'd sidelined me. Purposefully left me out. And it was grating. So, I wanted to grate back.

"*Or*," Seraphina continued sharply. "Whether there were any places she hung out regularly. We need to look for patterns in her behavior—just like we'd look for patterns in a monster's behavior.

It'll help us understand what happened to her." Seraphina crinkled her brow as she studied me critically. "This is common sense, Nix. You know this..." She inclined her head. "What's wrong? Didn't you and Cole fix—"

"Fine." I scowled and stomped over to Drew's laptop. I jabbed at the mouse pad. "I'll look through her computer."

Seraphina muttered something behind my back. I glanced over my shoulder. Her face was hidden behind the diary. "What was that?"

"Nothing."

I rolled my eyes and turned back to the computer as Drew's screensaver flashed on the screen. Another picture of her with her boyfriend at the beach. "I'm pretty sure you said something..." I mumbled moodily.

Seraphina groaned. "Well, my God, Phoenix. The poor girl's *dead*. If you think combing through her life is a waste of time, then go. Go poke around downstairs and goggle at all the blood stains with the guys if you think that's more worthy of your precious time! But I happen to feel like this girl deserves whatever time it takes to learn about her—as a person. Not just some random monster victim. In fact, I think she was a sweetheart. A good, decent girl. One who certainly didn't deserve to be shredded to pieces all over her living room floor. And so, I'm going to thumb through every photo in her nightstand, read every single social media post on whatever profiles she has, and peek through every page of her journal if it means finding some kind of clue to help us get her a little bit of justice!"

I spun around in the pink velvet swivel chair. "It's not about wasting my time!"

Seraphina cocked an incredulous eyebrow. A dubious smirk crept onto her face. She waited.

My cheeks burned. "Okay, okay. It's not *just* about wasting my time..."

A rueful smile pressed into her cheek. "It's about Cole."

"No!" I snapped, my face hot. And it wasn't. "It's about wasting Mary Tran's time. And the other six kids who are going to disappear if we don't figure this out fast enough. This is important to me." My voice wavered as emotion clogged my throat and blurred my eyes. "Finding Mary Tran alive and bringing her home to her sister? That's everything." I shrugged and swirled back to face the computer. "So...I'm sorry if I'm being a hag."

"Thank you."

I clicked into the laptop and checked Drew's internet history. I cleared my throat. "What have you learned from snooping through her diary?"

"Well, funnily enough, I think you might like her. She'd just started reading *The Shining*."

I nodded approvingly without turning around. My eyes moved over the searches.

"She had it hidden away in the top drawer of her dresser because it was freaking her out."

I snorted in appreciation.

"But she was excited to finish it. It was the only book she'd ever read that actually scared her..."

"Well, I hate to say it, Phin, but her good taste in literature isn't going to help us figure out—"

"And she really missed her parents. They're off on some remote, meditative, new agey retreat thing. They aren't allowed outside world contact until they get back. So, she's been alone in this house for months..."

"Well, that's—"

"And she was dealing with some guy—"

I glanced back at her, my finger frozen on the mouse.

Seraphina's eyes flickered across the page. "She only calls him 'S.' Like she didn't want to name him. He was making her uncomfortable."

"He did it." I turned back to the screen. "Case closed."

"If only it'd be that simple, right?" Seraphina sighed. "This guy really was a creep...but so far there isn't anything that might identify him from any other guy...ugh. A few girls have been giving her problems, too."

I nodded sympathetically as I only half-listened. I read through Drew's history and scanned her most recent website visits, my cheeks warming with my awkwardness. I hadn't realized, until that moment, how personal someone's internet searches could be. Most of it was...dating advice. Like the kind of things I'd ask Mama way before I'd take to typing a question like these into a search engine. I chewed on my cheek. She was alone. Her mother was gone. My stomach soured at the thought. I cleared my throat and clicked on the first link that didn't make me blush: *The Blood Farm*.

The website flashed on the screen. Literally. The name flickered with graphics and the information shot and swirled onto the page. Clearly whoever designed it had no concept of proper website aesthetics. The whole thing hurt, physically hurt, to look at. I squinted as I scrolled. My stomach lurched as I read. "Phin...I think I have something..."

4

# YOU CAN'T SPELL SLAUGHTER WITHOUT LAUGHTER

It was sick. Demented. Disturbed.

The first thing I saw: A long, detailed blog post describing what the author imagined might have happened at the Graham house on the night of the attack. It read like a bad short story. Entertainment. For clicks. My stomach churned in disgust.

And it didn't stop at Drew and Nathan.

There were sections on other missing kids, connecting them all in some way to a local legend of some witch and a place called the Blood Farm. But it all came off as exploitative. Using the kids to prove a point instead of honor or memorialize them. Rather than educational, it was sensationalized. Several different "theories" about what the witch does to the children she takes. But they didn't stop at a wicked witch; there were several tabs about what other monsters might be locked away in the Blood Farm. There was even a tab on what to do if you thought you might be next. Classic fearmongering.

I couldn't look anymore.

Seraphina was still mumbling to herself as she turned each journal page.

"Phin...I think I have something..."

She looked up with a start. I cocked an eyebrow. "Is Drew Graham that good of a writer, you forgot I was here?" I smirked. "Or is her life that filled with drama?"

Phin shut the book and slid off the bed. "What do you have?"

I snickered. "Drama then."

She smacked the back of my head with the book. "Nix!"

I rolled my eyes and waved a hand at the screen. "She visited this website...the night before she was attacked."

"The Blood Farm?" Seraphina muttered as her silver eyes moved across the page. "What's that?"

I scrolled farther down the page. "It's a local legend. This website..." I clicked a tab. "It was created by these two idiots. As of this year, they are juniors at Gloria Godwin School."

Seraphina grabbed a rose-gold pen off the desk and a pale-pink sticky note. She leaned over my shoulder and, without taking her eyes off the computer, she scribbled down the website. "We can check it out back at the motel—we should get the guys."

I frowned up at her as I swatted her silky, blonde hair away from my face. "Why?"

"Because we've been in this house too long already." Seraphina straightened and tucked the sticky note between the pages of the journal. "Last thing we need is to get arrested for messing with a crime scene or something." She headed for the door.

I shut down the browser, switched off the computer, and hurried after her. Instinctively, I cast the bedroom one last glance, my heart sore in my chest at the sight of the top drawer of her dresser, where she'd hidden the book she'd never get to finish.

When we made it downstairs, the guys were just heading up to get us.

"Find anything useful?" Logan's eyes were on Phin, so, of course, I answered.

"Actually, we did. Phin's quite the snoop when she wants to be."

Logan cocked an eyebrow. "And here I thought that was your expertise, Streaky."

Seraphina eyed me with a cool, amused smirk.

Logan jutted his head in the direction of the hallway. "I want to show you the scene."

He led us down the hall and down a handful of steps into a large living room with plush, expensive furniture. It was rich, but cozy. Lots of whites and browns. Built-in bookshelves lined one side, and a glass fireplace was nestled in the center of the back wall between two long windows that stretched floor to ceiling. I couldn't help but imagine how cozy it'd be on a snowy afternoon. I smiled slightly at the thought, until Logan nodded at the floor. I moved around the couch to see. My mouth fell open.

Whatever I'd expected...it wasn't that.

I hadn't been prepared. I wasn't ready. I recoiled, instinctively taking a step back and bumping into Cole, who squeezed my shoulders hard. I was going to be sick. The room spun slightly as I struggled to remain standing.

The middle of the carpet was shredded to pieces. Threads and chunks of material flopped over like peeled skin, brown with blood. So much blood. A huge dark pool in the center of the room. Then I saw the couch. The cushions were ripped apart and stained with more old blood. Buckets and buckets of blood. The stains streaked down the front of the upholstery and splattered the floor.

Logan cleared his throat. "This is your case, Grey. Tell me what you see."

I licked my lips and blinked furiously as I tried not to think too much about Drew's smiling face, a kiss pressed into her cheek. I tried to speak, but my mouth was dry. I took a breath and tried again. "One of them was on the floor...killed on the floor. The other on the couch. The door was locked. No sign of forced entry.

They let them in...or at the very least opened the door for them... so, they either knew the attacker, or they trusted the look of them."

Logan nodded. "Right, so that narrows your monster down to what?"

I chewed on the inside of my cheek and tried not to look at the blood splatter on the walls I hadn't noticed before. "A humanoid... with claws." I eyed the tattered carpet. "Huge claws."

"It also wasn't random," Phin murmured from behind me. Her voice was soft as the hum of a hummingbird, and still I flinched. I glanced back at her. She swallowed. "It happened in her home. It's personal. A personal attack. Most likely, right?" She glanced at Logan almost shyly for confirmation.

Logan gave her a soft smile. "Most likely."

"What do you think?" I looked at Logan. "I mean, what has claws like that?"

Logan frowned, his eyes on the mangled couch. He was quiet for a moment. It freaked me out. He was the expert. Logan not knowing made it even more disturbing. Finally, he looked up at us, his green eyes hard. "We have to see the remains."

We couldn't all go. Apparently. Logan said that four was too big of a group. We'd look suspicious. I said that was a bunch of bat poop. He said he didn't care what I said. But luckily for me, Seraphina has the most striking silver doe-eyes in the world. He couldn't say no to her. Just barely.

So, we all loaded up and headed to the funeral home. It was a bit of a drive, nestled deep in the woods on the outskirts of the rolling hills of the mountainous Watertown. And across from the Gloria Godwin School, which was a bit weird.

Cole turned the van off the back road and down the long cemetery driveway. The gravel road twisted through the trees and bumped and dipped with deep potholes. We exchanged an uneasy glance as our teeth rattled. What was it like when a hearse jittered down this road?

I looked out the window as we continued to bounce down the road, everything in the back of the van slamming and banging along with us. Out across the graveyard grounds, tombstones stuck out strangely among the thick, tall trees, like random teeth bursting from the ground. They were all old headstones, aged by time and style. But they weren't dirty or overgrown or littered with fallen leaves from the autumn-stripped trees. Every single one was maintained with meticulous care.

Cole pulled the van up to the funeral home. It was an old Victorian house, tall and looming above us in the gray afternoon light, the third story trapped in a thicket of branches from the barren maple trees leaning overhead, its spindlework and intricate columns, bay windows, towers and turrets, and wrap-around porch, all pale in the gloom of the cloudy sky.

"Finally," I muttered moodily. The place was positioned at the very end of the dirt road and the very back of the cemetery. "We must've passed a thousand dead guys to reach this place."

Cole scoffed and shook his head. He shifted the van into park and pushed open his door. "Come on."

I jumped out of the van and shoved my hands in the front pocket of my Lacuna Coil hoodie as we all gathered in a small huddle in the tiny gravel parking lot. There were only two other vehicles: a battered old beater car and a shiny, old-fashioned, black car with ample curves and small, round headlights. I smiled slightly. I wasn't much of a car person...at all. But I could appreciate a nice one...and I knew my movies. And that old car put Hell's Chariot to shame.

I glanced at Logan. He was eyeing Cole and me with a tight jaw and grim apprehension in his gaze. I scowled underneath his scrutiny. "What?"

Logan rubbed a hand over the side of his face. "If we're going to be believable...the both of you will need to not look so—"

My eyes widened. My mouth fell open before pursing into a tight pout. I folded my arms tight across my chest and glared up at him. "What's wrong with how we look?" Before he could answer, I slapped the back of my fingers down the sides of my hoodie. "This is comfy!" I snapped, lamely.

Logan rolled his eyes. "You look like the two of you just rolled out of bed after a grunge concert. No one is going to take us seriously, let alone poke around dead bodies with you dressed like that."

I glanced back at Cole. He shifted awkwardly, tugging at the corners of his jean jacket that he'd pulled on over his old Metallica T-shirt. Then he shoved his hands in the pockets of his baggy dark-green pants. My eyes slid sideways to Logan. "Fine. We'll dress like lumberjacks next time. Where do you shop for all your Paul Bunyan cosplay?"

Logan's jaw twitched, but Cole spoke up then. "He's right, Nix. We have to start preparing for these kinds of things."

"Maybe lose the red chunks, too, Streaky." Logan reached out and rumpled my hair like I was an overgrown puppy dog.

"Whatever," I scoffed, my cheeks hot with the insult. "I don't care what you all say...there's no way I'm going to have *boring hair*."

Cole burst out laughing.

I gritted my teeth together. Anger prickled along my arms. I had half a mind to hex every one of them.

Logan snickered. He slapped Cole on the back. "Let's go, before she hexes our heads to our butts..."

Cole chuckled and followed Logan.

My fingers clenched at my sides, digging into my palms.

Seraphina bit her lip on a grin. She draped her arm around me. "Come on, Nix." She led me up the path toward the old house. "Don't worry. No one is going to mess with your hair."

I was sour and grouchy as we clumped together inside the doorway of the funeral home.

Logan looked around the entryway as he decided which direction to go. He had four choices. "Hello?" he called out into the old house.

There was no answer. We all exchanged glances. Cole nodded toward the right. A placard on the wall read: Employees Only. The archway beside the sign opened and turned sharply to the left and ended abruptly in a staircase. With Logan at the head of our pack, we rounded the corner and descended the stairs.

As soon as we got to the bottom of the stairs, Logan hesitated. And I laughed. Loudly.

In the middle of the room, a girl, in a Halestorm tank-top, plaid mini-skirt, and fishnet stockings, stood at a table, preparing the body of an old woman for burial. Her hair, pulled back into high pigtails, was streaked like a sunset of hot pink, soda-pop-orange, and fuchsia. She smacked her lips as she chomped on a big wad of bubble gum the exact shade of the pink streaks her hair. I grinned and shoved Logan out of the way.

She had an old set of headphones on her head, blaring a catchy beat. Totally absorbed in her work and her music, she didn't notice us. The girl blew a giant bubble and it popped on her face. She licked it up expertly with her tongue.

"Excuse me, ma'am?" I waved to get her attention.

She looked up, flinching slightly. Then she pulled the headset down around her neck with a bright, happy smile.

"Nice hoodie!" She nodded toward me, grinning. "I love that movie." Then she inclined her head as she studied the four of us. "Can I help you guys?"

I hurried forward to extend my hand. "Hi, Phoenix Stephens."

She shook my hand with a slightly perplexed smile. "Lenore."

I jutted a thumb behind me. "We're pre-med students from Syracuse University." I pulled my lanyard out from underneath my hoodie and leaned forward, so she could inspect the fake ID.

She raised her perfectly shaped eyebrows in interest and took the badge in her hands. Satisfied, she dropped it, and I tucked it back beneath my collar.

"Professor Anthony sent us to—"

"Oh, Professor Anthony?" Lenore grinned, her dark eyes dancing. "He's a peach, ain't he? The old fart."

I beamed back. "Yeah, ain't he?"

She moved around the table so she could stand beside us. She put her hands on her hips and looked at each of us in turn. Then she inclined her head, her brow furrowed and her sunset hair swinging. "Aren't you all a bit young for—"

I rolled my eyes to the ceiling with an embarrassed shrug. "We're advanced placement. See, we three are juniors in the independent study program. Dual-enrollment homeschool students, technically."

Lenore glanced over my shoulder at Logan, with a flirty smirk. "And tall, tan, and golden?"

Logan stepped forward, but I slapped his chest with the back of my hand. "Aw, he's just your average college frat boy." I shrugged with a downturned smile. "Definitely below average intelligence. Just barely scraping by...my sister does all his homework—"

Logan's hands squeezed my shoulders as he guided me over to the side. "Lenore, you'll have to excuse Phoenix. She just can't seem to close her mouth half the time. It's too big, you see."

I pursed my lips into a tight smirk as I eyed him sideways.

Logan cleared his throat before he continued, "See, Lenore, Professor Anthony sent us to examine the remains of Drew Graham and Nathan Campbell."

Lenore opened her mouth in a small circle, then she bit her lower lip. Her brow crinkled. "Oh, well...Mr. Wollstonecraft...he's not here today. He takes Sundays off..."

Logan was good. Really good. Even I had to give him credit. He looked down at her with a lopsided, boyish grin that crinkled his golden-speckled green eyes just right. He ran a hand through his thick James Dean hair and massaged the back of his neck. "You know, this is really embarrassing, but Phoenix is right. I'm not the best student...I'm failing, actually. And this report, it's due on Sunday. Tonight. Online message board, you know? Is there any way we could just...glance at them real quick?"

Eyebrows raised and an amused smile tickling my cheek, I looked at Lenore.

She cocked her head with an indulgent smirk, her sunset pigtails swinging. "Fine." She stretched her gum out with her tongue and blew a bubble that burst with a loud pop. "But, just you, Frat Boy. The nerds have to wait upstairs."

My jaw dropped. Lenore smacked her gum and grinned, her eyes only on Logan, who flashed me a cocky smirk, coupled with a shrug that made me want to hex his face. My fingers itched for my wand as I hissed through my teeth. "Are you serious—"

"Forget it, Phoenix," Phin muttered low in my ear, so only I could hear.

With a disgusted sniff, I shut my mouth, eyebrows raised in disbelief. Without another word, Phin looped an arm through mine and tugged me back toward the stairs. Cole gave Logan a curt nod, barely managing a straight face, and headed up after us. By the time he made it up the top step, his face cracked into a stupid smile.

I glared at him as I paced the sitting room, or receiving room, or whatever the hex the place was called. "You think that's funny? That bimbo leaving us out like that? Just because we don't look like a greaser from the '50s?"

Cole struggled to keep a straight face as he dropped into an empty chair. "Hey, without his greasy good looks, Lenore would've kicked us all out. You should be grateful his hair's so shwoopy. And thank Phin for keeping his edges straight." Cole chuckled to himself with a shake of his head.

I scoffed and rolled my eyes toward Phin. She wasn't laughing. Seraphina sank into the love seat, her back uncomfortably straight as though she were literally on edge, and without a word, she pulled Drew's diary out of her messenger bag and opened it. I stared at her as she stared at the page. Her eyes weren't moving.

My irritation burned like a sunburn on the surface of my skin. I had to get outside. The room was suffocating. "I'll be right back."

I marched toward the door.

"Where—"

"I forgot something in the van," I snapped as I wrenched open the door and slammed it behind me.

I stomped down the porch and kicked through the crunchy fallen leaves, scratching along the stones in the cool November wind. The air was cold and damp. I squinted up at the gray sky visible through the naked trees. The clouds looked just dark enough to drizzle. Perfect. I stalked toward the van. I leaned against the side and stared sullenly out into the cemetery.

That's when I saw him.

A guy raking leaves a few yards away. He was too young to be "Mr. Wollstonecraft." But clearly, he worked here. I pushed off the van and walked over to him as slowly as my patience would allow. He didn't turn as I approached. He continued to rake at the dried leaves slick with grassy dew. I stood just behind him, dangerously close to getting poked by the handle of the rake.

I cleared my throat in an obnoxious way. "'Cuse me."

Nothing.

I bobbed a bit to avoid the handle. I muttered nastily under my breath and rapped him hard on the shoulder.

To say he jumped would be a complete lie. He full-on fell. Scrambling away from me on the grass before he turned a wide-eyed, terror-stricken face toward me.

Torn between surprise and hilarity, I stepped back from him with my hands up in surrender. "Sorry...you didn't hear me..." I pointed to my ears as I fought to keep a straight face. "Earbuds..."

The guy fumbled up from the grass, finding his feet beneath his short, spindly legs. He bent down to snatch up his fallen rake and held it up like a wizard staff. I studied him for a moment, still fighting against a smile. Like Logan, the guy's face was sharp and angular, but where the lines of Logan's face were strong and masculine, this dude's features were thin and delicate. His cheekbones were so prominent, they almost cast a shadow across his ghostly white skin, stark against his long, wavy, black hair. He looked like a vampire straight out of that Anne Rice movie. But instead of lace and knee britches, he was dressed in ripped jeans too big for his slight frame and a black Ghostface T-shirt he could've borrowed from Cole, underneath a dark flannel shirt that would've made Logan proud. He forced his fingers through his hair, shoving it back out of his gray, sunken eyes. "You scared the bejeezus out of me!"

I cocked an eyebrow as the corner of my mouth twitched. "I need your help."

The guy blinked his heavy-lidded eyes.

Then I saw it. I shook a finger at him as I struggled to remember. "You run that—that website...uh, *the Blood Barn*?"

"*The Blood Farm*, yeah..." The guy's sharp, sulky face split into a delighted smirk. He swapped the rake from one hand to the next and stepped forward, closing the distance between us. "Well, I mean...my buddy, he's the main developer—he's got the way with words. I just do the historical footnotes. They're listed at the bottom...if you, ya know, scroll a bit." He extended a hand, and we shook. "Rory Meeks. Always nice to meet a fan."

I scoffed in amused disbelief. "Right."

He smoothed back his hair against the sides of his face. "So, how can I help you?"

I hesitated. "I'm in an advanced study program at the high school and—"

Rory crinkled his eyebrows together and gave me a thin-lipped smirk. "You don't go to Gloria Godwin."

"I homeschool." The lie came quickly because it wasn't one. Then I added, "It's a program through the school—university, dual-enrollment—" I waved a hand with an easy smile. "It's complicated, but anyway, the point is: I'm taking a class at Syracuse on forensic anthropology. Professor Anthony sent me, my sister, and two of our classmates to study the remains of Drew Graham and Nathan Campbell but—"

Rory nodded sympathetically. "Lenore wouldn't let you work without Mr. Wollstonecraft." Rory leaned back on the rake, his eyes half closed as they crinkled on a downturned smile. "Sounds about right. Might not look it, but that girl is a stickler for the rules."

I turned my head and glanced at him sideways. "And what about you?"

Rory gave an almost modest shrug, a lopsided smile piercing his dimple. "Well, as you know, I'm a local historian and investigative journalist—"

I snorted. "And here I thought you were a part-time groundskeeper?"

Rory's pale cheeks pinched pink as he glanced sheepishly at his rake. "And there's also that..." He closed his eyes and waved a hand through the air. "But every genius needed a day job...or rather, a weekend...and afterschool...job..." He paused as he considered this and then held up his hand again. "But that's not the point. Point is, I can answer your questions." He winced, shrugged, then glanced up at the sky and added, "Sort of. In a way."

Eyebrows raised, I waited a moment to be sure he was done rambling. I opened my mouth, but shut it a second later as he continued, "My sister." He nodded, his dark hair swaying. He gripped the rake in both hands and leaned on the end. "She's, uh, the—well, *a* deputy. Watertown Sheriff's Department."

I blinked, stunned stupid by his mumbling. Then I grinned. "Seriously?"

Rory smiled and smoothed his hair behind his ears. He held the rake to his chest. "As a journalist...I am quite experienced in obtaining information...through whatever means necessary."

I scrunched my smile into a smirk. "Meaning?"

"Meaning..." He bounced a bit on his heels. Then he pointed the rake at me and then pulled it back into his chest. "I can get you the files. Autopsy notes, photos, anything."

I gave him a sharp punch to the shoulder. "Let's go."

Rory blinked, his gray eyes wide and round. "I...I'm sorry—now? You want to go *now*?"

"Yup." I looped an arm through his and dragged him across the grass, through the trees, and toward the parking lot.

"But—" Rory stumbled over his words as much as his feet.

"Which car is...oh, this one." I snickered as I pulled him toward the tiny, rusted beater. "You drive, I'll follow, okay?"

Rory's brow wrinkled as he glanced back at the discarded rake and leaf pile in the distance.

"We won't be long. I promise. And then you can get right back to your raking—"

"Groundskeeping," Rory mumbled weakly. He was barely taller than me. His gray eyes met mine as he hesitated.

"Please, Rory. I really need this. For my paper."

Rory sighed, clearly conflicted. "Okay." He held up a finger. "But you have to be cool, okay? The sheriff is a real witch."

I chuckled and slapped a hand on his shoulder. "Whatever you say, boss."

With that, I turned on my heel and hopped in the van.

Finally, I was getting somewhere.

## 5

# IF I TOLD YOU THIS WAS KILLING ME, WOULD YOU STOP?

It was small. At least, it seemed small to me. I'd never been to a sheriff's station. Back in Nile, I didn't even think we had a sheriff's station. Sheriff Vantine and his deputies—his sons—just kind of patrolled the island, made small talk with the islanders, and then went back home. Standing in the parking lot with Rory, I eyed the cop car next to us, my hands twitchy and impatient. We were about to steal police records from the sheriff's department. This was big.

And I was nervous as hex.

Sure, I was known to snoop (occasionally), listen at keyholes (maybe), and eavesdrop (of course, a girl can't help hearing), but pretending to be someone else for information? I'd only done that once—to Logan and his brother. The funeral home didn't count. Lying to the *police*? I'd never done anything like that before. I swallowed thickly, but I couldn't get rid of the lump in my throat. I licked my lips as I studied the station. A female deputy in her khaki uniform, with her badge and gun, came out of the building, shooting a suspicious glance our way as she headed for her car. At least Rory's rust bucket blended in a little bit. Cole's van stuck out like a teenage Kurt Cobain at ROTC camp.

"So, what's the plan?" I looked at Rory as we huddled awkwardly beside his beat-up, old junker. The officer shot us one more look, before she slipped into her car and drove away.

"Uh, okay..." Rory straightened his dark flannel shirt, pulling at the collar flaps with both hands. He raked a hand through his hair, and then another. "I'm going to see my sister. And you are my friend...who is, what? Like, doing research on the recent kidnapping...for the...uh, school paper...maybe?" He glanced at me with a wince. "Does that sound believable?"

I grinned and gave his arm a good smack. "Yup."

Rory flinched with a guilty smirk, and we walked up to the station. "Honestly, I've never done anything like this before." He choked out a chuckle. "I mean...I've done plenty of breaking and entering...even snuck around the station a handful of times...but never when people were like—paying attention."

I opened the door for Rory and bit my tongue on a retort I would have readily shot at anyone else. This anxious, mumbling, vertically-stunted, teenage Ichabod Crane was *clearly* not used to asserting himself in *any* situation, much less a grand theft of classified documents. But, somehow, I had a soft spot for him. Maybe it was because he'd dropped everything to help me. After being abandoned by my sister for a demon, blown off by my best friend, and ditched by the monster hunter equivalent of Qui-Gon Jinn, it was nice to have a sidekick...however awkward and greasy his hair.

The plan was solid. A high school student researching the kidnappings? It wasn't even a lie, really. I totally had this handled. And if not...I could always toss a little Jedi mind trick here or there.

I flashed Rory a smile and gave him a nudge as we slipped inside the station. "You got this, Meeks," I whispered.

"Hey, Rory! What cha doing here?" A young officer smiled up at him from where she sat behind the front desk. She was a plump blonde with a pretty face that lit up in a way that warmed the whole station. I liked her energy. It was dramatically different from her little brother. She was sunshine, and he was a rain cloud. Yup. I liked it.

Rory went up to the desk and gestured almost shyly toward me. "Uh, Heather, this is—"

"Hi, Officer Meeks." I flashed an easy grin and held out my hand over the desk. "I'm Phoenix. Rory's friend."

Officer Meeks chuckled and nodded eagerly. She grasped my hand in both of hers. She had a pleasant laugh that matched her smile. "Oh, please. Call me Heather..." She looked between the two of us. "I thought Rory had work today? It's Sunday, isn't it?"

Rory nodded and folded his arms on top of the counter as he leaned in close, eying the other officer at work in a nearby cubicle. "Right. See, Phoenix is new to town...researching Drew Graham and Mary Tran for the school paper." He raked a hand through his dark hair and glanced back at me. "I was hoping you could help her out with that?"

"Of course!" Heather jumped up and waved us around the desk. "Come on, I'll take you to the back room—Abigail, would you mind watching the desk for me?"

Heather Meeks grinned cheerfully at the officer. The young woman, Abigail, had hair like carrot sticks and a face as sour as pickles. She looked like she'd rather rip Heather's happy face off than do anything else, but she nodded stiffly.

"Thank you so much!" Heather gushed, completely indifferent to the hatred in Abigail's eyes. She turned back to me as bright and bubbly as ever. She looped an arm around me and led me across the room, past cubicles and shelves of office supplies. "You see, we don't have many officers, so with the Graham/Campbell case and missing Mary Tran...we are spread kind of thin. The sheriff isn't in right now. She takes charge of all the big cases like that—'course, we never usually have anything like this in Watertown. We are a small, quiet community, after all. But as head of our media relations, I'd be happy to help you out and answer any—"

"Just Phoenix, Heather..."

Heather and I both stopped short to stare at him.

Rory turned pink. He shoved his hands into the pockets of his oversized jeans and shrugged. "I gotta use the bathroom."

Heather scrunched up her face and inclined her head, her blonde ponytail swaying. "All right, Rory...you know where it is...around that corner, past the sheriff's office."

Rory bobbed his head as he smoothed his hair against the sides of his face. Then he hurried, shoulders hunched over and head down, in the direction of the sheriff's office.

Heather looked at me and grinned. "Shall we?"

"Honestly, ma'am, I'm just grateful for your help..." I bit my lip like Seraphina and tried to mimic her earnest enthusiasm. "I'm a bit nervous. I've never interviewed before...and these cases... they're such a big deal. So important. I want to get it right, you know?"

Heather nodded with a soft smile. She placed a gentle hand on my shoulder. "I'm sure you'll do just fine." With that she guided me into a small, empty break room and shut the door behind us.

She waved a hand at the round table in the center of the room. "Go ahead, sweetie. Take a seat. You like coffee?" Without waiting for my answer, she waddled over to the small kitchen and started up the coffee maker.

"I'd love some!" I settled into an empty chair and dropped my backpack at my feet. I started to rummage inside for a notepad and pen. I slapped the pad onto the table and clicked my pen, holding it poised and ready.

Heather, meanwhile, was ripping open packet after packet and dumping sugar into her mug. I grinned. I liked her a lot. After my cup was done pouring, Heather plunked the steaming mug in front of me along with a big handful of sugar packets. "You take sugar, hon?"

My eyes glittered as I took in the pile of packets. "Absolutely."

Heather snorted. "Oh, good. The other girls? Abigail, Clara, and the sheriff? Nope. They like it dark and beany. Bleh." She made a face as she took a seat across from me, her mug cupped in her plump hands. "They leave the sugar all to me, and you know what?" She raised her eyebrows and smiled with a glint in her gray eyes. "I say that's fine."

I chuckled. "More for you!"

Heather nodded with an appreciative smirk. "Exactly, my girl." She paused to take a sip and murmured over the top of her mug, "But it is nice to have company. I do enjoy the camaraderie of sharing a cup-a-joe, don't you?"

I raised my mug to her before taking an eager sip.

Heather gulped her coffee and chuckled softly. "Truth be told, at first I thought Rory had brought you here for that website of his." She made another face.

I snorted. "Yeah, no. I have nothing to do with that."

Heather smiled down into her mug. "You know, I get it. I understand how it works—kids making up stories to bring a little drama to this dull, little town. But, eventually, it all gets too much."

I blinked as I took a quick sip. I had no idea what she was talking about. I cleared my throat and frowned thoughtfully. "You know, I haven't read a lot of the website...what is it about, anyway? Some local legend?"

"Gosh, I forgot you're new, aren't cha?" Heather rolled her eyes and gave me a gentle smile. "On the outskirts of town, there's an old stone building, kind of looks like an old church or a meeting house from the old days...folks call it the 'Blood Farm.'" She wiggled her fingers in bunny-eared air quotes. "They say long ago, way back to the founding of the town, when the Godwin family first settled this place, a witch used to live there... luring young ladies and little girls to her with the promise of work...only to sacrifice them and bathe in their blood..." Heather winced and stuck out her tongue. Then she shook her head. "It's all nonsense, but Rory and his buddy, Keirian. They go on and on about that place. I really wish they wouldn't. It's only drawing more attention to it. My mother says it helps him process his emotions...says it's a healthy outlet for him, and all, but I wonder..."

I leaned forward in my seat, pen and pad forgotten. "So, people think Mary Tran was taken by the witch?"

Heather's eyes shined with emotion as she sniffed and looked toward the ceiling. "Well, you know how things go. When something doesn't make sense, folks always need to make up a reason. Like I said before, we don't usually have tragedies in Watertown. The most drama we see is drunk and disorderly. But occasionally, kids go missing...and when they do..." Heather shrugged as she stared sadly into her mug.

She was quiet for a moment, as though she couldn't bear to say any more. Then she cleared her throat, shook herself, and met my eyes with a steady, gray-eyed gaze. "Some say it's the Blood Farm witch—but then the kids'll get bored, and the story will change. Now they're saying it's not the witch, but a creature she locked inside the place. They say if you open the Blood Farm door, you'll let it loose. And it'll hunt you down and drag you to Hell to meet her..." As her words faded, Heather frowned. A tear slid down her cheek. She swiped at her face and forced a watery smile. "Gosh. Look at me. I'm sorry, sweetie. It's just been a hard few weeks. Drew Graham. I used to babysit her." Heather sniffed and choked on a weak laugh. "Rory had the biggest crush on that girl. But all the boys did, didn't they?"

A sober silence settled over the room. We sipped our coffee. Heather was quiet in her sadness over Drew and Mary Tran, but I was quietly trying to make sense of what I'd just heard. I picked up the pen as I gulped more coffee. I scribbled down as much of Heather's monologue as I could remember.

"So." Heather licked her lips and set down her cup. She folded her hands. Then she sat up straight. "What is it you'd like to know, Miss Phoenix?"

"Who owns the farm?"

Heather cocked an eyebrow. "I meant about the Mary Tran kidnapping, my dear…"

Right. Oops. Hastily, I put down my coffee and cleared my throat. "First, how many officers do you have here in Watertown?"

"Well, as I said, we're a small town…we have three deputies, including myself, underneath Sheriff Godwin."

I blinked as I scribbled. "Missing children…tends to be a regular thing for Watertown, doesn't it? What do you have to say about that?"

Heather's happy face faltered. "You know, grown-ups tell little ones—warn them they'll get snatched if they misbehave…" Heather bit her lip and stared at the center of the circular table, stuck in a memory. "But my mother never did that. When we were little…my mother always used to say, 'the monsters only take the good ones, Heather Ann' and 'you're too good for your own good'…'just like your brother'…" Her eyelashes fluttered. A tear spilled down her round check. She slapped it away and met my gaze with a wavering smile. "I think she was right. They always seem to go missing…the sweetest of us." Heather put a hand over her eyes and groaned. "Oh, gosh, sweetie, I'm sorry. I'm blubbering like a baby at bedtime—"

"No, no. Please. It helps me understand…the community pain and everything. Keep going." I crinkled my brow and gave her a sympathetic smile.

She folded her lips tight. She shook her head as she glanced off to the side. "Every few decades…little ones go missing. Cases of lost children pile up. And every single one is unsolved…except for Justine."

My pen froze on the page. "And she still refuses to speak?"

Heather nodded sadly with a downturned smile. "Mmhmm. It was way before my time…gosh, my mother was best friends with Justine's big sister!" She laughed lightly and cleared her throat. "When I was growing up, some of the kids had theories, you know? If it wasn't the Blood Farm witch, it was her monster. If it wasn't that, it was the town undertaker, Victor Wollstonecraft, or the giant cockroach that skitters inside the walls of the school—" Heather scoffed and scooted close, leaning over the table. "Some of my girlfriends even suggested Justine Kilpatrick!" Heather rolled her eyes to the ceiling. "Kids can be nasty little creatures...and Justine keeps to herself. Doesn't talk to anybody. The only time anybody ever sees her is when she goes to visit her sister."

I blinked, pen slipping on the paper. "I thought her sister was taken—"

Heather held up a hand as she gulped her coffee. "Excuse me, I wasn't clear: her sister's *cenotaph*...you know, her memorial marker at the cemetery." Heather sighed and looked down into her cup. "Justine visits it once a year...on the day she was rescued." Heather checked her phone with a scrunched-up face. "This week, I believe...was it?"

My eyes skimmed over the scribbles on the pad. I should've come with a list prepared. It was hard to think of all my questions on the spot. I cleared my throat as an awkward silence settled. "Now, I know all about the past missing kids, how they went missing from school..."

Heather nodded sadly over the top of her mug. "Yes, sometime after breakfast. They ate and weren't seen after that."

"But Mary Tran—"

Heather closed her eyes briefly and inhaled deeply. "Yes, little Mary's case is different..."

"And do you think Nathan and Drew—what happened to them—do you think that is connected to Mary Tran's kidnapping?"

Heather lifted her mug to her lips but set it back down without taking a sip. "And you've hit your first hot button question, and I'll have to give you the official answer: We have no comment on that at this time."

Before I could try again, Rory peeked his head inside the room. "Hey, sorry Phoenix, but I gotta get back to work..."

I stood quickly, scooping up my notepad and pen. I dropped them into my backpack. I plucked up my mug and plopped it into the sink. Heather hesitated, getting slowly to her feet. "Sorry I couldn't answer more of your questions, sweetie."

I waved away her concerns. "No worries. I have all I need." I flashed a cheesy grin which she returned weakly.

"All right, I'll walk you kids out...and be careful out there."

Rory and I followed her through the small station and to the door. Officer Abigail eyed the two of us with a sour, pinched expression. She didn't say a word as we passed by the desk. She didn't speak when Heather thanked her and settled back into the chair. And as Rory opened the door, and we both slipped outside into the dark gray of the late afternoon, I could feel her cold eyes on my back.


They were all on the porch when I pulled up. Cole slouched on the steps across from Phin who sat, her back straight against the pillar, and Logan standing on the ground off to the side, arms crossed and scowling. I smirked as I prodded the ignition with my finger and the van died. They looked like the cover of an emo album.

I hopped out of the van, files in hand, my Converse crunching on the gravel. I gave a small wave to Rory. He returned it with a twitch of his hand from across the hood of his rusty old car as he eyed the gang on the steps—Logan in particular, who I had to admit, looked slightly intimidating. As I made my way over to them, Rory hurried off, weaving through the trees, back up the grassy hill to his rake.

Logan's jaw pulsed.

I grinned.

But before I could flash the files, Logan grabbed me by the arm and tugged me toward his truck. "You and me. Talk. Now."

"Fine." I elbowed him hard in the stomach and shoved him off me. The two of us marched around to the truck bed. I stopped short and glared up at him as he towered over me.

"Explain." Logan's nostrils flared, his voice barely below a shout.

I snorted and rolled my eyes up to the darkening sky. I took a deep breath. "Look, I'm sorry I took off without—"

Logan scoffed and looked away from me. He punched his fists into his hips. Then he shook his head. "You don't get it, do you, Phoenix?" Logan's arms fell to his sides, and he shrugged. He met my gaze with hard emerald eyes and a downturned smile.

"What?"

Logan rubbed a hand over his eyes. "We—" He poked a finger into my shoulder and then into his chest to illustrate his point. "—are a team. Okay? You, me, your sister, Cole...we agreed to be a team. Work together. Get this job done. I invited you all along to be in this with me."

I gave a sarcastic smirk. "Yeah, so?"

"So, that means I need you to be smart and use your brain and not act like an idiot."

I blinked. My smirk slipped into a dark scowl. "Excuse me?"

Logan cocked an eyebrow, his face hard. "I need to be able to trust you not to make stupid decisions that could get you killed."

I recoiled, making a face. "What are you talking about?"

Logan pointed up the hill at Rory. "I'm talking about that. How long did you know that guy before you let him lead you off to God knows where?" He shrugged, raising his eyebrows in mock interest. "Like a minute? Two?" Logan held up a hand with a cruel, half-cocked grin. "Oh, no wait. Let me guess—as soon as you saw his grungy, boy band T-shirt, you figured he was all right."

"Actually, it was Ghostface," I snapped back sarcastically. Then I raised an incredulous eyebrow. "Are you serious? That's what you're so mad about?" I tossed my arm out, pointing at Rory off in the distance. "Logan, I had a lead! I did exactly what you would've done!"

He scoffed and rolled his eyes. He shook his head in disbelief. He shifted his stance, his boots crunching the gravel. His jaw tightened, and he spoke through gritted teeth, "You have a lead. You tell somebody. Doesn't have to be me, but you tell Cole, you tell Sam, you tell the damn cat—I don't care, okay? But you tell *somebody*."

I groaned and crossed my arms, crushing the files into me. I jutted my jaw to one side and stared off in stony silence. This was unbelievable. I looked back at him. "And *you* would tell somebody? If you had a lead that was time sensitive with a flake, who could easily change his mind and back out in a second?"

"I would." Logan nodded, his eyes hard and squinted. "I'd give everybody the freaking courtesy of knowing where I was running off to...that's how a team operates."

I chewed on my cheek, struggling to contain a retort, a secret I couldn't help but spill. "And what about Syracuse?" Oops.

Logan's face darkened. "What are you talking about?"

"Oh, come on." I smirked. "You know what I'm talking about, Logan. You disappeared for hours. Phin pretended like she didn't care, no big deal, but you *vanished*. Where'd you go? You didn't tell anybody then, did you?"

Logan's jaw pulsed. His mouth twitched. "Cole. I told Cole, okay? Because that's—"

My eyes narrowed, looking for a lie that wasn't there. I hesitated. "Cole said he didn't know where you were..."

"Because that's what I told him to tell you." Logan flashed a cocky grin that crinkled his dimples as he held out his hands. "Point being: you tell—"

"Oh, yeah?" I tilted my chin up, forcing all thoughts of Cole's lies out of my head. "And who'd you tell when you worked jobs without your brother? And don't say you never worked alone because I know for a fact you worked jobs on your own all the time!"

Logan scowled. He glared down at me, but he didn't answer.

"Exactly." I jabbed a finger into his chest. "You didn't tell anybody. So, this one time, I don't ask for a bathroom pass, I get chewed out and—"

"God, Phoenix, it's not about that!" Logan threw his arms out and groaned. "This isn't some power trip I'm going off on! You're new to the job, okay? Our experience levels—despite what your inflated ego may tell you—are a bit different. I can handle myself, okay? Because I have experience dealing with all of it. And I've proven that over and over since I was even shorter than you. So, you voluntarily putting yourself in a stupid position, one in which you could end up like Drew Graham? It's not happening. I'll drive your butt back to Nile myself if I have to...I'm not dealing with it."

I laughed. I couldn't help it. This was ridiculous. "I'm a *witch*, Logan!"

Logan froze. Something flickered across his face as his golden-green eyes flashed. Understanding.

Before I could call him out on it, question what had just passed through his mind, Cole and Phin came around the truck. Phin slipped her arm through mine and pulled me close. "Let's take this back to the motel."

Cole nodded as he nudged Logan. "Come on, man."

"We're done here, anyway," Logan muttered coolly. He turned his back on me and stalked to the front of the truck. My fingers itched for my wand.


"He cares about you." Phin glanced over at me as her hands gripped the wheel. Cole's tangle of keys clinked as the van bumped over potholes impossible to avoid. "Phoenix, you know that right? He's just trying to teach you. Like a mentor."

I snatched up a bag of potato chips from the giant snack box on the floorboards and popped it open. I stuffed a handful in my face and didn't bother to answer.

Phin sighed and switched on the stereo. The Offspring blasted from the speakers. Over the grind of the music, I shouted to be heard, "He thinks I'm an idiot."

I slid my eyes sideways to study Seraphina. She didn't bother to argue. But after a moment, she switched off the stereo, licked her lips, and tried her best. "He thinks you *acted* like an idiot."

I snorted into my bag of chips. Then I poured a mouthful onto my tongue.

"And Phoenix, you did. You *know* you did," Phin murmured imploringly. "Going off with some random guy? In the middle of a monster hunt? God, Nix, forget Logan, *Mama* taught us better than that."

I scrunched up my mouth into a sideways frown. I glared at her. "And how many times did you go off by yourself when you were dealing with that demon back home?"

"Never." Seraphina looked at me with a small smile before moving her eyes back to the road. "Not once did I ever go anywhere with a stranger without someone I trusted knowing where I was."

I stared at her—back straight with pride in being the perfect, obedient daughter. I snickered darkly to myself. Yeah, okay. I tilted the bag, shaking the last bit of crumbs into my mouth. "Your best friend was possessed," I quipped dryly through the crunch.

Phin's fingers tightened on the wheel. If she had magic, she'd have hexed me. But she didn't. And that's why she didn't get it. None of them did. And I couldn't explain it to her. It would hurt her too bad.

I took a deep breath and huffed out a sigh. "Listen, I'm sorry, Phin. Okay? But it wasn't some joyride. I was working."

"So were we!"

I snorted. "By sitting on an old couch waiting for Logan to sweet-talk that bimbo mortician apprentice?"

Seraphina's jaw clenched. She pushed a hand through her honey-blonde hair. "He examined the bodies...the remains," she corrected herself with a wince.

I flipped open the file on my lap and thumbed through the papers for the pictures. I smacked the back of my hand against the top photo. "These remains?"

Seraphina glanced at my lap. She gasped, swerving the van slightly. She snapped her attention back to the road and readjusted her hands on the wheel. Her face was pale. "Where did you get that?"

"That's what I'm trying to tell you." I shut the file quickly, covering up the grisly image. "Rory Meeks—that greasy-haired Ichabod at the cemetery? His sister is a deputy. While I interviewed her, he made copies of the case files."

Seraphina turned into the motel parking lot, her eyes shifting suspiciously toward me. "He stole—and illegally copied—case files...because you asked him to?"

Shaking her head, she pulled into a parking space. She slapped the van into park and turned to stare at me.

I opened my mouth to argue, but nothing came out. Was it weird that he went to all that trouble...? I tried again. Still nothing. I frowned thoughtfully and inclined my head. "He..."

Seraphina cocked an eyebrow, her rosebud lips pinched in a skeptical pout.

I screwed up my face and shoved her shoulder. "Oh, who cares! I got the files. Let's go."

Seraphina was slow to leave the van. When she did, she didn't even bother stepping up onto the curb.

I stopped and turned back to face her. "What?"

Phin flipped her hair over her shoulder. Her silver eyes slid to the truck. "Logan and I are going to pick up dinner."

I made a face as I followed her gaze. The truck was still running with Logan in the driver's seat. Cole, meanwhile, was crossing the street to meet us, his backpack slung over his hunched shoulders. At the sight of him, I remembered what Logan had said. Cole had lied to me. My fingers crushed the edges of the folder, magic humming in the tips.

I looked back at Phin. "When did you decide this?"

The corner of her mouth twitched. "When we were sitting around for an hour waiting for you to show up."

I winced. Before I could apologize (again), Phin turned on her heel, gave Cole a little wave, and ran across the parking lot for the truck. I scowled. They better bring back something good. This whole afternoon had soured my stomach.

6

# ADMIT IT!!!

"Coffee?" Cole held up a mug as we settled back into the motel room. Icarus was curled up on Seraphina's pillow, asleep. His ears had twitched as we'd come in, but he hadn't bothered to wake up.

"Sure." I tossed my bag onto Cole's bed. The bed squeaked as it bounced.

Cole fired up the coffee machine. I sank down onto the mattress. It groaned underneath me. I watched Cole as kept his back to me and his head bent toward the coffee machine.

The silence was irritating. Grating. Like a hex paste. I scowled at the back of his head. He refused to turn around. Like I wasn't even in the room with him. Fine. Let him be mad at me. Let him lie to me. I had to bite my tongue to keep from shouting at him to take his dumb van back to Nile right then. I was so tired of it. It was Seraphina all over again. Me, listening to whatever she said, being on my best behavior, making sure she didn't find a reason to leave. Again.

I slapped the case file on the bed and flicked it open. Mouth pinched and eyes narrowed, I read through all the information Rory had copied for me.

I didn't bother to look up when Cole passed me my mug. And I didn't say thank you.

Out of the corner of my eye, I saw Cole take a seat at the tiny table and fire up the laptop.

I tried to focus on the words, but I was so angry with Cole, it was almost impossible to process the information. Plus, whoever wrote the report had to be the most boring person in the world. I snatched it off the bed, held it close to my nose, and squinted hard at the words. I had to read it through several times to make any sense of it.

I peeked over the papers at Cole. He scowled at the screen, his mug gripped in one hand.

"I'm sorry I took the van," I blurted out.

"Stole." Cole glanced at me sideways. "Sorry you *stole* the van." He looked back at the computer screen.

"Whatever." I rolled my eyes. "Sorry."

Cole sighed and dropped his mug onto the table with a loud thud. He turned in the seat to face me. "It's not just that—"

I groaned and hid my face behind the report. "Yes, Cole. I know. Logan already gave me the lecture. And Phin." I lowered the pages and winced. "I don't need to hear it again from you, okay?"

Cole scoffed. "Fine." He turned back in his chair toward the laptop and began clicking away on the keys.

I stared stupidly at him. I had no idea what to say to fix whatever was broken between us. I chewed on my cheek, struggling to come up with something to talk about that wouldn't remind him of how mad he was at me. Or remind me of how mad I was at him. I cleared my throat. "You didn't want to get dinner with Logan?" I asked lamely.

"I wanted to work the case," Cole muttered.

I nodded awkwardly. I tried to think of something else to say, desperate to break the tension that'd hardened around the both of us. He must've felt the same pressure because Cole spoke up first.

"And I kinda got the feeling that he wanted to..." His voice trailed off with a sheepish shrug.

"Get the girl alone?" I quipped, taking a gulp of hot, sweet, beany goodness.

He snorted and nodded. "Something like that."

More silence.

Awkward, awful, uncomfortable silence.

I frowned down at my mug.

"Not enough sugar?" Cole asked quickly.

I looked up at him in surprise. My cheeks burned. Silently, I cursed my open, honest face. "No, it's not that..."

Cole gave me a weak twitch, sorry excuse of a smile. "I'm sorry, too. And I'm sorry it's so..."

"Awkward?" I took a long sip.

"Right." Cole put down his mug. He dropped his elbows on the table and bent his head down, smoothing back his thick hair with both hands.

Silence. The steady rhythm of Icarus's purrs was loud in my ears.

I watched him, eyes sharp over my coffee cup. "You and Logan have gotten close over these past few weeks, huh?"

Cole glanced at me with a lopsided smile. He shook his dark hair from his eyes. "Yeah...he's a good guy."

I gnawed on my cheek, then forced a polite smile. I gritted my teeth. Keeping my mouth shut was hard.

Cole twisted a bit in his seat to face me again. "Did you know his mom's gone, too?" Cole closed his eyes briefly as he corrected himself, "Well, she's not *dead*...that he knows of..." Cole snorted, his face dark. "But apparently, Logan's old man was a lot like mine. I mean, swap out the stone hauling for monster hunting and you basically have the same guy."

I raised my eyebrows as I lowered my mug. "That's...kind of a huge difference, don't you think?"

Cole shrugged and waved away my words with a smirk. "Naw."

I folded my lips together as I considered this. Cole never mentioned his parents. His mom had died shortly after he was born, but he never liked to talk about her. We didn't even know how she died. I mean, it's not like we could ask him...and Rachel didn't know, either. And as far as his dad, Cole didn't talk about him, either—mainly because Mr. St. Claire hated us Greys, but also because his dad was always gone for work so there wasn't much to say. He didn't see his dad much, if at all. It made me uncomfortable to hear Cole talk about them so easily now.

"Well, that's good." I tried to smile. "I'm glad you finally got a decent dude to hang out with, Cole." I bit my lip as I struggled to keep my mouth shut, but once I'd opened it, I couldn't keep my question quiet: "Why did you lie to me?"

Cole's face fell. "What do you mean?"

I winced. It was out there now. The room was so small, from my seat on the bed, I reached over and plopped my mug on the table beside Cole's. "For Logan. In Syracuse. You lied to me for Logan...er, about Logan...uh, you know, where he—*whatever*." I waved my hands between us as though to clear the air of my fumbled attempts at communication. My face burned. I put my hands on my thighs and shrugged. "You lied to me. Why?"

Cole inhaled so deeply his whole chest visibly rose. Like he was puffing himself up in defense. "Some hunter buddy of his called him with a tip on the demon—"

My hands slipped off my thighs. "The demon? *Our* demon?"

Cole nodded patiently. "Yes. The one that killed his brother. It's why we were in Syracuse in the first place—"

I jutted my head forward, slumping my shoulders with my mouth agape. "On a tip from some random hunter? Syracuse was a bust!" I furrowed my brow and shook my head in disbelief.

Cole sighed. He tossed his hair to the side. "He met with the hunter and...yeah. Realized it'd been a bad tip."

I scoffed. "You think? Why would—wait, no—why would he ask you to keep his little hunter meeting a secret?" I cocked my head to the side. I eyed him with narrowed, suspicious eyes. "From me and Phin..." I straightened as the pink pinch of Cole's pale cheeks answered me. My jaw dropped. I closed my mouth slowly and hissed through clenched teeth, "Oh, what a—"

Cole held up a hand. "Nix, it wasn't—"

"Some 'hunting buddy'...right. He didn't want you to say anything because it—or rather, *she* wasn't just a buddy, huh?" I rolled my eyes to the ceiling and muttered, "Unbelievable." I leaned up off the bed and snatched my mug off the table. The bed groaned as I sat back and guzzled my tepid coffee.

"Nix, it wasn't like that."

I snorted. "Sure."

Cole eyed me warily. "And you can't tell, Phin, all right?"

I lowered my mug and licked the sugar from my lips. I scoffed. "Right."

"Seriously, Phoenix." Cole's eyes were sad, his face as somber as his voice was serious. "You can't say anything. Please."

His tone made me hesitate. I studied him with my jaw jutted to the side. Impatience and irritation itched beneath my skin.

"He asked me to keep it between the two of us...and I feel like if we're going to be in this for the long haul—"

"Then we shouldn't be keeping secrets from each other!" I held up my mug in salute. I flashed a wide, sarcastic smirk, before I took another sip.

"Then we should be able to trust each other," Cole countered firmly.

"Trust means not lying!" I snapped furiously. "You know I hate keeping secrets, Cole. Especially from Phin. And I'm horrible at it!" I tossed up a hand in erratic frustration.

Cole just looked at me, his face impassive.

I groaned. "Fine. But I'm not lying to her. If she asks, I'll send her to you."

Cole gave a weak smile. "Thank you."

"Yup." I held my mug up to my mouth but didn't drink. Instead, I just muttered behind it.

"Nix...it really isn't what you think—"

I raised my eyebrows and blew my bangs out of my face. "Let's get to work, huh? I mean, that is why you stayed behind, right?"

"Yeah, but—"

"Great." I jumped up off the bed, papers in one hand, coffee in the other, and plopped down into the empty chair. I dropped my mug onto the table and slapped the papers down beside it. "Here."

He blinked in surprise. He looked from the stack to me and back again.

I waved a hand at the papers. "You read through the notes, and —" I grabbed Logan's laptop and fired it up. "I will check out *The Blood Farm*."

"Is this..." Cole lowered the pages to stare at me. "Nix, where'd you get this?"

I smirked, not taking my eyes off the screen as I typed in Logan's password. "I wasn't taking the van on a joyride, Cole."

I pulled up the Blood Farm website and scrolled through it. I glanced around the tiny table for something to write on, and with, but there wasn't anything. I groaned and hopped up from the chair. I snatched my backpack and pulled out my pad, pen, and while I was at it, the printouts from the library. I organized the papers across the bed, the maps on one side, the articles separated by year.

Cole, meanwhile, scribbled a few things on the motel stationary and got up to stick them to the wall next to Mary Tran's missing poster.

I squinted at the note.

Cole caught my eye as he slid back into his seat. "What we determined back at Drew's house...and Logan's take on the creature after viewing the remains."

"Which was?" I took my seat and stared into the laptop screen.

I scrolled down the Blood Farm website without really seeing anything.

"Well..." He shuffled through the case notes and found the photos. "It looked like an animal had eaten Drew's entire torso. Official cause of death is dog mauling...they were eaten alive. But Lenore said it looks more like a grizzly."

"A bear?!" Without thinking, I shut Logan's laptop to blink wide-eyed at Cole. "What monster has a bite like a *bear*?" The idea sent a shiver down my arms.

Cole nodded with a dark wince. "And there were bones missing."

I made a face and fixed him with a quizzical stare. "Like the creature *took*—"

"No." Cole shook his head. "The bones were crushed. Eaten."

My stomach lurched. "What could crush..." I blinked at him and repeated stupidly, "*Eaten* bones?"

Cole set the papers off to the side and lifted his laptop, turning it toward me. "A ghoul."

I reached over the mess of notes and pens and snacks for Cole's computer. I turned in my seat and rested the device on my lap. The image was grotesque: a hunched up, human-like creature with oversized jaws bulging out of its face and fingers that curved into claws large as sickles, leering over a gravesite. As I scanned the screen, Cole explained, "They originated in the Middle East. Mentioned in *One Thousand and One Nights*. Then they were found in Europe. But they didn't pop up in the US until the early 1800s. Edgar Allen Poe described them as neither man nor woman...which is because they can shapeshift—"

I looked over at Cole skeptically as I passed him back the laptop. "But ghouls eat the dead. Dead bodies. Drew and Nathan were alive when they were attacked. And eaten *alive*. Ghouls are scavenger monsters. They aren't predators...not like werewolves or vampires or—"

Cole set the computer back on the table and nodded grimly.

"That's what we were discussing when you pulled up at the funeral home. Ghouls stick to gravedigging. They eat the dead. And they certainly don't crawl out of their tunnels to crash a teenage date night."

I raised my eyebrows with a downturned smirk. "So, it's not a ghoul..."

Cole frowned with a shrug. "I'm going to dig through the books and stuff, but Logan hasn't heard of anything else that could come close to doing that kind of damage to a person."

I scrunched up my face as I considered this. I pointed a finger at Cole. "And it doesn't explain Mary Tran and the other missing kids. Justine Kilpatrick was kept alive for weeks...so we have to assume that the other kids were, as well. Including Mary Tran."

"Right."

I opened Logan's laptop again. Then I shuffled through my notes from Officer Heather Meeks. "Wait, there's a local legend..." My voice trailed off as I checked my untidy scrawl. Holding the pad up against the screen, I scrolled through the website to find something on the witch's creature. "They say there was a witch, an Elizabeth Bathory kind of thing...you know the psycho countess who bathed in blood? Yeah. Ew. Anyway, the Watertown legend goes that this witch—ah, here." I clicked on the tab and read, "'As Dracula manipulated Renfield, so the Blood Farm witch had a familiar in which she entrusted her secrets; the familiar who assisted her in all of her dark deeds'..." I rolled my eyes despite myself. "And it goes on, dripping with melodramatics. But it says the Blood Farm is located somewhere in the woods off an 'Adelaide Road.'"

I grabbed my pen and added the address to my notes. Then I scribbled "Blood Farm" on the motel stationary and pushed off the chair. I stuck it to the wall.

"Wasn't Justine Kilpatrick found on that road?" Cole took a sip of his coffee, typing one-handed. "Yeah. Right here. But...I don't know, Nix."

I slapped at the maps and rifled through the stack. "We should check it out. Obviously, this place must have something to do with the case." I grabbed my bag and shook it empty. Then I went around the room and started stuffing things inside that we might need: silver pen, hawthorn stakes—

Cole glanced up from his screen. "What are you doing?"

I cocked an eyebrow at him. "Getting ready. I mean, granted with my magic we won't have to worry about much...but I still think it'd be a good idea to—"

An incredulous smirk dimpled Cole's left cheek. "Nix, we can't just head out without everybody."

The bag sagged in my arms. "Wait, what?"

"I know you didn't want to hear it from me, but we need to talk about these things before we walk into who knows what."

My jaw tightened. "I thought everyone's issue was communication. Telling someone before you go somewhere. Well, I'm telling you, and you're coming with...I'll even wake up Icarus and tell him," I quipped with a dry smile. "Logan said that'd be enough."

Cole didn't move. He just shifted awkwardly in his chair. "Nix, this is different from research. Visiting the potential location of a creature...I feel like we need to wait for Logan and Phin."

I scoffed, my whole body deflating in disbelief. "You're scared."

"Absolutely." Cole smirked. "If you aren't scared, then you're not doing the job right." He shook his dark hair out of his eyes. "But that's not what this is about..."

I frowned. "Cole, you do remember I'm a *witch*, right?" I held out my hand and wiggled my fingers, my orange magic dust glittered in between them.

Cole grinned. "Nix, I still have the scar from when we were thirteen and you hexed me for eating the last apple cider donut." He held up his finger. "I couldn't possibly forget it."

I lowered my hand and raised my eyebrows with a downturned smirk. "Well, then—"

"We need to make a game plan as a group." Cole shrugged

easily as though it were all common sense. "Before you storm the castle, you assemble the troops. Discuss things. I mean, how mad would you be if they went right now, without saying anything to you?"

"You seriously are okay with sitting around and waiting for orders?" My lip curled in disgust. "From *Logan*?"

Cole laughed. His face was brighter than it'd been in weeks. He stood from the chair and wrapped an arm around me, squeezing me sideways. "Come on. Not orders. We still aren't sure what this thing is...that's priority number one. Research possibilities. And I know you hate to study—"

"I *don't* study," I grumbled.

He walked me over to my chair and woke up the laptop. "—but this is important. We can't hunt something until we know what it is, right?" He picked up our mugs and headed for the coffee machine to fill them back up.

"Fine." My whole body sagged. My shoulders hunched forward with the weight of my disappointment. Cole set the fresh cup of coffee beside me and with his cupped carefully in hand, he dropped back down in front of his computer and picked up the police report. And I started clicking through the blog posts on the website. I drank deeply from my mug and, with a sulky sigh, picked up my pen to scribble more notes.

By the time Logan and Phin got back with dinner, Cole and I had gone through all the pages in the case files and picked apart the Blood Farm website and still had nothing conclusive.

I blew my bangs out of my face and raked a hand through the chunks of hair that'd fallen from my topknot. "The MO matches a werewolf...but that doesn't fit because the lunar cycle is wrong... the actual bite and the manner of the attack match the features of a ghoul..."

"'MO?'" Seraphina raised an eyebrow. A smile teased the

corner of her mouth. "Nix, do you even know what that stands for?"

I narrowed my eyes. "Yeeesss."

Seraphina grinned, nodding knowingly. "Oh, so you know it means modus operandi?"

Logan laughed. Even Cole hid a smile.

My cheeks burned. I stuck my tongue out at her, before returning to the articles in my hands. "Whatever—the attack matches the *habits* of a werewolf...minus the moon thing...the actual state of the remains matches a ghoul, and then we have the kidnappings, which—"

"Are completely different."

I looked at Logan.

His face was hard as he surveyed the new notes we'd added to the wall. "We need to view this as two cases."

I made a face. "But they're clearly connected. Mary Tran was—"

Logan shook his head. "Until we can find something to *actually* connect them—the missing link between them—we need to approach the kidnapped little kid and the mauled cheerleader and her boyfriend as two separate cases."

Before I could argue, Logan reached out his hand expectantly. I slapped the police report into his palm. He brought the folder to the table and sank into the seat beside Cole, who was hunched over his laptop.

"I still can't believe that dweeb stole these for you..." Logan muttered as he scanned the papers. "He must have a thing for bad hair dye."

My mouth dropped open in outrage, but before I could snap a retort, Seraphina whacked a big, brown bag of Chinese takeout into my chest. "Here. Dish out the food."

Anger instantly forgotten, I smiled eagerly. "Excellent!" I clapped her on the back. The force knocked her off-balance. I grinned. "I'm starving." Then I pulled out cartons and grouped them together on the little bit of empty space left on the kitchenette. "So—how was it? You both were gone for a while...did you get lost?"

They both spoke at once.

"Fine."

"Nothing."

A smirk slid across my face as I eyed the two of them. Seraphina ran a hand through her hair, then shoved her hands into her jean pockets. She nibbled nervously on her lower lip. Logan's jaw tightened, and his cheeks tinged pink. *Something* interesting had happened...and not food related, either.

I continued to organize the takeout while Logan cleared his throat. "All right, enough small talk—let's get to work."

I passed out the food and plastic forks, and we all ate as we combed through everything: the books, the internet, the articles. But I couldn't shake the nagging feeling that we were missing something.

# SPARE ME THE DETAILS

After a while, Logan put down his carton of fried rice. "So, this guy that snagged the case file...he runs this website with this other nerd? Uh—" He squinted at the laptop screen. "Keirian Cullen?"

"From what I can tell...it's all mostly garbage," Cole muttered.

"I think the Blood Farm legend explains a lot of it." I shoveled several plastic spoonfuls of white rice, dripping with sweet-and-sour sauce, into my mouth. "The missing kids—and if the witch had some kind of creature locked up, and Drew and Nathan let it out...that explains them."

Seraphina frowned thoughtfully as she sat cross-legged on the bed beside me. "Why would Drew do that?"

"Because kids do dumb stuff, Phin; you know this better than anybody. Especially the ones that aren't homeschooled." I shrugged, scooped up more sticky, sweet rice into my mouth, and spoke around a mouthful. "She was probably dared to do it. I mean, she visited that website, like, the day before she died."

Phin shook her head. "I don't think Drew would do that."

I glanced at her sideways with a skeptical smirk. "Why not? Because of all the pink lace and stuffed animals?"

Seraphina scrunched her mouth off to the side in an impatient frown. "No. Because I've been reading her journal all day, and I feel like I have a pretty good sense of what kind of person she was... and Drew Graham would not succumb to peer pressure like that. She goes on and on about this clique of mean girls she's dealing with on the regular. Not once does she ever even hint that she wants to impress them. Quite the opposite, actually. And she was—"

"Maybe the boyfriend made her do it?" Cole suggested. "Or he did it on his own, and it followed him to her house?"

I shrugged. "Either way." I popped a fried ball of pork into my mouth and packed it like a chipmunk in my cheek as I continued, "Blood Farm witch and her monster. That explains the disappearances *and* the maulings."

Logan shook his head and held up his plastic spoon. "One case at a time. And the Blood Farm theory doesn't explain why a witch would suddenly start snagging kids from the school, when she'd been grabbing people at random for, like, a hundred years prior. And if she *did* have a monster locked up in the Blood Barn—"

"Farm..." I mumbled through my mouthful.

"—why did it wait until now to attack? There haven't been any other weird maulings in the entire history of Watertown."

I swallowed my giant bite as I struggled to keep up with his arguments. "Maybe—"

"Forget the barn. It's a distraction. And honestly—" Logan made a face at the screen. "These idiots look like they're making half of this up for attention."

"But—"

"We need to start at the beginning." Logan glanced at Cole. "How far back do the random disappearances go?"

Cole winced as he scrolled. "They seem to go back forever... like, as far back as the town was settled there were missing people. Dozens. Every year. All year long."

"When did they first mention a witch?" Seraphina pushed off

from the bed, small carton of rice in hand. She walked over to Cole and leaned over his shoulder. "Did you check the penny papers?"

The three of us stared at Seraphina. She blushed prettily as she twisted a long, blonde strand around her finger and shrugged. "The penny papers were kind of like the tabloids of the 1800s...if there was anything gossip worthy, it'd be in there."

Logan snickered as he stabbed a spicy chicken. "Nerd..."

"Okay—Watertown Public Library database." Cole started tapping away on the computer. "There were two papers circulating Watertown in the 1800s...*The Watertown Times* and..." Cole glanced up at Phin with a smile. "*The Watertown Leaker.*"

Logan choked on his pork fried rice. He grinned and leaned forward to read it himself.

Cole nodded. "Looks like...the first mention of a witch was in the late 1850s. The town held a meeting to discuss the problem..." He hesitated.

Seraphina frowned at the screen. "They burned a Brunhilde Wollstonecraft at the stake in 1862. She was seventy years old."

"Wait, they *burned* her?" I inclined my head.

Logan frowned. "Why didn't they hang her? That's weird."

"Why is it weird?" Cole looked between the two of us, his brow crinkled. He tossed his dark hair.

Seraphina took a deep breath and offered Cole a gentle smile. "Contrary to pop culture—the punishment for witchcraft in the United States was hanging. They burned witches in Europe. Not here."

"Well, unless you count Nile..."

Seraphina glanced sideways at me. "Not at first."

I was quiet for a moment as I chewed. Back home in Nile, a lot of our ancestors had been brought out to Bird Island and hanged under suspicion of witchcraft. But then the islanders had gotten bored and started burning them. None had been wickeds...but people didn't care back then. And now? I was grateful every day that the world didn't believe in us anymore.

"Well, whatever they did—if the old woman was truly a wicked, burning at the stake?" Logan gave a downturned smirk. "That wouldn't have killed her."

Cole glanced at Logan. "Right. Because—"

Logan nodded and stabbed a spicy chicken. "You need to take their heads. Quicksilver. That's the only thing that can kill a witch gone darkside."

I dunked a fried pork ball into the sweet-and-sour sauce and popped it in my mouth. I chewed in silence, staring down into my rice carton. The topic of witch hunting turned my stomach. I understood the need to end wickeds...but that didn't make it easier to hear. There was a natural balance between the good witches and the bad. The balance was necessary, and the High Council that governed us ensured it was maintained. They only ever intervened on a wicked witch if she drew attention to herself. Otherwise, the High Council allowed them to work in the shadows. And it also helped prevent another witch war. But Phin and I couldn't explain this to Logan—that the light couldn't exist without the dark. He wouldn't understand.

My eyes widened. "Wait, did you say, Wollstonecraft? Isn't that the undertaker's name? Victor Wollstonecraft?"

Logan nodded slowly, chewing a mouthful of rice.

I looked between the three of them, excitement mounting. "Well, that's something! Look up the Wollstonecraft family. How far back do they go?"

Cole began typing furiously on the keyboard. Seraphina bent lower over the computer, her golden-honey hair falling over Cole's shoulder like a curtain. She cleared her throat. "The first mention of Wollstonecraft was around the founding of the place. Brunhilde Wollstonecraft emigrated from Germany and arrived in the area around the same time that the Godwin family founded the town. She bought a bunch of property...and a farm..." Phin's voice trailed off and she exchanged a glance with me.

I pointed my fork at Logan. "Farm! She was the witch. And if she was a witch, her great-grandson will be, too. And we'll know it as soon as we see him. He could be carrying on the family kidnapping tradition!"

Logan frowned. He popped another spicy chicken into his mouth and shrugged dubiously.

I rolled my eyes at his lack of enthusiasm.

"Maybe..." Seraphina murmured thoughtfully. Her gaze moved across the screen. "But Phoenix...she didn't have any relatives."

I made a face. "But—"

"Brunhilde Wollstonecraft came to America by herself. She didn't have any relatives. No husband. No children. She lived alone."

"So, the name Wollstonecraft is, what, a *coincidence*?" I scoffed.

Cole typed away and clicked several times. "Victor Wollstonecraft..." Cole inclined his head. He glanced over at me. "Are you sure it's *Victor*?"

I looked at Logan for confirmation. He nodded. "Why?"

Cole raked a hand through his hair. "Well, there isn't much of a record of him at all. It's like he just appeared..." Cole narrowed his eyes and bent closer toward the computer. "He was the one who found Justine Kilpatrick on the side of the road."

My jaw dropped. I pointed my pork ball at each of them in turn. "He's connected! I knew it!"

Seraphina winced. "Nix, why would he help rescue the little girl if he was involved in kidnapping her? That doesn't make any sense."

"What? Of course—"

"According to this," Cole interrupted loudly. "Victor changed his name to Wollstonecraft that year. So, he isn't even technically a Wollstonecraft. Sorry, Nix."

He didn't sound sorry at all. I glared at him with clenched teeth. Before I could find an argument, Logan arched his neck and leaned over the table to peek at Cole's laptop.

"How did you find that out?" Logan mumbled through a mouthful of rice.

"Cracked into the database...it wasn't hard, just—" Cole shrugged sheepishly as he went on about his computer nerd nonsense with Logan looking on, grinning with impressed appreciation.

Phin and I weren't listening. We never did when Cole went into computer mode.

"So, it's not Victor." Seraphina gave me a sympathetic smile that made me want to jinx her face that way.

"Just because he changed his name...I mean, that's weird." I made a face as I continued, "Why would he do that? And for him to randomly find a kidnapped kid—the only one to ever be found? That *screams* suspicious."

"And Brunhilde Wollstonecraft, as the witch herself, that doesn't fit, either," Seraphina added softly, clearly not listening to any of my arguments.

"What are you talking about?" I scoffed in disbelief, stuttering over my words. "How doesn't it fit? Wickeds can live for hundreds of years!"

Seraphina shook her head with a patient frown. "It doesn't explain the pattern shift."

Logan nodded in agreement, his cheeks full of chicken. My eyes shifted back to Phin. A scowl twitched in the corner of my mouth. "What do you mean?"

Seraphina gestured to Cole to keep scrolling. "Why would a witch, who had previously been content with kidnapping dozens at random, completely change her pattern of behavior so dramatically? A pattern that she'd kept consistent for a hundred years?"

Cole glanced up at Seraphina as she towered over his shoulder. "And it changed again in the '60s."

"Right." Seraphina crinkled her nose. "So, why?"

Logan was quiet for a moment as he dug into his fried rice carton. He looked up suddenly. "Check those penny pinchers—"

"Pages."

"—for anything that happened after they burned the witch."

Cole shook his head with a frown. "Nothing...except that the Godwin family had started the first printing house...that was exciting, I guess."

I scoffed.

"Oooh, juicy." Logan rolled his eyes and shoveled more rice into his mouth. Cole held up a finger, his eyes still on the screen. "Okay, so the last person who went missing *prior* to the school snatchings...was a 'Bonnie Butts.'"

I snorted, inhaling some rice. I choked on a laugh. "Bonnie *Butts*? What a name."

"Wait...Bonnie Butts?" Logan stuck his fork into his rice carton. "I know that name." Logan dropped his carton on the table and went over to the piles of books and journals Phin and I had organized earlier that morning.

I shook my head and held up a hand. They were missing the point. "Local legends are usually spawned from truth, right? The Blood Farm—which was probably owned by Brunhilde Wollstonecraft—is the source of superstition in this town. We need to check out that Farm."

Cole nodded grimly. "We should at least take a look at it. See what we can find."

Seraphina looked at me. "And what kind of creature do you think this mysterious witch is hiding?"

I shrugged as I munched on a pork ball, ooey and gooey with sweet-and-sour sauce.

"Because it seems to me..." Seraphina frowned, looking down her nose at me as I chomped. "...that Brunhilde Wollstonecraft was just a poor, ordinary, old lady—a scapegoat for whatever has really been going on in this town."

I rolled my eyes. "Fine. Well, let's move on to the maulings then. You brought up the creature. What could it be? Looks like a ghoul. But doesn't. Not much to go on. Jaws like a grizzly bear, claws like that creep in *The Village*...that's a ghoul. But it's *not* a ghoul because ghouls don't eat fresh meat. So, dead end."

Seraphina straightened and picked up her forgotten carton. "It could be a grim," she murmured softly as she stared down at her rice.

"A grim?" I repeated. "Like the grim reaper?"

"No." Seraphina's voice was soft and solemn as she went on to explain, "They aren't the same creature. Reapers harvest a soul when it is a soul's time to be harvested. But grims are soul stealers. They *take* them." Seraphina picked up her fork and poked at the rice. "Demons use grims to snatch sacrificed souls. They're like demon familiars." Seraphina was quiet for a moment, her eyes downcast. Then she lifted her eyes to meet mine. "They look like... the raptors in *Jurassic Park*, but with fur...like giant cats on hind legs...and forked tongues that flick back and forth like serpents. Think of hairy, human-sized, wingless dragons."

I studied her as she sank into the bed. She continued to fluff her rice without taking a bite. I frowned. Something was bothering her. "How do you know so much about them?"

Seraphina's eyes darted to Cole and then back down to her rice. She cleared her throat and shrugged. She smoothed back a strand of honey hair, tucking it neatly behind her ear. "We read through all the monster books since we left Nile, remember?"

I raised a skeptical eyebrow. I looked from Cole to Phin. Clearly, I was missing something. "Yeah, but not enough to—"

"Found it!" Logan shouted as he smacked the dresser.

Phin and I jumped, flinching toward him.

He hurried forward, an old scrapbook held open in both hands. "Look."

I hopped to my feet, carton and fork in hand, and we all gathered around him. Peeking over the book while I scooped a mouthful of rice, my eyes scanned the pages of the hunter notes. The writing was awful.

"Uh..." I squinted. "What does it say?"

Logan tapped the page impatiently, as though it were written in plain English. "My dad heard about this place from my uncle. He'd wanted to check it out, but my uncle told him that the case had been taken care of—" Logan furrowed his brow and moved the book closer to his face. Apparently, it wasn't just me who couldn't read it. "Taken care of by a hunter named Westley Thomas. The last victim was Bonnie Butts. Thomas killed the witch—" Logan winced as he read, "—losing his wife, Persephone, in the process..." He cleared his throat. "The random disappearances stopped. But Dad didn't think it was over...he made a note here about the kids, the possible new pattern, and to come back this year in time for the next cycle." Logan's jaw pulsed slightly. He tossed the open scrapbook onto the bed. Like Cole, Logan didn't mention his dad much. Phin and I still weren't certain exactly what had happened to him, only that he'd been killed by the same demon that had killed Logan's brother, Traven, just weeks ago.

"So, it wasn't a witch? Or it was?" Cole sank back into his seat. He rubbed a hand over his eyes.

"It could be a grim, Logan." Seraphina's eyes were on the book. "Maybe the witch bound a grim?"

Logan winced as he considered this. "I don't know...maybe. It's all very strange. Like there's a lot more buried beneath the surface that we aren't hitting yet."

Seraphina sat down beside the old hunter's scrapbook and pulled it gently into her lap. "You know, I think we should shift our focus to Drew. Her circle was small. She lived for school, Nathan, and cheerleading."

"So?" I mumbled around my mouthful of sweet-and-sour pork. My eyes were on my carton as my fork scraped the bottom.

"So, we've established that her attack was personal. The creature was after her and Nathan for a reason."

"Exactly, we should check out the Blood Farm tomorrow morning, first thing." I shoveled my last bite of rice and smiled like a chipmunk at Cole. "In the daytime, so it's not so scary."

Cole stuck his tongue out at me.

I snickered.

"Well, Logan and I were talking when we went for dinner—we were thinking we should check out the high school first."

"Ick." I made a face. "No way."

"Nix, we need to talk to her friends. Figure out what she might have gotten into, or where she might've come in contact with the creature—"

"I know that one." I rolled my eyes and tossed my empty carton into the can. "The Blood Farm."

"Phoenix," Seraphina murmured patiently. "All the kids have been taken from the school—"

"And I told you before—" Logan dropped into the chair beside Cole. "The Blood Farm is a distraction. We need to focus on the cases before we go chasing down fake urban legends."

"Fake?" I scoffed.

Logan twisted his laptop, so I could see the screen. Rory and his buddy, wearing a Ghostface mask with a leather jacket and jeans, stared stoically out from their 'about me' section. "These guys made half this stuff up. And you know it."

I groaned. "Fine. Whatever. Phin and I will go to the school as new students." I snatched up a monster book and jumped onto the bed. I crossed my legs and opened the book in my lap. My ears prickled. No one was talking. I looked up, eyes shifting from one to the next. "What?"

Seraphina hesitated. Her silver eyes slid to Logan, who shoveled more rice into his mouth.

He coughed, choking on his full mouth. He pressed his fist into his chest and swallowed thickly. He winced. "Sam and I are heading to the school in the morning. New transfer students..."

My eyes narrowed, my hand froze mid-page flip. "You already set this up?" I looked at Phin. "For just you two?"

Seraphina smiled weakly. "Logan thought—"

I scoffed, slapping the page back. "Believe me, I know what he thought." I tossed the book off to the side, plucked up my empty coffee cup from the nightstand, and stalked to the kitchenette. I shoved the mug underneath the coffee machine and jabbed at the buttons. "And what are you expecting me to do while you guys work my case?"

"Logan set you and Cole up with the school staff—"

I rounded on Phin, my fists jammed into my hips. I blinked incredulously. "I'm sorry, *what*?"

Logan gave a lazy shrug with a smirk to match. "The school's K-12. It's divided into different wings. Phin and I will work the high school kids for information on Drew and her boyfriend. You and Cole will work the elementary wing; look for signs of a spirit, or creature, and scope out the kids—you know, because that is the current victim pool...and, judging by the pattern, six more will be taken before this is over."

I frowned. Seraphina stood from the bed and made her way over to me. I shook my head, still not understanding. "But what am I going to be doing there? It's not like I can pretend to be a teacher, much less a student..."

Logan waved a careless hand in my direction. "Ah, don't worry, you're short enough—you'll blend right in."

Seraphina rested a hand on my shoulder and squeezed, keeping me from lunging at him. "Cole's a volunteer music tutor...and you're..."

Slowly, I turned my head and glared up at her. "I'm *what*?"

Logan grinned, his eyes sparkling with mischief in the bad motel light. "A lunch lady."

My eyes widened in horror. My mouth fell open. I stared at him, stunned into silence by mortified outrage.

He couldn't keep it in any longer. Logan doubled over with laughter. Across the tiny table, Cole rubbed his chin, barely obscuring his grin. He struggled to straighten his face. "Nix, that's perfect for you..." Cole's mouth twitched. "You love food..."

Logan guffawed, tears leaking from his squinting eyes. Hand

still squeezing my shoulder, Seraphina started to shake with silent, stifled giggles. Then Cole burst out laughing, which sent Logan over the edge, and the whole room dissolved into gales of laughter.

My cheeks scorched as I scoffed. "Unbelievable."

Seraphina gave me a one-armed hug, crushing me into her. "Aw, Nix—*we love you.*"

I pursed my lips and looked up at her sideways. "Mmhmmm."

Despite myself, I felt a little tickle in the corner of my mouth. And I smiled. And I kept smiling as I walked to the bed, grabbed the pillows, and chucked one at Phin.

And another at Cole.

And the last one at Logan.

Hard.

# I'LL TAKE YOU EVERYWHERE

I woke up in the middle of the night.

Cole was moaning in his sleep in the bed opposite me.

I peered at him through the blue glow of the TV. He'd taken the somnum. I'd given it to him myself.

He shouldn't be dreaming.

I slid out of bed and kneeled beside him. His face was slick with sweat. His brow furrowed as his mouth moved. I brushed his damp hair from his forehead. I grabbed his shoulder and shook him.

His eyes flashed open. He gasped for air as though he'd been drowning. His hand snatched my arm, and he squeezed.

"Hey, hey—Cole, it was a dream!" I hissed. "Just a dream!"

He nodded. He closed his eyes and licked his lips.

"You shouldn't be dreaming..." My eyes searched his face. I swallowed thickly. My heart hammered in my ears. "What was it about?"

Cole sat up in bed. He raked his hands through his hair. His eyes were on the TV. "Go to bed, Nix. We've got a big day tomorrow."

I pushed up from the floor. I opened my mouth to argue, but I closed it. I didn't want to fight anymore...but that potion—Seraphina had brewed it. Her potions were flawless. There's no way Cole should've dreamed, much less had a nightmare. I bit my lip, gave him a brisk nod, and slipped back into bed beside Seraphina.

I didn't bother to close my eyes. I wouldn't be able to fall asleep. A nightmare unaffected by somnum...it seemed beyond unnatural. I continued to turn it over in my mind. What kind of dream would be impervious to magic? A magical dream...like a psychic premonition...or something.

Cole wasn't a witch.

He wasn't psychic.

But ever since the demon possession, he'd been tormented by dreams. And now they weren't just dreams, but prophetical...and magic resistant. The idea that the demon had given Cole some kind of power...left behind some kind of demonic dream curse was more than unsettling.

It was disturbing.

But the priest had checked Cole that night. Looked him over for any lasting demonic damage. He'd said there was nothing wrong with him.

I turned over to stare at Cole.

Something flew at me in the darkness.

I flinched and inhaled sharply as Icarus bounded onto the bed. His eyes shined fluorescent in the TV light.

"Outside. Now." Just as quickly as he'd pounced at my face, he slipped off the bed on silent paws and padded his way to the door.

I groaned through clenched teeth and tossed the covers off me. Seraphina mumbled in her sleep as the blankets thumped heavy on her head.

I didn't bother fumbling around the table for the motel key. I could unlock it with a magical prod of my finger. But I did scoop up a jacket. I tugged my *Return of the Jedi* hoodie over my head and stomped moodily outside. I was going to be an exhausted mess in the morning. And I wasn't a morning person to begin with... ugh. I didn't even want to think about the little kids. I hated kids. Except my sister, Fawn. Kids were annoying. I gritted my teeth, scowling into the darkness.

I yanked open the door and stomped out of the room. Icarus was already halfway down the breezeway. Being a familiar, the cat had his own magic. Magic beyond the understanding of witches. And he didn't need doors to get where he needed to go. His tail disappeared around the corner. I shoved my hands in my pockets and muttered to myself.

By the time I'd reached the parking lot, I was way past annoyed. Icarus sat patiently on a sidewalk bench beneath the solitary streetlamp overlooking the parking lot. I plopped down onto the cold bench and waited, shivering in the wind.

Icarus's tail flicked. "The boy is—"

"Cole," I snapped. Icarus didn't like him. And he would never use his name. Normally, I didn't bother with it. But I was tired and cranky, and this is what he got from me at whatever o'clock in the morning it happened to be.

Icarus's fur bristled as a cold gust of dying November wind pushed against us. "He's dreaming of things he shouldn't. Dark things."

I glanced down and out of the corner of my eye at the cat. "Icarus, I'm surprised at you...you say *I* have the eavesdropping ears?"

Icarus's whiskers twitched. His tail lashed back and forth. "I can feel them. In the night. His dreams make the air busy."

I snorted and cocked an eyebrow. "Busy?"

"Like bees. The air buzzes around him whenever he has one. They're not natural nightmares, Phoenix. They're—"

"I know. Okay?" I rolled my eyes as I bounced my legs up and down to fight off the cold. "I get that they're something—"

"Evil."

"Evil?" I scoffed and leaned over onto my knees to look him in his lamp-like eyes. "You think Cole St. Claire is *evil*?"

Icarus blinked slowly at me. His eyelids drooped and raised with the weight of his annoyance. "No, Phoenix. I do not think that over-grown, shaggy dog is evil. I think that he's having evil manifestations. And I'm telling you..." He paused and closed his eyes briefly as though searching inside himself for patience. His nose twitched. He opened his eyes again. "I'm *advising* you. As your familiar inherent...you need to reach out to your grandmother about this. The High Priestess of the House of Grey would know what should be done in a case like this."

"Be *done*?" I scrunched up my face.

"He took somnum this evening. An ordinary, non-witch human should, therefore, have a dreamless, undisturbed sleep...but that is not what happened, is it? The somnum didn't work."

I opened my mouth to argue, but I had no argument.

Icarus nodded his head. "Something must be done."

The moment I managed to finally drift off to sleep, the alarm blared.

As always, Cole and Seraphina were out of bed with the first chirp of the alarm clock. Cole went straight for the coffee machine, and Seraphina went for the shower. Logan and I, on the other hand, were a bit slower to get up. But I didn't see a point in stumbling out of bed when Seraphina was hogging the shower. I snuggled deeper into the bed in a tight ball of covers, the blankets over my head and my eyes squeezed shut.

I fell back asleep...for like a minute, only to gasp awake as Seraphina slammed a pillow on my head.

"Phoenix, come on. You're going to be late."

I moaned and crushed the pillow down over my head to hide.

"Now!" Her whine was muffled just enough by the pillow. "*Nix, come on.* We have to get through a whole school day. Then after we're done at the school, we're heading to the sheriff's department. I set up an interview with Sheriff Godwin. We're Phoenix and Seraphina Stephens: dual enrollment, independent study, homeschool students. You're volunteering in the cafeteria to earn some community service hours. Remember that."

I grumbled incoherently from underneath the pillow. Seraphina yanked it out of my clenched hands. I scowled and squeezed my eyes tighter. Then I sniffed at the air. "What is that—did you..." I squinted up at her with sleepy eyes. My nose crinkled in disgust. "Did you put *perfume* on?"

Seraphina frowned and flipped her shiny hair over her shoulder. "It's a lunaria elixir...we need to get answers. I figured it'd help."

I rolled my eyes. "I thought Logan didn't like magic."

Seraphina glanced over me toward the cot at the foot of Cole's bed. "He likes this one...I mean, this idea. He thought it was a good one." She looked back down at me, her brow furrowed and mouth in a pretty pout. "And it's not magic. It's chemistry."

I scoffed and buried my face in my pillow. "Five more minutes."

"No." She smacked her pillow into the back of my head. "Now. I'm not your wake-up service."

With a loud groan, I chucked the pillows and blankets off me onto the floor and stomped toward the shower. I glanced back to see Seraphina bend over Logan. She touched his shoulder gently and murmured a soft 'good morning.'

I grinned darkly and slammed the bathroom door so hard, the noise made *me* flinch. I hoped it freaked Logan out so bad he fell off the cot.


Cole parked the van in the faculty parking lot at the back of the building. Gloria Godwin School was nestled in the woods, down a backroad, a bit isolated and removed from the thick of the town, across the street from the cemetery and beside a cow farm. I crinkled my nose at the sight of the miserable, muddy beasts, standing stupidly in their own muck, beside the parking lot. It must stink bad in the summertime.

I surveyed the back of the building, my mouth in a grim line.

Cole shut off the van and pocketed the keys. He smiled at me. "Hey—it'll be fun, going undercover and all, right?"

I snorted. "Sure. Lunch lady. Awesome."

Cole grinned and gave me a playful nudge. "The kids'll love you...you're always generous with your helpings."

I rolled my eyes. "Whatever."

The lunch lady was a plump, older woman with grizzled gray hair and black cat-eye glasses, studded with rhinestones. She had a happy face and a round nose that crinkled when she smiled.

She put her hands on her hips and sized me up as soon as I trudged into the kitchen. "Aren't you a bit young to be working during school hours?"

I forced a smile that didn't reach my eyes. "Volunteering. Independent study stuff."

"Hmm. Well, I'm Ms. Margaret..." She held out her hand.

"Phoenix." I shook her hand, wincing as her warm hand crushed mine. She gave my hand a good yank that sent me stumbling forward.

"Good to meet you, Phoebe."

I gritted my teeth on a retort. "What's first, ma'am?"

Ms. Margaret rubbed her hands together and grinned. "Well, the kiddos will be heading in for breakfast in about an hour." Ms. Margaret gave me a list of prep jobs and cleaning tasks to keep me busy.

My mood was sour, and my face was grim. Ms. Margaret kept glancing at me as we sorted through the breakfast prep. Finally, I looked up at her, my eyebrow raised.

She smiled. "You're new in town aren't cha, Phoebe?"

I forced another smile. "My friends and I are just passing through...grabbing some volunteer hours in the spirit of Thanksgiving. Right now, we're working on a paper for our investigative journalism class." I studied Ms. Margaret. She looked old enough. I licked my lips and took a chance. "We're researching the missing kids...er, kid. Mary Tran. Have you ever seen anything like this before?"

Ms. Margaret sighed and nodded. She didn't say anything else.

I tried again. "Do kids go missing a lot around here?"

Ms. Margaret's hands froze on the boxes of cereal she was organizing. She looked over at me, her happy face stern. "No."

I nodded, sullenly wishing I had the tact of my twin. But I didn't. "Who do you think did it?"

Ms. Margaret slapped down the cereal box and put her hand on her hip. "Philomena, we have about a hundred little ones coming in for their breakfast in thirty minutes...do you think this is the proper topic of conversation to be having right now?"

I smiled awkwardly and shrugged. I shut my mouth and got back to sorting.

But to my surprise, Ms. Margaret said softly, "Things like this don't ever happen."

I looked up sharply in time to see a tear slide off Ms. Margaret's round nose.

She sniffed and rubbed her nose on her sleeve. "But, when they do—" She shook her head. "You know, I started working here sixteen years ago...when my boy was in third grade. My husband didn't want me to work. I was pregnant at the time, and we had a little girl still at home. But two babies had already gone missing...I wanted to keep a closer eye on my boy." Ms. Margaret gave me a shaky smile. "Because when *I* was a girl...my friend disappeared. Her and her little sister. Vanished from the school. So, I wanted to keep my baby boy close. Just in case..." Ms. Margaret shrugged.

"But he was taken anyway." Her face shined as her eyes blurred. She blinked at me with a rueful smile.

I could only stare. Whatever information I had hoped to get out of her...that had not been it. "I'm so sorry." My heart hurt for her, but I had to ask, "Ms. Margaret, you must have some idea—"

Ms. Margaret bit her mouth shut and shook her head. She slapped at the pockets of her dress and pulled out a wallet. "Here. Forgive an old lady, but I like to show him off..."

I took the wallet in my hands. An old picture of a goofy boy with a wide, open-mouthed grin beamed up at me. A smaller, second picture of a chubby girl with wisps of blonde curls around her smiley face. I smiled back at her, and then looked up at Ms. Margaret. "Her hair, it reminds me of my little sister."

I passed the wallet back. Ms. Margaret grinned down at them as more tears leaked from her eyes. "Oh, my Heather." Ms. Margaret pocketed the wallet. "She has a mallen streak on the back of her head."

I hesitated.

Ms. Margaret laughed. "A black streak of hair, dear."

I scrunched up my face as I tried to understand.

Ms. Margaret waved a hand. "It's rare, not many have heard of it...my grandma used to say it was a sign of witchcraft." She rolled her eyes and chuckled softly.

I smiled, slightly bemused. Then I remembered. "Wait, I'm sorry, is—are you Officer Meeks's mother?"

Ms. Margaret cocked an eyebrow. "Yes, I am...why do you know a Watertown deputy, Phoebe?" She put her hands on her ample hips. "Are you in some kind of trouble?"

I shook my head. "No, I just—I met Rory at the cemetery and—"

"The cemetery! Goodness, girl, what are you going on about?"

My cheeks burned as I grinned sheepishly.

Ms. Margaret jerked her head to the side as she sized me up.

"Are you working with Rory on that blasted Blood Farm nonsense of his?"

My eyes widened. "No, no, ma'am...just got a nose too big for my britches as my grammy would say...heh." I smiled weakly underneath her sharp eyes, gray like her children's.

"Hmmph."

"Honestly, Ms. Margaret, I saw Mary Tran's missing poster... and she reminded me so much of my little sister. And I understand how it feels to lose someone and have no answers..."

"Mmm." Ms. Margaret gave a slightly suspicious, slightly sad, downturned smile.

"You still have no idea who took your son?" I looked at her with sympathy wrinkling my forehead.

She cleared her throat and got back to work. "I *will* tell you —the Wollstonecrafts...and I'm not one to judge, but there's something unnatural about a family that keeps to itself, hides their children in so-called 'home' school, and doesn't ever leave the house." Ms. Margaret tilted her head. "Come to think of it, in all these years, I've never even seen his wife...wherever he found her."

I frowned as I fumbled a few boxes. "So, because they home-school their kids...you think they—"

Ms. Margaret looked up. "It's not right. Children should be schooled at school, immersed in their community. Not kept isolated and alone. Locked up far away from folks in that old, rundown house of theirs."

I scoffed, biting my tongue on my retort. Not only was *I* homeschooled...but I'd homeschool a hundred kids before I'd ever let them set foot in *this* place.

Ms. Margaret's happy face vanished. Her round, jolly features hardened. "Sheriff Godwin thought the same thing. But she could never prove anything."

I licked my lips and tasted my words carefully. "But, Ms. Margaret, a family with young children—that keeps to themselves...*away* from the school...how could they have been snatching students over a span of—"

"They could if," Ms. Margaret bit her lip. Her eyes darted between the kitchen doors. She bent in close to me and whispered harshly, "they're not human..."

"Not *human*?" My brow furrowed.

Ms. Margaret nodded curtly, dabbing her eyes with the corner of her dress. "It's the blood. My friend who went missing? Her baby sister, Justine Kilpatrick, was found by the Wollstonecraft man when he was a boy. Back then he was going by something different...he was a grade or two older than Jillian and me. He was the heir to an important family, a good family, one that I won't name because I'm not a gossip. But the boy, he was a loner, a delinquent, and a screw up. A trickster! The black sheep and stain on that good family. Then shortly after the girls vanished, Victor ran away from home, and he came back with a new name. New identity. And no longer human, if you ask me." She shook her head in disgust. "Somehow, he stumbles upon the only child to ever be found...missing almost all her blood? Psh. Please. Too much of a coincidence, if you ask me. And poor, little Justine...she was never the same again. And why 'Wollstonecraft?' Why did he pick that name?" She scowled darkly and leaned in close to me. "I'll tell you: to honor Brunhilde Wollstonecraft...the vampire witch that lived in the Blood Farm...that silly legend. Why, the man *lives* in Brunhilde Wollstonecraft's old house, for goodness' sake!"

I screwed up my face, trying to process what she was saying. "Wait, Victor Wollstonecraft lives in the Blood Farm?"

Ms. Margaret shook her head. "No, no. Brunhilde's actual house...on Adelaide Road. The Blood Farm is hidden in the woods nearby. That was her lair."

I cocked an eyebrow, uncertain how to separate superstition from supernatural.

Ms. Margaret shook her head again. "I tell you, sweetie, it's all about the blood."

"What do you mean, the—"

The bell rang. We both jumped.

Ms. Margaret wiped her face on her sleeve. "All right, Phoebe, let's feed those babies. Start their day off with a smile, hmm?"

She rolled out the breakfast cart. I hurried after her. Then we passed out the cereal boxes and bananas and milks, and I collected the tokens and placed them in the jar. It was mind-numbing work. All I could think about was the Wollstonecrafts and blood. What did she mean? I'd have to look over the articles again.

I stood up straighter as a small group of third graders, huddled tight together, moved through the breakfast line. They seemed skittish and sad. I smiled brightly and passed them cereal boxes and milk. They only nodded in return. Then they handed me their tokens and hurried off to a table.

Ms. Margaret nudged me. "Mary Tran is from their class. Connie, Robin, and—" She nodded toward the smallest girl. "That's Agatha Godwin. She was adopted by Dr. Godwin over the summer. Just started school in September. Stuck to Mary Tran like gum on a shoe. They were the best of friends. Poor thing's a mess. Of course, I know just how she feels and then some. Losing Jillian was awful. Losing my baby boy...a nightmare I never wake from." Ms. Margaret sighed heavily. "They say little Agatha was the last one to see Mary before she vanished."

I watched the three girls leave the line, headed for a table in the far back. I chewed on my cheek as I considered my options...I had no excuse to go linger by their table. I'd have to do it a different way.

My way.

I palmed the tokens the girls had handed me, clutching them tightly in my hand. "I'll be right back. Bathroom." I cut through the kitchen and ducked into a closet.

I'd only tried it once before, but it wasn't too hard. Of course, the first time had been back when I was a little girl, during a temper tantrum...an explosion of accidental magic. But the point was: I'd done it, so therefore, I could do it again. Right?

I pocketed the lunch tokens and covered my face with my hands. Orange magic shimmered in front of my eyes. Then I held my eyelids up and rolled my eyes into the back of my head.

It took a minute.

Several.

It was hard.

Painfully hard.

The concentration required made my brain hurt and my nose bleed.

But I did it.

I could see them at the lunch table and hear their whispers as the three girls leaned in together. Agatha in particular stood out. Though the other two girls wore bright colors and trendy clothes with way too many butterfly barrettes clipped all over their heads, Agatha had her dishwater-blonde hair perfectly plaited in two neat braids and wore a pink, plaid sweater vest over a crisp, white button-down shirt with gray slacks. She looked like she was ready for a business meeting...but she couldn't have been more than eight. Fawn's age. Yet, she dressed like a stuffy, old lady.

But, despite her polished clothes and perfect hair, her pale face was blotchy, and her eyes were red, bloodshot from crying. And the only behavior that gave away her age was the occasional nose wipe on her white sleeve.

One of her friends gave her a small nudge. "Don't worry, Agatha...I'm sure they'll find her. Right, Connie?"

"Yeah...totally, Robin." Connie nodded earnestly.

Agatha rubbed her nose again and sniffed. Tears leaked from her blue eyes. "You know they won't. And if they do, she'll be ripped apart like Drew Graham." She winced, her pale face shading a light green.

The other two girls exchanged wary glances. "Agatha—"

"You don't think she was taken to the Blood Farm, do you?" Connie whispered, wide-eyed.

Agatha sniffed and shrugged.

Robin nudged Connie. "It's that creepy homeschool family..."

"The Wollstonecrafts?" Connie nodded in agreement. She licked her lips, relishing the power of whispered secrets. "I heard my mom and dad talking...kids didn't start disappearing until the Wollstonecrafts moved to Watertown, like, hundreds of years ago. It's gotta be them. They say the Wollstonecraft witch kept a monster in the Blood Farm. It's still there, just waiting to drag kids to her, so she can—"

Agatha let out a breathless little gasp as she dissolved into silent tears.

Connie cast an uneasy glance at Agatha and swallowed.

"The Blood Farm." Robin glanced around them. "They call it the *Blood* Farm."

Agatha winced, more tears leaking down her face. "Mary's sister, Lizzie, doesn't think it's them..."

Connie made a face. "How do you know?"

"Connie!" Robin nearly dropped her milk. "Agatha's older brother, Sid, is *dating* Lizzie–"

Connie crinkled her nose. "But Agatha's adopted. Sidney's not really her—"

"Connie!" Robin squealed.

"What?" Connie shrugged. "It's not a secret or anything. Dr. Godwin adopted the twins, too. So, what?"

Agatha swallowed and rolled her eyes, wiping at her cheeks with her snot-stained sleeve. "Sidney said Lizzie wanted to skip school and ask M—" Agatha stopped short and cleared her throat. She sniffed and rubbed her sleeve across her nose. "She wanted to ask M-Mrs. Wollstonecraft if she'd see anything weird...you know, since their house is almost next door to the Blood Farm." Agatha gasped for another shaky breath that she couldn't seem to catch.

She licked her lips and stared hard at the table as more tears leaked down her face.

Connie and Robin grabbed each other and peeked over at Agatha. They both squealed at once: "They're going to *talk to her*?", "Is she *nuts*?"

There was a lurch, and I was snapped back into my body.

"Hey! Phyllis! Phyllis!"

I blinked, eyes wide. The lunch lady was shaking me so hard my bones rattled and my neck and head knocked back and forth.

"Oh, thank the Baby Jesus!" She gasped and gave me one last shake. She covered her heart with both hands. "You looked like you were possessed! Nose leaking blood! Eyes rolled back, nothing but white! Are you prone to seizures or something?"

I put a hand to my head and nodded. I swiped my finger underneath my nose to wipe the blood. "Uh, yeah. I guess this job is too much for me, Ms. Margaret...sorry."

I pushed past her.

"Wait—"

I didn't wait.

I had to find Cole.


"You want to go *where*?"

"Forget the barn. We have to check out the Wollstonecrafts. Mary Tran's sister is planning on stopping there today—" I hesitated as I remembered. Agatha hadn't actually said *today*. Whatever. "We should be there, too, just in case."

Cole shook his hair out of his eyes and pulled out his phone. "Let me text, Logan—"

I made a face. "Why?"

Cole smiled patiently as he tapped on his phone. "Because, Nix, we need to keep communicating. You think cops shut off their radios when they go investigate things?"

Cole sent the text and lowered his phone. "So, you got all this from the lunch lady?"

I stared at him coolly, my arms crossed. I tapped my foot impatiently.

Cole's phone buzzed. He slid his finger across the screen. "He says to stay put until they can meet up with us after school. He wants to go to the Wollstonecrafts' together. And then he wants to check out the Blood Farm."

I scoffed. "I'm not waiting around until—"

The bell rang, and Cole flinched. His hand went to Jean, slung around his neck. "I gotta go. Meet me here after class, okay? I want to check out the basement of this place...maybe we can find something there. Like where a creature might be moving in and out of here or something."

I nodded begrudgingly.

Cole grinned and gave me a little wave. I wiggled my fingers in return and watched as he disappeared into the classroom down the hall, followed by a stream of chattering little kids. Then I turned on my heel and ran for the parking lot.

9

# DEATH OF A BABYSITTER

I turned onto Adelaide Road just to get a feel for the place. The road was a long stretch of dirt, rolling up and down like a wave, with fields and forests on both sides, mountains curving high in the distance. As the van rumbled down the road, a cold cloud of gravel kicked up, making it hard to see out the rearview mirror. I drove almost the whole length of the road before I saw a farmhouse. I slowed down a bit to study the house, knowing the kids were probably pushing their noses against the windows to watch me, as well.

The house was set back, far from the road, amid a mess of overgrown grass and weeds. A few random crooked trees staggered around the front, and a tangle of forest stretched behind it. And it was falling apart: an old, weathered farmhouse, gray from age and abandonment rather than from origin. The structure was interesting in that there were several different elements to the house as though pieces of different houses had been pushed close and stitched together to make something new and improved. There were at least three stories and a small, covered porch beside a boarded-up bay window. I squinted at the house as I leaned into the steering wheel. Most of the windows were boarded. Except—

Something darted into the road.

My heart stopped.

I slammed on the breaks and scrunched up my face, bracing myself for tragedy. The van skidded in the dirt, spitting up a storm of gravel, before it jerked to a stop. My hands white-knuckled on the wheel, I stared wide-eyed at the road in front of me.

A little girl stood rooted just feet from the headlights. Instinctively, I slapped the van in park, jumped out, and hurried over to her. But the look of her...the look in her eyes made me hesitate. I stopped short. The girl just stood there—her head bent forward, eyes narrowed, and dirty, matted hair hanging in her face in chunks. Her clothes matched her hair in that they were shades of brown but from filth rather than design. Her pale face looked almost gray as she squinted up at me.

She gritted her graying teeth. "You shouldn't be here."

I took a step back. "Are you okay? You should look before you run out into the road."

"I'm okay." The girl grinned. Her smile curved up her face. "But you won't be."

I frowned and hooked my thumbs through my belt loops. "Do you know a little girl named Mary Tran?"

She giggled darkly. Then she ran off the road for the house. I stared after her as she skipped and jumped through the overgrown grass and disappeared around the back of the house.

The old, busted mailbox impaled by a 2x4 had the name Wollstonecraft across it in peeling paint. I looked down the deserted road, left and then right. Lizzie Tran and her boyfriend, Sidney Godwin, weren't here, whatever Agatha Godwin heard. And sneaking around this place would be next to impossible. Unless you were on foot. At night.

I cast one last look at the farmhouse. The driveway was a straight shot to the house with barely any space to turn around at the end of it. A quick getaway wouldn't be easy either. I scowled impatiently. Whatever. I was here. And I needed answers. I hopped inside the van, shifted back into drive, and turned down the Wollstonecraft driveway.

I parked and got out. My eyes went to the boarded windows and shifted to the back of the house where the girl had disappeared. I walked up the busted, broken front porch steps and knocked sharply on the door.

There was a flurry of activity from inside.

I knocked harder.

The door opened a crack. A haggard woman, with heavy-lidded eyes and a sharp, square face, framed with matted, dishwater-blonde hair, peeked out at me. She squinted into the weak November sunlight and fixed me with a mean glare.

Her voice was slow and cold, gravely as a dirt road. "Yes?"

I smiled sugary sweet. "I'm sorry to bother you, ma'am. My phone died, and I'm not from around here—I was wondering if I could use your house phone?"

"No." She went to shut the door, but I shoved my foot in the doorway. I winced as she pressed harder.

"Please—" I whipped out Mary's missing poster and held it in front of her face. "Have you seen this girl? I heard she was last seen down this road..."

"I already told the sheriff." The woman's eyes narrowed to snake-like slits. "We're doing everything we're supposed to, everything that's asked of us, and we're not doing anything wrong." She kicked my foot out the way.

Before she could slam the door in my face, I grabbed the doorknob and held it fast. "Well, then could you just write down the best way to get to I-781? Like I said, I have no idea where I am..."

I slung my backpack in front of me and rummaged through it for my silver pen and notepad. Silver burned most evil things...if I could just get it in her hand... I clutched the pen and thrust my hand through the crack, narrowly missing her skin.

The woman's lip curled in disgust. Her eyes shifted from the pen, to me, and back again.

She moved fast. So fast, I couldn't process what was happening. She stuck a rusty steak knife straight in the air.

I yanked my hand away and backed up a step.

A nasty smirk twisted onto her face. Then she threw the door wide with a bang. A cat sprang out at me, dashing between my legs. The woman clutched the knife with long, bony fingers. "If you don't get your nose out of my business and off my porch, I'll take it off myself! I'll slice the skin between your fingers! I'll cut off your eyelids! Then I'll cut off your head! *You stay away from my girls!*"

I held up my hands and backed up, careful not to fall off the porch.

She followed me, her teeth gnashing, the knife in her hand. "And you tell the lot of them—we're doing everything they ask! *So, you don't hurt my girl!*"

As I backed up, I bumped into someone at my back. I flinched and nudged away from them. They held me fast, strong hands on my arms, hugging me to them. I turned to see a girl my age, clearly *not* a Wollstonecraft, smiling coolly at the woman as she brandished the knife at the bottom step.

"Good to see you, Mrs. Wollstonecraft," the girl said in a low, soothing voice. "I see you're done with entertaining this afternoon, but I was wondering whether you'd seen my brother around?"

The woman sneered and pointed her knife at the girl. "*You—*"

"Fine." The girl held up a hand in surrender as she gripped me in the other and walked us backward. "Fine. We're going. Happy?"

The woman spat at our feet.

The girl turned us around and guided me back toward the van. I shoved her off me.

She scoffed. "You're welcome."

The door of the house slammed.

"I think I was handling her just fine, thanks." I stopped at the van, leaned against the side, and crossed my arms as I studied her closely. "Your brother is missing?"

Judging by her clothes, her family had money: tight designer jeans, flowy white shirt, golden watch, rings on every finger of her left hand, elaborate dangly earrings, and a scarf tied around her head. She tossed her hair as it caught on the wind, shimmering like sheets of molten gold. Her face was fair and heart-shaped, strong, yet distinctly feminine with round, full lips and striking green, almond-shaped eyes.

She put her hands on her hips and jutted her chin forward, her jaw set. "He's not missing. I'm *looking* for him. There's a difference—especially in this town." She pursed her lips and looked me over. "What are *you* doing here?"

I wrenched open the van door. "Leaving."

"Fair enough." The girl grinned, flashing a broad, brilliant smile. She held out her hand. "I'm Billie Godwin."

I tried to hide my surprise. Her brother must be Sidney...Lizzie Tran's boyfriend. I smiled slightly and shook her hand. She didn't look anything like her little sister, Agatha. Then I remembered Agatha was adopted. "Phoenix Stephens."

She scrunched up her forehead as she smiled. Billie leaned over to peek at the painting blazed across the side of the van. My cheeks burned. She cocked her head. "So, *Phoenix*—who are you missing?"

I hesitated.

Billie's eyes crinkled with a sad smile. "My mama's the town doctor. My grandma's the mayor. My aunt's the sheriff. Her cousins are deputies. My second cousin is the head of the girls' home down the road. Her sister is the town librarian. I know every girl in this town...but I don't know you. That means you're a ways from home." She glanced back at the old farmhouse. "And if you're stopping in to see the Wollstonecrafts...it means you're missing someone."

"Mary Tran."

Billie furrowed her brow.

My cheeks burned again. I pushed a hand through my hair. "I'm a cousin...just trying to help."

Billie only stared.

I waved my hands in exasperation as I stumbled around an explanation as to why I wasn't Asian. "Well, I'm a *stepcousin*, really. See, my mom married her uncle's...brother's...half-sister..." I cleared my throat uncomfortably. "It's a long story. The point is... I'm just trying to help. I—well, I was supposed to be enrolling at the school today, but I just had to do something. Sitting in school all day when Mary is out there somewhere—" I shrugged, my face grim. "Just seemed wrong."

"Yeah, Lizzie's taking it pretty hard, too. I'm sure you know." Billie shivered in the cold November sun. "If you see her, can you tell her to be careful, it's almost Thanksgiving—and the sibling is always next."

I nodded slowly. *Was* the sibling always next? "Sure—"

"Here, let me give you my number." She held her hand out for the notepad and pen still clutched in my hand.

I passed them over, my eyes on her hand. The pen didn't burn her. She scribbled her name and number on the pad, her rings sparkling in the cold sunlight. "Here's my address, too. Just in case." She handed the pad and pen back to me. "I wish I had a heart like yours, Phoenix Stephens." She smiled slightly. "If more people did...the world would be a much better place."

"Yeah..." I looked down at the pad and glanced at my watch. Almost lunchtime. I smiled up at her with my easiest of smiles. "You know, I'd really like to check out the high school. Talk to Lizzie. Are you heading back there?"

Billie scrunched her smile to the side in a small smirk. "I might be." She nodded her head toward the main road. "Follow the green car." Then she turned on her heel and headed up to the road. "If you can keep up, that is."

.   .   .

She wasn't kidding. Billie drove fast. Like Logan, she seemed to be either in a hurry, or just showing off, and judging by the flashy, lime-green car of hers, it was the last one.

I pulled the van into an empty space beside Billie and shifted into park. I scanned the cars and spied Logan's truck. A smirk snuck into the corner of my cheek. This would be fun.

By the time I'd grabbed my bag and hopped out of the van, Billie was already waiting for me at the entrance. I hurried across the street, shivering slightly in the gray November afternoon. From the front, the school was impressive, looking more like a massive courthouse than anything else. The brown brick building was several stories tall with long, rectangular windows cut into the sides and curling ivy creeping along the length of it, stretching all the way up to the roof. A modest stack of stone steps led up to the double doors of the entrance, which was flanked with thick, looming, white columns and stacked with giant windows stretching up to the pediment.

Billie leaned against the railing at the top of the stairs, her black designer backpack slung over her shoulder, and a smirk on her face. "Come on, Birdie. We might just make it in time for Thanksgiving."

I blew my bangs out of my face and grinned up at her as I trudged up the dozen steps. "I don't need an escort, you know."

"It's lunch." Billie straightened and shrugged. "I'm hungry. And I figured you could use a tour guide."

I considered this for a moment. Checking out the high school kids with an inside perspective could give me insight into Drew Graham's life that we couldn't find in the pages of that journal Phin kept reading on repeat. With Billie's help, I could find out why Drew was targeted a lot easier than investigating from the outside.

Before I could argue, Billie's green eyes glittered as she added, "Plus, I've got a good feeling about you."

I stopped at the last stair and adjusted my backpack with an eyebrow raised. "What do you mean?"

Billie grinned. "I figure a girl who's willing to lie her butt off to get answers about a missing girl must have a story worth hearing. You've got a good heart." She shrugged with a smirk. "I wish I had one."

I scoffed, smiling incredulously. "How'd you—"

"Like I said, I know every girl here." Billie draped an arm around me and led me inside the school. "And Elizabeth Tran can't even find a set of parents, let alone some random stepcousin."

My cheeks burned. I glanced sideways at her and flashed a guilty grin.

Billie snickered. "It was a good effort, though—is Phoenix even your real name? Or did you rip that off the van you're driving?"

I laughed and shoved her arm off me. "Yes. It's my real name."

"You sure?" Billie arched a perfectly shaped eyebrow.

I scrunched up my face on a smile. "What about you? I don't know many girls named 'Bill.'"

She crinkled her nose and gave me a playful push. "It's a nickname. For Wilhelmina."

My eyes widened. "Wow...okay. I'd go by Bill, too."

Billie giggled and nudged me left toward a pair of huge oak doors. "Let's go, Birdie."

I reached for the door, but flinched as the bell rang—and continued to ring—in an eardrum-shattering scream for several seconds. I glared up at the thing as we passed underneath it into the cafeteria. Reason a billion why homeschool was superior to mainstream: no obnoxious alarms.

The alarm had triggered what could only be described as a mass exodus. We had barely passed through the doors before a sea of teenagers flooded through behind us, rushing past and surging toward the lunch line. They pushed and shoved and elbowed us from all sides. Eyes narrowed, I struggled to shoot dirty looks at all of them. Billie caught my eye and leaned into me, chuckling. She pointed to the table at the far end of the room. "You go grab us some seats." She raised her voice, practically shouting over the chaos of kids, "Wait for me. I'll bring you a tray."

Then she disappeared, lost in the sea of students. I scowled and stuck my elbows out, knocking as many kids as I could on my way to the table. This cafeteria was different from the elementary one, but I supposed it made sense to keep the older kids separate from the younger ones. My eyes flickered from face to face, searching for Phin or Logan, but I couldn't see them anywhere.

When Billie finally emerged from the lunch line, she was leading a pack of kids. A guy as tall as Logan, and a few inches taller than Billie, followed close behind her. But unlike Logan who was broad and built like a grunt, this guy was lean like an athlete, agile and quick on his feet. His hair stuck up like spikey straw, unnaturally so, like he styled it that way intentionally. His golden face was long and angular like Logan's, too, but his features were softer and round.

Like Billie's.

I looked between them, amusement teasing a smile in the corner of my mouth. Aside from the expressions, they looked like "his and hers" copies of the same human. Billie, feminine sunshine...and this guy, masculine grumpy. Big time. His scowl clouded his face and darkened his bright-green eyes as he smacked his tray down and slumped into a seat.

Billie didn't seem to notice the guy's bad mood. She smiled and dropped two trays piled with potatoes and gravy on the table and slid one in front of me.

"Thanks." I grabbed a grape and popped it in my mouth.

"No problem. Thanksgiving specials today and tomorrow. Then Thanksgiving break starts Wednesday." Billie scooped my backpack off the chair I'd saved for her, passed it over to me, and slid into the seat. The four girls, who'd followed them, each took an empty chair and scooted it under the round table. The girls were all different shades of the same color. And all of them watched me with eager, hungry eyes. Which made sense because their trays were empty.

Billie glanced at me and then jutted her chin toward the guy. "So, where's Elizabeth?"

"Home sick." The guy glared down at the center of the table, clearly bothered by something. Then he shoved back in his seat and jumped up to his feet. "I'll see you later."

And he left. He stalked through the ebbed flow of students still wading aimlessly around the tables, pushing people as he passed. When he made it to the wooden doors, he smacked them open with a bang so loud, the whole cafeteria looked up as he disappeared into the hallway out of sight.

I cocked an eyebrow. "I think something's bothering your boyfriend."

The girls around the table all dissolved into giggles. I eyed them warily. Billie snickered. "Sidney's my brother, actually."

"They're twins," murmured the girl with perfectly curled bangs and an extremely high and tight ponytail overflowing atop her head with shiny platinum hair.

"And of course, Sidney's upset," another girl cooed sympathetically. She pursed her lips as she cast her eyes to the side. "His girlfriend is a nightmare."

"Totally," the next girl chirped shrilly. "She has—"

"Wait." I looked at Billie as she took a big bite of turkey. "Your brother—isn't he dating Elizabeth Tran?"

Billie's bite bulged in the pocket of her cheek as she nodded. "She and I aren't the best of friends." Then she swallowed and shot the girls across the table with a dark, cold stare. "But that doesn't mean she's a nightmare." Billie munched on a scoop of potatoes and spoke around the bite, "And you'd think you guys would cut her a bit of a break considering her little sister is missing."

I glanced sideways at the girls, who eyed each other awkwardly.

"Sure, Wilhelmina."

"Right. You're *so* right."

"Of course, she's right."

"Whatever—" The girl with the thick, auburn curls made a face. "You don't have to live with her. Ever since the Tran sisters showed up at Gossamer House, they've been causing problems. Snooping around the House at all hours of the night. Sneaking into—"

"Amanda. Enough," Billie snapped. "Her sister is *missing*."

Amanda shrugged with a snooty crinkle of her nose. Then she leaned over the table, her eyes on Billie. "Did you see him?" The stench of her perfume made my eyes water. I scrunched up my nose in disgust. What'd she do, take a bath in the bottle? Bleh.

"Who?" Billie eyed her warily.

Amanda smiled slyly at Billie. "*The new guy*. He looks like he walked right out of a Tarantino movie."

My ears prickled. I fought to keep a straight face.

The girl with the straight brown hair and wide, round eyes sighed dramatically. "He's totally taken. Did you see that girl he was with? The blonde tree?"

Then the girl with short cropped black hair burst out laughing. "More like giraffe."

"Big Bird."

"Guys." Billie made a face. "What is *wrong* with you?"

I watched them, my face stony and eyes hard.

"It's his sister. Duh." Ponytail girl rolled her eyes. "Got to be. You don't start a new school halfway through the year with your girlfriend. That doesn't even make sense." She blew up her bangs and waved the other girls away like they were flies. "Anyways, I had class with him—Logan, is his name. You'd like him, Wilhelmina. He's kind of like Sidney, except way more manly."

"He's really into occult stuff."

Okay. I'd had enough. I leaned over the table and whispered, "He's actually undercover."

Billie snorted into her milk carton. As I glanced back at her, she hid her smirk behind her hand. I turned back to the girls, eyes wide and serious. "He and his girlfriend travel all across the country looking into paranormal activity. They film it and post it on their website. Stream it and everything." I licked my lips, pausing for effect. "They came to Watertown because of the Blood Farm. Missing kid...no suspects. A *dog* mauling? Pssh. They think it's darker than that."

Amanda crinkled her nose and flipped her auburn curls. "Like what?"

"Vampires." Mousy Brown Hair squeaked. She bit her lip and lowered her big eyes. "Everybody knows Victor Wollstonecraft is a vampire. They keep the kids in their basement, feeding on them, until they're dead and dry—"

"It's gotta be them." Black Crop nodded earnestly. "It's why they homeschool their kids and keep them locked inside that rundown farmhouse of theirs."

"—then they stuff the dead bodies into unmarked graves in the cemetery."

"They went for Mary, but Drew and Nathan were in the way... so they ripped them to pieces."

I made a face and shook my head. "Nah, vampires are too easy. Logan thinks it goes deeper than that."

"Like the Blood Farm witch?" Amanda asked dubiously.

Ponytail Girl nudged Amanda. "I bet she's a Cullen groupie."

The two of them grinned nastily.

I smirked. "Eviler than an old witch."

The girls exchanged glances. Then Ponytail Girl jutted her chin out. "How would *you* know?"

Amanda scoffed. "I bet you don't even *know* Logan."

"You're just some lame Hot Topic cashier." Mousy Brown Hair snickered. "No guy in his right mind would even talk to a loser like you."

"Who are you, anyway?" Black Crop raised a suspicious eyebrow as she looked down her pointy nose.

"The camera guy's assistant." I popped another grape in my mouth. "You know, the guy who drives the van?"

Amanda snorted. "That dude always dies."

"Well, that makes sense." Ponytail Girl swung her hair and glanced at Amanda with a sly smirk. "She's so not 'final girl' material."

I smirked at the joke. Clearly these girls were horror film buffs. Well, thanks to the lovely Rachel St. Claire, that was a game I could play...and win. "Yeah, no." I slapped at my Freddy Krueger hoodie with a sheepish grin and a one-shouldered shrug. "Fresh out of white tanks and jeans."

Billie chuckled and touched my arm. "Nice."

Amanda frowned, her eyes cold. Ponytail Girl crinkled her nose at me. "So, the girl knows her horror tropes. Big deal."

Mousy Brown Hair wasn't listening. Her eyes, large in her head, were on me. "So, you're undercover, too?"

Black Crop leaned over Amanda to talk to Mousy. "Annie, she's *lying*. If she was really undercover, then she wouldn't tell us." She turned her attention to me. "How stupid do you think we are?"

I grabbed another grape. "Very."

Billie spat out her milk and choked on her laughter. I slapped her back as she coughed, gasping and laughing.

The girls stared at me with piercing, icy glares.

I flashed a cheesy grin.

The girls all leaned together whispering loud insults for me to hear.

I shrugged and added seriously, "You know...there's only one way to find out what really happened to Drew, Nathan, and all those little kids..."

Billie's eyes crinkled as she fought to keep a straight face. "How's that?"

I reached down into my backpack and pulled out my tarot deck.

Billie's eyebrow cocked in interest.

I watched the girls as I began to shuffle. My hands slapped the cards over and over each other. Their eyes shifted uneasily between each other.

"Go ahead. Ask a question." I didn't look away, my hands moving fast and familiar.

Black Crop pursed her lips into a smirk. She opened her mouth, but the question died on her lips. A guy with a thin, narrow face and a thin, dark mop of unkept hair leaned into the table and fixed me with a deadpan stare.

"Did Sidney Godwin kidnap Mary Tran?"

# IMMORTALS

I furrowed my brow and glanced sideways at Billie.

Her face was hard and impassive. Her full mouth twitched as her jaw tightened.

I looked back at the guy, who leaned his forearms on the table, his backpack slumped forward onto his neck. He nodded for me to go on.

I cut the deck and flipped the cards.

My eyes moved across the spread; the colors and symbols blurred, illuminating different meanings like flashes of lights in my brain.

"What does it mean?" the guy prompted impatiently.

"Blood. Loss. Betrayal." So much blood.

He scoffed. Then he ran a hand over his mouth. He inclined his head, looking remarkably feline. Like a stray, disheveled and mangy, crawling out of a trash can...after being run over a few times. He fixed me with another stare and repeated slowly as though I was stupid: "*Did Sidney Godwin kidnap Mary Tran?*"

I didn't flinch. "No." But he knows who did...

The guy pushed off from the table and shook his head as he walked away. The girls all turned to glare at him. He stopped abruptly at an empty table far away from ours and he dropped into a seat. I scooped up my tarot cards and tucked them back into my bag. My heart quickened uncomfortably in my chest. Sidney Godwin knew who took Mary...but did he *know* he knew it? I had to find Sidney. Talk to him. I cleared my throat as I tried to straighten my thoughts. "Who was that guy?"

"Keirian Cullen." Ponytail Girl blew up her bangs and tossed her ponytail. "He's a total bum. Works for Victor Wollstonecraft at the cemetery. He's, like...some kind of grass janitor." She rolled her eyes.

"Groundskeeper, Pamela."

"Whatever." She waved a careless hand, flashing pointy, painted nails. "He and Rory Meeks run that creepy Blood Farm website. He's been spreading rumors about Sidney having something to do with Mary going missing since last week. Sidney dropped Mary off at Gossamer House. Why would he kidnap her after bringing her home?"

I glanced over at Keirian. He wasn't eating. Instead, he gnawed on a pencil as he read a beat-up copy of *It*. The only kid in the whole cafeteria who sat by himself.

"He's harmless," Billie muttered coolly. "Just like Victor."

Amanda scoffed. "I don't know, Billie. Keirian keeps talking—it's going to force your aunt to take him in...blood or not."

"Not. We're adopted, remember?" Billie smiled sarcastically.

Pamela snickered as she twirled her ponytail around her fingers. Her eyes glittered. "Lucky."

"I'll be right back." I snatched up my bag and left the table, slipping in between kids as they flitted from table to table, gossiping with friends. I dropped into the seat across from Keirian Cullen.

"What do you know about Mary Tran?"

Keirian looked up from his book and snorted as his eyes found my Freddy Krueger hoodie. "Nice."

"Well?"

His eyes slid to the side, toward Billie and her friends, then back to me. "Nothing."

I cocked an eyebrow and leaned back in the chair, arms across my chest.

He put down *It* and stuck the pencil he'd been chewing behind his ear. "Aren't you supposed to be the fortune teller? What do *you* know about it?"

"I already told you. Now it's your turn."

Keirian scrunched up his face into a thoughtful frown. But before he could decide whether or not to answer, a kid came up to him with a swaying, bobbing swagger, and smacked him in the arm. "Hey, Keirian...you got those Lit notes for me?"

Keirian glared up at him with an impatient scowl. "*You* were supposed to take the notes. I was—"

The guy wasn't listening. Instead, he slid into the chair beside him and leaned across the table toward me, his hand outstretched. "Hey, I'm Stuart. You're, like, the third new kid I've seen today. That's gotta be some kind of record in this town."

"Hey." I took his hand and gave it a shake. He held my hand fast, his thumb smoothing over mine. He turned my hand over and examined the lines of my palm. I yanked my hand back with an impatient scowl.

Stuart grinned a sly, wolfish smile that crinkled his eyes. "I knew it."

"What?"

Stuart nodded toward my hand, now clenched and hidden in my lap underneath the table. "It's written all over your hand."

I frowned. My jaw tightened.

Stuart sat back in the chair and threaded his hands behind his head. "You'll see."

"Right..." I raised my eyebrows and chewed on my cheek. I shook my head. "Well, Keirian and I were talking, so if you could—"

"Oh, don't tell me Keirian already made a move..." Stuart

looked back at Keirian in disbelief. Keirian was looking up at the ceiling with a surly expression. Like he was wishing the both of us would go away. Stuart jutted his thumb at Keirian. "You can't go out with Cullen. He's like one promotion away from makeup artist of the dead." Stuart made a face.

"We were talking about Mary Tran," I muttered. Each time the guy opened his mouth, I liked him less and less and wanted to hex his face more and more.

Stuart leaned back in his seat again with a nonchalant wave. "Pfft. Another copycat kidnapper." Stuart cocked an eyebrow at Keirian. "Or are you telling her it's my cousin?"

"Your cousin?" I prompted, interested despite myself.

Stuart flashed a cocky grin. "Sidney Godwin...his mom is my mom's sister..."

"Sister—" I struggled to remember Billie's list of relations. "So, your mother is the sheriff?"

I crinkled my nose as I studied him. He was a tall, golden boy built like a quarterback. His features were strong and defined, and he had that same lionlike look that Billie and her brother had about them. But unlike his twin cousins, Stuart had a thinness and a hunger about him that made him look starved. The most dangerous kind of lion.

He grinned. "So, what's Keirian been gossiping about now?"

"He hasn't told me anything thanks to—"

Something caught Stuart's eye in the crowd behind me. He sat up straight in his seat and gave me a little wave without looking. "I'll catch you later."

I rolled my eyes as he stood from the chair and hurried after a tall blonde, with his looping, bobbing gait that was almost as annoying as his mouth. I turned back to Keirian but did a double take. Seraphina. The idiot was bouncing after Seraphina. Good. Maybe Logan would knock him on his butt. I bit my lip as I craned my neck to see where she was heading, but a herd of kids cut in front, and she disappeared. I sighed heavily, impatience twitching in the corner of my scowl. I looked back at Keirian.

He was gone.

With a low groan, I snatched my backpack, swinging it over my shoulder and pushed through the kids after Keirian. I could just barely see his shaggy black head moving toward the double doors. I hurried after him, unable to run through all the bodies. I finally managed to catch up with him down a dark, side corridor lined with lockers. I snatched him by the bag and tugged. Hard. Slamming him into the lockers.

His bag slung low on his arm as he glared at me, tossing his hair out of his eyes. "You mind?"

I shook my head with a downturned smirk. "Not at all. Please, continue." I pushed a fist into his chest. "What do you know about Mary Tran?"

He sighed. His nostrils flared like a dragon as he stared moodily off to the side. His eyes flickered back to meet mine. "Does it matter?"

I made a face and pushed him harder into the lockers. "Of course, it matters!"

He shrugged, his eyelids heavy with callous indifference. "Does it?"

My nose crinkled as my lip curled in disgust. I shoved him. His head knocked against the lockers. He closed his eyes briefly, his mouth thinning into a grim line. He opened his eyes again and fixed me with a cool stare. His jaw pulsed as though he were just barely keeping his hands off me.

I didn't flinch. My voice was low as I hissed through gritted teeth, "I'm not playing this game with you anymore. You tell me what you saw. Or whatever it is that you know. She's a little girl. What is the matter with you?"

"How cute." Keirian scoffed, an amused glint in his hazel eyes as a smirk twitched in the side of his face. "You cosplaying Gale Weathers with those streaks?" He jutted his pointy chin toward my hair. Then he shrugged again with a dismissive shake of his head. "Why do you care? You can't do anything about it. Kids get taken. They go missing for a while. Then they don't. That's Watertown. It happens all along the highway, too. But nobody's paying attention."

I inhaled deeply, struggling to find patience. Fighting against every instinct to hex his pencil halfway up his nose.

Suddenly, Keirian laughed. A loud, barking laugh. "Fine. Okay. Let's just say, if you want to know what's really going on...check out my website, *The Blood Farm*."

I scoffed in disbelief. "So, you *are* that dude on the website with Rory? Wearing the stupid Ghostface mask in the publisher photo?"

A crooked smirk curled across the side of his face. "You've certainly done your homework, haven't you?" He crossed his arms and leaned down close to my face, his neck twisted to the right, his head cocked at an angle so he could study me sideways. "And *you're* that girl Rory met yesterday...homeschooled pre-med...hah. I don't believe that for a second..."

I scowled and stepped back. "Would you please just—" I took another deep breath and closed my eyes, searching for patience. "Tell me why you think it's Sidney."

"I don't." Keirian chuckled. "But it *is* an angle that I'm pushing. Definitely boosting our hits on the website. Good for business."

My eyes narrowed. "That's it. That's all you have to say?"

He shrugged with a bored, disinterested air. "Mary Tran disappeared. Sidney didn't. Hours before that Drew and Nathan were shredded to pieces by a dog that doesn't exist. You tell *me* what that means."

"*That could mean a lot of things...*" I muttered through clenched teeth.

"Not really." Keirian tossed his hair out of his hazel eyes. His mouth stretched in a curious kind of smile. "The Godwins own this town. Their women run *everything*. Always have. So, if Sidney Godwin, pretty boy prince, is getting kicks out of kidnapping little kids—you really think they're going to do anything about it?" Keirian shook his head with a downturned smirk. "Nah. All they're going to do is cover it up for him."

I cocked an incredulous eyebrow and scoffed. I folded my arms across my chest. "So, you think Sidney Godwin—"

"Superstar, All-American Athlete, heir to the Godwin dynasty." Keirian nodded with sarcastic encouragement. "Just like his sister. The two of them are built like Greek gods. Do you know Billie is the only girl on the football team in, like—ever? That girl may look like a beauty queen, but she can kick butt like a *beast*." He snickered and ran a hand over his chin as he added, "She's also a secret cinema freak." He cocked his head thoughtfully. "And I have to admit her paper on women and the golden age of slasher films was *mind-blowing*. But I think she doesn't—"

I rolled my eyes. "Whatever *Sidney* is, you think he's kidnapping kids? For what? And like you say on that ridiculous website of yours, this has been going on for years. So, you're saying he's some kind of copycat kidnapper?"

"*I* never said he's a copycat," Keirian murmured, his hazel eyes cold. "My family might not have the notoriety of the Godwins... but we've been here just as long. And one thing about old families, we like to tell stories about the old days. And one of those stories is that when this happened back in 1996, Victor Godwin was involved—"

I scrunched up my face and waved a hand in frustration. "Victor Godwin? Who's Victor—"

"—but the mayor covered it up...disowned him. *Her own son,*" Keirian clucked his tongue against the roof of his mouth. "And she forced him to change his name to Wollstonecraft...like the witch. For shame."

"Wait." I did a double take. "Wollstonecraft, the *undertaker,* is related to the Mayor of Watertown?"

Keirian smirked. "There's a reason the Godwins are all women...their men seem to go bad..."

"You're pretty chatty for a guy who doesn't care," I muttered, my mouth twitching in amusement. "What's your theory...*officially.*"

Keirian raised an eyebrow. It disappeared into his dark, feathery waves, frumped in a clump on top of his head. "Well, it's all on the website...unbiased, hard-earned, dedicated research. Dozens of different possibilities and ideas. But—" A slow smile slid across his pale face. "Off record?" He leaned in close and whispered, "I think it has to do with the Gossamer House."

"What's that?"

"The Gossamer House for Girls. Run by Catherine Godwin? Nestled neatly in the woods across from the Blood Farm...home to our five resident foster girls: Lizzie Tran, Pamela Bradford, Annie Collingwood, Amanda Thompson, and Tiffany Crane. Little Mary Tran lived there, too, of course...before she disappeared." Keirian slapped a hand on my shoulder as he bent forward to whisper loudly in my ear. "See—Drew had a fight with Annie and Pamela. Annie and Pamela are cheerleaders. Drew was the new cheer captain. The girls had a little mutiny on the squad when Nathan ditched Annie for Drew. And Mary?" Keirian made a face and gave a lazily one-shouldered shrug. "Well, unfortunately for her—her sister, Lizzie, is Sidney Godwin's girlfriend...and Amanda has a thing for Sid. Always has. Guards him like a Pit Bull."

The bell rang.

I flinched.

Keirian pushed past me and headed down the hall, leaving me staring after him as the sea of students flooded through the corridor.

It wasn't hard to find the Gossamer House. It was on the same backroad as the Wollstonecrafts', just farther down the dirt road.

And, just like Keirian had said, it was nestled neatly in the thick of the woods, half hidden by the naked branches of the trees. It sat a bit back from the road, the gravel driveway curling around to the side of it instead of leading to the front. The house itself looked like a large, three-story box with white siding, black shutters, and a dark-red door. It might have been impressive when it was first built, but not anymore. Now it just looked sad and lonely; a giant, old house tucked back in the thicket of dying November trees, in the middle of nowhere. And unkept, judging by the chipping paint and splintering wood. The garden was just a clump of overgrown, mangled bushes. And brown, dead leaves blanketed the ground, and coated the drive as the van bumped along, all the way up to the house.

I put the van in park and prodded the ignition with my finger. The van shuddered and then stilled. I eyed the side of the house as I chewed the inside of my cheek. There was a thin, black back door, leading into the side of the house, standing tall and ridged at the top of a handful of cement steps. I grabbed my backpack and stepped outside.

The cold, damp breeze of the grisly afternoon rushed to greet me as I slammed the van door. And there was something else...a low hum, like static in the air. Magic. Faint, just a trace, but I could feel it. I tucked my red tendrils behind my ears and double-checked my wand was still secure in my topknot.

I squinted against the chill as I adjusted my backpack higher onto my shoulders. Then I trudged along the broken stone slab walkway, around to the front of the house. As I approached, the curtain fluttered in the window beside the dark-red front door. I frowned and jabbed my finger into the doorbell. An echoing chime vibrated from inside at the same time I realized, I probably should've done some research on this place.

Before I could change my mind and head back to the van, the door swung open. A woman—not a witch, and even shorter than me, stood in the open doorway. Her head inclined slightly as she studied me with wide, gray-blue eyes. Her face was square and angular. The only thing soft about her was her full mouth, everything else was sharp, even her bangs and the ends of her thin, straight, black hair.

She pursed her lips. Her jaw tightened as she took in the sight of me. "I'm sorry, sweet girl, but I don't have any beds available. We're full..." Her brow furrowed beneath her bangs. She leaned outside to peer around me. "Where's your social worker? I didn't even get a courtesy call—"

"Yeah...she's awful at her job." I gave an ironic downturned smirk and shrugged. "And she's late. Can I come in? It's cold."

The woman hesitated and then forced a pinched smile that didn't touch her cheeks. "All right, come on in..."

She led me through the entryway, past a giant staircase that curved out of sight. I couldn't feel the magic anymore. Whatever it was must've been outside. We passed through a narrow hallway and into a sitting area. The bones of the house were old and dated, but the insides were fresh and new. The furniture gave off a cozy, welcoming vibe that you'd see in a catalog, but it was only surface deep. I dropped down into the nearest loveseat, slinging my backpack to the ground. I flinched as my butt hit the hard cushion. I glanced around the room with a suspicious frown. Did they even *use* this room? Did they know how awful this couch was?

The woman sank slowly into the loveseat across from me, a neat glass coffee table between us. Her back was pin straight, and she folded her hands in her lap. She smiled sweetly at me. I winced. Her smile freaked me out. Like her face was a mask...fake and hiding something.

I averted my eyes from her, looking everywhere and anywhere, but her bizarre face. I cleared my throat. "So, this is a pretty old place, huh?"

"Yes."

I hazarded a glance at her. "When did you buy it?"

"I didn't." She continued to smile with that same sly sweetness that made my teeth hurt.

I pouted impatiently. Clearly, she wasn't going to make this easy. Lucky for me, my social worker wouldn't be here anytime soon. "I heard the place is haunted." I chuckled. "Kind of glad you don't have room for me."

Her smile slipped for a second. It was so fast I almost missed it. Hah. Got her. I grinned and leaned back into the couch, only to sit back up when the cushion jammed me painfully in the back.

"The Gossamer House has been in the Godwin family for generations. It is our ancestral home, built when the town was first settled in the early 1800s." Her smile didn't slip again, not even as she spoke. It was like watching a doll talk. Creepy.

I nodded again as though I was impressed. "And how long has it been an orphanage?"

Her eyes narrowed. She inclined her head. "It has been a *foster home*...for troubled and lost young girls like yourself...since 1930."

"Hah! Lost." I snickered rudely. "Mary Tran...she is definitely lost, for sure."

The woman's smile vanished. "May I have the number for your social worker?"

I waved away her question with a lazy shrug. "Nah, don't have one. I'll see myself out. Oh, you know what? Where's your bathroom?"

The woman fixed me with a blank stare as she answered in a monotone, "Down the hall. To the right by the staircase."

I snatched up my bag and left the room quickly. I followed the hallway back toward the staircase, but instead of heading into the bathroom, I headed up the stairs, two at a time. The staircase twisted around the entryway, the banister the only thing between me and a drop to the first floor as I reached the top step. It opened into another narrow hallway with doors on the left and windows on the right. Each door had a name placard. I passed Pamela, Amanda, Tiffany, and Annie. The last door had two names: Elizabeth and Mary. Sidney Godwin had said Lizzie was home sick. I reached up to knock on the door.

"I think you know that's not the bathroom, sweet girl."

I froze, closing my eyes briefly. Jinx it, she was fast. I spun on my heel to face her with a sheepish shrug. "I thought you said up the stairs. None of these were it, but then I saw Mary's name and—"

"I think..." Her small, almost squat stature filled the entryway. She was cast in shadow and, with the trick of the gray afternoon spilling in from the windows scattered along the hall...I could've sworn I saw her eyes shine. "It's time to go."

I nodded, conceding her point, and headed back down the hall, my thumbs hooked in the straps of my backpack. As I passed her, she eyed me coolly. I almost shivered. I gripped the railing tightly just in case she got the urge to toss me over the side. The floorboards creaked as she followed me down the stairs and to the door.

She opened it wide. A cold blast of air rushed into the house. I shuddered with a wince. I glanced at her, my nose crinkled. "You sure I can't wait inside?"

"We both know you aren't waiting for anyone." The woman jutted her head toward the outside. "Please leave."

I swung my backpack around to the front of me. Hugging it in one arm, I dug into the bag and pulled out my silver pen. "Here, hold this? Please, just—thank you." The woman took the silver pen begrudgingly, her eyes fixed on me, coupled with an impatient scowl.

I jammed my hand deeper into the bag. "Ugh, nevermind. I was going to give you her card—you know, my social worker...but I can't find it." I took the pen back and tossed it into the bag. Her hand was fine. The silver hadn't burned her. My heart sank a bit. Scratch that off the list. I swung the bag back onto my shoulders, knocking her slightly off-balance, and I headed outside into the cold.

As I rounded the corner of the house, back toward the drive-way, I felt it again.

Magic.

Faint, but there.

My sneakers crunched on the gravel as I made it to the van. I hesitated. There was something here. I looked back at the house. The curtains were drawn and still. I craned my neck off to the side, peering around to the backyard. I couldn't see much. I glanced again at the house. Then I walked past the van and hurried around the back of the Gossamer House.

The leaves were slick on the ground, sticking fast to the soles of my sneakers as they crunched on dead grass. The backyard was the same as the front, only more so, with tangles of tall grass and barren bushes cropping up everywhere. There was a back door and several windows lining the backside of the house. I felt exposed and increasingly uncomfortable with every step, but I couldn't be sure if it was the fear of getting caught or the magic that was affecting me. But then with every step, it grew stronger, and I knew. It was the magic. Just enough to irritate my skin. Just enough to unsettle me. This was dark magic. I stopped short and surveyed the yard. It wasn't even really a yard because the forest had overtaken it. Several maple trees towered here and there among the bushes and tall grass, their branches reaching down to the ground, weighed down by the wet, dead leaves still hanging from them.

There was nothing here.

I cocked my head as I studied the nearest maple. Maybe it was an enchanted tree? I approached it and placed a hand on the bark. Nothing. I walked farther across the yard, nearer to the forest.

Then I saw it.

I couldn't believe I didn't notice it right away.

It was right there.

"You lost?"

I jumped and whirled around, slipping slightly on the leaves. My heart hammered hard against the hollow of my chest.

In her flannel pajama bottoms and oversized football sweatshirt, she looked a lot different from when I first saw her at the mall—but I recognized her right away. Lizzie Tran, arms folded and eyes suspicious. I backtracked across the yard, back toward the house to meet her. "Hey, I'm Phoenix Stephens." I held out my hand, and she took it reluctantly. "You handed me Mary's missing flyer at the mall."

"So, you decided to visit me at home?" Lizzie's voice was rising with impatience.

I shook my head with an easy smile. "I'm actually interested in the history of the Gossamer House."

"Why?" Lizzie cocked a dubious eyebrow and flipped her shiny, black hair over her shoulder.

"Rory Meeks called me. My sister and our friends, we're paranormal investigators."

Lizzie shifted where she stood. Her arms unfolded and fell to her hips. "You mean like ghost hunters or those Bigfoot freaks?"

I scoffed. "No. More like Scooby-Doo."

"Right." Lizzie almost smiled. "Okay. Well, why are you here?"

I squinted up at the house behind her. "How long have you and your sister lived here?"

"Long enough."

"Have you noticed anything weird in the house? Cold spots or electrical problems or—"

"Listen,—Phoenix, right?—the only thing messed up about this house is the people in it."

"What do you mean?"

"Exactly what I said. Catherine Godwin and the Gossamer girls. They're like a pack. They target someone and make them suffer."

"Is that what they did to you?"

Lizzie rolled her eyes. "Let's just say, I'd rather deal with a house full of monsters than deal with them."

"So, why are you home sick?"

Lizzie smirked. "You talked to Sidney?"

"I tried to; he's a hard kid to track down." I hesitated. "Do you think he knows what happened to Mary?"

Lizzie's dark eyes flashed. "You've been talking to Keirian Cullen, too, huh?"

I found an easy smile. "I told you. Paranormal investigator. Talking to people is a big part of the job."

Lizzie pursed her lips and crossed her arms again. "Well, what other leads do you have, Velma Dinkley? Because it isn't Sidney."

I glanced over my shoulder and then back at Lizzie. "What do you know about that old well in the woods back there?"

Lizzie made a face. "What do I *know* about it?"

I nodded. "Have you ever noticed anything strange about it?"

Lizzie hesitated.

I licked my lips and pressed them together in a knowing frown. "I thought so."

"Whatever. It's just a well." Lizzie shrugged uncomfortably.

I waited.

She licked her lips and shrugged again. "I don't know. I guess, sometimes Mary thought she'd see something at night. She used to like to play back here...in the trees, you know? But a few months ago, she stopped. When I asked her why, she said her friend, Agatha, told her it was dangerous."

"Hmm." I turned around and headed back toward the well. Lizzie hesitated before hurrying after me.

"What—do you think she fell down the well?" Lizzie stammered anxiously. "Because I'm telling you, she wouldn't go near it after—"

We neared the large, stone circle; the traces of old magic stained the air around the thing, sticking to my hair and scratching at my skin. I crinkled my nose and peered down into the depths.

Darkness.

That's all there was to see.

Lizzie inched forward, coming up close beside me. She craned her neck over the side to see better. "What is it?"

I straightened and backed away from it.

It was a witching well.

I looked at Lizzie. But before I could come up with a lie, something rustled behind the trunk of a tree a few yards away. I grabbed Lizzie's arm and stepped in front of her.

"Hey, what—"

Long, thin fingers curled around the curve of the trunk, gnarled and old as the tree itself. Then a little old man peered around the bark, his eyes squinted into the light of the gray, drizzly afternoon. He blinked beadily at us. He had a starving, rabid look about him that made my skin prickle uncomfortably. He bent himself around the bark of the tree and inclined his head to the side as though deciding whether or not he could eat us.

"Hey!" I shouted, my voice high and thin. "Who are you?"

"Shhh!" Lizzie pushed me to the side and waved a hand hastily at the old man. "That's just Catherine's father. Come on!"

I glanced at her sharply. "*What?*"

Lizzie looped her arm through mine and tugged me away from the well and the creepy old man lurking behind a tree.

"That's her *father*?"

Lizzie leaned into me and whispered harshly in my ear, "He's got some kind of dementia. The poor man can't talk. He comes to visit her sometimes to wander around the yard."

"He comes here to *wander around the yard*?" My voice was high and thin with alarm.

Lizzie marched me all the way back to the driveway and pulled me to a stop in front of the black back door. She jutted her chin in the direction of the backyard. "He's crazy. But harmless. And Catherine will freak out if she catches us harassing him."

"Harassing *him*?" I gaped at her, struggling to catch my breath. "He's the one hiding behind trees, spying on us like—"

Lizzie rolled her eyes. "Just trust me. Catherine can be a beast when she wants to—just leave it alone."

I shook my head and glanced back at the old man. His hand still clutched the bark of the tree like a small, skeletal child playing hide-and-seek. I shivered in the cold and hugged my Freddy Krueger hoodie tighter around me. I checked my watch. I was running out of time. I had to get back and meet Cole.

Lizzie shifted awkwardly in the stone driveway. "Look, I appreciate you looking into Mary's disappearance. But if you really want to help me, you and your buddies should be checking out the Blood Farm."

I raised my eyebrows, tempted by the suggested. I hesitated. Maybe I had time to check it out before I met Cole at the school. Especially if she could give me directions. I cocked my head to the side. "Well, I have to—"

The black back door opened sharply. The two of us winced at the sudden noise and turned toward the door. Catherine stood in the archway, her sharp eyes piercing each of us in turn. "Elizabeth. You asked to stay home sick today."

Lizzie looked away from Catherine and faced me. She closed her eyes and exhaled deeply.

Catherine's jaw tightened ever so slightly, but her voice never lost its gentle tone, "Unless you are feeling up to attending class, I suggest you head back upstairs to your room."

Lizzie slowly opened her eyes, staring off into nothingness, her mouth set in a grim scowl. She didn't answer.

Catherine clucked her tongue against her teeth. "Now, my sweet girl."

Lizzie met my eyes and gave me a small wave. Then she turned on her heel, like a soldier doing an about-face, and marched through the doorway without looking at Catherine as she passed.

Catherine stared at me. "I don't want to see you here again."

I grinned. "Don't worry. You won't."

I didn't move. She didn't either. A cold gust of November air blew by her into the house. Her spiky straight hair fluttered slightly in the breeze, but she didn't flinch.

Clearly, she wasn't moving until she saw me leave.

I sighed heavily and glanced back at the woods. The witching well positioned ominously in the center of the scattered trees, far back in the backyard. My eyes slid back to Catherine.

She continued to flash that frozen, sugar-frosted, fake smile.

Fine.

I trudged around the side of the van and hopped inside. I poked the ignition with my finger. A burst of orange magic sparkled to the floorboard as the engine rumbled to life, and I drove away.


Cole was waiting on the steps, in full view of where he'd originally parked the van. His shoulders were hunched forward, his elbows propped up on his knees, and his guitar case leaned against his chest, upright between his legs. He squinted at me as I pulled the van into its old parking space. I flashed a cheesy smile, broadened with guilt.

He didn't smile back. He stood briefly and headed for the driver's side. I hopped out quickly, holding the door open for him like a carriage.

He didn't say a word.

I shut the door behind him and hurried around to the passenger side, half expecting him to drive away without me.

But he didn't.

Because he was Cole.

Patient and loyal and better than me.

Because I would have.

I jumped inside and hugged my backpack to my chest as I maintained my wide grin. "Were you waiting long?"

"No."

"Well, that's good!" I chirped brightly as I gave him a small nudge.

Cole continued to stare almost blankly out at the road. He left the parking lot and turned onto the street. "You left the school as soon as you talked to me this morning, didn't you?"

I rolled my eyes toward the window. I watched as the woods of the cemetery passed by in a blur of gray. "Cole—"

He sighed heavily and shook his head, mumbling under his breath.

I looked at him with a scrunched-up frown. "I'm sorry, okay?"

Cole scoffed with a smirk. "No, Phoenix, you aren't. Because if you were, you wouldn't keep running off when you know you shouldn't."

"I had a lead!" I tossed up my hands in exasperation, smacking the backpack as I dropped them back down. I twisted in my seat to face him, my excitement rising slightly. "Which led to another, and *then* I found—"

"Just...wait. Okay? Just tell everybody when we get back to the motel."

I recoiled and made a face. "Why?"

Cole didn't answer. He just turned onto another road.

I did a double take. "Isn't the sheriff's department—"

"We're going to the motel."

I inclined my head. "Really? Why? I thought Phin set up a meeting with—"

"Logan called from the Campbell house. Change of plan. The sheriff interview is rescheduled for tomorrow morning before school hours."

I blinked, jaw dropped. "Wait, he went to Nathan Campbell's house? Without me?"

Cole glanced at me sideways. "I guess he was following a lead..."

# I DIDN'T SAY I WAS POWERFUL, I SAID I WAS A WITCH

"You went *where*?" Logan's jaw tightened, the lines of his angular face sharp and distinct.

I rolled my eyes. "Again—I was following a lead."

Cole averted his gaze, keeping his focus on his laptop.

Logan put a hand over his eyes and massaged his temples. "Putting aside the fact that going off by yourself was an incredibly stupid thing to do, I told you to check out the school. How are we supposed to work both cases at once if you aren't working yours?"

I scowled moodily. "I'm a titled witch, Logan—I think I can handle myself just fine."

Logan pointed a finger at me. "That's it—right there!"

I scoffed. "What?"

Logan shook his head and stomped to the coffee machine.

"What!" I snapped. His testosterone temper tantrums were getting old.

Seraphina, seated quietly at the table across from Cole, finally spoke. "Phoenix, is it possible your magic is making you reckless?"

I scrunched up my face. "That's the most ridiculous thing—"

"Nix, reverse the roles." Seraphina gave me a patient yet pointed look. "Mrs. Wollstonecraft could've been a monster. Or the foster woman, Catherine Godwin, even. What would you say if *I'd* done what you did today?"

I made a face. "That's completely different—"

"Because of your magic, right?" Seraphina prompted gently.

Logan snatched his mug out from under the machine and leaned against the kitchenette to glare at me. "Stupidity gets hunters killed. If you're going to be dumb, you can go back to Nile."

I pushed off the bed and stalked over to the books. I snatched one on monsters and started thumbing through it. "Look—I got a lead that some kids might be sneaking around the Wollstonecrafts' place. I didn't think they should be out there alone. I didn't have time to wait around for the rest of you because there's a rumor around town that the Wollstonecrafts—"

"Are vampires..." Seraphina looked over at Logan. "We heard the same thing."

Logan drank deeply from his mug, his eyes narrowed over the top. I held up the book to the vampire section. "Vampires can't feed on witches—to them, the magic in our blood is like drinking acid. So, they couldn't hurt me if they tried. And I didn't go there empty-handed, okay? I had a silver pen and—"

Logan snorted, blowing bubbles into his coffee.

I glared at him and jabbed my finger into the book. "I did my research. In fact, a lot of monsters can't stand the taste of witch blood."

"And you agree with the rumors? You think this man and his family are monsters, just because they homeschool their children?" Seraphina asked, a quiet challenge in her question, not needing to point out the irony of our own homeschool education.

"*No, not because they homeschool!*" I rolled my eyes at her. "It's—"

"It's not vampires," Logan said flatly.

My shoulders slumped, and the book sagged in my hands. I blinked up at him stupidly. "What?"

Logan gave me a sarcastic smirk. "Yup. And if you would've *waited*, I would've told you: the sixteen-year cycle doesn't fit with vamps at all. And the victim profile doesn't match—"

I ran to the articles and started flipping through them.

"—Vampires don't typically feed on children because people tend to look for their missing kids. Vampires are solitary, but on the rare occasion that they aren't, their number one priority is to protect the colony. Hunting and feeding anywhere near their roost put them at risk. So, they travel out of town, lurk around truck stops, dive bars, and snatch their victims at night."

"But look—" I held up the article underneath his face. "Justine Kilpatrick had puncture wounds, and her blood was almost completely drained—"

"Vampire bites don't look like Dracula pinpricks, Grey," Logan interrupted with grumbled impatience. "Justine Kilpatrick had puncture wounds. Not a bite mark."

"Victor Wollstonecraft found her! And..." I paused for dramatic effect as I glanced around the room. "Victor's really a *Godwin*."

"What?" Seraphina looked at me blankly.

"Yup." I nodded, eyes wide. "Keirian Cullen told me. Victor Godwin was kicked out of the Godwin family by the mayor—his *mother*—when he was a teenager, and she forced him to change his name. They all disowned him. Probably because he was some kind of monster!"

"Keirian Cullen..." Logan furrowed his brow with a down-turned smirk. "That creepy film geek who runs that website?" He snickered. "Super reliable source."

"Anyways..." I shot Logan a murderous glare as I shook the article still clutched in my hand. "That's not the point. Point is, Victor Wollstonecraft found a *blood-drained* Justine Kilpatrick *randomly* on the side of the road? Come on. *And he works at the funeral home across from the school!*"

Logan lowered his mug as he took the article from me with his free hand. His eyes moved over the pages, his eyebrow cocked dubiously.

I looked from Logan to Seraphina. "So, who's to say the Wollstonecrafts *aren't* hunting outside of town but have some kind of family ritual in which they sacrifice the town's children or something—" I waved an arm at Seraphina. "Witches have coming of age things, cultural rituals, traditions unique to Houses—maybe these vampires do, too!"

Seraphina gave me an uncertain shrug. "Maybe—"

I turned back to Logan and jabbed a finger into the page he was skimming. "And maybe Mary Tran was onto him...and she told her babysitter, Drew Graham. So, Victor went to Drew's house and killed her and her boyfriend. And then headed for the Gossamer House and grabbed Mary." My voice trailed off as I heard myself. It wasn't very solid. Or convincing.

Logan shook his head. "Phoenix, it doesn't fit. Do you realize how many 'maybes' your theory needs to even *almost* make sense?" He slapped the article back into my hands. "And vampires can't crush bones, much less eat them."

My jaw jutted to the side as I glared up at him. "Well, forget vampires. I still think it's the Blood Farm witch and/or her monster..." My eyes shifted from face to face. "But, of course, nobody else thinks so." I folded my arms across my chest. "Still, I don't hear *you* coming up with any ideas."

Logan's jaw tightened. "If you would've been at the school, then we would've told you—"

"Here it is." Cole looked up from the screen, turning the laptop for us to see.

Logan put down his mug and walked over to him. "Excellent."

"What?" I snapped, tossing the papers back onto the bed.

"I had Cole dig up some information on Justine Kilpatrick."

"Justine—" I recoiled. My eyes widened as I stuttered, "The survivor?"

Seraphina smiled slightly and nodded. "She still lives in Watertown."

"Seraphina and I are heading there now. And then we'll pick up some dinner..." Logan bent down to make a note of what was on the screen.

I put my hands on my hips and frowned. "I suppose you want Cole and me to wait here and do more research?"

Logan grinned and tousled my hair. "Look at you; finally using your brain."

I shoved him off me. I looked sharply at Seraphina and jutted my thumb toward Logan. "Phin—any thoughts?"

She twisted a strand of blonde hair around her finger and bit her lip. "It's not that I don't think you should come—it's just that Justine Kilpatrick is supposedly very wary of people...she keeps to herself. It'd be best if only two of us went, so we don't overwhelm her."

I rolled my eyes. "I can't believe this—"

"And research is so important at this stage, isn't it, Logan?" Seraphina forced an encouraging smile.

Logan nodded and clapped me on the back. "Sure is!"

Seraphina groaned at his gleeful condescension and pushed up from her chair. She put a hand on my shoulder, but I shrugged her off.

I looked at her hard. "If they keep with the pattern, there are still six kids who are going to get taken. And soon. You really think Cole and I are better off stuck here *researching*?"

"Yes," Logan answered flatly. The laughter gone from his face, he stared at me with a cool, stony seriousness that made me shiver. "Two reasons." He stuck up his thumb. "Number one—as of right now, we have no idea what this thing is...which means it's *your* job to figure that out."

"But—"

"How? By sticking your nose in a book, for once, and researching what it is we're dealing with. And number two?"

Logan's eyes narrowed, and he stepped toward me. "You're using your magic as a crutch."

I made a face and opened my mouth to argue, but Logan kept going. "It's making you sloppy. And until you start using your head, instead of leaning on your magic, you're staying in this motel room."

I turned to Phin and waved an impatient hand toward Logan, who swapped his usual rucksack for an old backpack and started packing. Seraphina winced and shrugged. "Phoenix, I'm sorry—but I think he's right...you could've gotten hurt, or worse..."

I scoffed, staring wide-eyed at them as they got ready and headed for the door. Logan held the door open for Phin, who gave Cole and me a little wave before she slipped out of the room. Logan pointed at Cole. "If she gives you a problem, call."

I stuck my tongue out at him.

Logan grinned, gave me a sarcastic salute, and then slammed the door behind him.

Scowling, I glared down at Cole. He turned quickly back to the computer screen.

I pursed my lips into a pout. "You were awfully quiet..."

Cole nodded to the empty chair. "Sit. Grab some stinky chips. And let's figure out what we're up against, so we can stop it before any other little kids disappear."

I sighed and snatched a salt and vinegar chip snack pack from the box. Then I stalked over to the bed and flipped open Logan's monster book. As I poured chips into my mouth, I scanned the pages. We were at it for hours and still came up with nothing new.

And by the time Logan and Phin walked through the door with a stack of pizzas, I'd just about given up. My stomach had been grumbling just as much as my mouth, which only added to my bad temper. Logan dropped the pizzas on the empty chair, and I snatched up a box.

"So?" I dropped back onto the bed and flipped open the pizza. Excellent. Phin got my special. I ripped out a slice of pizza so gooey it'd put the Ninja Turtles to shame. Mood instantly boosted, I closed my eyes and took a big bite. Hot, oozy cheese and spicy, orange buffalo sauce. Delicious.

"Well..." Seraphina glanced awkwardly at Logan, who looked pointedly at the pizzas. "Let's just say, Justine didn't want to talk."

Logan scoffed and piled pizza onto a paper plate. "She shot us off her porch."

"What?" I gaped at them.

Cole pushed back in his chair, his brow furrowed, eyes on Seraphina. "Are you okay?"

She nodded. Her eyes shifted to me as she hesitated. "We headed to the Blood Farm after that."

Cheese string hanging from my chin, I snorted. Figures. After all that grief about strength in buddies, or whatever... "Unbelievable," I muttered.

Seraphina had the decency to look abashed. "Nix, it isn't what you think—"

"What'd you get from the barn?" Cole grabbed a pizza slice from a box and a soda from the mini fridge.

"It's not a barn..." I mumbled moodily.

Logan spoke around a mouthful of pepperoni pizza. "Best guess—dark witchcraft. Ceremonial sacrifice."

"Wicked witches?" I frowned as I chewed. "*Now* you're onboard with the Blood Farm thing? You said it was just a distraction."

Logan shook his head as he chewed. "No, I said the *website* was a distraction. That whole thing is just the made-up ramblings of two chuckleheads. Anyway, Sam finally found us some concrete evidence." Logan raised his gooey slice to Seraphina who blushed prettily as she rolled her eyes.

I cocked an eyebrow. "Is that so?" I doubted it. Very much. There was one thing I could never forgive, and certainly never forget about Logan: up until recently, he'd held very firm, anti-witch beliefs. And he probably still believed them but gave Phin and me a pass. He viewed us as the exception, not the rule. And the rule was: witches were wicked, if not now, then they would be later. I shot Phin a disapproving frown.

"Well, it was more of a combined effort..." she muttered defensively as she slapped a slice on her plate and dropped onto the bed beside me.

"*Sure.*" I furrowed my brow and nodded fervently, mouth downturned in sarcastic understanding. "Right."

Logan wasn't listening to me. Instead, he waved Phin's words away. "Don't listen to her. She did great. Sam, tell 'em—" He nodded encouragingly as he chomped down on his pizza, cheese strings dangling down his chin.

"Yes...please, Seraphina, tell us everything," I mumbled sarcastically through a mouthful of cheesy goodness. My eyes closed. It was so good; I was having a hard time holding onto my bad mood.

"Well..." Seraphina paused as she tore her pizza into pieces and popped one in her mouth. She glanced at Cole. "The place reminded me a lot of Alice Grey's shed off Hyde Road—"

Cole nodded curtly and chewed silently. Alice Grey, our aunt. A witch without magic, who'd gone darkside. Made a demon deal for magic. She had used an old shed in the woods to work her spells. It was there that Cole was first possessed by a demon. At least, that's the jist of what Phin had told me—*after the fact*...I hadn't been there.

"—there weren't any books or herb jars or anything like that. But the place had been touched by evil magic. I could feel it."

I thought of the Gossamer House. My heart hummed slightly in my chest. "There was a witching well!" I blurted through a mouthful of cheesy sauce.

"A witching well?" Seraphina stared at me. "You found a *witching well?*"

I nodded rapidly as I took another bite with rising excitement. I'd been so busy arguing with everybody, I'd forgotten all about it.

Cole scrunched up his face and looked between the both of us. "Care to explain?"

Seraphina studied me uncertainly as she spoke. "A witching well is an enchanted portal...a lot of the time, they lead to other worlds—"

I snickered. "Where do you think Carroll got his Wonderland inspo, eh?"

"But they're very rare..." Seraphina spoke softly, unease wavering her voice. "It takes an incredibly powerful witch—like, god-like level power—to create one..." Seraphina shook her head, silver eyes wide. "Phoenix, are you *sure*?"

"Mhmm." I nodded as I sucked pizza grease off my thumb. I shrugged. "I think it's dead. But I could still feel it. Traces of it, like you said you felt around the Blood Farm."

"You could *feel* it?" Cole prompted as he reached for another slice.

I swallowed a hard bite of crust, wincing as it scratched down my throat. "Witches can feel magic. Witch magic, at least. That's partially how we can identify each other. We can 'see' another witch." I waved a dismissive hand as I grabbed a new piece from the box. "It's hard to explain."

Cole made a face and struggled to follow. "Like how your magic is an orange color and Fawn's is copper?"

Seraphina smiled indulgently at him. "Not quite..."

"Phin doesn't have magic, but we can still see her as a witch. She looks like one because she is one." I explained vaguely, taking a big, gooey bite.

"She *looks* like a witch?" Cole shook his hair out of his eyes as he looked at Phin. He scrunched up his face. "What do you mean—"

I snorted as I watched Cole study Seraphina as though he might suddenly notice a witchy wart on her nose.

Logan rolled his eyes. "Sam, keep going."

"*Anyways*," Phin smiled at Cole, who shrugged, clearly still confused. "The point is—the building has been touched by dark magic. Which means whether human or monster, the kidnapper could be using magic. And when you factor in the sixteen-year cycle, the children—all innocents—the number seven, it screams ritualistic sacrifice."

I licked the cheese string off my chin, unimpressed. For all my talk about the Wollstonecraft witch...and *now* they think it makes sense. "So, now you believe in the Blood Farm legend? The witch and her monster?"

Phin winced and glanced at Logan, who shook his head. "Not in the slightest. None of it is believable. None of it is making sense. And if it doesn't make sense, it's not true. We're still missing something."

Seraphina nibbled her lip. "Drew had been writing a lot about four specific girls. Tiffany Crane, Annie Collingwood, Amanda Thompson, and Pamela Bradford. They have a kind of mean-girl clique at school. And from what Logan and I could get out of kids this morning, those girls aren't just mean, they're *sadistic.*"

I cocked an eyebrow. "Isn't that a little harsh?"

Seraphina shook her head. "Mind games and public humiliation. Drew's best friend, Mandy, told me one girl they bullied changed schools. Like, *moved out of town* to escape them. So, it's possible the girls are messing with dark magic." Seraphina winced skeptically as she continued, "But they aren't naturals...so they'd have marks from working the dark magic. We just have to check their hands—"

"Nope." I shook my head. "I had lunch with all of them this afternoon. Hands are clean. I would've noticed the dark marks right away."

"The marks don't always show up on the hands," Logan muttered.

"Right." I scoffed. "I'm sure you know all about wickeds, don't you?"

Logan muttered again under his breath, his face darkened and angles sharp.

"I'm sorry—what did you say?" I demanded, temper sparking.

Logan's eyes narrowed. "Just eat your pizza, Grey."

"Why don't *you*—"

"It's true," Seraphina cut in loudly, "that, in some rare cases, dark marks can appear on other parts of the body—"

I glared at Logan as I took an obnoxiously big bite of pizza. He rolled his eyes and grabbed another slice, his attention back on Seraphina.

"—but it still doesn't fit perfectly," Seraphina continued, "because they came to town as infants. Foster girls. So, it's not like they're ancient, ageless, wicked witches."

I made a face. "They got dropped off at that creepy, old place as *babies*?"

Seraphina sighed. "It could explain their behavior issues..."

I rolled my eyes. Another dead end. "So...it's not the mean girls. And we're back to no suspects."

"Not no suspects." Logan held up his pizza slice before he took a bite. "Stuart Godwin was stalking Drew...we found that out from Rory Meeks."

I sat up straighter. "Yeah? What's that story?"

Seraphina reached into her bag and pulled out Drew's journal. She passed it to me, and I flipped through it as she spoke. "I told you before...a guy she called 'S' was freaking her out. He was obsessed with her. So much so, she took out a restraining order on him."

"And according to Nathan's football buddies, Stuart wasn't the only guy creeping up on her. Rory Meeks and Keirian Cullen wouldn't leave her alone, either."

Seraphina crinkled her forehead as she tried to follow. "So, it could be Rory or Keirian?"

"Probably not Rory..." I frowned thoughtfully. "His older

brother was one of the children taken in 2012...he wasn't even born yet. His mother said she was pregnant at the time."

Everyone stared at me, then the three of them exchanged glances.

"What?" I frowned, clearly missing something.

Logan cleared his throat and fought against a smile. "The dude introduced you to his *mother*?"

My eyes widened and then narrowed with understanding. My face burned hot. "Hah hah. *Hilarious.* But no. Rory didn't introduce me to his mother. She's the lunch lady...Margaret Meeks..."

Seraphina bit back her smile. Logan snickered. And Cole shook his head and went back to the computer.

I chomped off another bite of pizza. "*Anyways*—Keirian is spreading rumors that Sidney Godwin had something to do with Mary Tran's disappearance." I blurted through cheese and sauce. "Keirian's the one who told me to check out the Gossamer House. He also said the Godwin boys always go bad...whatever *that* means. But Sidney and his sister were adopted...so they aren't technically Godwins..."

Logan considered this a moment. "I haven't looked into Sidney yet..."

"He didn't do it."

Logan cocked an eyebrow. "Oh, no?"

"Nope. But he knows who did it...though, I don't know if he *knows* he knows. I haven't been able to find him since he ditched lunch this afternoon."

Logan scowled suspiciously. "And how do *you* know he knows—"

"I checked the cards." I shrugged. "I met his twin. She's cool—"

Logan tossed his half-eaten pizza back into the box. "Wait, wait." He waved one hand and rubbed his forehead with the other. Then he squinted over at me. "You checked your tarot cards, and the *cards* told you that Sidney Godwin is innocent—but he knows who did it...whether or not he *knows* he knows...”

I pursed my lips into a disapproving pout. “Yes...”

Logan scoffed. He shook his head and rolled his eyes to the ceiling.

“What?” I demanded furiously.

Seraphina glanced between the two of us. “Logan, Nix's readings are usually pretty accurate...she wouldn't accept a reading if it wasn't clear...”

Logan looked between the two of us and sighed heavily. “I don't think we should be relying on magic to the point where we exclude a potential suspect...you know what I mean? I think it's dangerous.” He shrugged. “It could narrow your focus. Limit potential connections.”

There was an awkward silence.

Then Cole cleared his throat. He looked uneasily from me to Logan and then to Phin. “So, what do we do? How do we figure this out?”

“Well, what do we know?” Logan dunked his crust in the marinara cup.

“You want to go over it all *again*?” I rolled my eyes. “Fine. People go missing all the time, from anywhere. Then in the 1930s, only girls go missing and only from the school and on a time cycle. Then in the 1960s, the victims switch again—now it's not just girls...but they are all little. And now, there's a double mauling in a locked house...with injuries that don't match any monster we know.” I shook my head in frustration.

Logan pointed his crust at me. “You forgot my dad's hunter log. He said that in 1916 a hunter killed the witch after she killed his wife.”

“Westley Thomas and his wife, Persephone,” Seraphina reminded him softly.

“Right.” Logan nodded at her appreciatively. “Thomas took

care of it. But, obviously, it didn't work...so, that got me thinking..." Logan hesitated, glancing at Seraphina.

Seraphina winced ever so slightly. She inhaled deeply, her nostrils flaring. Then she met my eye pointedly. "Logan thinks he knows someone who might have insight into what happened all those years ago..."

Logan nodded. "We wanted to talk it over with you guys first, but I'm going to make the call tonight."

I cocked an eyebrow as I watched Seraphina shift uncomfortably. "To who?"

"Look," Logan sighed heavily and massaged his temple. "I really was hoping to avoid it, but I think the Bloodstone will have a record of what happened in 1916. So, I'm going to call this hunter I know...and they can put me in contact with a specialist at the Bloodstone."

"The *Bloodstone*?" I scowled, my eyes narrowed. "What in the hex is the—"

"It's an organization of mages and..." Logan rolled his eyes and made a face. "They call themselves 'slayers,' but they're really just hunters with a paycheck."

"*Paycheck*? How do we get on the payroll?" Cole quipped, only half kidding.

Logan frowned. "Trust me, I'd rather nasty motels and bad gas station food, then have to report to Bloodstone."

"Why?" I snapped, unable to hide my rising annoyance with a soft tone and gentle expression like my sister.

"The money comes with strings." Logan shrugged. "They tie you up like a puppet. The Bloodstone has complete control of their 'contracts.' Slayers go wherever and do whatever they are told, and nothing else. Just, trust me, okay? It's not as great as they make it out to be...and besides, you have to be born into the order. Slayers are born, not made like hunters."

I crinkled my nose. "So, why call them if they're so lame?" My eyes slid to Seraphina. She'd been quiet and was now staring down at her hands.

"Like I said, it's the last thing I want to do, but they probably have some record of what happened back then when Westley took out the witch. When they aren't sending slayers out on hunts, they are sending their mages out to record everything. And honestly, they just know a lot in general." Logan shrugged and continued begrudgingly, "I mean, hunters? We pick up things as we go, spread the word around to other hunters when we can, teach each other...but we only know what we've seen. It's all trial and error. We don't know everything. The Bloodstone, on the other hand—" He shook his head in disgust. "They hoard supernatural secrets and paranormal lore like a mawkit hoards souls. And all that knowledge? They keep it locked away and only privy to their mages. And the mages get to sit back, safe in the Bloodstone Temple, while the slayers do all the grunt work. Every slayer gets assigned to a mage...it's a whole thing."

"If they keep it all to themselves, why would they tell *you*?" Suspicion creased my forehead as I studied Seraphina who still hadn't looked up. There was something they weren't saying.

"Like I said...I know somebody." Logan's jaw tightened as he tore off a new slice. He brought it to his mouth but lowered it before taking a bite. He tossed it back into the box. "I always reach out to other hunters before I bother with the Bloodstone. And this hunter is sort of a specialist in the subject. Hopefully, they can give us some idea of what we're looking for..."

"Specialist?" Cole scoffed with an amused smirk.

I raised my eyebrows and my mouth sagged as I finally put it together. I inclined my head at Seraphina in disbelief. Phin finally raised her gaze and met my eye. I shook my head and pursed my lips into a disapproving pout. Then I turned to glare at Logan. "And when you say specialist, you mean *witch* hunter, don't you?"

# THE FUTURE FREAKS ME OUT

"Wait, what?" Cole's face hardened. He looked sharply from me to Logan.

Logan shoved a hand through his sandy-blonde hair and rubbed the back of his neck.

I tossed my crust into the empty box. "You're actually thinking about calling a *witch* hunter here to help us?"

Logan's eyes shifted to me. He scowled darkly. "Obviously not. I'm going to ask questions, not ask them to come here."

"No." I shook my head. "No way." I crushed the pizza box in half. I stood from the bed and stalked over to the tiny trashcan. I stuffed the box inside and started digging for my pajamas.

"Nix, he's not going to put us in *danger* or anything." Seraphina looked to Logan for confirmation.

"Of course, I'm not." Logan's face lined with irritation, his jaw tight with indignation.

"I don't know, dude." Cole shook his dark hair from his eyes. "I think a call could potentially be taken as an invitation..."

Logan shot Cole a pointed stare.

Cole gave a one-shouldered, sheepish shrug. "You know them

better than me...but I'd advise not disclosing our location, if you get my drift..."

"It won't be an issue," Logan muttered with a scowl. Then, his face moody, he looked between me and Cole and Phin. "Well, everybody cool with this?"

Cole nodded slowly. "As long as you keep them away from the girls, I trust your judgment." Then he straightened his laptop and started typing again. His eyes on the screen, he added, "But either way, I'm sure we could figure it out on our own..."

I scoffed. "Cole, we've been at it for hours." I shoved my balled-up pajamas underneath my arm and waved a hand angrily. "Days, technically."

Logan smirked. "My point exactly."

I glared at him with a nasty sneer. "But we've been looking for the demon for weeks. I don't see you calling in any help for that!"

Logan shifted where he stood, his eyes narrowed, but before he could argue, Cole cleared his throat. "Oh! About the demon—" He gestured to his laptop. "I've been working on something that might actually help with—"

I snapped my head in his direction. "Cole, now is not the time for your inner computer geek to come out!" My eyes slid back to Logan. "And it certainly isn't the time to be calling witch *murderers* to—"

As always, Logan only had eyes for Seraphina. "Sam, what do you think? Honestly. If you think it's not a good idea, I won't do it. You're tie-breaker."

I snorted, muttering darkly under my breath.

"More kids are going to go missing." She hesitated. "I suppose if you feel like this is the best thing to do—"

I groaned with an incredulous smirk. "*Oh, come on!*"

Phin looked at Logan, her face apprehensive. "I trust you."

Logan stared at her for a moment, a mixture of surprise and something else softening the hard lines of his angular face. He smiled slightly.

I scoffed. My eyes darted between the three of them: Logan, eyes on Phin; Phin, doe-eyed and downcast; Cole, glued to the computer; and then there was me...furious and clearly out-voted. Without another word, I marched into the bathroom and slammed the door behind me.

I couldn't sleep.

Logan insisted on having the television on while he went to bed. Something about an old banshee injury. Bedtime silence made the ringing in his ears unbearable. TV helped.

*Him.*

Not me.

I found it annoying. Like everything else about him. But if I was being honest, it wasn't the TV that was keeping me up.

My blood was burning, barely containing my rage.

How could Seraphina think that Logan calling a *witch* hunter would be a good idea? It was like a betrayal. Like, once again, she was choosing something (someone) else over me. Leaving me all over again. Metaphorically or whatever. I tugged the covers tighter around me. Phin grunted at my back. I pulled harder. She elbowed me in the spine.

I didn't bother yelling at her.

She was asleep.

I could tell. Let's just say: I wasn't the only Grey sister who snored.

Sleep took almost all night to come to me, and just as my eyes began to droop, there was a low moan in the darkness.

My eyes flashed open, wide and alert.

I looked over at Cole.

He'd rolled over in his bed, his face illuminated in the blue glow of the TV.

His eyelids fluttered. He mumbled. Then he began to thrash.

He was dreaming. *Again.* Even after taking the somnum.

Cole was right. There was something wrong with these dreams...in that, they couldn't be dreams.

I slipped out of bed and shook him awake.

Cole's arms lashed out. His hands crushed my shoulders. His eyes bulged out of his head, black in the dark.

"Dream!" I hissed. Fear seeped into my heart and sharpened my words. "COLE! DREAM!"

He let me go immediately, like he'd been caught doing something wrong. Then he pushed up on his elbows and sat with his back against the headboard. His chest rose and fell rapidly as he stared straight ahead, his face haunted and harrowed.

He'd seen something. And it hadn't been a dream. It was real. I was sure of it.

"Tell me."

Cole closed his eyes, his nostrils flaring as he inhaled and exhaled, struggling to find a rhythm. "There was, uhm." He licked his lips, white in the TV light. He gritted his teeth, his jaw tight. "There was a girl, like—our age. She was sneaking into the Blood Farm—then it changed...and the girl was tied up, then like a cave or something...dirt, lots of dirt everywhere...and there was this *woman*. She was stroking her hair—and the little girl." Cole covered his face in his hands. He racked his hand through his hair. "It was Mary Tran. And the woman was..." Cole trailed off. He looked like he was going to get sick.

"Drinking her blood?"

Cole looked at me sharply, his eyes shining in the glow of the TV. "She was chewing on her throat. Like, *eating* her." He closed his eyes, his head swaying as he whispered, "Blood gushed from her teeth."

"Show me."

Startled, Cole's eyes blinked open. He shook his hair from his dark eyes and cocked his head to look at me better. "What?"

"There's a spell..." I pushed off the bed and stumbled through the dark for my Book of Shadows. I grabbed the book from the stack and made my way back to Cole's bedside. I plopped on the bed and thumped the book open. "It's supposed to be for telepathy, but Mama used it for dreams...with Fawn, when she was a baby. Fawn used to have these horrible night terrors and—ah, yes, here." My eyes skimmed the page. "It forms a telepathic connection, so we can send thoughts back and forth..." I chewed on my cheek as I read through the method, squinting in the dim glow of television flashes.

"Nix, no." Cole shook his head, his mouth curled in disgust. "You do not want to see this. Why would you want—"

I waved a hand dismissively, not bothering to take my eyes off the page. "Because you aren't having *dreams*, Cole. You're having premonitions. Visions of the future." I looked up from the book then, and I met his eyes. "And you just saw what's going to happen to Mary Tran if we don't stop it."

Cole winced. "Okay, maybe. That doesn't mean *you* need to see it."

I scoffed and returned my attention to the spell. "Yes, I do. Because these—these *visions* or whatever—have you all messed up. You don't want to see them, so you aren't looking at them hard enough. I might be able to see something you haven't noticed. And I need to see who the woman was that..." My voice faltered as I struggled with the words. "You know, the woman who was with Mary Tran."

"And how long does this last?" Cole asked uneasily. "This brain connection?"

I looked up sharply with a smirk. "What's wrong? You don't want me snooping inside your head?"

Cole forced a smile that didn't touch his eyes. I passed Cole the book and went to the dresser for some ingredients. "Don't worry. It shouldn't last longer than a day or two."

As I started to brew the tea in the low light of the oldies channel, Logan, still asleep, grumbled from the cot and rolled away from the noise to face the wall. I looked back at Cole. His brow furrowed, he held the book up close to his face and squinted in the darkness. As the water poured into the mug, I turned back to the kitchenette to finish. I crushed skullcap into the tea and stirred it with my finger. Then I carried it over to Cole.

He wrinkled his nose. "Nix, I don't know—"

I groaned and grabbed his hand, forcing the mug into his palm. "Six kids, Cole. Six more kids will be taken."

"But Logan said—"

I rolled my eyes. "I don't care what he says."

"But it was just a dream—"

I gave him a scathing stare. "You and I both know it was not just a dream."

Cole flinched.

I shrugged impatiently. "I don't know what's going on with you, okay? I don't know why this is happening to you. I'm going to get a hold of Grammy as soon as this is all over...she'll be able to help. But if there's even a *chance* that I'm right—that this is a vision of the future, of what might happen to Mary...?"

"Fine." Cole took a deep breath. He pointed the mug at me. "But no reading my mind without asking first..."

I grinned. "It doesn't work like that."

Cole frowned, eying the mug in his hand.

"You'll see." I waved him on. "Drink."

Cole crinkled his nose and drank deeply. He didn't come up for air until it was gone. He made a face and stuck out his tongue. "Blech." He shoved the mug back at me and held his stomach.

I put the empty mug on the nightstand and chuckled. "Okay, now repeat after me...*videre quod vides sic video.*"

Cole stumbled over the incantation, but he managed it well enough.

"Okay, it'll be easier if we hold hands." I grabbed hold of him and gripped his hands hard. "Now—close your eyes and imagine what you saw like a moving picture...and send it to me."

Cole scoffed. I squinted through my closed eyes. "Come on, Cole—please."

"I'm trying..."

I breathed in deeply through my nose and exhaled, nostrils flaring. Meditations were never my strength. Clearing my mind was nearly impossible for me. But I had to.

Blank.

Blank.

Blank.

I continued to breathe in a steady rhythm.

Blank.

Blank.

Then something flickered behind my eyes.

It flashed like a channel change.

Again and again.

Closer each time.

I squeezed my eyes shut, tight as I could.

On.

Off.

I flinched.

On.

Off.

My fingers crushed Cole's hands.

Then I saw it.

The Blood Farm.

Bruised clouds blocked out the sun overhead, giving the strange feeling of night in midafternoon. It wasn't a barn, not really. It was an old stone building with large double doors and high, boarded-up windows on the sides, more like a church, but without any sign of a cross. There was a giant bell in a tower off the side of it that, for some reason, felt ominous. Silent as it hung, it seemed to radiate, vibrate with darkness. But in the vision, I couldn't feel what it was exactly. Though, I had a guess...

Two lanes of pressed grass like tire tracks curved through a tall field surrounded by woods on all sides, a well-worn path leading from the forest, through the field, up the hill, and straight to the double doors. It was like a clearing had been cut just for this field, for this path, for this building with its bell.

A girl, slim and small, her face shrouded in long sheets of black hair, framed by a headband fashioned from thick, green ribbon, hurried forward toward the Blood Farm, hugging her jacket around her. She turned to look behind her, revealing the pale of her face.

Lizzie Tran.

A guy as tall as Logan, followed close behind her. He shoved his hands into the pockets of his letterman jacket, glaring up at the building. His tan skin looked olive in the darkness of the black clouds. His hair stuck up like spikes of gold. His face was long and angular, yet his features were soft and round.

It was Sidney Godwin.

"Lizzie, this is a bad idea," he muttered, his voice nearly lost in the wind. He eyed the way they'd come. "We shouldn't be here."

The girl stopped short in the middle of the path. Strands of black hair blew in her face as she glared up at him. "Sid, I'm doing this. Either help me, or go back to school and have lunch with your sister."

He gritted his teeth. His jaw pulsed with frustration as he studied the determination on her face. His eyes slid toward the Blood Farm. Thunder rumbled in the distance.

"All right." He held up a finger in warning. "We walk inside, have a look around, and then we leave. Okay? In and out. Promise?"

Lizzie nodded earnestly. "Promise."

He wrapped a protective arm around her, holding her tight to him. Then together, they made their way through the waving, graying field, huddled against the old November wind, and up to the double doors.

They hesitated at the threshold. A lifetime of legend holding them back from reaching out for the door. Lizzie looked back down the path that snaked through the grass. In the distance, the path leading through the woods was dark and ominous as a cave. She looked back at the building. Her round, black eyes striking against her fair skin. Her jaw set in her oval face. Her rosebud lips pursed. "Let's go."

Sid forced a smile that looked more like a grimace. "Monsters don't come out in the sunlight, right?"

They shivered in the cold as the dark clouds passed over them, covering them in shadow. Lizzie tried the door, but Sid put a gentle hand over hers. "Let me."

She stepped back, and he grabbed the curved handle with both hands and pulled. Hard. There was a creak and shower of dust as the door was yanked from its frame. Sid held an arm up to shield her from the debris. Lizzie swiped at her phone, turning on the flashlight. She held it in thin fingers and a slightly trembling hand. Sid turned on his own phone flashlight and stepped in front of her. "Stay behind me."

It was empty. Literally. A big, wide-open space with nothing inside.

Exposed wooden rafters in the ceiling, dim light pouring in from the cracks in the high, boarded window slits and streaking the stone floor, there was nothing there. But I could feel it. The vibration of power. It rose up like steam from the ground. And I knew it was evil.

Lizzie shined her light all over, but there was nothing to see. Except the stains. Dark on the floor and smeared on the walls as though someone had tried to clean it...but couldn't.

"Is that—"

"Blood." Sid scowled, wincing in the harsh phone light. "She's not here, Lizzie. Mary's not here. We need to leave."

Lizzie shook her head and quickened her pace. She ran along the length of the building, her phone light swaying from side to side, sweeping the entire place until she got to the farthest corners.

Sid stopped behind her. He put a hand on her shoulder and squeezed. "Lizzie, I'm so—"

"Don't be." Lizzie scoffed. "I'm the one who's sorry..." She sniffed, her voice watery and thick with her tears. "I let those witches get to me. *Again*. They've been taunting me about it all week. Ever since she disappeared." She cleared her throat and continued in a mocking, high-pitched squeak, "'Mary's rotting away in the Blood Farm because you're too chicken to save her.'" Lizzie groaned. "I had to be sure they were wrong...God, I'm an idiot." Lizzie lifted her gaze to meet Sidney's. "But if she's not here, where is she, Sidney? I know she's not dead. I'd *know* if she was dead."

"You're going to find her, okay? Hey, no, listen to me, Lizzie." Sidney pulled her toward him. He bent low to look directly into her eyes. "I promise you, okay? I swear—if it's the last thing I do— I'm going to make sure you get her back."

She pushed him away with an impatient eyeroll. Then she bowed her head, her whole tiny frame caving in on itself underneath the weight of crushing disappointment and grief. She turned her phone over to slap off the flashlight. In the glow of the phone, her dark eyes glittered with tears as they spilled down her cheeks and slipped down her broad nose.

Then there was a shadow in the darkness.

A movement at their backs.

Something slammed into Sid. Knocked him to the ground. Pinned him to the floor as he roared, "LIZZIE, RUN!"

Stunned, Lizzie turned to her side to stare down at Sid struggling on the ground. Then something grabbed her, yanked her head back by her raven hair, exposing her white neck, glowing ghostly in the dark. Before she could scream, teeth tore into her throat, black blood gushing and bubbling, leaking down her neck.

Then I was falling.

Screaming.

I blinked, unseeing, staring blindly into sharp motel light.

"NIX!" Seraphina was leaning over me, tapping my cheek, smoothing my hair back from my forehead.

Her face was upside down. It was making me dizzy. I swallowed thickly, heart hammering, chest heaving with labored breath. I licked my dry lips. I struggled to sit up.

Seraphina's hands lifted me underneath the armpits. She moved to sit next to me. Her silver eyes flashed with fear. "What happened?!"

Logan stood on the opposite side of Cole's bed, arms crossed and his face hard. Cole was apparently suffering from the same after-effects I was—he clutched at his head and blinked rapidly around the room.

Logan nodded toward the nightstand. "What's in the mug?"

I held my head. It throbbed painfully. How hard had I hit the floor? "Nothing now."

I scowled as my thoughts cleared. I hadn't seen who it was. I hadn't seen who—what?—had attacked them. It'd been too fast. Too dark. *Jinx it.*

"Phoenix—" Seraphina frowned disapprovingly. She reached for the fallen Book of Shadows and glanced over the page we'd left it open to. Her eyes moved from Cole to me.

The disappointment in her eyes was too much. Condescending. Annoying. I snatched my book from her. "I was trying to help Cole with his nightmares. No big deal."

Logan cocked an eyebrow as he tossed Cole a water bottle. "Is that so?"

He didn't believe me. Didn't trust me. What else was new. I blew my hair out of my face. "Yup." I pushed to my feet, fighting to remain balanced. My head spun.

Cole cracked open the bottle and drank deeply. He didn't say anything. He pointedly avoided my eye.

Seraphina stood slowly. She turned to Cole. "You shouldn't still be dreaming…"

Cole winced and chugged more water.

Icarus's voice startled us all. "He isn't dreaming."

We all turned to look at the cat. Icarus sat stiffly on the table, his tail flicking back and forth as it dangled over the edge. "These visions aren't nightmares. They are something else."

Seraphina inhaled deeply and turned back to Cole. Logan, his face stony and scowling, looked between Icarus and Cole with increasing irritation. "Then what are they?" he asked gruffly, obviously annoyed at having to converse with a cat.

Icarus paused to scratch his ear with his paw. "I don't know."

Seraphina went to the books and pulled out *her* Book of Shadows. It was hefty. Bulky. A lot more filled her pages than mine. Of course, that was because she'd spent years padding it with everything she could, hoping the harder she studied, the harder she worked, her magic would somehow reveal itself...but it never did.

She ran her finger along the index (mine didn't have an index) and then swiped away the pages with an urgency that made the back of my neck prickle. Her hand froze as she stopped at a page somewhere toward the end. Silver eyes moving rapidly, flickering back and forth, she slowly sank backwards, down onto the bed as she read.

Logan's jaw jutted to one side. He gnawed on the inside of his cheek. His sharp eyes pierced into Cole with such intensity, I scowled. "It's not his fault, you know," I snapped coolly.

Logan's eyes shot to mine. He didn't speak, simply stared at me.

I shifted underneath the weight of his gaze. I shrugged and tossed my hands at my sides. "Well, it isn't," I muttered moodily.

Logan nodded curtly. "Obviously. But these nightmares—"

"They aren't nightmares," Icarus replied from the shadows.

"Whatever." Logan rolled his eyes, not bothering to acknowledge the cat. "It started after the demon." Logan ran a hand through his hair and dropped down onto the bed beside Cole. "Dude—why didn't you tell me it wasn't...they weren't...normal. I mean, you said you had it handled."

Cole chucked the empty water bottle onto the nightstand. He bent forward, his head in his hands. "I do have it handled. I'm dealing with them. Phin's potion isn't working for me, that's all."

"And that is the problem," Icarus muttered in the background.

Logan closed his eyes briefly, his jaw tightening. "Yeah, so you keep saying—" He glared at Icarus, who blinked back. "But you aren't exactly clear about why that is...so if you've nothing *helpful* to add—"

Suddenly, Seraphina looked up from the book. "Icarus." She stood from the bed, her book clutched in both her hands, held out in front of her like a High Priestess at a ceremony. "You need to go to Grey Isle. You need to ask Grammy about this. Tell her *everything*."

Icarus blinked slowly, his tail flicking back and forth. "I can only tell her everything once the boy has told *us* everything." Icarus stared at Cole.

Cole shrugged. "What do you want me to say?"

"What, exactly, have you been seeing?"

Cole's jaw pulsed. He tossed his dark hair out of his eyes. "Before we came here, I saw a town flooded with red water. And dead little kids floating through the streets."

"He saw Mary Tran." I blurted angrily. "He saw her face before he even saw her missing poster. I think they're premonitions." I bit my lips together and shrugged beneath the weight of every eye. "Psychic visions. I think he's having psychic visions of the future, and we should be using them to our advantage."

Logan scoffed. He shook his head and covered his eyes with his hands as he muttered, "Of course, you do..."

I rounded on him. "*How could we not*? Cole just saw Lizzie Tran attacked at the Blood Farm!" There was a dark silence. I winced underneath its weight. "How could we *not* try to stop that from happening?"

Logan hesitated, considering this for a moment. Seraphina nibbled anxiously on her bottom lip. Hope swelled in my heart...

"No." Icarus blinked steadily at me.

And then it burst.

I blinked stupidly at the cat, my mouth sagging.

Icarus's fur bristled as he regarded me with heavy eyes. "Phoenix, you must understand...*these visions cannot be trusted.*"

Logan scowled with increasing impatience, looking from me to Cole and back to Icarus. "I'll take care of Lizzie Tran. I'll watch her. Make sure she doesn't go anywhere near the Blood Farm. But—"

"No." Icarus dropped down from the table and hopped onto Cole's bed. His tail flicked furiously, his fur on end. "Acting on these visions could lead to an even worse outcome. Until we know what they are—*precisely what they are*—you all need to ignore them. And you most certainly should not make any decisions based upon them."

"Are you serious?" I scoffed incredulously. "So, even though I know that Lizzie Tran is going to get *attacked by a monster*, I have to just—" I tossed my hands in the air. "What? Pretend I didn't see anything?"

Icarus's eyes bored into mine. "Yes."

I recoiled. "That's—" I scrunched up my face in disgust as I stammered for words. "That's—!"

"Icarus," Seraphina interrupted sharply as she moved around the room in a sudden rush of activity. "Go to Grey Isle. *Now.*" Her back to us, she rummaged through our collection of potions and herbs. "And don't come back until you have answers." She shoveled plants and spices and various other ingredients onto the pages of the open book. Then she shuffled through the cramped space to the kitchenette.

I glanced back at Icarus, but he was already gone.

Logan spun around, his neck craning around the tiny motel room searching for a glimpse of the cat. "Where did he—"

"He's gone," Seraphina murmured. She didn't bother to look up. Focused on her task at hand, she measured and chopped. Her eyes shifted back and forth between her work and her book, now propped up against the wall in front of her.

Logan looked at me, his brow creased in confusion.

"Icarus is a *familiar*." I smirked at Logan's blank stare and spoke slowly as though he were an infant. "He has magic of his own."

Logan waved me off and walked over to Phin. He stopped behind her just close enough to peek over her shoulder and still maintain a respectful distance.

Seemingly sensing his presence, Seraphina spoke softly, her voice kind. "I'm brewing morsmort. Somnum clearly isn't strong enough." Seraphina paused then. "Which is interesting because it doesn't work on witches, either..." She glanced back at Cole, who stared off into nothing, a broody darkness settled around him. "So, whatever is happening to him, it must be supernatural in nature. But whatever is the cause, morsmort should work. It's a potion that puts the drinker into an unconscious state until awoken by an outside stimulant...like an alarm clock, or even a voice or a touch."

"So—" Cole scoffed darkly. "I'll be *knocked out* every night?"

Logan turned back to Cole, his face grim. "It's the best option, dude. You can't keep having those visions every night...especially when we don't know what they are or where they come from...and we can't do anything about them. That'll drive us crazy."

Cole sighed heavily. "Right."

An awkward silence settled around the room as Seraphina worked. Then the sweet smell of roses and apples wafted through the room. Then she brought a steaming mug of morsmort over to Cole. She gave him a gentle smile as she sank down onto the bed beside him. She passed him the potion.

He looked from the brew back to Seraphina. "You promise I'll wake up in the morning?"

Seraphina placed a hand on his knee and squeezed. "As soon as your alarm goes off."

Cole inhaled deeply. His nostrils flared as he stared down at the mug cupped in his hands.

"You won't have to take it forever, man," Logan added quietly from the kitchenette. "Just until the cat comes back with something actually helpful." Logan paused and shook his head. "Well, that is one of the weirdest things I've ever said..."

Cole's jaw tightened. Then, without a word, he downed the brew in one long chug. Then he passed the cup back to Seraphina and scrunched down into the covers. He turned his back on me, flopping pointedly to the other side of the bed. He tugged the covers up over his shoulder. And then he was still.

Seraphina's eyes met mine. "You heard what Icarus said?"

My mouth pinched in a pout, I returned her stare without comment.

"Phoenix!"

I looked away, jaw jutted to the side. "Yes. I heard what he said."

Phin grabbed my chin and forced me to look at her. "Are you going to listen to him?"

I shoved her hand off me. "Maybe."

"*Phoenix*!"

I rolled my eyes to the ceiling. I shook my head in disbelief. "So, I watch Lizzie Tran get her throat ripped out...and I'm supposed to just—" I looked from Logan to Phin with a down-turned smirk. "Just forget it? Let it happen anyway?"

"Yes." Phin didn't flinch. The word was short and cold and so...unlike her. It was disturbing.

I did a double take. "You're *serious*? You want me to just let her—"

"Yes." Seraphina's hands gripped my shoulders, and she squeezed. Hard. "Yes, Phoenix, and you know why? Because if you make your decisions based upon this vision—you're changing the future—"

I snickered darkly. "Yeah, that's kind of the point—"

"—and something worse could happen!"

I smirked. "Like what?"

Seraphina groaned and rolled her eyes in disgust. "God, Phoenix, don't you get it? *These visions aren't a good thing.* They aren't happening to Cole for a good reason...they're rooted in evil. And you change one thing about the future, you change a million things. How would you feel if you interfered and made something even worse happen?"

I snorted in disgust, biting my lip as I shook my head. I looked at Logan who stood off to the side, his arms crossed like Phin's bodyguard. "And what does your Wookiee think?"

Logan continued to stare at me with his stupid, stoic face. He was quiet for a while. So long I couldn't stand it any longer.

I marched over to him and shoved his shoulder. "Come on, Logan. You know we have to help her. That's our job!"

Logan stared down at me, his expression impassive.

He knew I was right. I knew he knew. I tried again. "If you'd seen—"

"No." Logan shook his head. "No. You shouldn't have seen it in the first place. And until the cat comes back, we're not going to do anything."

I took a step back, blinking slowly in defeated disbelief. "How can we just let her—"

"We don't know what those visions are, or where they're coming from, okay? Do you not get how seriously messed up this entire situation is?"

"Oh, I get it." I snickered and shrugged. "It's *extremely* messed up that you're just going to sit on your butt and let a girl get—"

Logan stepped forward, closing the distance between us, so he could loom over me. "Say you follow her, hmm? Say you ditch Cole at the school again, and you chase after this girl... meanwhile, you leave all those little kids behind...and six more are taken because you weren't there to stop it?" He shrugged with a downturned smirk. "Maybe Cole gets jumped and eaten alive in the process, all because you weren't there to have his back?"

I chewed on my cheek as I considered this.

Logan kept going. "You say it's a psychic vision of the future? Where's the proof of that?"

"Cole saw Mary Tran!"

Logan smirked. "But did a town actually fill with red water? Do you see any dead kids floating around—or whatever he said? No. So, I'm going to listen to your mom's creepy cat and wait this out. And so are you."

"But—"

"And in the meantime, I'm going to do what I *can* do to stop all this. What I was going to do in the first place: call up Frankie and get in touch with a mage who can give me intel on Westley Thomas and his witch hunt, and maybe tell me how to stop this before it continues. And you're going to go to that school with Cole...and you're going to dig through every inch of that place until you find out where these kids are vanishing from. Understood?"

I shut my mouth on a retort. I didn't trust myself to lie. I gave him a curt nod instead.

Seraphina cleared her throat. "That spell...Phoenix, you should take it easy in the morning. You're going to feel it tomorrow."

"It's okay." Logan flicked on the TV. "They've got elementary duty—that'll be plenty relaxing."

I regarded him coolly. "And you guys will be—"

"Heading to the sheriff's department." Logan smiled smugly.

I scowled and tossed my book into the corner and slapped off the light switch.

Seraphina switched off the lamp.

I plopped into bed and yanked the blankets over my head. My heart was still racing. I couldn't get the image of Lizzie's bloody throat out of my head. Those teeth...short and stubby and gushing red. I closed my eyes, and that's all I saw. I peeked out through the covers at the TV and stared unseeing at the infomercials as they flashed on the screen. They all could believe whatever they wanted about Cole's nightmares.

It didn't matter what anyone said.

Tomorrow, I was going to save Lizzie Tran.

13

# OKAY, I BELIEVE YOU, BUT MY TOMMY GUN DON'T

My eyes flew open at the sound of the alarm. I tossed the blankets off me, covering Seraphina as she sat up in bed. She looked like a little kid in a ghost sheet costume. I snickered as she grumbled and fought her way out of the covers. Then I slipped into the bathroom and locked the door before Phin even realized what'd happened.

As I switched on the water, Seraphina jiggled the knob. Then she banged on the door. "Nix, what the hex! We're leaving before you!"

"What?" I shouted back with a grin as I tested the water temperature. "I can't hear you! Tell me when I get out!"

I stripped and slipped underneath the spray. She shrieked in frustration and slammed against the door. I bit my lip on a smirk.

By the time I got out, Phin and Logan were gone. I chuckled to myself. Cole was on the computer. He glanced at me as I came out of the bathroom. "You did that on purpose."

My mouth fell open in mock shock. My eyes widened with feigned innocence. I put a hand on my heart. "Me? *Never.*" I laughed and snapped my finger. My backpack, shimmering with

184

orange magic, dumped itself onto the freshly made bed. I snatched up the now-empty bag and began to pack.

Cole watched me quietly. I looked over at him. His face was stern, his full mouth in a round pout. I rolled my eyes and continued to raid our supplies for potions with healing properties. Just in case. I dropped to my knees, sitting back on my heels. I opened the rucksack and gingerly felt my way through Logan's weapon stash. My hands closed around the cold metal of a handgun. My stomach did a small flip.

As soon as we'd gotten on the road, Logan had taken time to teach us how to handle everything from a shotgun to a crossbow. And although I could definitely carry my own, I still didn't like them. Guns. I always had an uneasy reaction to them. Physical. Visceral. Guns...bullets...were too final. Like those moments that crash into your life and change everything. No do-overs. And I, Phoenix Grey, was a girl who *needed* do-overs. My hand moved to the quicksilver machete.

"Here. You take the blade. I'll take the hawthorn stakes." I put the machete aside for Cole and grabbed a bundle of stakes for me and dumped them in my bag. "It could be a number of things... but quicksilver and hawthorn weaken most monsters..."

Cole didn't move. "I take it we're—"

I looked up at him, my mouth twitching with impatience. "Yes, Cole. We're going to the Blood Farm, and we're going to stop those things from attacking Lizzie and Sid."

His jaw tightened. His disapproval hardened his face. He looked like Johnny Depp in *Cry Baby*: all broody angst and cheekbones.

"Cry baby..." I mumbled under my breath. A smirk tickled the corner of my mouth.

"We aren't supposed to act on what I saw." Cole shut the laptop.

I rolled my eyes and continued packing.

"A really messed up dream." He turned in the chair, resting his forearms on his thighs and threading his hands. "We need to be at the school keeping an eye on those kids and figuring out why, where, and *how* they're disappearing."

My backpack stuffed full of hawthorn stakes, I zipped it shut and slung it over my shoulder. The keychains and enamel pins clattered together; some snapped me in the arm.

"You know I can't just forget what I saw." I shook my head. "I don't know why, or what's going on with you—we'll figure it out later, but right now we have to go with what we know. And we know that you are having premonitions in your sleep."

Cole scoffed and raked a hand through his thick black hair. "Nix, nothing I've seen has come true. And you know why that is? Because I'm not a witch. I'm not a psychic. Okay? We need to focus on our job. And our job is to keep those kids safe." He pushed up from the chair. He stomped over to his guitar case and threw it over his shoulder.

My eyes narrowed as I watched him head for the door. "Lizzie Tran will get her throat mauled by a monster. Unless we stop it. How are you going to feel if—"

Cole rolled his eyes, his hand on the doorknob. "And how would *you* feel if a little kid gets snatched because we weren't where we were supposed to be?"

My jaw jutted to the side, and I marched across the room to stand toe to toe with him. "Why are you so—so stubborn?!" I held my hands up between us, fingers clenched like claws as though I might squeeze his head. I groaned and slapped my arms to my sides.

"Stubborn?" Cole cocked an eyebrow. "*Me?*"

I had to smile despite my increasing irritation. Cole was the most easygoing, laid-back guy on the planet. He was a lot of things, but stubborn was definitely *not* one of them. Still. "Yes! Why are you refusing to see what's right in front of your face?"

Cole's face constricted, his high cheekbones prominent in his face. His dark eyes slid to the door.

"Why?!" I shoved him. Hard. He staggered but didn't grab me back.

"Because." His eyes met mine with a cool anger. "*Because*, Nix, okay?"

I shrugged. "Not good enough."

He snorted. "Of course, it's not." He flashed a sideways smirk as he shook his head.

I scrunched up my face. "What?"

Then Cole looked at me, really looked at me, meeting my fiery gaze with one to match. His face marred with a strange mixture of hurt and anger. I'd never seen him look that way.

I recoiled slightly. I'd hurt him somehow. "Look, Cole, I'm sorry if I'm pushing too hard or whatever, but—"

Cole shook his head again, his mouth downturned. "Nah, Phoenix, don't worry about it. You're right. Not good enough." He licked his lips and looked off to the side again, unable to meet my eyes. "If I *am* having some kind of prophetic sixth sense, or whatever..." Cole's gaze moved to mine. "Where do you think that came from?"

His dark eyes looked almost black in the weak motel lighting. Instinctively, I took a step back. I remembered when those dark eyes had glowed demonic like molten gold.

Cole scoffed with an ironic smile. "*Exactly*. Any special ability I have? It had to have come from the demon." He shrugged. "That's the only thing that makes sense, right?"

I hesitated. I had no answer. Because he was right.

Cole grinned darkly. "Why do you think I didn't mention this to Phin before? I mean, she would be the better one to talk to about something like this..."

I frowned, my brow furrowed moodily. Sure, maybe Phin would be more understanding, and blah, blah, blah. But that didn't mean I couldn't be sympathetic...if I tried...

Cole waved his hands up in exasperation. "Or even Logan?

After all, he's become pretty much like a brother to me since we hit the road."

I made a face. Logan? That seemed a bit of an exaggeration. I opened my mouth to argue this, but Cole didn't stop there.

"Phoenix, the *last* person I would talk to about this would be you. But you forced it out of me. And I shouldn't have let you. But that's what I do. I let you push me around, and I go along with whatever you say. Well, not this time, Phoenix. I'm not basing my actions, my decisions, on demonic dreams. I'm working the case. I'm keeping those little kids safe."

I flinched as his words hit me. Hard.

Cole didn't wait for me to recover. "But it's early. School doesn't start for a while. And clearly, I can't trust you to stay put, so we might as well head over to the sheriff's department and crash their interview."

He wrenched open the door and walked out, leaving me staring stupidly after him.

"Afternoon, Officer Meeks." I leaned over the desk with a warm smile. "Good to see you!"

Heather grinned in genuine delight at the sight of me. "Well, hello, girlie. You're up early. Good to see you back so soon! Are you looking for Rory?"

"We're actually with—"

Heather beamed brightly and continued as though she hadn't heard me. "You know as much as that boy held a torch for poor, sweet Drew...he hasn't been able to shut up about you, Miss Phoenix! All dinner long, he just kept going on and on—why my mama had to—"

"Uh...no." My smile slipped slightly into a grimace. Ew. Not creepy at all. "Uh, we're actually with—"

"And who's your friend? Gosh," Heather's smile slipped into a knowing smirk. "I'll have to tell Rory he's got no chance at all if this is the kind of company you keep, my girl."

At that, Cole stepped forward and held his hand out across the desk. "Hello, ma'am, Cole Oberst."

I blinked. Then my eyes slid sideways.

"Good to meet you, Cole. Are you with the school paper, too?"

"Yes, ma'am, we're actually with two other students who came here ahead of us—"

I lifted onto the tips of my toes and peeked over the desk and several cubicles in between us. I jutted my chin in their general direction. "The model and the sasquatch."

Officer Meeks chuckled and nodded. "Right, Miss Stephens and Mr. Craven..." She did a double take and then flashed another smile. "Wait a sec—is that blonde beauty your sister?"

I nodded with an almost boastful, broad grin. "We're twins, actually."

"No, kidding!" Heather's gray eyes burst big. "Well, come on over, sweet girl." She stood up, then, and waved us around the desk, but hesitated. She scrunched up her face and inclined her head, her blonde ponytail swaying. "But they didn't say to expect cha?"

I smirked. "Honestly, ma'am, they didn't expect us to make it..." I jutted a thumb toward Cole, who'd saddled up beside me. "Oberst, here, drives like his nana."

Cole glanced at me out of the corner of his eye. His mouth twitched in amusement.

Officer Meeks giggled. "All right, well, come on over—looks like Sheriff Godwin just took 'em back."

She led the way past a handful of desks piled high with files and littered with coffee-stained papers. Then she opened an office door and poked her head inside. "Sheriff? We got two more for ya!"

I hurried inside with Cole right behind me. The office was the same beige as the main building. The far wall was lined with big windows with slanted shades pulled tight. The desk was as neat and orderly as the woman who sat behind it. I had to do a double take. This was the sheriff. The mother of Stuart Godwin. The woman didn't look anything like her son. He was lion-like. She was more crow-like than anything else. Her black hair was slicked back in a bun so tightly it gave her face a lift. Unlike my go-to topknot style, in which I was constantly battling wisps of hair falling into my eyes, not a single hair on her pointed face was out of place. Her cold eyes moved over me, her thin lips pinched, judging me from the tips of my chunky cherry streaks all the way down to my unraveling shoelaces hanging limply off scuffed-up Converse.

My very existence irritated her.

And I loved it.

A lopsided smirk slid onto my face, and I nodded in greeting. "Hiya! Phoenix Stephens, how ya doing?"

"Cole Oberst. Thanks for waiting." Cole rushed forward and stuck his hand out.

The sheriff leaned forward and gave his hand a hard shake. "Sheriff Godwin."

Cole glanced back at me. "We would've been here sooner, but—"

"Oberst drives like a girl," I quipped with an obnoxious wink.

I turned to Logan and Seraphina perched in identical chairs in front of the desk. Phin balanced a notebook on her crossed leg as she clutched a pen in her hand and looked up at me with a pained expression, framed by a few tasteful golden tendrils spilling from her fishtail side-braid. Logan had a tape recorder in his hand. He'd slicked his hair so it was extra shwooshy, looking like an action star on the cover of GQ. The angles of his face were sharp and defined as irritation lined his clenched jaw. I beamed at them and gave Logan's shoulder a good smack.

"Hey, guys!" I bent over Sheriff Godwin's desk and plucked up a pen. "You mind?"

Sheriff Godwin's face pinched tighter. "Ehm."

I sat down on the armrest of Logan's chair, my butt forcing his arm off it. I grinned down at him. His temple pulsed. His jaw twitched. I bent down a bit to whisper loudly for all to hear: "Nice edges; did Phin do your hard part before you left?"

"As I was saying—" Sheriff Godwin snapped, her voice cool and cutting.

"Drew Graham," Logan sat up straighter, his recorder held out in his lap. He clicked it on and spoke in a crisp, clear voice. "Your official stance is that it was a dog attack."

Slowly, Sheriff Godwin slid her icy-blue eyes away from me and rested them on Logan. "Yes."

"A dog...that you haven't been able to track down. That neither Drew nor Nathan owned. And a dog that made sure to lock the door before it left..."

Sheriff Godwin blinked slowly. She regarded Logan coolly through half-closed eyes. "What are you suggesting, Mr. Craven?"

"Your nephew was the last person to see Mary Tran before she disappeared. He was also at the Graham house just before that, picking Mary up."

"At this time, we can officially state that the attack at the Graham house and the disappearance of Mary Tran are completely separate tragedies. There is no connection between the two of them. Whatsoever."

My lip curled in disbelief. "You seriously—"

Logan elbowed me in the butt. Hard. I slid off the edge of the chair. Cole grabbed me underneath the armpits before I hit the ground. I regained my footing and smacked Logan in the back of the head.

He didn't flinch.

His eyes were on Sheriff Godwin. "Except for Sidney Godwin. Who was at both scenes, within hours—possibly minutes—of each other."

Sheriff Godwin met his hard stare with one to match. "Sidney Godwin is not a suspect in either of these cases."

"Very good." Logan nodded, his brow furrowed in sarcastic understanding. "Now, we've gotten reports from several students that Drew was being harassed by a clique of girls in her class. A clique of girls from the Gossamer House...run by your cousin, yes?"

"Catherine Godwin runs the Gossamer House. And bullying doesn't necessarily equate to a dog attack, Mr. Craven...does it?"

Logan scoffed. "Depends on if they have a dog. Now, you said that Mary Tran, Drew Graham and Nathan Campbell, not connected...but there's more to it than just Sidney Godwin, isn't there?" He glanced quickly at Phin at his left.

"Mary Tran lived at the Gossamer House," Seraphina murmured. "Sidney Godwin dropped her off that night, while Tiffany Crane, Amanda Thompson, Annie Collingwood, and Pamela Bradford were all home and present."

Logan looked back at the sheriff. "Right. The same girls who were harassing Drew Graham were also at the scene of Mary Tran's disappearance."

"They were at the Gossamer House because they live there, Mr. Craven." Sheriff Godwin's jaw tightened as she shifted ever so slightly in her seat. "The girls have all been questioned, and the four of them all have solid alibis. Their stories all line up."

Logan tilted his chin so he could squint down his nose at the sheriff. "And who corroborated their alibis?"

Sheriff Godwin was silent. She stared unblinking at Logan.

"Catherine Godwin, wasn't it?" Logan didn't stop there. He rubbed a hand over his forehead as though he were just recalling something. "And wasn't your son, Stuart Godwin, *stalking* Drew Graham for weeks, all the way up until her death?"

I leaned down, hands gripping the back of Logan's seat. "She got a restraining order on him." I looked back at Sheriff Godwin. Her face was rigid and hard.

But before Sheriff Godwin could say another word, Logan shifted topics so abruptly I blinked slowly trying to process the question. "What can you tell me about the Blood Farm?"

Sheriff Godwin pursed her thin lips tightly as she shifted her mouth to one side. "I take it you've been listening to local legends, Mr. Craven?"

Logan and Phin exchanged a quick glance.

"Well," Seraphina hesitated as she furrowed her brow. "The stories are hard to ignore, when you consider everything...don't you think?"

"What I think, Miss Stephens, is that I have a missing child to locate. I don't have time—"

"So, you don't find it," I shrugged, frowning ironically. "Odd that there are missing kids just up and vanishing every sixteen years? That doesn't raise any—"

Sheriff Godwin's eyes slid to mine. "Are you suggesting that our history of disappearances—occurring over the span of two centuries—are all committed by some kind of witch?" Sheriff Godwin's thin lips twitched. "Or better yet, a *monster*?"

Logan snorted, a sly smirk in the corner of his mouth.

Seraphina didn't flinch. "We are suggesting that maybe you are missing something that connects the crimes. Location, number, and—"

"If you'd truly done your research, Miss Stephens," Sheriff Godwin's words cut sharply, yet with a dismissive air that strongly suggested boredom. "You'd know that in each case the students had expressed unhappiness at home, or depression at school, or were prone to wandering into the woods surrounding the school grounds. More likely than not, it's just more of the same— runaways and lost children."

Logan snickered. "Well, that's convenient."

"Right?" I smacked his shoulder. I grinned down at him. "I was gonna say!"

Logan gave me a wink.

Sheriff Godwin continued as though she couldn't hear us. "In addition—"

"Scott Tyler was last seen going down into the school basement," Cole cut in as though he'd been waiting for his turn and decided to finally take it.

I looked at him in surprise. Scott Tyler? What was he talking about?

Cole didn't look at me. Instead, his dark eyes bored into Sheriff Godwin. "Why do you think he went down there instead of heading to his first class?"

She stared at him with a strange, interested tilt of her head. Like she didn't know what to make of him. For the first time, she was truly unsettled. "Scott Tyler...is, as of this moment, not considered to be missing. There is a strong likelihood his mother took him early from school yesterday. As of now, we have not been able to reach her. And no missing child report has been filed—so unless you know something we don't know—"

Cole didn't flinch. "I know that a bunch of little girls in his music class are worried that Scott went down to the basement and never came back up—"

Sheriff Godwin interrupted, her voice rising, sharp and crisp, "And the basement of the school has been thoroughly searched. It isn't uncommon for the students to be caught exploring the off-limit areas of the school. It was once a boarding school, Mr. Oberst. The history of the place has a certain mysterious fascination for the littlest ones." Sheriff Godwin eyed him coolly. "As I was saying, it must be noted that Watertown has the lowest crime rate in the state. These things are tragic, Mr. Oberst, but they aren't some sort of norm for this town."

"And yet, they are..." I muttered.

Seraphina smiled politely. "But don't you think—"

"Again, as I said..." Sheriff Godwin's gaze drifted to Seraphina. The judgment in her ice-cold eyes was chilling. "The cases have no connection. And now, we have idiotic, sorority girls with their moronic, frat-boy boyfriends making road trips across the state to exploit missing children."

"Can I quote you on that, Sheriff?" A cocky grin pressed into Logan's right dimple, his narrow green eyes crinkled in the corners.

Sheriff Godwin blinked, looking remarkably like a starving cat. Now she looked like Stuart. She stood slowly. I half expected her to pounce. Scratch Logan's eyes out with her perfectly manicured nails.

"We're done here, Mr. Craven."

Logan nodded curtly, his mouth in a downturned smirk. He stood in one fluid motion. Seraphina followed his example. They looked like some kind of TV crime fighting couple. Like Booth and Brennan. Mulder and Scully. Jane and Lisbon.

I half-hid a smile.

Sheriff Godwin stalked to the door and yanked it open for us, her ponytail swishing like a black cat tail.

"One more thing, Sheriff..." Logan shrugged, still grinning. "Because you brought it up, the guys back at the frat house would love to know—there seem to be an awful lot of *females* at this station..." Logan sauntered up to stand over her. She was a tall woman, but he still had her by a couple inches. Logan was only eighteen, but he had all the strength and presence of a hardened soldier.

Sheriff Godwin glared up at him venomously. Her irritation only encouraged him.

He bit his lip on the smirk sneaking across his face. "What are the gender demographics of the Watertown sheriff's department? And do you think that the overwhelmingly *female* force may play into the fact that you are all in *way* over your head here? And obviously unable to solve the case before more kids go missing—"

"Alex!" someone called through the doorway. "I'm glad I caught you—oh, I'm sorry, are you in a meeting?"

I snorted, snickering quietly as I studied the woman who'd just approached. She was a doctor, judging by the Nightmare Before

Christmas scrubs underneath her white coat. Her long, dark hair and big, round blue eyes made her fair features stand out. Her face was angular like the sheriff's, but it had none of the sharpness. Instead, it was delicate and friendly.

The sheriff didn't take her eyes off Logan. "They were just leaving."

I hurried forward and held my hand out to the woman. "Phoenix Stephens."

The woman inclined her head at my name and grinned. "My daughter just mentioned you! Billie Godwin?"

I smiled, slightly taken aback. "Oh, yeah…"

The woman laughed. "What brings you here?"

I gestured to the rest of the group with a shrug. "We were interviewing the sheriff for our website on mysterious cases of the supernaturally inspired."

The woman's kind face softened with sadness. She ran a hand through her raven hair, and then took my hand in both of hers. "Penny Godwin. Any attention you can give to the case is greatly appreciated. By everyone, I'm sure." She sighed and shook her head as she released my hands. "The children are weighing heavily on all our minds. Actually, I just came from the school. My youngest—" She glanced at Sheriff Godwin. "Agatha is struggling."

Sheriff Godwin didn't react. If she cared at all, she hid it well.

"I love your scrubs," Cole commented from just behind me.

The woman managed a small smile. "Thank you—"

"Getting into the holiday spirit?" Cole smiled and tossed his hair out of his eyes.

Dr. Godwin grinned. "Never too early to spread a little Christmas cheer."

"Definitely in the top ten Christmas movies of all time." Cole nodded appreciatively. "I've always had a thing for Sally."

"What can you tell us about Mary Tran, Dr. Godwin?" Seraphina asked gently.

Penny Godwin's face fell. "Not enough. Alex is handling the case. I'm just the town pediatrician."

Logan scoffed at that. He bit his lip on a grin. "Ma'am, can you tell me the gender demographics of your practice?"

Penny scrunched up her face at the question, taken aback.

Before she could answer, Seraphina stepped forward slightly, keeping her voice even and soft. "I'm so sorry, Dr. Godwin. This must be hard for you."

The doctor inclined her head as she studied Phin—almost as though she were confused by her. "That is very kind of you to say." Her blue eyes shined, and she blinked rapidly. She shifted her stance and crossed her arms over her chest as though to hug herself. Then she nodded, giving Phin a rueful smile. "It's been extremely hard. I know each and every one...every child in town...and—" A tear spilled down her face, and she quickly pressed the heel of her hand into her cheek. She gave a small, sad chuckle. "I'm sorry—"

"No, no!" Seraphina rushed forward and snatched a tissue from a box on the nearby desk. She passed it to the doctor, who took it and dabbed her eyes.

Seraphina placed a gentle hand on her shoulder.

Penny sniffed and pocketed the crumpled tissue. "We are a small town. I've helped deliver most of these babies. I've literally watched them as they grew." She shook her head. "We're all connected here in Watertown. My son, Sidney, is dating Mary Tran's older sister, Elizabeth. My daughter, Agatha, is best friends with Mary." She cleared her throat, eyes downcast as she added softly, "It's particularly hard on Agatha."

"But what can you tell us about Mary Tran and Scott Tyler?" I held my hand out and my pen up, the point pressed into my palm. "Are there any similarities between them, anything at all you can think of as to why these specific children were taken?"

Penny raised a perfectly shaped eyebrow at my makeshift notepad. I grinned cheekily. Penny scoffed in a mixture of amusement and disbelief. "Uhm." She touched her head lightly as she considered my question. "Uhm, no—Mary and Scott...they are both wonderful, bright, active kids. I'd just seen them for their fall sports physicals. Uhm, I'm sorry, did you say Scott Tyler is *missing*?"

Sheriff Godwin shook her head firmly. "He has not been reported missing, Pen."

Penny let out a big breath of relief. "Thank goodness." She gave a nervous chuckle and waved a hand toward Sheriff Godwin, who stood silent as a pinched statue, glaring at the four us, Logan in particular. "Like I said," Penny gave a warm smile that didn't quite reach her eyes. "Alex would have stitched the pieces together before I could. But—" She glanced at her watch. Then she placed a hand on Phin's shoulder. "It was nice to meet you all. I've got to get back to the office. Here, Sheriff." She passed Sheriff Godwin a large manila folder packed full of papers. I tried to read the label, but the sheriff grabbed it and covered it with her hands. Then she practically shoved us out the double doors.

The four of us exchanged glances, amused at the irritation of the sheriff. Then an awkward silence settled around us as Logan remembered I wasn't where he'd told me to be...again.

Phin noticed the shift and slapped a hand on my shoulder with a cheerful smile much too bright for the early hour. "All right— breakfast meeting before we break for the day?"


Cole and I didn't speak the whole drive to the bagel cafe. Beauty and the Bagel was a little specialty bagel shop, squished in between an ax throwing place and a tattoo parlor called Ink Drunk. The whole street gave off that old-timey, New York City kind of feel with the smushed shops and the streetlights and iron benches and trees stuck in cement. The parking was limited and metered, with most of the spaces somewhere in the back of the buildings. It was early, and we got lucky. Just as a car pulled out, Cole whipped the van right in and shoved it in park. Logan passed us in the truck and signaled he was going around the back to park. Cole waved him on as he unbuckled his seatbelt.

I didn't move.

"Come on, Nix. You love breakfast."

I grunted.

"And you *know* a nice cheesy egg sandwich always puts a smile on your face." Cole leaned on the wheel, his eyes on me.

I looked at him. "You didn't tell me about Scott Tyler."

Cole closed his eyes for a moment. Then he shrugged. "He isn't technically missing."

"But you thought he was. You think he is."

"Yes."

"And you think I should've been there yesterday."

Cole inhaled deeply. He opened his mouth to answer but nothing came out.

I didn't bother arguing anymore. I opened the van door just a crack, squeezing through the gap. Parking was obnoxiously tight. I shut the door and stalked toward the sidewalk. Cole stuck some coins in the meter and hurried after me.

By the time we got inside, Phin and Logan were already seated at a booth with trays full of food, deep in discussion about the sheriff and her department. Cole left to grab us food, and I slid into the booth beside Phin.

Logan rolled his eyes and stabbed a sausage. "Figures that sheriff was so stuck up. The Godwin family's probably been running this town for centuries. She married into money and power. Went straight to her head. Also, what's with all the women at that station, huh?" Logan shook his head as he took a big bite of his bagel sandwich.

My eyes narrowed. Cole passed me a tray and scooted into the booth beside Logan. I glanced down at the offering of food. My mouth twitched with appreciation despite myself. Cole did good. He did good. I grabbed the bacon-egg-cheddar cheese bagel and took a gigantic bite.

"Explain?" Phin scowled.

Cole looked uncertainly between the two of them. "Explain what?"

"Logan is a chauvinist," I quipped through salty, crunchy, eggy goodness, my eyes half-closed, savoring the deliciousness.

Logan, still chewing, glanced over at us girls, his breakfast sandwich packed into one cheek. He rolled his eyes. "This isn't like a guy/girl thing, it's a *statistical* thing. Something's off about that department."

I exchanged a pointed look with Phin. Her face was hard. She turned back to Logan, her head inclined. "I thought you were just trying to get at her with all that gender demographics junk...you seriously think that because the department is run by women that there's something wrong? That their investigation isn't solid?"

Cole smirked, hiding his face with his hand as he ducked his head back to his computer screen.

I rolled my eyes and chomped a big bite of my bagel. My eyes shifted toward the clock. It was still early. I had time before the high schoolers headed into school. While everyone had gone over the case—again—I'd been silently planning my rescue mission.

Step one, head to Gossamer House before Lizzie even left for school. Cut her off there and convince her not to bother with the Blood Farm.

Somehow.

Easier said than done.

If Fawn was missing, no one would be able to stop me from finding her. I chewed slightly, savoring the crunch of the bagel as I planned. My eyes flickered up, and I caught Cole looking at me over the top of the laptop screen with a deadpan stare. I scowled, took an obnoxiously big bite of bagel, and flashed a stuffed, cocky smirk his way. He frowned. Whatever. He could think what he wanted. It didn't change anything. My ears prickled as I realized I was missing half the argument. My eyes shifted from Logan to Phin, eyes glittering with amusement.

Logan stumbled around his words as he tried to explain. "No... it's not—Sam, you saw the woman! She's clearly hiding something."

"Now she's *hiding* something?" Seraphina scoffed. "Unbelievable."

Logan looked at Cole and raised his eyebrows expectantly.

"Uhh." Cole hesitated. Then his eyes darted back down to the computer. "Oh, okay. Forget the Godwins. Here—" Cole held up a finger, his eyes still on the screen. "Scott Tyler's mother."

I looked at the computer, and my heart dipped into my stomach. What was left of her...had been found on the side of the highway off Exit 45.

Now, *officially*, Scott Tyler was missing.


When we loaded up into the van, Cole told me the plan in a cold monotone that made my lip curl. After the elementary breakfast rush, we'd meet up in the conference room and head to the basement. Cole was convinced that Scott Tyler had disappeared when he snuck down there yesterday morning.

I didn't say anything.

What could I say?

I wouldn't be meeting him there.

Scott was missing.

But Lizzie wasn't yet.

We went our separate ways at the school without another word. It was awkward. Clearly, Cole had some kind of underlying issue with me that he hadn't ever bothered to explain, so we couldn't do the mature thing and work it out. The whole morning left a bad taste in my mouth, souring my face as much as my mood. But I couldn't think about that now...I had less than an hour before the high schoolers headed inside the building.

I had to get to the Gossamer House.

I had to get to Lizzie.

# THANK GOD IT'S CLOUDY BECAUSE
# I'M ALLERGIC TO THE SUNLIGHT

N o one was home.

At least, no one answered the door.

And the cars were all gone from the driveway.

So, I probably passed Lizzie on her way into school. Not a great start to the rescue mission. Cursing myself and muttering maniacally, I drove *back* to Gloria Godwin School.

The high schoolers started later than the elementary students, so there were plenty of kids still trickling up the stairs and into the building when I pulled back up to the school. I pushed past several on my way up the stairs. My head was spinning trying to think of how I would find Lizzie. But luckily, I didn't have to think long. I yanked open one of the heavy oak doors and spied a sulky-looking Keirian slumped over on the bench outside what I could only assume was the principal's office.

I hurried over to him and gave his shoulder a light shove. "Hey."

Keirian glared up at me from his book. "You again?"

"I need to know where Lizzie is."

Keirian snorted. "You know, she has a boyfriend. Why don't you ask *him*?"

"Okay, where's he?"

He rolled his eyes. "You think I keep tabs on these people?"

"Yes. Because you're the outsider. The creepy loner who knows things. Nobody sees you, so you see everybody."

Keirian's bushy eyebrows disappeared into his scruffy hair. A smirk pressed into his left dimple. "And let me guess, you're the formerly-homeschooled novelty, shooting high into popularity just because you're untouched by societal norms. You stand out in a deliciously corruptible way."

I groaned. "Listen, I don't have time to—"

Keirian stood from the bench, shot a glance over his shoulder at the office door, and jutted his chin toward the left corridor. "Come on. Lizzie has art with me."

He led me down several hallways with tall, stretching ceilings, lined with doors to match. Then we took one final turn, and the walls were suddenly slapped with random paintings and artwork, all stuck on with sticky tack. He opened a classroom door for me, and I slipped inside.

All the students, bent over watercolors with paint brushes in hand, looked up as one to stare at us. Then they whispered to their neighbors as their eyes followed me to the teacher's desk.

Keirian put a hand on my shoulder, guiding me toward the teacher. "Mr. Mann, this is Lizzie's cousin—"

"Phoenix!" I smiled brightly.

Keirian snickered. "—yeah, that. She just got into town and was hoping to say 'hi' for a minute..."

"Lizzie's cousin..." Mr. Mann raised a curious eyebrow at me, his mouth downturned and thoughtful.

My smile grew wider as he took in the obvious differences in our appearance—namely race. At the end of his assessment, he smiled politely and spoke kindly. "Well, Lizzie hasn't shown up to class, yet, but you're welcome to wait—"

I didn't.

Without a word of thanks, I turned sharply on my heel and

bolted for the door. My Converse squeaked loudly on the waxed wood floors as I took the turn, backtracked down the various hallways. Lizzie was home, and she hadn't come into school today. Because she had other plans. And thanks to Cole, I knew exactly what they were.

"Oi! Wait!" Keirian's shouts followed me along the hall. "Phoenix!"

I didn't bother to slow down. But I should've because as soon as I turned the corner, I ran right into Rory Meeks.

He bent his head down to stare at his phone at the same moment I'd turned back to make sure Keirian wasn't close behind me, and we collided. Our heads knocked. Painfully. Rory stumbled with a yelp. The books he'd been lugging toppled to the ground. I grabbed my head and cursed under my breath.

Keirian caught up easily and clapped me on the back with a snicker. "That'll teach you to run in the halls."

"Sorry..." Rory dropped down to scoop up his books. He straightened and smoothed back his hair. His eyes widened as he recognized me. "Phoenix! Jeez. Sorry! I didn't see...uh, what are you doing here?"

Massaging my forehead, I winced. "Uh, just looking for Lizzie Tran. It's nice seeing you, Rory, but I really have to go."

"Lizzie? Oh, well, if you're looking for Lizzie, I think I know where she is..." Rory licked his lips and smiled eagerly. "I heard her talking during homeroom. Amanda was pestering her about her sister again. I'm pretty sure she ditched to go check out the Blood Farm."

"Ok, thanks, Rory." I gave him a weak smile and sidestepped him. "I'll see you."

"I can take you there!" Rory called breathlessly.

I stopped short, sneaker squealing like a breaking tire. I looked back over my shoulder. Keirian draped an arm around Rory and grinned. "No better Blood Farm tour guides than us."

I faced forward and closed my eyes, searching for patience. I couldn't bring them with me. But behind me, they started making plans.

"Dude, this will be awesome for the website. Thank God I remembered my camera…" Keirian chuckled.

"Exclusive, behind-the-scenes access!" Rory whistled.

I inhaled deeply, eyes half-closed, weighed down with annoyance. I gritted my teeth. Then I whirled around to face them, arms folded across my chest. "You're not coming."

Keirian made a face as he guided Rory forward, closing the distance between us. "Yeah, okay."

Rory shot me an apologetic, sheepish wince. Then he glanced up at Keirian as he led him past me. "Uh, Kei…maybe we should just—"

I spun on my heel and marched after them. "You aren't coming!"

"Heh, actually, I think *you* are the one who isn't coming." Keirian snickered. "Good luck finding the place!"

I grabbed him by the arm and pulled him to a stop, yanking him and Rory apart in the process. "Listen, I don't care about your lame website, okay? This is serious, and I have to find Lizzie. I don't have time to babysit you people!" I gave him a shove to accentuate my point.

Keirian snorted. His hazel eyes glittered. "You have two choices: watch us leave without you, or come with us." He gave a lazy, one-shouldered shrug. "Pick one. Fast, if you're in such a hurry."

My nostrils flared as my lip curled into a nasty sneer. My fingers itched for my wand. I wanted to hex his face. Give him a nice case of shiny, red acne. I clenched my fists, stiff at my sides. "Fine."

This was bad.

Now, not only were Lizzie and Sidney in danger, but I was

bringing two other people into the equation. Which is exactly what everyone had warned me about in the first place.

I muttered madly to myself as I turned onto Adelaide Road. We passed the Wollstonecrafts' house. Then, after several miles, we passed by the Gossamer House. It wasn't long after that, Rory swerved his rust bucket over onto the side of the road. I pulled the van up behind him and shoved it in park.

The boys got out, lugging their backpacks and film gear. Keirian stuck his phone to some kind of tripod-stick-thing. Rory had a camera strapped around his head that puffed up his hair like a little kid in a skiband, the camera positioned dead center of his forehead like a headlamp.

Eyes on the boys, I twisted my grip on the steering wheel, squeezing it tight. How was I going to do this? I shook my head. This was so bad. But I had to save Lizzie. So, I had to babysit two more. I could handle it. I grabbed my backpack and hopped out of the van. The air was cold and damp. The clouds were darkening over the woods. I shivered slightly as I approached the guys.

"Hey...glad you could join us." Keirian grinned.

Rory smiled shyly, waving his hand toward the road. "We park here and then walk a bit along the road, and then the path is there..."

"Okay, listen." I licked my lips and bit them together in a tight pinch. How could I explain in a way that would get through their thick skulls? Inwardly, I groaned. Nothing could possibly penetrate the density of these two knuckleheads. I'd have to bash them over the head with it. "The Blood Farm monster? *It's real.* And it's going to attack Lizzie if I don't stop her." I swung my backpack to the front of me and unzipped the pocket. "And because you idiots insist on coming," I dug into my backpack and passed them both hawthorn stakes, keeping one for myself. "You take these. I can't promise they'll do anything, but they might."

Keirian and Rory exchanged glances, snickering and smirking.

"Yeah, okay. You lead the way." Keirian held up his camera stick and started filming.

I scowled. Then I gave him and his camera the rudest gesture I could, before charging down Adelaide Road, sneakers scuffing the asphalt. All along the roadside, the overgrown grass was waist high, leaning into the road. But then suddenly, there was a gap. I glanced toward the trees. The path was just big enough for a vehicle to drive down. Exactly like in Cole's vision.

I looked back the way we'd come. The van and Rory's car were nearly out of sight. I looked ahead, farther down the road. There weren't any other cars. If Lizzie and Sidney were here...then how'd they gotten here? Walked? From Gossamer House? Or had they driven up the path?

Suddenly, doubt crept into the back of my mind. Maybe I was wrong...maybe Lizzie wasn't here at all. I chewed on my cheek, gripped the hawthorn stake, and shifted my shoulders, hoisting my bag higher up on my back. Then I stepped down onto the clearing, and the boys followed me down the path.

As soon as we crossed through the tree line, we were submerged in the hazy gray-brown of the November woods. The sun streamed weakly through the barren tree branches, casting a cold light overhead. I held the stake low at my side and continued to scan the woods as we walked down the overgrown dirt road. I was ready. It wouldn't take any effort at all. Launch the stake with a blast of magic. I could impale anything. The smirk faded from my face as Rory pushed forward to keep up with my pace.

His gray eyes slid sideways, and he smiled. "So, you're a believer, too, huh?"

"Uh, yeah." I forced a pained smile. It was literally painful.

"Was it the crime scene photos? Did they convince you?" He nodded grimly. "Lenore—the mortician assistant? She told me there was *no way* a dog could...like, make that kind of damage...the bites and all? She said it was like a bear attack."

Keirian shoved between us and took the lead. "Yeah, well,

Drew should've listened to us. I told her Nathan Campbell was a dirtbag."

I frowned at his tone. "Ah, that's right. You had a huge crush on her or something. Bitter much?"

Keirian shot me a dismissive smirk. "Psh. Nah. I mean, sure, Rory and I both shot our shots...Drew wasn't interested. No big deal." Keirian forced a chuckle. "I didn't sic the Blood Farm monster on her, if that's what you're suggesting."

I narrowed my eyes. I hadn't, but now I considered it. The motive wasn't reflected in the children. The little kids weren't personal. Drew Graham and Nathan Campbell. That was personal. And Lizzie Tran...an attack on her, *that* could be personal...unless it was just 'wrong place, wrong time'...but then, Phin and Logan had checked out the Blood Farm yesterday. There wasn't anything lurking in the place. If something had been there... they would've been attacked, too.

I glanced at Rory. "So, I know what Keirian thinks is going on...sort of." I rolled my eyes. "What do *you* think is going on, Rory?"

"Oh, well, heh." Flustered, Rory shuffled the stake from one hand to the other. Then he tucked it underneath his armpit as he smoothed back his hair. He stopped for a moment as though he forgot we were walking somewhere and then hurried to catch up. He cleared his throat. "Well, you see...the Drew Graham attack... that's where the legend truly came to life. Before her, it was only really a ghost story. People talked about the witch's monster...whispered about the missing kids...but no one had been taken from anywhere other than the school since the '30s. And how would a monster get in and out of the school, dragging kids with it all the way to the Blood Farm?" He scoffed and tucked strands of limp, dark hair behind his ears. "That just isn't logical. And when my brother was taken—"

I looked at him sharply. I'd forgotten. Margaret Meeks lost a child. Rory's older brother. "Rory. I'm—"

"Oh, that's okay." Rory's eyes darted from the ground to mine. "Please. I mean...my sister, Heather...she actually, like, *knew* him...I wasn't even...yeah. It's okay."

My pace slowed. Now I understood. His obsession made sense. Logan always said hunters were made, not born. Formed from personal tragedy. And Rory was essentially a hunter, albeit in a really *weird* sense. He was hunting for answers for his own supernatural loss in a less vengeful, violent way than the norm. But, I mean...that's because he was Rory.

Rory's rambling fell silent, his eyes back on the ground as we walked.

"And your theory?" I prompted gently.

Rory stumbled a bit on a tree root and smoothed back his hair. "Ah, yes, well. As I was saying, the Graham attack. It brought the monster to life, in a way. Before, it was just the story. More than likely, the witch's ghost snatching the children...but the case with Justine Kilpatrick—you know, the survivor? She was *also* an anomaly. Based on my research—and Keirian refuses to let me publish it on the website—" Rory added with a grumble.

"It's too complex for the fans." Keirian tossed back at us over his shoulder. "And too boring!"

Rory rolled his eyes and muttered something under his breath.

"Rory."

"Right. Sorry. I believe there was a witch in Watertown since the founding. I believe she had a monster that she kept as, like, a kind of familiar, an, uhm, like an assistant?" Rory glanced at me nervously as though to see if I was keeping up with his explanation.

"Okay..." I fought to keep a straight face and forced a thoughtful nod. "Like Dracula and that Renfield dude..."

Rory's face lit up. "Exactly!"

I smiled weakly.

Rory nodded and continued with zeal, "Okay, so she and this monster would feed on the townspeople. Then the townspeople started to put things together, and in 1862 they burned Brunhilde

Wollstonecraft at the stake. *But that didn't work!*" Rory turned to me, his excitement growing. He paused a bit and had to hurry to keep up. He stumbled over his feet and slipped on the damp leaves along the path. "Because, Brunhilde Wollstonecraft...wasn't the witch! They'd never found the real witch!"

"Yes, she wasss," Keirian groaned.

Rory shook his head. "See, popular opinion and legend has Brunhilde Wollstonecraft as the witch. But she wasn't...and I know this because the disappearances continued—just the same as before —with no change. *Until*!" Rory held up a finger to emphasize his point.

Keirian moaned good-naturedly. "Here we go..."

"*Until 1916, when the witch herself finally disappeared.* Now, I've been looking through records..."

I raised an eyebrow in surprise. Rory had uncovered more than he'd realized. And I'd bet anything Westley and Persephone Thomas had shown up in town at that time...

"No, no. Roar—" Keirian slowed his step and wedged between us. He draped his arm around Rory's slight shoulders. Keirian glanced at me sideways as we walked. "You see, Rory gets all hung up on the *school*, and what *changed*, blah, blah. But see—he's missing the big picture."

"And what's that?" I asked dryly.

Keirian grinned. "The Gossamer House. Did you look into the history of it like I told you?"

I hadn't. I should've. Instantly, the witching well flashed in my mind.

Keirian scoffed and tossed his dark wispy curls out of his face. "Rookie mistake. That House...has been steadily filling with girls every couple decades...and you know what happens to most of them?"

"What?" I crinkled my forehead and eyed him uneasily.

"They never get adopted...until the Godwins finally snatch them up."

I blinked. "Wait, what?"

"The Godwins adopt them." Keirian shrugged lazily as though what he said was just common sense. "And they initiate the girls into their family cult."

Rory rolled his eyes. "That's ridiculous."

Keirian burst out laughing.

I made a face. "That doesn't even make sense. And what would that have to do with anything?"

Rory leaned forward looking past Keirian to me. "Don't listen to him. He still thinks Annie opened the Blood Farm door, let out the monster, and sent it to kill Drew and Nathan."

"Hey, hey!" Keirian looked down at Rory with mock seriousness. "Jealousy is a powerful motivator, and no one was more jealous of Drew than Annie Collingwood. Everybody knows Nathan ditched her mousy butt the second he saw Drew at Homecoming."

"Using that logic, we'd be suspects," Rory muttered.

Keirian leaned down and whispered loudly in Rory's ear, "*Maybe we are...*"

"Dude, breath mints! Eat a handful." Rory punched him in the side and shoved him off him.

Keirian laughed loudly, clutching his side. He continued to chuckle as the three of us quieted. We walked on in silence. Without the conversation to distract me, I realized how eerie it was inside the woods. The farther into the thick of trees, the stranger the air felt.

We were getting close.

I walked faster, pushing ahead into the lead.

My grip tightened on the stake as the path opened up to the field. Phin wasn't kidding. I could feel the darkness all around me. It was like walking into fog. Behind me, Keirian and Rory chuckled and laughed as they made jokes. Guilt twisted in the pit of my stomach. I shouldn't be taking them with me. But I had no other choice. I had to get to Lizzie. And they were going no matter what I said. But by bringing them, I was putting them in danger. Hawthorn stakes or not. And the thought scratched at the back of my brain as we passed out of the woods and into the open field.

I lifted my gaze to the Blood Farm, high on the small, rolling hill, a mass of black clouds at its back. The stone, dark gray, and the weathered wood of the double doors ashen and decayed. I eyed the bell warily. It was the same feeling I'd had in Cole's memories... except immensely stronger.

The bell hummed with a dark energy that made my head hurt. My pace slowed despite myself. I angled the stake up at the ready. I hadn't expected to be affected so much. The tan grass, high at my sides, swayed back and forth with the cold wind as it raced across the clearing, pressing against me, urging me back. I didn't care. Whatever magic marked the Blood Farm, I had to save Lizzie.

I swallowed and licked my lips as I hiked the hill and neared the building. Where had they come from? The monsters that'd jumped out from the darkness? When Lizzie and Sid had entered the building, there'd been nothing inside...I'd seen it. The place had been empty. I glanced around the trees surrounding the glade like a wall. Had they rushed out of the woods? I stopped short of the threshold of the Farm. I choked up on the stake and checked my watch. Lizzie had said something about lunch. It was almost noon. I looked back down the worn path to where it met the woods. They weren't here yet.

The boys huddled around me. Keirian held his camera up at an angle, so the Blood Farm towered over it.

"I'm sorry, Phoenix...I assumed she'd be here..." Rory squinted back down the hill toward the woodline.

"No, it's okay." I waved away his concern. "I thought the same...but, hey, why don't you guys head back to the car, and I'll catch up, huh?" A flashed a cheesy grin and eyed them hopefully.

Keirian snorted. "Can't ditch us that easily."

I scowled. "Why not?"

"Well, I'm pretty sure you're going to open these doors...and

—" Keirian grinned as he glanced from Rory back to me. "We've never had the nerve to actually do it...because of the curse and the monster and whatever else...but if *you* do it," Keirian panned the camera stick into my face. "Well, that's prime footage right there."

I smacked his stick out of the way. "*Are you kidding me?* This isn't a joke!"

Keirian snickered. "Hey, I'm laughing!"

Rory, meanwhile, stepped closer to the Blood Farm doors. He switched on the light of the camera strapped tightly to his head. Before I could stop him, he yanked open the heavy door with a low creak and a small sprinkle of dust and dirt.

Instinctively, I rushed forward and shoved him back. Placing myself in between Rory and the entrance, I didn't move.

Keirian had stopped laughing, his laughter cut short as soon as Rory had opened the door. "Yeah, uhm..." He cleared his throat. "Uh, I think I'm going to head around the back and get some more footage of that creepy, old bell..."

I didn't dare take my eyes off the darkened opening before me. "No. Wait, Keirian—"

But he didn't.

He took off and disappeared around the back of the Blood Farm.

Rory swallowed so loud it was like a gulp of water. "It's, uh, it's okay...he'll be fine. There's nothing back there...we've gone around the back loads of times."

"You can go with him, Rory," I murmured as I leaned forward slightly on my tiptoes. I lifted my head to squint into the dark and gritted my teeth. My mouth was dry. I couldn't shake the feeling that something was going to happen. Something bad. Because I knew it was...I'd seen it. "Go on."

Rory shook his head, his hair fanned underneath the camera strap like a skirt. "No. No. I need to do this."

I sighed heavily and resisted the urge to roll my eyes. "Fine."

Without sympathy, I grabbed him roughly by the arm and

pulled him close. He stumbled and staggered to regain his footing. Then, blindly, I held out my hand, my eyes still fused to the dark doorway. "Give me your phone."

He slapped it hastily into my hand. I held the phone up, shining the light into the black. The light was weak and nearly useless. I scowled. If he wasn't here, I could've lit the whole place in a second with my magic.

I chewed the inside of my cheek as I struggled to keep the annoyance out of my voice. "Make sure you move your head in each direction, slow and steady, all around us. There's something not so nice in this place."

"Well, really, I think it's—" and Rory stammered on about his theories on Brunhilde and Drew. I wasn't listening.

I palmed the stake and took a step forward.

Then another.

I took a deep breath as my sneaker crossed the threshold, and I stepped into the wide, open room. My heart was loud in my ears. My breath came quick. The camera light on Rory's head illuminated much better than the phone light I was holding, but there was still too much shadow for me to feel safe. My ears prickled as we moved through the room. My sneakers slid slightly in the grime that coated the stones. There was nothing here.

We made it all the way to the back of the building, submerged in the dim darkness of the boarded windows. It was just a big, empty space. Exactly like in Cole's vision. And precisely how Phin had explained it. I could feel the evil, the stain of dark magic, radiating up from the floor. It was so strong. Permeating the air, seeping from the bones of the place. Instinctively, I glanced down at my feet, shining the flashlight across the floorboards, wondering if there wasn't something on the ground that I'd missed.

"OI!"

I turned sharply, stake raised. Rory shouted and did a bit of a dodging motion. He jerked back and then tried to jump in front of me. And if I wasn't absolutely terrified, I would have laughed my butt off.

In the distance, a tall boy and a girl in a green ribbon headband, hanging just behind him, stood in the doorway, shining their phone lights in our direction.

"What are you doing here?"

Instantly, the fear washed over and churned into relief. It was them. Lizzie and Sidney. Now we could get out of the horrible place.

I hurried forward, but so did Sidney. As soon as we met in the middle, he grabbed me roughly by the shoulders and shook me. Hard. "I said, *what are you doing here?*"

I scowled up at him. "I'm here to help you."

Lizzie came up beside us, shining her phone light in my face. "Phoenix?"

Rory hopped into the group and stammered, "Hey, Sid, Sid, it's true...we're here to help—"

"What? Help with what?" Sid's brow furrowed, his round features hardened and cold.

"There's no time, okay?" I shoved him off me with the broadside of the stake for good measure. "We need to get out of here now."

Without further explanation, I took a hold of Lizzie and tried to pull her toward the door. She held her ground. "Uh, I don't think so!"

I rolled my eyes, wincing under the harsh flashlight as she swung it back and forth between me and Sid, casting herself in shadow.

*We didn't have time for this.* I gritted my teeth. "You're both about to get your throats ripped out if we don't hurry. I can explain once we get out of here."

To my surprise, Sidney didn't need to be told twice. "Come on, Lizzie." He took Lizzie's hand in his and dragged her with him, despite her sputtered, indignant protests.

We were almost at the door when a figure filled the doorway. Sidney tossed Lizzie back behind him. I held up the stake, praying it was Keirian.

The figure stepped forward.

It wasn't Keirian.

But I knew her.

So did Sidney.

It was Billie Godwin.

15

KEEP YOUR HANDS OFF MY GIRL

She came at us.

Sidney backed up. He planted himself firmly between his sister and Lizzie. "What are you doing here, Billie?"

I lowered the stake.

Billie scoffed as she came to a stop a few feet away, backlit by the dim daylight streaming in from the open doorway. She stuck her thumbs through her belt loops. "Don't worry, Sidney. I'm not here to kidnap your girlfriend."

"Then what do you want?" Lizzie snapped, stepping out from Sid's shadow.

"I'm here to drag my brother back to school where he belongs." Billie shook her head, her hair tossed in the breeze blowing through the boarded windows. "I *told* my mom you were a bad influence on him. She kept telling me it was just my jealousy talking, but she'll sure believe me now." Billie waved a lazy arm around the place. "Breaking and entering...into the *Blood Farm?*"

"I couldn't care less what you—*any* of you—think about me," Lizzie muttered. "And if you actually *knew* him, you would know that no one can make Sid do anything—"

"Ha. That's funny coming from you...wasn't it your idea for

him to drop out of his scholarship program? And ditch the football team right when he made varsity? He's become the worst version of himself because of you."

"That's enough, Billie." Sidney raised his voice over his sister, but she didn't stop there.

"Not to mention, his reputation is now in the trash because of you and your friends. I know what they've been saying about Sidney...hissing like snakes in the hallway that *he* took Mary?!" Billie crossed her arms over her chest. "Disgusting."

"Actually, Wilhelmina," Lizzie's words dripped with venom. "They think *you* took her."

Billie didn't flinch. "And now you drag him here—are you *trying* to get him arrested?"

"It's *your* friends that are the problem," Lizzie countered. "The four of them together, stirring the pot like a bunch of witches around a cauldron. I've seen them. Staying up all night, watching those messed-up torture movies you all love,—"

"Slasher films," Billie snapped.

"—taking *notes* and laughing when—"

"Oh, my God." Billie snorted. "Are you serious? It's for our freaking *film class*."

Lizzie laughed coolly. "That's not even—"

"Look, Elizabeth—"

"*Enough*," Sid snapped, stepping back in between them.

Lizzie sneered. "Why don't you just—"

I blinked between the three of them. I rubbed my forehead trying to clear my thoughts. Awkward family situation aside, we were in danger. I needed to take charge.

"I know you're upset about your sister." Billie's voice softened with genuine sympathy. "I totally get that, but the Blood Farm? What could you possibly gain by coming here?"

"Okay, listen." I stepped forward. "As nice as this little reunion has been, can we please discuss this outside...*where it's safe*?"

Sidney nodded.

Billie snickered. "Hey, that's all I'm here for..." She paused and inclined her head. "Is that you, Birdie?"

I moved to wrap an arm around Lizzie, but before I could answer Billie...the double doors slammed shut.

I flinched at the sound.

My heart sank.

I squinted into the sudden pitch-black of the Blood Farm. The only light came from the three phones, Rory's camera, and the streaks of weak sun, sneaking in through the cracks in the window boards.

"What the—"

Something slammed into Lizzie from behind us.

I staggered and nearly lost my balance with the impact. Lizzie slapped against the stone with a loud smack. Her phone knocked out of her hand, clattering across the floor. The light shined straight up at the ceiling, casting all of us in glare and shadow. We all shouted at once, stunned and scared and struggling to process what was happening.

In the same instant, something dark and cloaked in darkness launched itself at Rory. He screamed as the thing ripped at his arm. Hawthorn stake still in hand, Rory stabbed furiously into the creature. It cackled like a hyena before slamming him into the ground.

But Sidney wasn't worried about Rory. As soon as Lizzie had hit the ground, Sid whirled around with a furious shout of rage. And I acted without hesitation, firing the stake with a blast of magic into the dark.

But it was too fast.

And it was too dark.

And I missed.

Whatever had grabbed Lizzie, dragged her clear across the room in seconds. Lizzie's scream tore through my brain, adding terror upon terror. Her nails screeched against the stone. Her hands scraped desperately as she tried to claw her way back to us.

"LIZZIE!" Sidney charged after her. He jumped for her hands, sliding like a baseball player into a plate.

"Please, Sid," she shrieked and gasped through tears. "*Please!*"

I raced after him, my heart light with hope.

His fingers curled tight around hers.

Lizzie whimpered. "*Don't let me—*"

It was like slow motion.

I couldn't process it.

One second Sidney had her, their hands clasped tight.

And then he didn't.

Lizzie's hand slipped through his grasp. Her tormented scream pierced my heart. And she disappeared into the black. Her screams faded away as though she were lost, falling away from us.

I didn't stop.

I ran to the back of the room, scooped up the stake and gripped it hard in my hand. I felt along the wall for a door I knew wasn't there. I moved along the length of it, kicking the stones and slapping against them, praying they'd budge. My thoughts raced along with my heart. My breath came quick and panicked. She'd disappeared. *How could she disappear?* I stepped back from the wall, dazed. I stumbled back to where I'd left Sidney. He was hunched over. Broken.

I bent down and pulled him to his feet. "W-where did she go?"

Sidney didn't answer as he panted heavily, his breathing labored as it came in thick streams from his nostrils. Enraged and murderous, he shoved me off him and rounded back toward Billie.

She was crouched on the ground a few feet from Lizzie's phone, the light of which still pointed straight at the ceiling. Billie bent over Rory as she rocked back and forth on her heels, muttering nonsensically. As we approached, her voice got louder and more deranged. "What was that? *What the heck was that!*" Billie shrieked.

I went for Rory. I pulled him limp into my lap. But Sid went for Billie.

"You—" He grabbed her by the shoulders and shoved her backwards, rushing her toward the wall. "*You tricked her into it!*"

He slammed his sister against the stones and shouted in her face.

But I couldn't hear anymore. I could only see. And all I could see was Rory, with his goofy headstrap puffing up his hair like a little kid. In the shine of the headlight, he looked dead. But he was breathing. His heart was steady. He'd fainted. Just fainted.

His camera light glared in my face. I swiped the stupid thing off his head and used it to look him over. I recoiled at the state of his arm. Right below his shoulder, there was a chunk of meat missing as wide as my open hand. Straight down to the bone. And he was bleeding out. Fast. His life oozing out of him in thick gushes of blood, black in the darkness. I slapped at my bag and, with fumbling fingers, ripped open the zipper and dug through the front pocket for Phin's potions. One hand on his headlight, the other smoothed over the labels as I squinted through the glare of light and dark. Then I found it. Bungleweed.

I dumped the whole bottle onto his bite. I shook it furiously, willing it to empty faster. When the bottle was empty, I chucked it to the side, and my fingers moved over the rest of his arm, checking him for other injuries. There were claw marks, gashes in his leather jacket, like he'd been attacked with a dozen butcher knives. The claws had cut deep. Scratches in his skin were visible beneath the tears in the leather. But they weren't life threatening. I could fix them later. I pointed the light back at his upper arm. The bungleweed was working...but not as fast as it should've. There must be something in the saliva of the creature that was slowing it down. Preventing it from clotting. He needed a doctor.

I looked over at the twins as they continued to argue. Though Sidney shouted violently an inch from her, Billie was impassive and cool. As I watched, he slammed her against the stone. She winced at the impact but wasn't fazed by his rage. Instead, she glared back at him with a ferocity to match. She spoke through gritted teeth, words stilted and choppy. "*We need to tell Aunt Alex.* No one will think it was you. Phoenix will be able to back us up."

Sidney cast a glare at me as I scrambled to my feet, and then his head snapped back to Billie. He screamed in her face, showering her with spit. "Why? WHY!"

She didn't even flinch.

I made my way over to them, uncertain how to calm the confrontation.

"Hey, hey, we need to—"

"Sidney..." Billie's voice lowered and softened. "I'm sorry about Lizzie. Okay? I am. It's awful. But Sidney, think about what her friends have been saying about you...think about what just happened and where we are...it's lucky Rory and Phoenix are here. Otherwise...Aunt Alex might've been forced to arrest you."

His expression didn't change. In the dark of the shadows, he looked like he might kill her. I licked my dry, cracked lips and stepped forward. "Sidney—"

His hands squeezed Billie's shoulders. She closed her eyes briefly, then met his fierce stare. He screamed again and shook her so hard she rattled like a doll. Then he shoved her into the wall again and stalked away from her in disgust. He scooped up Lizzie's phone, slapped off the harsh light, and marched toward the doors. He punched his fist through one of them, knocking it open with a bang. I squinted outside into the dull brightness of the blue-black clouds.

I hesitated and looked back at Billie. She rubbed the back of her head. I rested a hand on her shoulder.

"Are you okay?"

"I'm fine..." She glanced back toward the far wall where Lizzie had disappeared. "What *was* that?"

I shook my head as my eyes darted around the empty room. I walked back to Rory. "Help me get him up."

Billie gently nudged me aside and lifted Rory up with a small grunt, slinging him over her shoulder in a fireman carry. She jutted her head toward the open door. "Come on, let's get out of here before those things come back."

I hesitated. I wanted to stay behind and look for clues...traces of the creature that had taken her. What kind of creature could disappear? A familiar. A witch's familiar could disappear. But could a familiar be a monster?

Billie touched my arm. "Hey, I know this is messed up—but we need to catch up to Sidney. If you aren't there to back us up...things could get bad for him."

I nodded and followed Billie out of the Blood Farm, my heart aching with guilt and self-loathing. I hadn't saved Lizzie, and I'd made everything worse.

But I would fix it.

I would fix everything.


I'd forgotten about Keirian.

But as soon as we made it back to the cars, I remembered.

I stopped short just out of the woodline as Billie hurried down the road toward Rory's car.

"Wait! Billie—did you see Keirian?"

"What?" she snapped back breathlessly, not bothering to slow down.

The walk was a long one, but we ran anyway. Well, I jogged when the cramp stabbed into my side, but Billie ran. And it was a good thing Billie had stamina from the football team because there's no way I would've been able to lug an unconscious Rory, however slight his frame, a half a mile down the road to his car.

"Keirian!" I struggled after her as she reached the car door, panting as I came to a stop beside her. I jutted my thumb behind us. "He's still back there somewhere—"

She yanked the passenger door open wide.

Something sprang up in the seat.

Billie screamed and stumbled backward down the incline. She

landed on her butt, and Rory slumped, headfirst, over her shoulder.

Instinctively, I swung my arm out at the thing in the car, my fist connecting with something soft and squishy.

Keirian's face.

He howled and grabbed his nose, which leaked blood in between his fingers. "Dude! *What*?"

*Keirian.*

My whole body burned hot with furious outrage. He dragged Rory along with me, only to wander back to the car for a *nap*? I grabbed him by the scruff of his jacket and yanked him out of the car. "*Where have you been?*"

"What? *What!*" Keirian winced. His hands cupped his nose. "It was a joke!"

Behind me, Billie helped Rory to his feet. Apparently getting dumped over a shoulder and landing on your head in a ditch is enough to bring you back to consciousness.

"I told you this would happen!" I shrieked in his face. "*And where the hex were you*?!" I shoved him back into the car. His head knocked against the doorframe as he dropped back into the passenger seat.

"Oi! A joke!" He rubbed the back of his head as he crouched in the seat. He wiped the back of his hand underneath his nose, smearing blood across his face.

Billie leaned Rory gently against the side of the car. "Guys, he needs to go to the hospital. At the very least, he should see my mom..."

"Not until this idiot starts talking!" I shoved Keirian's head to the side for emphasis.

Keirian shook his shaggy hair from his eyes and glared up at me. "I saw Billie head inside the Blood Farm, and I thought, 'Hey, wouldn't it be hilarious if I shut the doors on them and ditched?' Jeez. It was a *joke*. Okay?"

I blinked at him, heart pounding, chest heaving. "And you didn't hear the screaming?"

Keirian rolled his eyes sarcastically. "Yeah. That was the funny part." Then he snickered. "I slammed the doors and booked it for the car. You all should've heard yourselves. Oh, wait." Keirian held up a hand. "Don't worry. You can." He dug into the floor of the car for his phone, still on the stick. "I got it all on film."

"Phoenix!" Billie snapped.

I turned sharply to stare at her, eyes still wide in marvel at the stupidity of this kid. "*Huh*?"

"Keirian should take Rory to my mom. She's working until late tonight. She'll see him right away, no questions asked." Billie tilted her head to stare at Keirian. "Can you handle that, featherhead?"

Keirian screwed up his face and craned his neck around the car to peek at Rory. "Why would he need—what happened to him?"

I yanked Keirian back out of the car with both hands. Then I dragged him around to the driver's side, opened the door wide, and forced him inside. "Just do it!"

"Fine! Jeez." Keirian shook his head as he muttered more underneath his breath. He tugged the keys out of Rory's pocket and started the car. On the opposite side, Billie helped Rory into the seat and buckled him carefully before shutting the door.

A second later, Keirian peeled out. Tires screamed as he spun the car around and barreled down the road toward town. Dirt kicked up in our faces.

I winced and squinted through the cloud.

I had to go back to the Blood Farm.

I looked at Billie. "Listen, I know you want me to—"

"Save it," Billie said flatly. "You can't go chasing after Lizzie. That's insane. Plus, I need a ride."

I glanced around the van. There was no other vehicle. "How did you get here?"

"My car." Billie gave a sour, downturned smirk. "Which... Sidney stole."

I didn't want to take her. But I couldn't leave her on the side of the road. Priority one: get Billie to her aunt. Then I could get back to the motel and dig up a spell that might track where Lizzie went... maybe...if I got back there quick enough. My heart was like a stone stuck in the pit of my stomach.

And Rory.

I had to make sure Rory was okay.

When we got to the Sheriff's Department, Sidney was sitting in the front seat of Billie's car, staring straight ahead. He hadn't bothered to go inside the department alone. When we pulled up, he jumped out of the car and slammed the door so hard I could've sworn I saw it shake. I tried to leave, but Billie said I needed to be there as a witness...in case they tried to arrest Sidney.

An anxious impatience churned in my stomach as we hurried inside the station. Officer Meeks met us with a bubbly smile, which popped as soon as she saw our faces. "How can I help—"

"We need to see Sheriff Godwin," Billie interrupted.

Sidney was next to me fuming and restless as a caged cat. He paced the length of the desk, muttering to himself. It made me even more uneasy to see him so unraveled.

Officer Meeks seemed to feel the same. "Uh...Sid, you want a donut or somethin'?"

It was like he couldn't hear her. He continued to stalk back and forth.

Billie rolled her eyes and slapped the desk. "*Heather*! Is Sheriff Godwin in?"

Officer Meeks's brow furrowed almost fearfully. "She's in her office...did something happen?"

Billie stomped off toward the far room where I'd been earlier this morning. I shot Heather Meeks an apologetic smile, and I hurried after Billie, backpack keychains smacking together as I jogged to keep up. Guilt twisted in my stomach. Rory was Heather's little brother. And he was hurt because of me.

Billie didn't bother knocking. She wrenched open the office door and marched inside as though she belonged there. Her confidence and strength just radiated off her. From her thick, golden braids at her shoulders to her rich maroon coat and geometric leggings in knee-high boots, she was an impressive presence.

Sheriff Godwin stood immediately. "Wilhelmina, what—" Her thin features pinched at the sight of me.

Billie stopped in front of the desk, her hands on her hips. "Lizzie Tran was taken. It wasn't Sidney." She pointed a finger at me. "Phoenix was with him the whole time. Rory Meeks, too." Then she crossed her arms over her chest ready to fight anyone who dared to suggest her brother was involved.

The sheriff looked slowly, almost calculatingly, between the both of us. "Where?"

Billie and I exchanged a quick glance. "We were in the Blood Farm..."

Sheriff Godwin frowned, her pointed face lined with suspicion. "Wilhelmina...what in the world were you doing there?"

My eyes slid to Billie. What *had* she been doing there? She hadn't been in Cole's dream.

"The girls were teasing Elizabeth about her sister. They goaded her into it. And when I couldn't find Sidney, I knew Lizzie'd probably dragged him up there with her...I was just going to drive by. Sidney's car wasn't there. But then I saw Phoenix's van. Rory's car. I had a bad feeling."

The van.

So, *I* was the reason Billie stopped... I gritted my teeth at my incompetency. Not only had I gotten Rory ripped apart, I'd put Billie in danger, too. And I still hadn't managed to save Lizzie. I cleared my throat but couldn't swallow the guilt, much less stomach it.

Sheriff Godwin's sliver of an eyebrow cocked. She turned to me. She opened her mouth, but before she could ask me a question, Officer Meeks popped her head into the room. "'Scuse me, Sheriff…?"

Sheriff Godwin's icy eyes snapped toward the door and pierced Officer Meeks, who winced slightly underneath the severity of her stare.

"Sorry, ma'am, it's just…Sidney left so fast he forgot his phone." She squeezed in the room past me and Billie and made her way almost cautiously toward the sheriff. Then she leaned over Sheriff Godwin's desk and placed it gingerly in the center. Officer Meeks forced a weak smile. Then she bobbed her head and scooted back toward the door.

Billie looked past me, her braids swinging. She craned her neck to see out the doorway. "Wait, what? Sidney *left*?" Billie turned sharply to Office Meeks, who flashed an awkward smile.

"Sure did, Miss Wilhelmina. He—"

She didn't wait for her to finish. Billie pushed by Heather Meeks and went for the door. Her hand gripped the frame as her eyes scanned the empty station. "Did he say where he was going?"

"Oh, that boy." Officer Meeks let out a nervous chuckle. "He's such a sweet soul…he told me not to worry. He was going to save her. I can only guess he meant Mary…He says, 'even if I have to burn the world to get to her'…chivalrous, ain't he?" Officer Meeks looked at each of us in turn with a warm, sad smile. "If only, huh? He really is a good young man, Sid is, hmm? That Lizzie is a lucky girl."

Billie groaned and ran from the room. Not about to be detained for questioning by the hag of a sheriff, I left the office without a word and caught up with Billie at the front entrance. "Billie, wait! What—"

She threw open the glass door, and I caught it before it hit me in the face. I shivered slightly in the gust of cold. The black clouds had rolled over the trees and covered us in the strange darkness of an afternoon storm. Billie stopped on the sidewalk, her eyes on her brother's empty parking spot. His car was gone. Or rather, her car was gone. She turned back to face me. Her striking green eyes swam with tears. "I need to go."

"That's going to be hard without a car..."

Billie rolled her eyes to the dark sky threatening to split open. Saline spilled down her soft, round cheeks. All her strength, all her power, seemed to be leaving her, leaking out with her tears.

I grabbed her shoulders and gave her a gentle squeeze. "Hey. I'm here. Start talking."

She sniffed. Her eyes met mine. "He's going to burn it all down."

My heart dipped a bit into my stomach. I opened my mouth to speak, but Billie stepped back from me. Then she pinched her temples and waved a hand as though trying to regain her focus. "Uhm, I've got to...I've got to call my mom."

"Okay." I nodded firmly. "Get your phone."

She swallowed thickly and slapped at herself as though she couldn't remember where her pockets were. She slipped her hand into her jacket and pulled out her phone. Her fingers fumbled clumsily across the screen as she tapped in her passcode and swiped at her contacts. Before she could dial, the phone rang in her hands. "It's mom."

She brought the phone up to her ear.

I flashed her an encouraging smile.

"Hey..." Billie glanced at me. "Yeah, Rory was attacked...but Mom, I need to tell—uh, I don't know, hang on!" Billie groaned and held the phone away from her mouth. "Did you put something on Rory's bite?"

I froze slightly. "Uh, just a medicine...first aid thing...that I carry." I shrugged with a sheepish smile and tried not to look too guilty.

Billie made a face and then rolled her eyes impatiently as she went back to the phone. "Yeah, first aid; I don't know! *I don't care about Rory right now.* Mom, something happened to Lizzie. She—she was taken...yeah. Taken, Mom. I'm not—" She gripped the phone in one hand and held her forehead with the other. "No, that's not...yes, of course we went to Aunt Alex. But then Sidney left...He freaking left, Mom...no! No, Mom, *because he didn't take his phone!*"

While Billie argued with her mother, the wind began to pick up, blowing so hard it bent all the trees surrounding the station. Then there was a low rumble, and the clouds burst apart. The rain poured down on us. I couldn't help but look up. I flinched as the cold water soaked my face. Billie paced along the sidewalk, unfazed by the cold spray as it blew around us from all sides.

All I could think about was Rory.

She waved her hand as she spoke. "I mean, yeah, no question." Billie stopped as she listened to her mother. Her face wet with rain, darkened with annoyance. "But, Mom, I—ugh. Fine. Yes. All right. Let me know. Love you. Bye."

I squinted through the downpour. "What'd she say?"

Billie flipped a damp braid over her shoulder, her shoulders hunched forward in the cold. "She wants me to head to the cemetery."

I made a face. "Why?"

"Rory left his stuff at work. She wants me to bring it to his house for him." Billie's smirk twisted to a scowl. "But the real reason is because she doesn't want me to go after Sidney." Billie cursed under her breath.

I glanced at the van and winced in the icy, wet wind. "Why don't you ask Meeks to drive you to the cemetery, and I'll go hunt down your brother."

Billie scoffed. "Like you could find him without me."

I shrugged. "I think it's obvious he went back to the Blood Farm. And I think I should get there before..." The anxiety crawled up and down my arms. My skin itched.

Billie hugged herself in the wind and leaned in closer to me.

"What was that back there?" Billie grimaced. "Like, I can't even believe what happened...it *couldn't* have happened..." Then she started rambling, her words running together in a breathless rush. "Maybe there's some kind of hallucinogen permeating the air of the place or something. Like the Salem witch trials? I mean, I'm a closet film geek. Specializing in horror. I study it. Critique it. Write it, even, occasionally. Like, I've seen my share of monsters...but that's...it's not *real*. It's—"

I nodded without hearing. My brain couldn't process much other than the fact that I'd totally screwed everything up. Lizzie had been taken. Sidney was storming the castle without a sword. And I just had to hope Cole was having more luck than me. Maybe he found the vanishing point. Maybe we could still find Lizzie and Mary and Scott Tyler...if they were still alive. And what *were* those things? I had to get back to the motel. Or to a computer.

"Phoenix!"

"Huh?" I blinked at her and flinched from the sting of rain in my eyes.

Billie shook her head. Her teeth tore at her bottom lip. "I said: he won't go back there. I know where he went."

Before I could ask, she waved an impatient hand. "Mom's going to take care of it." Billie shivered in the wind as it blasted us with rain. She squinted at me through the water dripping down her face. "Can we go? I just want to get Rory's stuff, get home, wait for Sidney to show up, and pretend none of this nightmare ever happened. Because it couldn't have happened. There's no way any of it did."

I sighed and glanced from Billie to the van. I checked my watch. Rain splashed on the face. I wanted to get back to the motel, look for a spell to track Lizzie. But so much time had passed...I probably wouldn't be able to make it work. And I couldn't ditch Billie...unfortunately.

As though she guessed my thought process, she smoothed the

wet tendrils from her forehead and added, "Just a ride to the cemetery, Phoenix. Then I can get a ride home with Lenore. Please."

I forced a smile. "Fine. Get in."

By the time both of our seatbelts were clicked, her phone rang again.

They'd found Billie's car in a ditch.

And Sidney was missing.

16

# FRONTSEAT SERENADE

illie was silent after that.

She didn't say a word.

And I didn't really know what to say.

The car was abandoned, and Sidney was gone. That was pretty vague. I had to chew on my cheek to keep the questions contained. But there were so many.

When I turned into the cemetery, I couldn't help but glance over at the school as we passed. And then at the radio clock. School was getting out soon. A few hours. Cole probably knew I'd left by now. Taken the van. Again. Stranded him there to babysit. Again. I nibbled on my lip as the guilt ate away at my insides. I'd messed everything up so badly.

Billie cleared her throat as she nodded in the direction of the funeral home. "You can drive all the way through—yeah, just park by that tree."

I snorted. There were a lot of trees. The whole cemetery was essentially in the thick of the woods. I couldn't even see the school across the street, let alone the main road itself. But I pulled up close to the giant willow tree and I shoved the van into park. The forest formed a gnarled canopy beneath the black clouds rolling across the sky. I scanned the graveyard. Dozens and dozens of headstones stuck up in clumps, amid a splattering of old, slick leaves, between the dusting of stripped trees.

"And...he isn't here." Billie's voice was strained and thin as her eyes scanned the gloomy, gray woods outside. "I'd thought maybe..." Billie sighed. "He and Lizzie had this thing about that stupid willow tree."

I opened and closed my mouth several times, struggling to find something helpful to say. I cleared my throat. "I'm awful at...you know...saying things. But let's not think the worst. For all we know, he's fine. I think we have to go with that, until we know otherwise, right?"

Billie nodded stiffly, her eyes squinted and staring. "I should head inside for Rory's stuff."

She didn't move. Maybe she couldn't? Weighed down into the seat by all that had happened.

The rain was steady as it rapped readily on the roof, a soft drum in the background of the silence that settled around us.

I looked at Billie. "You okay?"

Billie's jaw tightened. She shrugged. "You're probably right. It wouldn't be the first time he's up and disappeared." She scoffed, rolled her eyes to the van roof, and sniffed. "I'm used to him running away from me."

I snorted. "I know the feeling. My sister is the same."

Billie glanced at me sideways, a small smile on her face. "At least your sister didn't leave you for another girl."

I burst out laughing. "Oh, trust me, she did that and worse."

Billie's smile warmed, but then it flickered and faded like a flame in the rain. "Sidney and I were so close...and then as soon as he found Elizabeth Tran...it's like he can't wait to get away from me." Billie winced and buried her face in her hands. "God, I'm a monster."

I had to laugh. "You're not a monster." I put a hand on her

shoulder and squeezed. "You're human. Humans feel all kinds of things that aren't rational or...you know, always kind..."

Billie dropped her hands into her lap and looked at me with a tear-streaked face. "Kind?" Billie scoffed. "My brother's girlfriend was dragged away by some rabid animal, possibly a witch's demon monster, and I'm sitting here whining about how he likes her more than me...that's just...evil," she finished dully.

I snickered. "Believe me, I've seen evil. You're not it."

Billie shot me a weak half-smile. "Thanks for that...even if it is a bunch of bologna."

I sighed and shook a hand through my damp, dripping hair. "Listen, I know how you feel." And I did. "People always leave. At least that's what it feels like..."

Billie cocked an eyebrow. "Who left you?"

"My sister." I ticked off my fingers. "Then my *other* sister. My mom. My—" I couldn't say his name. Daddy. I cleared my throat. "Just everybody, you know?"

Billie smirked. "I'm adopted, Phoenix...I get it."

"Right." My cheeks burned, and I shifted in my seat.

Billie jutted her chin toward a parked car in the distance. "I didn't realize it was today..."

"What?"

Billie peeked at me sideways with a grim smile. "I assume you've heard of Justine Kilpatrick?"

I sat up in the driver's seat, arms wrapped around the wheel, squinting into the foggy window. "The survivor from 1996?"

Billie nodded. "She's visiting her sister, Jillian, today..." She winced. "Or whatever it was that they buried."

I inclined my head as my thoughts blurred. "Do you know her?"

Billie snorted. "Nobody does. She has a shotgun to make sure of that."

I chewed my cheek as I watched the woman. It was hard to see her through the graying downpour. The only thing I could tell for sure was that she was thin in her oversized raincoat with hunched shoulders. It was almost Thanksgiving, and she was standing alone in the rain, staring at a marker for her dead sister.

"She has to know something," I muttered.

Billie scoffed, her voice dark with disdain. "Justine Kilpatrick is only out for herself. She doesn't care about anyone else. Not even her sister. If she did, she sure wouldn't be standing out there."

I raised an eyebrow. "No?"

Billie sighed and slapped a hand to the door handle. "Thanks for the ride, Phoenix. I'll see you."

I nodded with a small smile as I watched her lean into the door, her shoulders rolled against the rain, and she shoved open the door. But before she could hop outside, someone jumped into the doorframe.

"Argh!" Billie shouted as the both of us flinched. "Stuart! You idiot!" She shoved his head back. His forehead hit the door still partially open. He bounced back, ducking his head inside the van as he laughed.

I swallowed hard and forced my heart back down my throat. I scowled at Stuart's grinning face.

His cheeks and nose were rosy from the cold and shiny with rain as he smiled wickedly at the two of us. "What do we have here?"

"Where've you been?" Billie winced with narrowed eyes as the rain sprinkled inside the warm van.

"Right where I was supposed to be..." Stuart backed up and shut the door. Billie rolled her eyes at me as Stuart slid open the side door and hopped inside. He slammed the door behind him to block out the rain. Then he leaned between the front seats, sticking his head in the middle of us. "Where were *you*?"

All I could think about, aside from his rotten breath, was how mad Cole would be that I let Stuart in the van.

"Sidney's missing, Stuart," Billie snapped.

He jutted his head forward in surprise. "Missing? What do you mean?"

Billie groaned. "God, Stuart, what does that mean to *you*?" She shook her head and muttered insults under her breath.

Stuart frowned in a moody, pouty kind of way, like Billie had genuinely hurt his feelings. "Well, that'll put a damper on the party tonight, won't it?" Stuart turned his head toward me.

My nose crinkled at the stench of him. "You're throwing a party? On a Tuesday night? Days before Thanksgiving?"

"No school tomorrow." Stuart smiled easily. "And it had to be tonight. The girls are hosting."

"The girls?"

"Amanda, Tiffany, Annie, and Pamela," Billie muttered with a weary sigh. "Catherine—their foster mom—is going to be out of town for the night. They always tend to go wild when she's not around to keep them in line."

"Yup." Stuart grinned.

My skin itched.

"You're coming, right?" Stuart squeezed my shoulder. "It's going to be epic."

I screwed up my face in disgust and smacked his hand off me. "Uh. No."

"Aw, come on. The best thing is: the kidnapper will probably show up. You know how these serial killer types like to immerse themselves into the action." Stuart snickered. "I know I would, if it was me..."

I rolled my eyes. "Actually, I have to go—"

"Oh, right. Yeah, sorry." Billie waved an apologetic hand my way. Then she glared at her cousin. "Stuart, get out."

He turned toward her with a sad pout. "Why?"

"Because Phoenix has things to do, and I need to get a ride home."

Stuart flashed a smug smirk. "Well, you won't be getting a ride from Lenore."

"What? Why not?" Billie tossed her hands up in exasperation.

"She left early. Something about Lizzie Tran going missing... did you guys hear about that?" Stuart looked over at me.

I gritted my teeth and didn't bother to answer.

"Yes, Stuart," Billie muttered in a monotone. "Great. Now what?" She covered her face in her hands.

"People are really starting to freak out...I heard a few kids say it's Keirian and Rory. Like they're doing some kind of tag-team, publicity, killing spree for their stupid website. Beefing up the Blood Farm legend for clicks." Stuart chuckled darkly. "Maybe I can force a confession out of them at the party tonight..."

Billie scoffed, her eyes shining with unshed tears. "It's not Rory."

"Lizzie's friends think it's you, Bill. And/or the rest of the girls." Stuart wiggled his fingers like a wizard. "Like they all sold their souls to the Devil for control of the witch's monster."

I looked at him. "And what do *you* think?"

Stuart shrugged. "Hey, before it was just kids vanishing from the school every generation or so...sure, it's a witch's ghost or whatever...but then Nathan and Drew ripped to shreds, then Mary taken from the Gossamer front steps, and now Lizzie. And you're saying Sidney, too?" Stuart blew a raspberry. "Now it's, like, *real*."

Billie scoffed and rolled her eyes to the ceiling. "You are such an idiot," she hissed under her breath.

Stuart smacked her shoulder. "And hey, it could be anybody." A slow grin curled up his face as he peered at me sideways. "Even me."

I snorted. "Now that you mention it—what are you doing here, Stuart?" I studied him with an eyebrow raised. "Why aren't you in school?"

Stuart gave a lazy shrug. "Stalking Justine...I think she's up to something."

I scoffed. "She's mourning her sister, you creep!"

Stuart snickered and then slapped my shoulder. "Look, she's

leaving. I say we go confront her at her house. Make her talk." Stuart giggled as he bobbed a bit with enthusiasm.

"What?" Billie snapped. "That's the stupidest thing you've said in a while."

I squinted through the window as Justine got in her car and drove away. Thoughts raced through my head. All the answers could be right here. "Where does she live?"

Stuart grinned. "Start driving."

I couldn't shake him.

Billie didn't know where she lived. And Stuart wouldn't talk, much less leave. And I didn't have time to argue with an idiot. So, with hands constricted tight around the steering wheel to keep from strangling Stuart's neck, I listened, teeth clenched, as Stuart giggled the directions.

When we finally pulled up, I did a double take.

Justine Kilpatrick's house was a wreck.

It looked like it'd been cruelly dumped in the middle of the otherwise picturesque, wooded neighborhood. Literally. And it was falling apart due to the violent impact. The wood siding was faded, the paint peeling off in big chunks. There were boards on the windows, and the porch was crumbling, leaning to one side. The lawn was wild, overgrown, and the fence was less picket and more pike, the wrought iron bars jutting up high like stakes.

The houses that flanked it contrasted so dramatically you could tell they were making a point. Their freshly painted sideboards, perfectly manicured autumn lawns, and elaborate Thanksgiving decorations, screamed: trying too hard to compensate.

I pulled the van up behind Justine's car from the cemetery. We sat in the van, idling, staring up at the old Victorian.

"How are we going to get her to let us in?" Billie muttered. "She refuses to answer the door."

I prodded the engine with a finger, disguising the movement

with a flick of the wrist as though I were tucking in a ring of keys into my palm. They didn't notice. All our eyes were on the busted front door. "Improvise."

The rain had ebbed, replaced with an overcast, white-gray sky and a scattered sprinkle. I ran a hand through my hair, shaking it out like a Labrador. We all left the van. Then the three of us walked side by side, trudged tentatively up the teetering steps, and huddled together at the door.

Billie moved to knock on the door, but I held up a hand. I dropped down to the keyhole and pulled out my pocketknife. Stuart started laughing.

Billie scoffed. "You've watched too many movies, Phoenix. There's no way that'll—"

I jammed the knife into the lock as though I expected it to do anything. I bent over the lock, my back to Billie to hide the sparkle of orange magic that puffed out from the lock. I slipped out the knife as the lock clicked open and stood back. I tucked the knife back in my pocket and waved a hand at the door.

Stuart hooted with appreciation.

Billie gaped. Her eyes shifted between me and the door. "But, how—"

"Come on." I opened the door.

Yet another mistake.

I flinched as I found myself facing down the barrel of Justine Kilpatrick's shotgun.

"You've got five seconds to get the Hell off my porch."

I swallowed thickly, hands raised in surrender. But I didn't move. "We need your help."

Justine had dark circles underneath her eyes. Her dishwater-blonde hair hung limp and damp past her shoulders, framing her thin, haunted face. "Five."

I licked my lips. I tilted my head toward Billie. "Her brother's been taken."

"Four."

My heart pounded loudly in my ears. "And I think you know where he might be."

"Three."

"Oh, for the love of—" Billie elbowed me out of the way. "We have some questions. And you're going to answer them, or I can promise you—the sheriff will pay you a visit instead."

Justine's thin lips pursed tightly as she considered this. She lifted the barrel and jutted her head toward the inside of the house.

I barely hid a smirk as Billie and I stomped through the doorway, with Stuart bobbing behind us in his odd, loping gait. The house was dirty, dusty, and dim. It matched the exterior perfectly: complete, hopeless abandonment.

Justine waved us over to the tiny dinner table. Billie sat down, back straight and green eyes cold, as she watched the woman move awkwardly around the kitchen that clearly hadn't ever been used for anything other than storage. Stuart leaned against the doorframe, his arms crossed over his chest.

I took a seat beside Billie and cleared my throat. "I'm sorry for —you know, forcing our way into your home...but you're the only one who can help us."

She sat back against the kitchen counter, her thin fingers clutching the edge like pale spiders. Her jaw clenched, pulsing in the hollow of her cheeks. "Why are you here?" Her sunken, angular face and hawkish eyes pierced into mine.

"I think you know." Billie frowned coolly. She waved a lazy hand in my direction. "My friend here is interested in the disappearances...the maulings...attacks...but me, I just want to know where my brother is...and I think you have an answer for me."

I cleared my throat and cut in sharply. "We all just wanted to ask you what you remember from 1996."

Justine's eyes flickered to Billie, then back to me. She anchored her eyes to mine, though directed her question at Billie. "Why don't you ask your aunt, Miss Godwin?"

Billie gritted her teeth, her anger boiling just beneath her words. "My brother is missing. He was taken. I need to know what you know."

Ever since we'd forced our way inside her house, Justine Kilpatrick had avoided meeting Billie's hard stare. But at those words, her eyes slid slowly from me to Billie. She looked at her with a deadpan stare, her eyes cold and glassy, her voice flat and rote. "I was walking upstairs to class from the elementary cafeteria, then I wasn't."

Billie and I exchanged a dark glance. "Well, where were you when you weren't?"

"I woke up in the Blood Farm. Alone. I don't remember anything else..."

"You just appeared in the Blood Farm?" Billie scoffed.

"Where did Victor Wollstonecraft take you? After he found you?" I prompted gently.

Justine inclined her head toward me, the harsh lines of her face softened. "He took me home." Justine blinked furiously, her brow furrowed as though she were struggling to recall the memory. She licked her lips, her voice quiet. "My mom would wake up early for work...she wrote books." Justine cleared her throat. "She'd take her coffee on the porch with a blanket and a book before she'd sit down to write...she said that after we were taken, she'd sit on that porch from twilight to twilight, watching the street, praying we'd come home. And I did."

Billie wasn't impressed, only impatient. "You must remember something else."

"Nothing."

"Nothing?"

Justine's jaw flinched as her lips pursed. "No."

Billie rolled her eyes in disgust.

I bit my lip and tried again. "What about your sister? Who was taken first?"

"I was taken first." Justine's voice rose slightly as though she were gaining confidence. Her eyes drifted to Stuart. "They take the little sister before they take the girl."

I did a double take, inclining my head. Her words were odd... like she misspoke. Before I could ask her to clarify, Billie slapped the table and pushed out of her chair. "Let's go, Phoenix. I'm wasting time here.

I didn't move. I studied Justine, the haunted, tormented eyes. She reminded me of Cole in a way. Then I realized. Maybe it wasn't that she didn't remember, it was that she *did*. Not that she didn't know enough, but that she knew *too much*. Maybe there was a *reason* why she never spoke...my eyes followed her gaze and rested on Stuart who could barely contain the cocky smirk sneaking up the side of his face. I looked back at Justine. "They?"

The hollow of her throat flexed as though she was struggling to swallow. Her jaw clenched. Her cheeks pulsed. Her mouth pinched. Her nostrils flared. Then she shook her head in tight, twitchy jerks.

Billie waved an impatient hand and tapped my shoulder. "Come on. You can drop me off at the sheriff's department. I'm going to be camping out there until they find my brother."

The shrill ring of her phone made me flinch. Billie pulled the phone out of her pocket and held up a hand, motioning for me to stay in my seat. "Hang on—I'll be right back." She hurried from the kitchen. There was a moment of silence before the front door squeaked open and then snapped shut.

"Whelp. I'm going to head home...it stinks in here." Stuart chuckled cruelly. He pushed himself off the doorframe and disappeared after Billie.

Justine stared after him, eyes unblinking, unseeing. Like she was lost in memories. Then her gaze rolled over me, and she sank into the empty chair. She clutched at the table with her spidery white hands and leaned toward me. I sat back a little, instinctively, to put distance between us. Justine didn't notice. She licked her pale lips and swallowed hard. "They're everywhere." Justine's voice was a harsh whisper that scratched at my ears like sandpaper and sent a shiver down my spine. "You need to be careful." Justine bit down on both her lips, sucking them inward.

"Who are they?" I bent over the table and breathed, "Who was it, Justine? Who took you?"

"No. You don't understand." Justine's eyes blurred and leaked down her cheeks, smearing tracks in the grit on her face. She opened her mouth to speak but froze; her eyes darted to the doorway as Billie burst through.

"You need to take me to the school." She looped her arm through mine and yanked me up to my feet. "Now."

"What's—"

"My little sister." Billie's eyes were big in her blanched face as she stared, unseeing, at Justine. "Agatha's missing."

17

CUTE WITHOUT THE E (CUT FROM
THE TEAM)

When we pulled up to the school, a horde of media trucks filled the lawn between the road and the building. The reporters and their cameramen stuck out around the property like creepy garden gnomes. A line of parents in cars stretched the length of the road's shoulder, curling all the way around the parking lot.

They weren't moving.

I sat up straight in the driver's seat to see over the stretch of vehicles. There were the two deputies at the front of the pick-up, standing like foot soldiers, guarding the school. There was no way we'd get through with all these parked cars in the way. But I wasn't in the mood to wait.

I floored it, whipping the van down the wrong lane, and cut off the minivan who was just about to turn. Cars all along the line honked obnoxiously. It was too congested to make it to the entrance. So, I cranked the wheel to the left and steered us onto the lawn, but we weren't parking like a media truck. I was headed straight for the front. The van skidded over the slick grass, and we caught air as it launched itself off over the curb and onto the road. I yanked the wheel to the left and the tires squealed as the back end swung forward. I mashed the breaks. The van jerked to a neck-snapping stop, right in the front of the pick-up line.

One of the cops hurried forward, hand on their weapon. Billie jumped out of the van and ran for the school without bothering to wait for me. The officers must've known her because they let her race right by...but I wasn't so lucky.

They waved for me to get out of the van. Great. I swiped at the ignition; an orange sparkle of magic flickered as it fell to the floorboard.

I plastered on a cheesy smile and hopped out. The taller of the two, with hair like carrots, grabbed me roughly by the arm and escorted me inside the building. I recognized her at once: Deputy Abigail, from the station. There was a loud rumble vibrating from behind the gym doors. She pushed me along with her down the hall. Then she shoved me into an office off to the side and yanked me back to stand beside her in the doorway.

"Excuse me, Sheriff. This one brought Wilhelmina...thought you'd want to talk to her."

Inside the room everyone paused to stare in my direction. The air was tense and almost sorrowful. Billie stood behind her mother, who was seated in a chair in front of the desk. Billie's hands clutched tightly to Dr. Godwin's shoulders as she stared blankly into space. The woman, who I could only assume was the principal of the school, sat at the desk, her face grim. Sheriff Godwin stood off to the side, next to an older woman with wavy, dark hair, streaked with silver. The two of them exchanged a glance.

Abigail shook me just a little. "Fit your description. Short. Tacky, red, chunky streaks—"

I scoffed and glanced sideways at the woman with carrots for pigtails. "You want to talk about *my* hair?" I rolled my eyes.

She jerked me so roughly my bones rattled. I couldn't help but yelp. For someone so lanky, she sure was strong.

The older woman stepped forward and rested a gentle hand on the deputy. "Thank you, Abigail. You can go back outside now."

Carrothead nodded and released me with a good shove that made me stumble off-balance. I regained my footing just as the woman put a hand on my shoulder and led me out of the room. She shut the office door behind her. I opened my mouth to speak, but she closed her eyes and shook her head.

"Young lady, my daughters have told me a lot about you." The corner of her mouth twitched in amusement. Her blue eyes sparkled. "Conflicting things, to be sure...but a lot, nonetheless—"

"And your daughters are—?"

"Sheriff Godwin and Dr. Godwin."

"Right." I nodded ironically as I studied her. Her black hair rolled in gentle gray waves around her strong, angular face. Her nose hooked at the end, downturned like an eagle. Her skin was smooth and shiny, with just enough wrinkles around her eyes and full lipped, too-white smile, to hide the fact that she'd clearly had some of those anti-aging procedures. "And you must be—"

"Mayor Godwin." She smiled.

I snorted and muttered underneath my breath.

"Now, I'd like to press upon you the severity of the situation we find ourselves in...my granddaughter is missing...as is my grandson. Along with the Tran sisters. I'd appreciate it if you kept your journalism outside with the rest of the media." Mayor Godwin held up a hand, silencing my objections. She was patient and gentle, but firm. "I realize the website run by Mr. Cullen and Mr. Meeks is...a necessity...an outlet for the older students to channel their frustrations, while at the same time to celebrate the historical lore and heritage of our beloved town, but this really is not the place to—"

"But I was—"

Mayor Godwin gingerly placed a finger to my lips, both silencing me and creeping me out at the same time. I took a step back from her. She smiled sadly. "Wilhelmina told me how much of a help you were to her. She said you have a good, strong heart. And I can see that your heart is indeed in the right place. But if you really want to help Wilhelmina, the best thing for you to do is step outside."

I hesitated as though considering this. "Can I get a quote?"

Mayor Godwin bent her head forward to give me an indulgent grin. "Spoken like a true journalist..."

I flashed my cheesiest, Cheshire smirk and gave a lazy shrug. "Just tell me when Agatha was last seen."

Mayor Godwin's eyes shined in the bad school lighting. Her jaw tightened as though the thought pained her. She pursed her lips thoughtfully. "Very well...off the record. I'm sure you'll hear it from Wilhelmina soon enough." She cleared her throat. Then she blinked back a tear. "Agatha's class has recess right after lunch. She was with the other students on the way to the playground. But somehow, she didn't make it to the structure. Her friends quickly realized she was missing. She's been gone for over an hour now."

I glanced down at my watch. "So, she disappeared shortly after Billie's car was found."

Mayor Godwin hesitated. Something flickered in her blue eyes so fast I wondered whether I'd imagined it. Then she nodded slowly, almost reluctantly. She held out her arm. "Now, please..."

"Yes, ma'am." I made to leave the building but stopped short at the entrance. I glanced back to make sure she was gone and ducked into an empty classroom off to the side. I plucked up the phone mounted to the wall and dialed Cole's number.

"Hello?"

I gripped the phone tight, my eyes on the door. "Meet me in the lobby."

"*Phoenix, where have you been?*" he hissed so loudly in my ear, I winced.

"Just meet me in the lobby!"

I placed the phone back quietly into the cradle and scooted to the doorway to lean against the frame, lurking just out of sight. The last thing I needed was to have the sheriff catch me and decide to detain me for being suspicious or something.

After a few minutes, one of the double doors to the stairwell cracked open, and Cole slipped out. I hurried out of the classroom to meet him. Cole flinched at my sudden appearance. His face darkened. He hitched his guitar case higher on his back and opened his mouth, but I cut him off.

"You can yell at me later. We need to leave. Fast."

Cole rolled his eyes and stalked toward the doors. We moved through the courtyard. I could feel the eyes of the parents follow us, anxious and irritated in their cars. The deputies turned as we approached. I waved to Officer Carrottop with a cheeky grin. When we got to the van, Cole slid the back door open and shoved his guitar case in the back as carefully as his patience would allow. Then we both hopped inside. As soon as the doors slammed, Cole revved up the engine. The van purred as though grateful for the key. Cole pulled out of the parking lot. Tires squealed as we slammed onto the main road past the snake of cars.

I glanced at Cole. He was fuming. Cautiously, I reached for the stereo dial. I switched on the music. Cole jammed the eject button and popped out the CD. Silence, angry and static, buzzed in the air.

"Cole—"

"Don't."

I made a face. "Listen, I—"

"Agatha Godwin was taken." Cole shot me a murderous glare. "And despite what these morons said, Scott Tyler is gone, too." He snapped his head back to watch the road. "And if you'd have been there yesterday? If you'd have been there to help me this afternoon, *maybe* we could've stopped it."

Guilt pinched my insides. I scowled. "How? It wasn't like she got nabbed from music class or the cafeteria..."

"Phoenix, she was taken in between classes. There were whispers she was heading for the basement."

I shrugged, irritation scrunching my face. "So?"

Cole sighed heavily as though he was fighting to find patience.

"She was last seen leaving the cafeteria. Where *you* should've been serving her lunch."

"Oh." It was all I could say.

"Agatha is on us."

I shook my head like I could shake off the sin. I held up a hand. "Well, I have another lead. That's something! Aren't you going to ask me where I've been all day?"

Cole's jaw tightened. "I did. You didn't answer."

"Okay." I rolled my eyes. "Well—"

"Phin and Logan have made contact with the slayer." Cole slapped at the blinker and took a right toward the heart of town.

My words died on my tongue as my mouth hung open. "Wait, what? The *witch* slayer?"

Cole nodded curtly. "It's not vampires, Phoenix, no matter how bad you want it to be."

I made a face. "That's not—"

"Just save it."

"Excuse me?" I glared at him, my brow furrowed and eyes glaring.

Cole snorted. "Phoenix, I'm tired. I'm ticked off about Agatha. I just...let me drive it off, okay? I'm not ready to hear about whatever it is you thought was more important than an eight-year-old girl."

I blinked stupidly, stunned into hurt silence. I jutted my jaw to one side and stared pointedly out the window. Fine. I wouldn't tell him anything.

When we got to the motel, Logan and Phin were busy packing bags. Logan had his phone wedged between his shoulder and his ear. He spoke in short, stilted sentences as he stuffed different things into a backpack. They both looked up briefly as we walked in the room, then exchanged a glance.

Logan straightened, taking the phone in his hand. "Gotta go."

He shut the phone and shoved it in his jean pocket. His face was dark with disappointment. Phin wore her disappointment differently, but it was there all the same, in the soft curves of her face and stormy silver of her eyes.

"So, Agatha's gone. And we all heard about Lizzie...so, you didn't manage to save *her*. And then, Cole said something about *Sidney Godwin* disappearing, too?" Logan cocked an eyebrow, his mouth in a hard line. He shrugged. "What's your excuse this time?"

I gritted my teeth as I shot Cole a glare. And he said *I* had big ears and big mouth. This was ridiculous. I tossed my bag onto the bed. It bounced off, keychains clattering loudly. All eyes were on me. Waiting.

My temper flared hot underneath the collar of my jacket. I threw up my arms and folded them across my chest with a stiff shrug. I shook my head. "I'm not making excuses."

Phin inhaled sharply. Logan scoffed. Cole bowed his head.

I held my chin high. "And I'm not going to apologize for making a decision I thought was right. Isn't that what this is all about? Following instinct, making choices based on your moral compass?"

Logan chucked his backpack to the ground and closed the distance between us, so he could tower over me. The flecks of gold in his emerald eyes burned. He spoke through gritted teeth. "You don't get it, do you?"

I glared up at him, refusing to flinch.

"This isn't some Nancy Drew cosplay. These are real kids. And it looks like we lost three of them today. And one of them is definitely on you."

My eyes blurred, and I had to look away. All of them were on me. I slapped at my cheeks and forced myself to meet his green glare. "Logan, I was following a lead. You'd have done the same thing."

Logan snorted and a cool smirk pierced his left dimple. "What lead, Grey? Tell me. What lead?"

I hesitated. "I told you last night. Lizzie Tran was going to the Blood Farm. I was worried she would run into trouble." I swallowed, forcing the memory of her sliding across the stone floor from my mind. I opened my mouth but couldn't find words. Her screams echoed in my head.

Logan gave me a deadpan stare. "Well, she did. Didn't she?"

"It was worse than that," Cole muttered from his seat at the table. His hands hovered above the keyboard. Cole looked at me, his eyes hurt. "Wasn't it?"

I licked my lips, folding them together. I gave a curt nod.

Logan's eyes shifted from me to Cole and back again. "What happened?"

My eyes blurred. I cleared my throat, but my words still slurred, watery with emotion. "Two guys followed me to the Blood Farm, and one kid was bitten."

Logan shifted where he stood, angling his head toward me as if he couldn't believe what he'd just heard. "I'm sorry—you brought two other kids with you...and one was *bitten*."

"I had Phin's bungleweed tonic. It stopped him from bleeding out."

"He was bitten." Logan raked a hand through his cropped, sandy hair. "Did you get a good look at the bite? Where is he now?"

It took the full strength of my pride to hold my head up and meet his eyes. "He was taken to Dr. Godwin. She sent him home."

Logan rubbed his forehead as he sighed. Then he checked his watch and pointed at Cole. "Check on him. As soon as we leave." Logan went over to our stash of books. What had been neat stacks along the wall were now a jumbled mess. He dug through them for the one he needed and plopped it on Cole's lap. "See if you can find a match. And watch for changes in behavior. Hit him with silver. Text me with what you find."

Seraphina winced. "Phoenix, I warned you not to—"

I scoffed, rolling my eyes to the side. "If you saw Cole's dream, or his nightmare—vision—whatever the hex it is, you would've gone after her, too."

Logan shrugged. "Maybe...but if she had, she wouldn't have gone by herself. Did you even bother to tell Cole? Or did you Grand Theft Auto his van?"

My cheeks blazed hot with shame. I groaned and stalked over to the kitchenette. I slapped on the machine and shoved a mug underneath it, my back to them all.

"Phoenix..." The soft sadness of Seraphina's voice made me wince. "How could you do that?"

I turned to glance at her over my shoulder and recoiled at the disheartenment in her face. She hadn't ever looked at me like that before. Usually, her disappointment was mixed with anger. I could handle that. Gave me something to battle against. But the beaten, doe-eyed look? It hit me like a hex in the face.

I plucked up my mug. Coffee sloshed down the sides as I took a fast sip. I scrunched up my face; the brew scalded my throat the whole way down. I leaned against the kitchenette and spoke over the brim of the cup. "Lizzie Tran was going to the Blood Farm...I needed—"

Seraphina shook her head. "That's not what I mean...how could you go off like that without even telling anyone?"

I sighed heavily. I couldn't keep the irritation from sharpening my words. "It wasn't like that—"

Cole's cool voice froze the words on my lips. "Phoenix had planned it ahead of time."

I lowered my mug and glanced sideways at him. This time, he didn't bother to look up from the screen.

Logan scoffed and raked a hand through his hair. "Figures."

"What?" I snapped furiously. I drank deeply from my mug.

Logan shook his head and snatched his bag off the ground,

slinging it roughly over his shoulder. "We don't have time for this." He nodded to Phin. "Get your bag."

She cast me one last puppy dog look, before she grabbed her things.

I licked the coffee off my upper lip. "Where are you going?"

Logan didn't answer. He went for the door. Seraphina gripped her backpack as she studied me sadly. "Phoenix, didn't you listen to anything anyone has said? After what happened at the church on Bird Island...you should understand better than anybody how a situation can go from handled to completely out of control...you think your magic makes you untouchable...indestructible. But—" She shook her head as she twisted up her hair into a topknot. "Magic didn't save you in that church and—"

I held up my mug. Coffee spilled down the sides. A smirk tickled the corner of my lips. "Actually, it did...you cast the summoning spell and—"

Her eyes hardened like silver blades. "Forget it. See you later, Cole." She headed for the door. Cole gave her a curt nod. Logan had a hand on the knob as he waited for Phin to slip on her jacket.

"Wait...where are you going?" I shifted my feet, barely resisting the urge to stamp my foot.

Seraphina didn't answer. Her back was still to me. In silence, she pulled her bag over her shoulder. Logan spoke up instead as he wrenched open the door for her. "We're meeting with the slayer up in Saranac Lake."

I choked on a mouthful of coffee. I wiped my mouth with the back of my hand. "A witch hunter you mean. *You're willing to risk Phin getting her head hacked off by some—*"

Logan snorted, his jaw tight as he shook his head. Then he slammed the door closed and stalked across the small space to meet me. His eyes pierced mine like emerald glass. "If you think I'm half as reckless as you, you're—"

Seraphina shoved her way between us. Her hand on his chest, she pushed him back. Then she turned to me. "The slayer wanted to come to him. To Logan. *To assist*. He refused. He didn't even tell her where we were, much less case details. We're meeting in a crowded bar, in the heart of town. Then heading back here to finish this. Completely safe."

"And what can a witch hunter possibly tell you that might help us? In case you haven't noticed—the only signs of magic have been old, faded traces. The witching well is dead..." I hesitated and rolled my eyes. "I mean, I'm, like, nearly positive it's dead. And there's been no magic signs at the school where most of the kids have gone missing. And the things that attacked me in the Blood Farm—definitely not witches."

Seraphina's face was impassive. "We don't think it's wickeds."

I made a face. "Again, my point exactly—"

"We think it's ghouls."

I recoiled, brow furrowed. I looked between them. Logan, jaw clenched and glaring, Seraphina, doe-eyes sad, but patient. I waved my hands through the air as though trying to clear it of my confusion. "Ghouls don't fit the pattern—*at all*." I scoffed. "The only thing that matches a ghoul is the bite force. And, okay, the strength of the claws. But ghouls don't even eat fresh kills. They literally don't kill anything. They scavenge and eat rotting corpses. And they don't go around snatching kids from classrooms...Why would you think—"

"Because as soon as he heard Agatha had disappeared, Cole went to the basement and started searching..." Phin flicked her eyes toward Cole with a warm, rueful smile. "He found a hole."

"A hole?" I repeated dully.

Seraphina nodded. "A hole in the wall in the basement. It was concealed, but it led to a tunnel. He texted pictures to Logan...and it matches some of the ghoul tunnels he's seen in the past."

Logan bobbed his head up and down begrudgingly. "Yup. And you're right, Grey. None of this makes sense, so that means something isn't true. There's something going on here...I can't put my finger on it, but—it's not a cut and dry case. We're missing something. That's why I need to talk to Frankie. Her experience with witches will help clear up the Wollstonecraft witch angle... and her mage contact can give us insight into what—if anything—would make a ghoul go completely bonkers."

Convinced and pumped for a win, I put down my mug and went for my bag. "All right. Then let's go."

Logan chuckled darkly. "You're staying here."

"What?" I demanded, my voice high and strained, overcome by a crushing wave of disbelief and disappointment. My eyes blurred as I chewed the inside of my cheek.

He shrugged, his mouth in a downturned smirk. "I told you, Grey. You need to rely on your head. Not your magic. Until then, I can't trust you out in the field."

I looked to Phin, brow furrowed, eyes blurring. "Phin?"

She winced. "He's right, Phoenix. You shouldn't have gone off on your own like that...and we need to figure this out before more kids are taken—before it's too late for all of them."

I scoffed, blinking stupidly in the face of her abandonment. I gave an ironic smile. "So...you expect me to stay here...*home*, essentially." I held up my hands and waved around the disgusting motel room. Then I gestured to Phin. "While you go off, leaving me—*at home*—again."

Seraphina rolled her eyes. "Nix—"

I frowned. Then I held up a hand. "Don't even bother." I scooped up my mug again and raised it to my mouth. I paused and spoke over the rim. "The case is here, anyways...so you're both just wasting your time."

"Phoenix...Agatha is only eight years old," Seraphina murmured, her silver eyes sad and cold. "You were supposed to be there for her. So don't talk to me about wasting time." Seraphina shook her head and followed Logan out the door. And this time, he didn't slam the door, just shut it with a quiet little snap. I flinched as though he'd bashed it against the frame.

# MR. BRIGHTSIDE

"We don't need a cover...Rory isn't going to need manipulating or convincing that there are monsters. He was just bitten, remember?"

Cole didn't answer. Instead, he continued to sort through the stuff on the table, packing his bag and putting some things off to the side. He slid Logan's book of monster bites—which was really just a photo album of grisly wounds—in the bag last and then zipped it up. He looked at me without looking at me. "Ready?"

I rolled my eyes as I scooped up my backpack. Keychains knocked every which way. "Yup."

It was the most uncomfortable ten-minute drive, ever. Cole, jaw taut and cheekbones sharp, refused to say more than an occasional grunt. And I, mouth scrunched in a moody pout, refused to let him sit in silence. Every few minutes I'd come up with a new question, not just to break the tension, but to annoy his butt off.

A quick call to 411, and we found the Meekses' house easily enough. It was in one of the dozens of neighborhoods splattered throughout the wooded, mountainous heart of town, just a few blocks from the sheriff's department. Cole pulled up to the curb and parked. We stared at the little brick Victorian, its lines, accented in black, popped against the gray trees that hugged the house. The yard, nestled inside an iron picket fence, was well cared for and neat, the browning grass cropped short and edged sharp. I glanced at Cole. "Ready?"

Cole gave me a curt nod and hopped out of the van. I grabbed my backpack and jogged after him. He was halfway down the Meekses' walkway before I made it to him. "Just let me do the talking, okay?"

Cole scoffed. "Right."

"What?" I glared at him sideways as we hurried up the porch steps. "I actually *know* Rory. It wouldn't make sense for *you* to check on him!"

Cole snickered darkly.

"What?" I snapped again. We stopped short at the door, and I jammed my finger into the doorbell. "Would you just talk to me!"

The door opened wide, and Heather Meeks appeared, flour smudged on her face, her honey-blonde hair piled high on her head, spilling tendrils all over the place, and an apron around her neck that read, "Smiles, Sunshine, and All the Snacks."

She smiled curiously at the two of us. "Afternoon, guys! You caught me just before my shift. What can I do for you?"

I hesitated. This was not the face of a woman whose little brother had been attacked. Maybe she didn't know.

Before I could figure out what to say, Cole finally found his voice. "Deputy Meeks, we were hoping to see Rory...well, actually, Phoenix wanted to see him." Cole gave a sheepish shrug and an easy smile that made his dark eyes shine.

I could've sworn Heather Meeks fluttered her eyelashes. She certainly blushed a bright red and blinked a bit.

I rolled my eyes. If it wasn't Logan getting the morgue girl all creepy...then it was Cole. Gross. Then Heather shifted her eyes to me with a knowing grin and it finally registered what Cole had just implied.

Now it was my turn to blush. My face burned hot with embarrassment. "Oh, no. It's not like that—"

Heather giggled like a little girl, grabbed me by the shoulder, and yanked me inside. "Come on in! I just made some peanut butter blossoms! Hot out of the oven—"

"Oh, no, Deputy, we really shouldn't be—" Then I stopped resisting, and my feet followed her obediently into the house. "Did you say peanut butter blossoms?"

Heather laughed a light, trickling chuckle. "Yup."

She swept us through the entryway, down a narrow hall so tight the three of us barely squeezed through, and into the kitchen. Heather's gentle hand on my arm, she guided me into a chair and sat me down. Cole sat across from me with a smirk piercing his dimple. I scowled at him.

Heather didn't seem to notice the tension. Humming sweetly and reminding me strongly of a Disney princess, Heather piled a plate with yummy cookies and set them in front of us. She stood over us, beaming bright, her hands on her hips. She nodded eagerly. "Go on, try one!"

I'd already taken a bite. With an eyeroll of appreciation, I scooped up several more. "Delicious," I moaned through the mouthful.

Cole grabbed a blossom and took a nibble. "Wow, these are great, Deputy Meeks!"

Heather waved a hand. "Oh, call me Heather. You're making me feel old."

I crinkled my nose as I smiled at her. For the first time, I realized, she couldn't be much more than twenty. "So, where's Rory?"

Heather frowned thoughtfully and inclined her head. "You know, I don't know. Usually, he's home before now. See, on Tuesdays I have the evening patrol, so when he gets home from school, we like to have some sweets together..." She scoffed and shook her head. "But not today. Today has been a strange day in the Meeks house, I'll tell ya. I got a call from the school this morning saying he'd skipped class! He's lucky Mama left for Albany this morning, or she would've raised a ruckus like nobody's business. I had half a mind to go down there and make sure he wasn't missing...but luckily, I called him first." She shook her head again. "That boy... he told me he and Keirian were playing hooky. And I told him, I says, 'Rory Raymond Meeks—'"

"Have you heard from him since?" I blurted out. Heather's brow furrowed at my tone. I flashed a cheesy smile and shrugged. "I just mean, with Sidney and Lizzie going missing...you think he's okay?"

Heather's face eased into a smile. "Gosh, you got it bad, don't ya, girlie?"

My eyes widened. I choked a bit on my cookie. Cole spoke loudly over my coughing fit. "She *really* does...you know, Heather, could you give us both boys' numbers?"

Heather nodded, "Sure, I don't have Keirian's memorized...let me go get my phone—"

As soon as Heather left the room, I shot Cole the nastiest look I could manage. "*Why did you have to make me sound like some kind of bimbo?*"

Cole snickered and shrugged.

Before I could hiss anything else, Heather hurried back into the room. She passed me a slip of paper with three phone numbers written across it, and Cole punched them into his contacts.

I pocketed the paper with a grateful smile. "Thanks so much, Heather."

"Oh, sure! I added our house number, just in case. Rory tends to forget his phone in odd places. Let me know if you need anything else...here, take some cookies home with you." She bustled around the kitchen filling two giant baggies with blossoms.

By the time we got back into the van, my sugar high had vanished. Keirian was supposed to have taken Rory home. Why hadn't he taken him home? I glanced at Cole as he clicked in his seatbelt. "Let me see your phone."

He passed it over without comment. I tapped the screen, pulled up his contacts, and pressed Rory's number. I held the phone up to my ear and waited. Cole stared out the window with a sour, stony expression on his face.

Voicemail.

I ended the call and tapped for Keirian's number. The phone rang loudly in my ear. My heart pumped just a bit harder. Where could he be?

"Hello?"

I flinched. I cleared my throat and answered quickly, "Hey, Keirian. It's Phoenix—"

"Who?"

"*Phoenix*, Keirian." I frowned. My eyes slid sideways at Cole as I muttered into the phone, "The girl with the Gale Weathers streaks."

Cole burst out laughing, doubled over the steering wheel. I smacked him hard on the back of the head. Cole continued to snicker.

Keirian laughed; the noise crackled loudly in the phone. "Yeah, yeah, I know. Just wanted to make you sweat a bit."

I groaned. "Where's Rory?"

"I dunno. His house?" he mumbled in a mocking monotone.

I gritted my teeth and crushed the phone in my fingers.

"He has a phone, too, Phoenix. Call him. I'm not his—"

"*He's not at his house*," I snapped.

"Well, that's where I left him. So, I don't know what to tell you."

I squeezed my eyes shut. My middle finger and thumb pinched my temples. "Did you *see* Rory enter his house?"

There was a pause. "Uhh..."

"Oh, you know what, Keirian? Why don't you call me next time you see him, all right? Can you handle that?"

"Oi! Now wait a minute! It's not like I just abandoned him,

okay? He wanted to go home. I asked if he was good, he said he was good...what happened to you guys, anyway?"

"Ask Rory next time you see him." I hung up the phone.

Out of the corner of my eye, I saw Cole side-eye me with a smirk to match. I inhaled deeply. "What?"

Cole grinned and reached a hand over to slap my knee. "There's my girl."

I rolled my eyes and stared out the window. Where were we now? And where was Rory? We were silent for a while, lurking like creepers outside the Meekses' house. We were quiet for so long, when Cole finally spoke, I jumped.

"I'm sorry."

I looked at him. "Me too."

"It just feels like you aren't hearing what we're saying..."

"You mean, what Logan is yelling..."

Cole furrowed his brow as he smiled sheepishly. "Sure. That."

"I'm not trying to be...*reckless* or whatever. I'm just trying to help, and it feels like no one agrees with the way I want to do things." I tossed my hands up and dropped them in my lap. Palms up, my magic hummed in my fingertips and without thinking, I held my hands one over the other. My fingers tingled. The warmth of my magic teased a twitch of a smile in the corner of my mouth. There was a small burst of orange glitter and then a cast of bright light, burning like a flame in the space between my hands. I played with the fire for a moment, mesmerized by the magic. "I can hide my talent. I can do my best to be the sister she wants me to be, but I always seem to come up short, don't I, Cole?"

When I looked at him, he was looking at me, his dark eyes intense and focused. He didn't answer. I forced a smile, but it was sad. "She's always going to leave me for somebody else, isn't she?"

Cole squinted his eyes, his face hard and serious. "You can do impossible things, Phoenix Grey, but you can't control what other people do."

I scoffed and flashed an easy, lopsided grin. "Well, *actually*—"

"It's your response to their actions that makes all the difference."

I closed my hands over the flame. The magical fire burst like a bubble of glitter, sending sparks of magic all over my hands. I stared down at my clasped hands and murmured softly, "Fawn always liked that spell."

Then I thought of Mary.

And Scott.

And Agatha.

I blinked back a tear and licked my lips. "I'm so sorry I wasn't there when you needed me, Cole." I sniffed. "I wasn't there when Agatha needed me, either."

"You were doing what you thought was right in the moment. We get it. Even Logan, for all his growling."

I glanced at Cole with a cocked eyebrow.

Cole smiled. "He does. He's just hard on you because he feels responsible for you. I mean, think about it, his whole life he had this hierarchy: Dad, brother, then him. Traven was his protector. Now that he's gone, he feels like it's his job to step into that role. If anything happened to you, think how he'd feel. He brought you here, he trained you, he taught you what to do, and if you mess up...it's like *he* messed up."

I stared at Cole. "That's dumb."

Cole burst out laughing. "After all that, that's all you have to say in response."

I grinned. "Yup." I slapped him hard on the back. "Thanks, Cole."

He nodded with a humble, downturned smile. "Anytime."

The silence was warm and heavy. I cleared my throat. "So..."

"What did Keirian say?"

"He said he dropped Rory off." I rolled my eyes. "But Heather clearly hasn't seen him at all. She doesn't even know he got hurt."

Cole leaned on the steering wheel. "And you believe Keirian when he says he dropped him off?"

I studied Cole for a moment, my mouth scrunched in a thoughtful pout. "What do you mean?"

Cole shrugged. "Well, I know you've been pretty much working the case solo, but when the rest of us have talked about it, based on the Campbell and Graham attacks...those are personal. Personal if you set aside the kids, because the kids have always been a constant in the pattern. Nathan and Drew break pattern, so—"

I twisted in my seat to face him and nodded eagerly. "Well, yeah. That's what we said from the beginning—it's personal."

Cole smiled slightly at my enthusiasm. "And considering Drew's world was centered around her social life...stands to reason, the only ones who'd want her dead are her peers at school..."

"Right..." It seemed so simple and obvious when he said it like that, I felt incredibly dense.

"Phin thinks it's the Gossamer House girls. Annie was upset that Nathan ditched her for Drew. And, apparently, the lot of them were bullying Lizzie Tran, too. But I think she's letting her experience with the girls at Mater Christi High bias her opinion." Cole chuckled with a small shake of his head. "Logan said Phin was like, first instant she saw them all in their mean girl huddle—*'it's them!'*" He snapped his fingers and grinned.

I had to smile. "I wish I'd seen her. Phin's funny when she's fiery."

Cole laughed. "Right? It hardly ever happens, but when it does—"

"Watch out." I grinned. Then I held up a hand. "Okay, okay. So, your question is, could Keirian be a possible suspect? I'd say yes...maybe? He had a crush on Drew—"

"A lot of guys did," Cole pointed out and began to tick them off. "Keirian Cullen, Rory Meeks, Stuart Godwin—"

I held up a finger. "Stuart was stalking her."

Cole nodded slowly. "Right, I forgot about that."

I frowned. Who could've hated Drew so much they wanted to rip her and her boyfriend to shreds? Who has that kind of capacity for rage? "Kieran thinks it has to do with the Gossamer House. He was pretty vague on why. But he's also spreading a rumor that it's Sidney..."

"Sidney Godwin? The kid who—"

I nodded. "Went missing, yup."

"Boyfriend of Lizzie Tran, who—"

"Was attacked and taken...right."

Cole smirked. "I'd say he's wrong."

"Right? He doesn't really believe it. He's spreading the Sidney angle for website traffic, but his theory was interesting."

"How so?"

I took a deep breath. "Well, Keirian said that his family had been around a long time, and they tell stories about the Godwins —how all their guys go bad." I waved a hand with a dismissive eyeroll. "Keirian's just a conspiracy theorist. He gets his kicks out of being scared."

Cole tossed his hair out of his eyes to meet mine. He held up a finger and shook it at me. "You know, that is something that stuck out to me."

I cocked a quizzical eyebrow.

Cole leaned one arm against the wheel and spoke with the other. "It's like Logan said before—we haven't met one adult Godwin man, have we?"

I considered this a moment. "That is weird..."

Cole raised his eyebrows with a hint of a smile in the corner of his lips. "You know what else has a female hierarchy?"

I glanced at him sideways. "Ghouls."

Cole nodded seriously, an eager grin on his face. "It fits, doesn't it?"

I burst out laughing. "No. Like I told Logan, and like Logan already knows—which is why he's running off for help—ghouls don't force themselves into society, and they certainly don't establish human towns! They live in tunnels and—"

"Like the one I found in the basement of the school," Cole cut in quickly.

"—sewers, and they don't come out in the daytime!" I finished firmly. "They eat decaying, dead people. That means people *already dead*. They don't kidnap kids or maul teenage babysitters or—" The memory of the Blood Farm flashed in my mind. Lizzie's screams echoed in my head. I winced and closed my eyes. "You saw what happened in your dream. Ghouls don't do that."

Cole nodded quietly. Then he glanced at me. "But they *could...* if they wanted to, couldn't they?"

"You only think they're ghouls because they have no men." I grinned at his persistence. "The House of Grey doesn't have many men; that doesn't mean we're ghouls!"

"But witches have a matriarchal society, don't they?" Cole inclined his head with a smirk. "Like ghouls."

I frowned. "Witches are usually born female...male witches are rare. That's why the lore calls our men something completely different, for a while people didn't think male witches existed." I shrugged. "It's why our family names get passed down the way they do...we have the family name of Blackwell, and the heir carries the House name..."

"You don't have any adult male relatives, do you?"

"I only know of one adult male relative, and that's my Great Uncle Richard..." I tossed up my arms and grabbed my bag of cookies. "But just because *we* haven't met any Godwin men doesn't mean they don't exist."

"This is true," Cole conceded with a shrug. "And you've met Sidney and Stuart...and they're almost men."

I stuffed a blossom in my mouth and spoke around the chocolate candy, "Stuart thought it was Keirian."

Cole scoffed with an open-mouthed smirk. "Oh, yeah? What was his reasoning?"

"He said Keirian was doing it to get clicks on his website. Bring credibility to the legend, or whatever." I rolled my eyes as I wiggled my fingers in air quotes.

Cole shrugged. "Could be. You said yourself he's spreading rumors to drive traffic. So, the real question is, do you believe Keirian when he says he dropped Rory off?"

I sat back in my seat. I inhaled deeply and meditated on the question for a moment. Then I answered without hesitation, "Yes. I do. But I don't think Rory went inside his house. And with all this conspiracy talk about the Godwins..." I shook my head as my thoughts kept racing. "I know where our next stop needs to be."

Cole shook his dark hair out of his eyes and inclined his head. "Where?"

"Justine Kilpatrick's house."

It didn't take long to find her house. Cole pulled up alongside the road and switched off the van. I held up a hand before he could unclick his seatbelt. He shot me a quizzical look.

"Wait here. I think this will work much better if I go in alone."

Cole's eyes narrowed. "How's that again?"

"Justine..." I frowned as I considered how to explain. "She's disturbed. Like, mentally traumatized by whatever happened to her. And the last time I was here, it seemed like she *wanted* to talk to me...but she was uncomfortable with an audience. I think she'll actually help if it's just me."

Cole inhaled deeply, his nostrils flaring and his cheekbones sharp. "Fine. But you're taking this—"

He dug into the glove box and fished out an old flip phone. He slapped it into my hands. "It's one of Logan's. He scrubbed it for you. Now, you're going to act like any normal, teenage girl your age and keep this glued to you, got it?"

A lopsided smirk slid onto my face. I stuck the phone into the baggy pocket below my knee.

Cole held up a finger in warning. "And I don't care what your mother says, phones are necessary in this line of work. Magical interference or not."

I pursed my lips into an amused smirk. "You know that's just an old witch's tale, right?"

Cole nodded. "Well, there you go. Now hurry up. I'd like to grab some takeout on the way back to the motel."

I chuckled and jumped out of the van, the phone bumping awkwardly against my leg. I hurried through the yard, up the porch, and knocked on the door.

I waited a moment and then tried again. "Justine, it's me—Phoenix, the girl from this afternoon?"

Nothing.

I knocked again. "Hello?"

I glanced over my shoulder at the road. Her car was still parked where it had been earlier that day. I looked back at the door, frowning thoughtfully. I placed my hand on the knob. Magic warmed in my palm and the lock unclicked. I turned the doorknob with one hand, reaching for my wand with the other.

Dred, the ominous kind that makes you sick to your stomach, seeped through me like a potion. I swallowed, my tongue thick and dry in my mouth. I peered into the dim living room. It was dark, barely any day made it through the window shutters. I reached out for the light switch and slapped it up. The blub overhead popped on, casting a rusty-yellow glow around the messy room. It had been in shambles before, strewn papers, old soup cans, and other hoarded things, but this was a different kind of chaos. This was a battleground. The couch was shoved into the far wall, the lamp was smashed on the floor, the coffee table was flipped on its side—everything in the room was either knocked around or shattered.

I wanted to call out for her, but I couldn't find my voice...and wasn't that the thing Rachel and I would always complain about? Final girls shouting for their friends when the monster was waiting around the corner? I held my wand out and stepped slowly into the room, my Converse crunching on crumpled papers, garbage, and glass.

"Nix?"

I flinched at his voice and whirled around with my wand to my lips. Cole's nose crinkled as he eyed the place. He reached for his hip and unsheathed a machete. He held it out low at his side. Together, we searched the house. It didn't take too long, but it would've been quicker if Justine hadn't hoarded so much stuff. A lot of the rooms upstairs were filled with boxes on top of boxes, which made many places for things to hide. We checked every room, every closet, but she was gone. Cole and I met back in the living room, which was the only place in the entire house that showed any sign of a struggle.

"Okay…" Cole glanced around the room. "She was taken… against her will. But why?"

I had a few ideas.

We moved around the room looking for something, anything. I made my way to the mantel. It was dusty and covered with cobwebs. The only thing on it was a single picture frame, knocked on its face. Gingerly, I picked it up and turned it over in my hands. It was Justine…

…with the Wollstonecrafts.

It had to be.

I easily recognized the crazy wife and the feral little girl from the road. And Victor looked just like the sheriff—his sister—all thin with sharp pointy angles, but unlike the sheriff, he looked happy. They were standing beside the giant willow tree in the Watertown cemetery, arms around each other and smiling. Three little girls in old, worn dresses and wild, matted yellow hair stood in front of the adults, the girls' dirty faces grinning.

Cole came over and peeked over my shoulder. "What is it?"

I met his eyes. "What does this look like to you?"

Cole smiled slightly. "Family photo."

My breath caught in my chest like a caged bird. Flighty and

desperate. I looked back at the picture. My thumb smoothed over the grimy glass. "This is Justine and the Wollstonecrafts...Victor... who is technically a Godwin." I shook my head. "What is going on here?"

Cole shrugged and tapped a finger on the photo. "I don't know, but those two are sisters."

I made a face as I stared down at Crazy Lady and Justine Kilpatrick. "What?"

Cole a smirk pierced his dimple. "Yeah, I mean...look at them."

"Cole, Justine's sister—"

Something creaked.

Cole's eyes darted to mine.

He heard it, too.

We both turned sharply toward the sound.

# YOU COULDN'T TEACH ME INTEGRITY

The front door opened a crack and Rory Meeks stuck his lanky, black-haired head inside, "Hello...?"

I exhaled the breath I'd held.

Cole muttered darkly beneath his breath.

"Rory, what are you doing here?" I crossed the trashed room to meet him. "Where've you been?"

Cole hung back, the machete still gripped at his side.

"Wait, what are you doing here—where's..." Rory ambled inside the house, cautiously teetering around the mess of hoard and destruction. He smoothed his hair back against the sides of his face. His eyes, wide and fearful, surveyed the damage. "Uh...what happened here?"

Cole was at my side so suddenly I flinched as he brushed against my arm.

Rory jumped and hesitated at the sight of Cole. His eyes dropped to the machete in his hand. He tucked a strand of greasy hair behind his ear. "Oh, hey. Who are—"

Cole didn't let Rory finish his question, much less answer it. Instead, he asked one of his own. "We were just at your house; you didn't make it home?" Cole tossed his hair out of his face and inclined his head as he stared Rory down with hard, dark eyes.

"I, uh, well, I was—"

I smacked Cole's shoulder with the back of my hand. "Would you give him a minute?"

I unzipped my bag and tucked the family photo into the small front pocket before swinging the backpack over my shoulder, knocking Cole in the process. "Sorry, Rory. Cole's manners are lacking. It's not his fault, he's just spent too much time with this meathead we know." I shrugged with a lazy grin. "How are you feeling, Rory?"

Rory shifted his eyes from Cole back to me. "I'm okay...I didn't want to go home because, well, I—"

"You didn't want to go home?" Cole asked, his voice taking on that gruff, guy tone dudes use when they're talking to each other. Posturing or whatever. Annoying.

Rory took a sharp breath as he crossed his arms and tucked his hands underneath his armpits. "Well, no. My mother's in Albany until Thursday, but I didn't want to worry my sister. Uhm, Phoenix...do you mind if..." Rory eyed Cole uneasily.

I got the hint. I slapped Cole on the back. "Cole, wait in the van. I'll be just a minute."

Cole glanced at me sideways. He scoffed. "Not happening. Try again."

My eyes narrowed. "Are you kidding me?"

"Dead serious. There's no way I'm leaving you alone with this dude." Cole jutted his chin toward Rory, who practically crumpled inward like a crushed piece of paper. "If you didn't go home, where'd you get the fresh change of clothes? I'd expect your clothes to be a bit of a mess after an attack..."

"These?" Rory grabbed at the corners of the clean (way too big for him) letterman jacket and held them up. "Oh, well, Keirian had a change of clothes in his bag."

"Lucky."

Rory, completely missing the irony in Cole's voice, nodded. "Yeah, he's on the football team, so he usually has—"

"By the way, which arm was it?"

Rory gulped, the knot in his throat bobbed up and down. "What arm?"

"I know if I got my arm chomped on like a chew toy, I'd sure be favoring it a little. And," Cole gave a sarcastic smirk. "doesn't really look like you're in all that much pain...at all."

Rory smoothed his hair behind each ear. "Right. That's actually what I wanted to talk to Phoenix about..." He pulled his arm out of the sleeve of the letterman and ran a hand over his arm, pushing up the short sleeve of his t-shirt so we could see his skin.

There was nothing there.

I grabbed his arm, yanking him into me. I moved my hands all over his bicep. It was completely gone. As though it never happened. I stared at him, eyes wide and mouth parted. I shook my head. "How?"

Rory licked his lips, eying Cole anxiously as he approached. In one motion, Cole sheathed his machete, snatched Rory's arm, and checked for himself. "I don't know. And that's why I wanted to see Justine—well, one of the reasons..."

Cole dropped Rory's arm. He studied him, his eyes narrowed.

"Weird." I blinked, still trying to process. It didn't make sense. "Uhm, well, Rory, it's not safe here. Something happened to Justine. The best place for you to be right now is at home."

Rory glanced around the room, shaking his head slowly. "No, no. Phoenix, can we just—"

Cole shook his head. "No."

Rory sighed and scooted closer to me. He leaned in slightly and tried to whisper, but I shook my head. "It's okay, Rory. Ignore Cole. Just say it."

Rory took a deep breath and blurted, "I think we should go to Stuart Godwin's party."

Cole scoffed. "Are you serious?"

For the first time since their interaction, Rory seemed to have found his confidence. He glared at Cole with a stubborn impatience that pinkened his pale cheeks. "Yes. I'm serious. This situation is a lot more complex than I'm sure you could possibly understand." Rory rolled his eyes and then turned his attention to me. "There's an old stone well behind the Gossamer House—"

The witching well. I nodded my understanding without comment.

"I think whatever is taking the children...I think it's accessing the school from a tunnel..." Rory shrugged and clarified, "A tunnel that connects the well to the school. The best way for us to get access to the well is—"

"To crash Stuart's party," I finished with a small smile. I clapped him on the back. "Excellent thinking, Rory."

Rory grinned as his shoulders relaxed.

I glanced at Cole. He was standing off to the side, moody and broody as ever.

Cole raised a skeptical eyebrow. "I'm still waiting for the complicated part."

Rory licked his lips. "Well—"

"It's not at all complicated; it just makes absolutely no sense." Cole snorted. "Why would you think there's a tunnel in the well... or a tunnel at the school—unless you've seen it?"

Rory's eyes narrowed. "Well, that's the complicated part—"

"All right." I cut in between them and guided Rory back out the door. "Whatever is going on here, the Gossamer House is a good place to start, regardless. Head home, Rory, and I'll call you when we're on our way."

Cole followed us out the door. "I'll call this in...report Justine missing."

Cole got on the phone and headed for the van. I walked Rory to his car, hugging myself against the cold. "Remember, Rory: Wait for me to call you, okay?"

Rory slid into the driver's seat and chuckled, smoothing his hair back from his face. "Trust me. I'm not going to go anywhere without you."

I smiled and shut the door behind him with a quick wave. As soon as I wrenched open the van, Rory drove away.

I hopped inside and slammed it shut.

Cole was off the phone. He leaned against the steering wheel, his eyes on Rory's car as it drove away. "We aren't going to the party until we talk to Logan."

I rolled my eyes and shook my head in disgust.

"Phoenix, I'm serious." Cole started the van and pulled away from the curb, heading back through town. "We're not going until we talk to Logan about it."

"My God, Cole, Logan isn't going to be here to hold your hand through this! I mean, if it's too much for you, maybe..." I shut my mouth and shrugged, staring pointedly out the window.

"You really think that's it, huh?" Cole snorted. "Think I'm too much of a coward to handle all of this?"

I didn't answer. Maybe. Yeah.

Out of the corner of my eye, Cole nodded curtly, his mouth pursed into a downturned smirk. He muttered under his breath and cranked up the stereo.

I scowled and turned it down. "Well, then what is it?"

Cole shook his head. His hands squeezed the steer wheel. "You didn't think it was a bit odd that the dude's bite is completely gone?"

"Well, yeah. He did, too; that's why—"

Cole snickered darkly. "If you weren't so anxious to jump face-first into every single situation, maybe you'd see things a bit more clearly."

I gave him a deadpan stare, my mouth pinched into a flat line. "I'm getting really tired of people insinuating that I'm some kind of dumb bimbo."

"*Nix, ghouls can shapeshift!*" Cole cried in exasperation. "They literally are what they eat. They eat someone, they can transform into them."

Now it was my turn to laugh. "You think that Rory wasn't Rory?"

"I don't know." Cole shrugged angrily. "That's why, before we let him lead us anywhere, we're going to wait until we hear back from Logan and Phin."

I shook my head. "Unbelievable."

"Well, think about it, Nix. Keirian Cullen drops the guy off at his house...but he doesn't go home. He randomly shows up right where *you* happen to be with some weak line about wanting answers? Doesn't make sense. And if it doesn't make sense, it's not true."

I made a derpy face and nodded up and down. "Yeah, okay, Logan."

Cole shrugged again with an unapologetic smirk. "Say what you want, I've had my nose buried in every monster lore book for the past month, and I don't know of *any* monster bite that magically heals itself...unless the victim is infected and turned."

"I poured a bungleweed potion all over him, so—"

Cole rolled his eyes. "Bungleweed clots wounds. It doesn't prevent scarring. You need goldthread for that."

I made a face. "Well, someone's been taking potion lessons from Phin behind my back."

Cole glanced at me sideways with a satisfied smile.

I waved a dismissive hand. "Either way. If Rory was a ghoul, he'd have just eaten us right there in the living room. He wouldn't need to lure us to some party and down a witching well."

"No." Cole held up a finger and shook his head with a down-turned smirk. "No, if he was a ghoul, he wouldn't be wandering around town in the middle of the afternoon—"

I stared at him blankly. "That's what I've been saying..."

"He *should* be crawling around a dark tunnel somewhere, digging up coffins, and munching on dead dudes. But he's not—

and *that's* the problem. That's what Logan is going to figure out from Frankie and her mage."

"Of course..." I cocked an eyebrow.

Cole's jaw clenched.

"Frankie. That's the same person who gave Logan the tip about Syracuse, isn't it? The tip that turned out to be a *bust*. The same person he *lied* about." I asked with a wide sarcastic smirk. I shook my head. "Unbelievable."

Cole's cheeks pinched pink, but he shook it off. "We aren't talking about that. Logan's business is his business. All I care about is whether or not she can give us the information we need. Because none of this case is coming together, and there's a reason for it. We're missing something. And what about Justine? She's *missing*, Phoenix. Something grabbed her. Something didn't want her around. Why? If it's the same thing that took her in the first place—they'd left her completely alone for, what? Thirty-two *years*? And *now* they come for her? Why?"

"She talked to me." The words slipped out before I could even think them. I looked at Cole, almost surprised. "Justine talked to me," I repeated.

Cole looked at me sharply. "What did she tell you?"

I held up a hand in correction. "Well, she didn't actually talk to me. But she almost did. I could tell she was going to. I told you! That's why we went back there. I was sure she would help..."

Cole frowned, considering this. "So, she almost starts talking, and then the creatures or whatever decide—that's it, she's gotta go." Cole winced. "I don't know, Nix. This is closer than you think."

My nose crinkled. "What do you mean?"

"I think these things know that you're onto them. I'll bet you anything that Rory dude is one of them. And that's why we aren't going to make another move, until we hear from Phin and Logan. Agreed?"

I snorted. "No." I glanced sideways at Cole. "But does that really matter?"

Cole didn't hesitate. "Nope."

That night, I tossed and turned in the bed. I was seething, my anger burning hot beneath the covers. All I could think about was how no one was listening. It was like I was a little kid, yapping at their ankles, desperate for attention. And on top of everything, Seraphina left me. That hurt more than I wanted to admit. It was like no matter what I did, she was always going to look for someone else. Nothing had changed. It was still the same.

But it didn't matter.

I didn't matter.

Mary. Lizzie. Sidney. Agatha. They mattered. And here I was, lying in bed, waiting for...what? Logan and Phin to get back from their little dinner date with witch murderer, Frankie. They should've called, but so far, it'd been several hours and nothing. No text. No call. No magical answer to our mysterious monster problem.

I twisted in the blankets. This was pointless. I wouldn't be able to fall asleep. I glanced at Cole. The only reason *he* was asleep was because of the morsmort. I knew he was asleep, even though I couldn't see him. The motel room was dark. It had been a welcome relief not to have to deal with Logan and his irritating television habit. But I couldn't see Cole. Was he having another premonition? He shouldn't be. Not after Seraphina's personalized potion. But even if he was...he wouldn't let me see it. Not after the last time. Not after I went rogue.

I reached over to the nightstand. My fingers found the remote. I clicked on the TV. The room was bathed in a blue light. I looked over at Cole. His eyelids fluttered rapidly. His mouth was in a grim line. His arms were pinned to his sides. His fists clenched the covers.

I bit my lip.

He was. I could tell. Despite Seraphina's potion, he was still dreaming.

I licked my lips, my tongue dry in my mouth. This was bigger than any hurt feelings or bruised egos. I slipped out of the bed and sank to my knees beside him. I smoothed the hair back from his brow and rested my palm on his forehead. I inhaled and exhaled, my chest rising and falling steadily. It was harder to clear my mind this time. Cole's forehead kept twitching underneath my hand. But then the darkness flickered.

It flashed.

Closer.

I flinched.

Closer.

My fingers tightened, nails digging into Cole's forehead.

I saw it.

# THE WORLD IS A STAGE, BUT THE PLAY IS BADLY CAST

The Blood Farm.

In the dark, the moon and stars blocked by the bruised clouds, it was somehow possible to distinguish. Like watching a dark movie scene. I could see everything, even when I shouldn't have been able to. A girl in all black hurried up the hill toward the ominous stone building. Hair like honey curled out from underneath the dark hood that obscured her face. She tugged the hood tighter, her silver rings flashing on her left hand.

Billie.

Then the scene changed. A quick cut. It was bright. Old, fashionable furniture, and kids all over the place. The Gossamer House. Stuart's party? The view floated above the crowd, down the narrow hallway, and into a room with two doors. A girl with chunky red streaks in her dark hair stood before a taller girl with golden hair twisted up high on her head. It was us. With Cole. He had his hand on my shoulder as though he were pulling me back.

Phin was scared.

Of me.

She backed up, bumping into the desk behind her as I neared her. I wanted to leave. Pull myself from his vision. I had to stop her...me? But I couldn't. I was stuck, eyes wide shut and staring, silently screaming overhead. I knew what would happen. And then it did. In an instant, I watched myself unsheathe a blade and swing. Seraphina's beautiful face, frozen in horror as I sliced off her head. Then I turned to Cole, the blade raised.

A blink, and the darkness was all I could see. It wasn't real. It couldn't be real. The visions were evil. They were wrong.

But they hadn't been. Not really.

The shadows cleared like a smoky room. And I could see the funeral home down the sloping, grassy, forest hill. And I saw Billie. She grabbed onto a girl with mousy-brown hair. Annie Collingwood. Annie stared owl-eyed into the dark. She spun on her heel, Billie clinging tight to her side. There were eyes, fluorescent and bright, like white lights shining in the dark, all around them. Four creatures emerged from the trees. They drew closer, closing in on the two girls from the black of forest. The creatures were hunched with limbs, protruding from long robes, hung forward with claws long as sickles. Then teeth, thick and stubby in wide jaws, gnashed from beneath hooded cloaks. And the creatures charged forward. And all I could see was blood.

Then it changed.

The interior of an old house flashed before my eyes. A lamp popped on, casting a warm glow around the room. A living room with aged, grimy walls, scuzzy, grayed wood floor, and piles of random junk shoved up in the corners. There was a mantel coated with dust above the fireplace. Faded sepia photos in tarnished picture frames stuck up randomly amid the cobwebs. A little girl with stringy, matted, dirty, yellow hair came into the room, dragging a body of a young woman, golden honey spilling out of the black hood over her head.

The girl and another one—the urchin from the road—lugged Billie across the ratty rug and heaved her into a chair. Billie's head lulled lifelessly to the side. Blood trickled from the corner of her mouth. They twisted coils of rope around her wrists and ankles.

Then from the shadows of the far doorway, an old woman emerged.

And the room changed like a channel.

It wasn't Billie.

It was me.

The old woman was coming for me.

Her skin was leathery, cracked, and clumpy like a Halloween mask, darkened around her sunken eyes and puffy lips. Her wispy, white hair feathered around her face from the poofy bun at the nape of her neck. She looked like a swollen corpse as she limped toward me with an uneven waddle. Her hands, shaky and unsteady, pulled back her hood as her glassy eyes bulged, and her fat, crusty tongue lapped over her lips. As she drew closer, she bared her teeth, blackened, oozy, chipped, and jagged. The vision was silent, so I could only imagine the sound she made. Then her teeth retracted into pits in her gums. She slapped her tongue around the gaping hole that was her mouth as her foggy eyes rolled back into her head and a second set of teeth slid from pits in her gums—stained and stubby and sharp. She gnashed her teeth and opened her mouth wide.

My eyes flashed open.

Something hit me.

Hard.

I was falling.

My head hit the thin, moldy carpet. Hard. I blinked in the darkness, stunned by the impact.

The lamp snapped on. A shadow loomed over me. I flinched, hands over my face. I curled tight in a fetal position.

"Nix, what—"

I lowered my arms and squinted up at him. Cole crouched down. Gentle fingers brushed my hair from my slick forehead. "What happened? I thought—did I—?"

I struggled to sit up, massaging my temple as Cole moved to help me. "It's okay...it was my fault."

Cole eased me onto the bed. He winced. "You don't look so good. Here, let me—" He hurried across the room to dig out a water bottle from the minifridge. Then he thrust it in my hands. "Drink."

I nodded and cranked off the cap. Afraid to close my eyes, I stared wide-eyed as I drank. Water gushed from the corners of my mouth and leaked down my chin.

Cole put a hand on his head as he sank down to sit beside me. "Wait, what were you doing?"

I continued to chug the water until the bottle crinkled in my hands. Then I lowered it, twisted the top, and tried to keep my stomach still. "You were having a nightmare."

"I was?" Cole tossed his dark hair out of his eyes. "But I took the morsmort." His thick lashes lowered over his narrowed eyes. "And you knew that. Did you do that brain connection thing?" He stood abruptly. He threaded his fingers behind his head. "You did." He slapped his forehead and rubbed hard as though he had a headache to rival my own. He stalked away from me and toward the bathroom and then over to the tiny table. He glanced back at me, hurt etched in the corners of his eyes. "Phoenix, how could you do that?"

I held my stomach as I tried to steady my spinning thoughts. "Cole, I—" Then I remembered. Billie. Annie. Blood.

I stood up from the bed. I swayed slightly on my feet. "I need to call Billie Godwin."

"What?" Cole's mouth hung open slightly, his lip curled in disgusted disbelief.

"You saw what's going to happen!" I snapped impatiently. I staggered to the nightstand and pulled my phone off the charger.

"Actually, I didn't. Phin's morsmort did its job and blocked it out—"

"Well, you were right. We *are* dealing with ghouls. At least four. And Billie Godwin and Annie Collingwood are about to get eaten if we don't do something—"

"Phoenix, we aren't supposed to do anything! We aren't supposed to *act* on these visions. We aren't supposed to see them at all! Don't you remember what happened the last time? Not only did you fail to save Lizzie Tran, you got Rory Meeks chomped on, Sidney Godwin disappeared, and Agatha Godwin was taken! All because you acted on what you saw!"

I shook my head, eyes off to the side. He didn't understand. He hadn't seen it. Seraphina's severed head flashed in my eyes. My stomach heaved, and I forced it back down. I couldn't think about that. One problem at a time. Billie. I had to warn Billie.

I looked over at him, amber eyes fusing to onyx. "Cole—"

"And that's not even the point...forget the visions." Cole inclined his head, his dark hair falling into hurt eyes. "Nix, how could you do that to me?"

I blinked stupidly. "Excuse me?"

His voice was soft, weighed down with his pained disappointment. "How could you sneak into my head like that?"

I scowled. I didn't have time for this. So over all the bruised male egos, I didn't bother to explain. I snapped my fingers. In the far corner, my backpack unzipped itself, and my notepad flew across the room. I swiped a quick hand and snatched it out of the air. I flipped through the pages for Billie's number.

"Unbelievable," Cole muttered.

Before I could look up, the door slammed.

Cole was gone. He'd left.

"Hello?"

"Hey." I blinked back a tear and cleared my throat. "It's Phoenix. Where are you?"

There was a pause. "I'm going to meet Annie. We're going to find Sidney."

"What?" I chucked the notepad onto the bed. I went to the dresser and dug for a change of clothes, grabbing whatever was on top. Flannel button down, tank top, jeans...and a leather jacket. It was cold.

"She's at the cemetery now. She said she found some kind of tunnel hidden behind that old willow tree. Rory told her he thinks those *things* are crawling around underground and dragging people into them. So, we're—"

"*Oh, for Fay's sake*," I hissed under my breath. "Billie, listen to me—" I gripped the phone and went for my backpack. "You can't—"

"Watch me."

I winced as I slung my bag over my shoulder. I had. "You can't go there by yourself. You'll get—"

"Then come with me. I'll pick you up."

I groaned and pinched my pounding head. "Fine. I'm at the Adelaide Inn. Pick me up at the corner."

I slapped the phone shut and shoved it in my pocket. There. I had a phone. Maybe that would make them happy. I flicked my hand, and the notepad flew off the bed and into my open palm. I smoothed my thumb across the paper. A smudge of orange glitter shimmered across the page leaving a brief note for Cole.

I twisted up my hair into a quick topknot and stuck my wand through it. Then I snatched a sheathed machete from Logan's ruck, a blowtorch, and a handful of lighters, and I left the room.

"You're going to wait in the car."

Billie glanced at me as she pulled away from the shoulder and merged onto the road. "What do you mean?" She shook her head, her voice hardened. "I told you. I'm going—"

I scowled as my hands moved blindly through my backpack, reorganizing everything. "Annie's already there..." I muttered more to myself than Billie.

"There's no way I'm waiting in the car! If there really is a *tunnel*—"

"Don't you remember what it was like when those things came for Lizzie?" I snapped.

Billie shot me a sharp look. "Of course." She shifted her eyes back to the road. "And that's why I'm going. It's my *brother*...I was sure he went to the Wollstonecrafts', but now—"

I stopped listening. My heart was pounding too loudly in my ears to hear, and my brain was blurring too fast to process. "How many people live in that house?"

"The Wollstonecrafts' house? Uhhh...Victor. And you met the wife." Billie snickered, rolling her eyes as she turned left. The lights in the windows of the old Victorians winked as we whizzed by way too fast. "Their daughters..."

"Is there a grandmother?"

Billie twisted her head to stare at me, swerving slightly on the street. "I'm sorry?"

"A grandmother? Like a freaky, mummy-looking, old lady?"

Billie scrunched up her face as she turned back to watch the road. She braked hard as a car in front of us pulled into a driveway. "I don't think so..."

The grotesque face flashed behind my eyelids. Then it was Annie and the four creatures in their hoods with claws like curved blades, jaws, and eyes like—

"Phoenix." Billie's gripped on the wheel tightened. "What aren't you telling me?"

I studied her warily. She was wearing the same black hoodie and black jeans from Cole's vision. I thought of the teeth. The blood. I bit my lip. "Just trust me. You need to stay in the car, and I'll get Annie, and then we can—"

"No." Billie shook her head furiously. "No. Phoenix I'm checking out that tunnel."

I pinched my forehead and squeezed hard. "It's not safe—"

"If it's not safe for me, then it's not safe for you."

I groaned as she turned onto the backroad that led to the school and the cemetery. For an insane moment, I contemplated jinxing her to her seat. Magically locking her inside the vehicle...I could do it. I *should* do it. I glanced at her out of the corner of my eyes.

"You don't understand." Billie licked her lips as she pursed them tight. Then she took a shaky breath. "I *need* to find him. I need to make things right." Billie's voice broke, and her lower lip trembled.

Then I realized: we were the same. Struggling to fix things. Desperate to end this nightmare. "Okay."

"I'm not kidding, Phoenix!"

"I said, 'okay.'"

Billie chuckled dryly. "Sorry. I'm used to having to fight a lot longer for what I want. You gave in a lot easier than most."

"But you have to be ready." I bent over and dug through my backpack. "Machete. Blowtorch. Fire is the best thing."

Billie's lip curled. Her nose wrinkled as she glanced over at my bag. "Right...and fire is the best thing for...what?"

"They have a really good sense of smell, so—" I fished out the bottle of skunk cabbage. "This is a mixture of garlic and..." I hesitated. "Just some other stuff."

"Who has? Phoenix, what are you talking about?"

"You were there. You know what we're facing." I eyed her grimly, wondering if I was doing the right thing by including her. "Ghouls."

Billie looked at me, clearly startled. Her hands slipped a bit on the wheel. "*Ghouls*? Like..."

"Like ghouls...but these ghouls aren't like any I've ever heard of...there's something, a piece we're missing." I turned the bottle of skunk cabbage over in my hands. "They aren't acting like ghouls."

She glanced at me sideways. "You...you're talking like you deal with this kind of thing...a lot."

I tried to smile but only managed to grimace. "Monsters. My sister and our friends, we hunt them."

She inhaled sharply and forced a laugh. "I want to say you're insane, but—"

"You were there," I repeated, finishing her sentence. I got it. The shellshock of reality. Been there. Of course, being a witch, it'd been easier for me to believe it. Monsters. Ghosts. Believing magic was easy.

Suddenly, she reached over and grabbed the bottle. Her thumb smoothed the label. She passed me back the vial, her eyebrow cocked and eyes curious in the shine of the streetlights. "What do these symbols mean?"

"Oh, just—" I struggled to come up with an innocent explanation for witch runes. The last thing she needed to know was what they said. Then she'd never drink it.

Billie saved me with another question. "We sprinkle that on our necks or something, right? We don't have to, like—"

"Drink it? Yes. We drink it." I smirked darkly. "But it'll keep them from smelling us, giving us a better chance at catching them off guard..."

She forced a smile, but it didn't touch her eyes. "And they...the ghouls...they live in the tunnel Rory found?"

I bit my lip as I looked down at the potion in my hand. "I think you should wait in the car."

"Again with that?" She glared at me, swerving slightly. "No way. I'm coming, Phoenix. Don't suggest it again, or I'll leave you on the side of the road."

I scoffed with a small smile. I'd hex her first, but— "Fair enough. First priority: grab Annie and get her away from the cemetery."

Billie turned down Godwin School Road and nodded curtly. "Okay. Then we clear the tunnel?"

I nodded. The images of Cole's vision continued to flash behind my eyelids. It was distracting and turned my stomach. I needed to focus. "Yeah."

"With machetes...and blowtorches?"

My heart sank a bit. Honestly, I'd planned on using magic.

She scoffed at my awkward silence.

I flashed a guilty grin. "Sorry, I was just thinking I didn't pack the stakes or an extra blowtorch."

She laughed darkly at the joke that wasn't one. "That's okay. Fire kind of freaks me out anyway."

"Heh. Too bad. You're taking the blowtorch. It's a lot harder to chop off a head than you'd think..." My voice trailed away as Seraphina's neck flashed in my mind. I cleared my throat.

Billie didn't bother arguing, but I think it was the look on my face that silenced her, rather than her conceding anything. She took the left into the cemetery. Her car bumped and jolted down the gravel road through the trees toward the funeral home. She drove the car right up to the willow tree just as she'd had me do the last time we were there. She forced a smile as she finally shoved the car in park. "Annie isn't here. That's good, huh?"

I frowned and scanned the dark woods all around us. Actually, it wasn't good. It was weird. "I thought you said she was already here?"

Billie shrugged. "I thought that's what she said...but her car isn't here, so—"

I shook my head, thoughts racing. Once again. Something wasn't right. I was missing something. "Annie told you to meet her here?" I repeated stupidly.

Billie nodded slowly, her eyes wide and her voice slow. "Annie told me to meet her here. She said Rory found a tunnel by the willow tree...Phoenix, what is it? You're freaking me out..."

I looked at her sharply. "Rory and Annie aren't friends."

Billie hesitated, her brow furrowed. She folded her lips together, her eyes fearful. "No...they aren't."

"Why would Rory and Annie be—"

Billie grabbed me to her, yanking me halfway out of my seat. My hip slammed against the middle console, and my head bumped against the roof. Billie's fingers fumbled behind her for the car door locks. She hugged me tight around the neck and pointed wildly at the passenger window. "*I saw it.* Eyes. *There were eyes.* Glowing outside the window. Like, *right outside.*"

I shoved her arm off me and pressed the blowtorch in her hands. "Here. Burn anything that comes close."

I grabbed the machete, fastening the sheath around my waist. I scanned the grassy hill. Maybe it scurried underneath the car? They were supposed to be fast. And they burrowed.

My heart slammed hard against my chest. I struggled to steady my breathing. I licked my lips and spoke with words thick on my dry tongue. "Back up."

Billie stared at me with wide, wild eyes. "Excuse me?"

I nodded and swallowed the lump in my throat. "Just, trust me. Back the car up."

Billie gave a shaky nod. Then she shifted the car into reverse and slammed on the gas. The car roared backwards. The headlights burnt white light into the cold, dark grass.

And the hole.

There was a hole, freshly dug, where the car had been parked.

Billie slammed on the brakes and shifted the car back into park. Both of our heads jerked with whiplash, our eyes on the hole.

"*Oh, my God...*" Billie hissed with shallow breath. "What in the—"

"It's a ghoul tunnel. They dig. They have claws, and they dig..." I looked at Billie. "Are you sure you want to do this? Because now is the time to back out. Last chance."

Billie shook her head. She took a breath. "I'm good."

I nodded and reached down to my pocket and pulled out the phone Cole had given me. I found Phin's number and sent her, Cole, and Logan a mass text. Then switched the phone to silent and tucked it back inside the oversized pocket. It felt like a rock against my calf.

I glanced over at Billie. She was eying the blowtorch uneasily. I smiled slightly. "You'll be fine."

Billie tried to smile. "I think I'd rather the machete. Have you seen me swing a softball bat?"

"Yes, I know. All-star athlete. But fire is safer. Trust me."

Billie tugged a charm out from underneath her hoodie and pulled it off her head. She held it up for me to see in the radio light. "Then you wear this."

I scoffed in confused surprise. I inclined my head. "Why? What is it?"

Billie eyed me anxiously. "You're going to think it's stupid..."

Kind of. We didn't have time for this.

Billie inhaled deeply, her nostrils flaring. "It's a good luck charm. I've worn it every tryout, every game. It never fails. I'll take the blowtorch if you take this."

I studied her for a moment. She was serious. I nodded slowly. This situation was dangerous enough. I wasn't about to force her to go out there with a weapon she wasn't comfortable with.

"All right." I undid the sheath from my waist and passed her the blade. "Here. You take the machete."

A ghost of a smile twitched at Billie's lips. "Thank you."

She pressed the blowtorch in my hands and slipped her charm back over her head. Meanwhile, I dug into the depths of my backpack, tucking lighters into all the random pockets of my baggy pants. I passed her one. At least she took the lighter. Then I passed her the bottle of skunk cabbage. "Drink this. Just a mouthful."

She took a gulp. I snickered at her face. Disgusted and gagging, she shoved it back into my hands. I tossed the drink back quickly, my teeth grinding on the bitter, metallic taste. I struggled to keep my tongue inside my mouth. I wanted to gag. But I didn't. I chucked the vial back into the bag. Then I slapped a tiny flashlight into her hand, slipping one into my overcrowded, oversized leg pocket. I passed Billie a knife and took one for myself.

Billie tilted her head curiously as she opened the pocketknife, watching the blade dangle. She cocked an eyebrow at me. "Silver?"

I made a face. "Cliche?"

"I love a good cliche. But no. I just know my metals." Billie chuckled as she pocketed it. "I thought we fought them with fire and head chopping?"

I shrugged. "Just in case. Like I said, these ghouls aren't natural —in a manner of speaking. And silver doesn't usually hurt ghouls...but it burns most things."

Billie smirked darkly. "Just in case. Gotcha."

I reached in the bag for one last thing. A bottle of lighter fluid.

All equipped for supernatural warfare, our eyes shifted toward the hole, illuminated by the bright headlights. Then I jutted my chin toward the ignition, and Billie shut the car off, cutting the lights, submerging the woods in total darkness.

"All right..." I cleared my throat again and continued, my voice low, "First thing—I'm going to light a ring of fire around that tunnel...so the ghoul shouldn't be able to get back out..."

Billie snorted. "A ring of fire, huh? Well, I like the song—why not the battle plan?"

I couldn't find a smile. All I could think about was how risky this was...like Cole had said (too many times) these ghouls didn't behave like other ghouls—so who's to say they had the same weaknesses. I nibbled on my lower lip.

Billie slapped a hand to my shoulder.

I flinched.

"Hey..." Billie squeezed my shoulder and forced me to meet her gaze. "We can do this."

I scoffed. "You have that much faith in me?"

"Not at all." A smirk twitched in the corner of her mouth. She yanked her charm up out of her hoodie again. "I have faith in this."

I burst out laughing and it felt good. Billie smiled. "We got this, Birdie."

I nodded and rolled my shoulders. "You're handling all of this monster stuff remarkably well."

Billie snorted. "What other choice do I have?"

My eyes moved past the dark tunnel toward the shadow of the

willow tree. The branches swayed solemnly in the darkness. It wasn't too far. "Okay—I'll light the ring, and then we'll head for the willow tree. That's where Annie said it was, huh?"

Billie gave a silent nod.

"Okay. Well, they know we're here. There's at least four. Anything comes at you, swing for the head. Got it?"

Billie took a gulping breath and nodded again.

We opened our doors and shut them quickly, cutting the car light and slipping into the dark accented by the slivers of moonlight streaming down in between the branches overhead. Cold and damp seeped through my Converse as I hurried for the tunnel.

"Keep watch," I breathed.

Billie moved to my back, following me as I shifted around the mounds of fresh dirt.

I finished pouring the lighter fluid and stopped as though I meant to fish out a lighter. But I didn't. I pointed my finger at the circle and flames shot from my fingertip. In an instant, magical fire ran around the tunnel in a brilliant, bright ring. Billie and I jumped back from the flames. Startled, she stumbled several feet away and stood for a moment, transfixed by the fire that roared high like a wall around the tunnel. Then she looked at me, her eyes wide in the light of the flames. "How—How is that—"

"Gasoline." I grabbed her roughly by the shoulder and tugged her toward the willow tree. "Come on. Eyes wide, head on a swivel. Remember what it was like when the thing jumped on Rory?"

Billie let out a little gasp as she nodded. Then she elbowed me off her and walked on her own. We hurried for the tree with a steady, synced rhythm.

The blowtorch in one hand, I fumbled in my pockets for the flashlight. I clicked it on and aimed it beneath the drooping branches at the base of the tree as we approached.

Nothing.

We moved swiftly, silently, in a wide circle just on the outskirts of the branches to the opposite side. There was a gap in the branches at the back of the tree, the leaves and limbs parting like an archway. I shined the flashlight at the base.

At first, I didn't see it.

Then I did.

Instinctively, I stepped forward, passing beneath the overhanging branches. There was a small hole at the bottom of the tree, like the one Alice fell through into Wonderland.

Billie pushed forward and grabbed my wrist. Hard. Her grip like a vise, she lifted my hand up so the flashlight shined on the trunk of the tree. Her hand shook as it crushed mine. The trunk of the tree curved slightly, splitting from the straight base into one thick branch jutting to the left like an arm.

My stomach heaved.

There *was* an arm.

And a leg.

And a mangled body, ripped and shredded, bones hanging by thin tendons, dangling over the side of the willow tree.

# STAY TOGETHER FOR THE KIDS

nnie Collingwood.

She was tattered and torn, tossed over the tree as though an animal had left her there for later.

Billie yanked my hand hard to the left, shining the flashlight on the grass below the thick branch. It was her head. But it wasn't. Billie gasped and stumbled backward. There was something wrong with Annie's face. Her eyes. Wide and terrified, they seemed to glow in the beam of the flashlight. Fluorescent. I approached her slowly, cautiously in a wide arch, keeping my distance from the small hole—the ghoul tunnel—at the base of the tree.

"*Phoenix, what are you doing*? Don't touch—"

I bent down and poked Annie's cheek with the nozzle of the blowtorch, pushing back her lip. Her teeth...human teeth... retracted, sinking into her gums and disappearing into her skull. My breath caught in my chest. I stood quickly and backed up. I looked over at Billie. "She's a ghoul...was..."

"*What*?!" Billie hissed as she backed up another step and bumped into a willow branch. She jumped and barely contained her scream.

I walked over to the rest of Annie still dangling in the tree. I gritted my teeth and prodded her remains with the blowtorch. Then I went back to the head. Gently, I pushed her head back with my shoe. I winced at the gore and looked back at Billie. "Her head wasn't cut."

"*What*?" Billie snapped again, her impatience and panic sharpening her voice.

"It was chewed off."

Billie heaved, grabbing her stomach. She doubled over and gagged into the willow branches.

I shook my head. "She was killed by ghouls."

Billie straightened as she gasped and wiped her mouth on her sleeve. "Oh...my God."

I glanced at the tunnel at the base of the tree and back at Billie, swinging the flashlight beam between both. "I'm taking you back to the car."

Billie hesitated but shook her head. She stepped toward the tunnel. "No. Sidney could be down there. I'm not leaving. Stop wasting time."

I exhaled deeply through clenched teeth. I'd have to hex her. There was no way I was going to take her down there. It'd been a mistake to let her leave the car. I'd screwed up with Rory. I was *not* going to screw up again.

"Billie, I'm not kidding. I'll knock you out and drag your butt back to the car if I have to, but you're not going down there. And you arguing with me is wasting time that Sidney and Agatha and all the other kids do not have. I can't focus on saving them when I'm—"

Billie groaned. "Fine!" She yanked out the machete and thrust it into my hands. She took the sheath and strapped it roughly around my waist. Then she stomped back underneath the willow branches toward the car, with me hurrying after her. I clipped the blowtorch to my belt loop and gripped the machete, eying the darkened shadows and pools of moonlight as we walked.

The fire still burned around the tunnel by the car. Billie eyed it uneasily. If she was freaked out about the lifespan or the height of the flames, she didn't say anything. When we reached the car, she yanked her door open and leaned on it as she turned to me. "So, what? I stay here?"

"No. You drive to the motel. Go to room eight. There'll be a guy there, possibly my sister and another guy. You tell them what happened."

Billie frowned. Her eyes flickered between me and the willow tree. "I can't just drive off and leave you here."

"You aren't leaving. You're going to get backup." I gave her the most reassuring smile I could and guided her into the car with my free hand.

She sighed with a sad shake of her head. Reluctantly, she snatched her buckle and clicked the seatbelt in place. She looked up at me, her bright-green eyes shining with hurt.

I nodded toward the wheel. "This is how you help. Go. Quickly."

Billie jutted her lower jaw to the side as she seemed to consider this. She wanted to argue some more. But she didn't. Instead, she reached down the front of her hoodie and yanked her charm off her neck. She held it out for me. "Take this."

"Sure." I scoffed, torn between relief and amusement. I slipped the charm over my head and held out my hand for my backpack.

Billie grabbed it from the passenger seat and tossed it out the door. I slung it over my back and gave her a little salute. Then I shut her door. She revved the engine to life and pulled onto the gravel drive. I watched for a moment as the taillights disappeared into the trees.

The quiet and the cold and the dark pressed down on me from all sides. The ring of fire, a handful of yards away, felt like my only company. I was alone. With whatever ghouls that lurked within the trees. Flashlight in one hand, blade in the other, I held the machete low at my side and headed back toward the willow tree. My ears prickled, alert for any sound distinct from the soft murmur of the flames or the creak of the branches in the cold.

I didn't know what I was heading toward, but I wasn't wasting any more time. I was going to figure this out now. Billie was off to the motel. I wouldn't have to worry about her. Cole would keep her with him until Logan showed up.

I ducked beneath the willow branch archway. The flashlight beam bobbed between head, body, tree, and hole. Where were all the ghouls? And *who* were they?

Annie Collingwood. A ghoul. So were the other girls ghouls, too? But what were the chances of four baby ghouls getting dumped at some girls' home? And that didn't explain the missing children. Or the *centuries* of missing children. Annie only explained Drew and Nathan. Maybe Lizzie...but barely. I started toward the hole. Nothing made sense. And if the boys were here, they'd say that meant something wasn't true.

I grimaced. Great. Now I was saying it, too.

I stood above the hole and shined the light down into the depths. I'd have to crawl inside. It seemed to go down. I scowled and sheathed the machete. Then I tossed the flashlight down the hole.

The flashlight beam dropped with a light thud onto a dirt floor. It was no Wonderland rabbit hole. It was just a few feet deep. Maybe six...but it was a ghoul tunnel, that was for certain. I dropped to my butt and slipped inside. My feet hit the ground, hard. I winced slightly at the impact and squinted through the dim.

The tunnel stretched forward, beneath the bottom of the willow tree. But the flashlight beam at my feet barely lit a yard or so ahead. Not enough.

Time for magic. I cupped my hands...

...and nothing happened.

I titled my head, my mouth parted and jaw jutted to the side. Uhm...excuse me?

I flexed my fingers and strained every muscle in my hands.

Nothing.

No ball of light to guide my way through the tunnel.

No warmth beneath my skin.

No magic.

Nothing.

I scrunched up my face and tried to pool my magic in my palms.

Nothing.

My heart began to pound loudly in my ears. My chest bounced up and down with my panicked breaths. *What was wrong with me?* It was like I couldn't reach it. Couldn't find it. My magic was gone.

Eyes wide, heart stricken, I snatched up the flashlight and held it out with a shaky hand. In all my life—the demon battle, the torture in the old, abandoned church, never—*never* had I ever felt fear as I did now.

It paralyzed me.

Powerless. Alone.

I was on my own in a way I'd never been before.

But I had to keep going.

Magic or no, I couldn't pause for a mental breakdown now.

I stuck the flashlight in my mouth and gripped it in my teeth. My hand went for the machete...but the tunnel wasn't wide enough. My fingers fumbled to the other side of me and found the blowtorch. I unhooked it and held it up, finger on the trigger. I was ready. Taking the flashlight from my mouth, I pointed it straight ahead down the dirt tunnel. I licked my lips and folded them tight together.

I could do this.

I was a hunter.

But—I was also a witch...and what the hex had happened to my magic?

I scowled at my impotence. It had to be the ghoul tunnel.

Maybe it was cursed in some way...that had to be it. A kind of defense mechanism. And as soon as I got out of here, I'd find my magic again. Right? Maybe? Whatever. I'd figure it out later.

I walked on down the tunnel, eyes squinted, searching the dark ahead, ears prickled for any sound. Every step, I was sure something would skitter out from the depths and rip me apart. Every movement, my muscles tensed, ready for pain. Teeth. Blood. But nothing came. Something wasn't right. The anticipation of terror was almost as horrible as the real thing. It was torturous.

And the tunnel was monotonous. It just went on and on...

Until it went down.

And I wasn't ready.

My foot stepped into nothingness, and I pitched forward and fell. Down, down the ghoul hole. My head smashed into the side of the tunnel. Loose dirt filled my nose, then I bounced back and landed hard on my feet. The impact rattled my joints and sent shockwaves through my bones. I gritted my teeth to quiet my cry of pain and only whimpered. I plugged each nostril and blew hard in turn, ridding my nose of the dirt. I snatched up the flashlight and waved the beam in front of me and continued on. For what felt like a mile or two. Then the tunnel sloped upwards and stopped at a dead end. I looked up and saw stars. Another ghoul hole.

I clicked off the flashlight and hooked the blowtorch to my pants. Then I climbed out.

And I still couldn't feel my magic. My heart dropped into my stomach. Whatever. I'd figure it out later. I needed to focus. Where was I? I blinked through the blue-black moonlight as I struggled to get my bearings.

I was in a ditch beside a backroad. The mouth of the tunnel was hidden within the tall grass that grew wild along the roadside. I turned around searching for a landmark.

The mailbox.

I was only feet away from the Wollstonecrafts' obnoxious mailbox.

I pulled out my phone and sent Billie a text. Then I tucked it back into my pocket and slipped through the shadows toward the cover of the nearest tree to survey the house. It was dark and quiet. Like everyone inside was asleep...or gone. There was no vehicle at the end of the driveway...but did they even *use* a vehicle?

There was a ghoul tunnel...that led from the funeral home to the Wollstonecrafts' house.

That was pretty hard evidence against them...but something still felt off. And Annie Collingwood was a ghoul...it's not like the Wollstonecrafts turned her...ghouls weren't made like vampires or werewolves. They were born. So, how could the Wollstonecrafts be connected to Annie Collingwood? And if Victor was a ghoul... then wouldn't the rest of the Godwins be ghouls? Unless...he was adopted? Like Sidney and Billie and Agatha? Wasn't that what Keirian had said? The Godwins tended to collect the kids from the Gossamer Home? So maybe it wasn't Victor? Maybe it was his wife?

I slapped the dark fallen tendrils off my forehead as I tried to think. My head hurt. It was like Logan had said—too many maybes to make the theory work. What did I *know*?

I knew that Annie Collingwood was a ghoul—killed by other ghouls.

I knew that she told Billie to meet her there because of something Rory Meeks had said about a tunnel.

And I knew that the ghoul tunnel literally led straight to the Wollstonecrafts' house.

That meant they were connected in some way. And that had to be my next move. Follow the clues.

I inhaled a deep breath of courage and slipped silently through the tall, overgrown switchgrass to the back of the house. I tried not to remember what had happened the last time I'd crept along the outside of a house. Back in Nile, Logan and I had gotten ambushed by a demon. Not a good night.

I bit my bottom lip. Hard. I didn't have time for paranoia. My heart slammed against my chest, loud in my ears. As I moved toward the back of the property, I could see a small, makeshift back porch with a handful of steps beside an awning window. I crouched down low to peer into the foggy glass. It was too grimy to see through. I bent down toward the window and pulled out my pocketknife. I fiddled with it in the side, sticking it in the crevice and wiggling it around. It took a minute. I hadn't had much practice with lock picking. But I did it. The latch popped open. I stuck the knife in the screws of the metal latch, working those for another minute. Finally, the hardware dropped to the ground.

I glanced around the tall grass, blue in the moonlight, swaying in the cold, November wind. My eyes moved across the trees just yards from me, like a black curtain in the dark. Still no ghouls. Where had they all gone? Home? I dug the flashlight out of my pocket, clicked it on and swung the beam through the open window, around the room as I peered down into the basement. No glowing eyes. No hunched shadows. No stubby jaws or sickle claws. I stuck my knife in my teeth, struggled through the small opening in the awning window, and dropped inside. I pocketed the knife and unsheathed the machete, holding it out in front of me in one hand while I gripped the flashlight in the palm of the other.

The basement was empty.

No ghouls. No caged kids. Just an ordinary basement...well, if you count stacks and stacks of banker boxes bursting at the seams and random junk stuffed everywhere 'ordinary.'

And it smelled. Like garbage.

As I moved through the basement toward the stairs leading up to the main floor of the house, I remembered Cole's vision. Icarus had said they couldn't be trusted...but in the vision, I'd seen Billie at the Wollstonecrafts' house...and now I was there. The two little girls had tied her up. And an old woman—a ghoul—had come to gnaw on her face. Or was that a different vision? I couldn't remember. The scenes were all blurring together. Was I walking into one of them now? Would I run into the old woman—and the girls... but I didn't want to think about them. Beheading an old lady seemed more palatable than severing the heads of two little girls. Ghoul or not. And how could I be sure they were ghouls? The only tell was their retractable teeth...and there's no way I'd get close enough to give them a dental exam. My stomach lurched as I weaved my way through the mess and headed for the staircase. As I neared the bottom stair, I clicked off the flashlight. I squinted, readjusting to the darkened space, the moonlight pooling over the outskirts of the basement.

My foot on the first step, I flinched.

The stairs creaked.

Of course they did.

I bit my lip as a trickle of fear slid down my spine and rushed down the lengths of my arms. I held my breath and ascended as slowly as possible. I gripped the grimy railing with gritted teeth. Ew.

At the top of the staircase, I hesitated. Where was I in relation to the front door? Nightlight slipped through the slated boards over the windows, highlighting the kitchen in black and blue. I maneuvered through the scattered chairs and filthy table and over-flowing bags of trash. Then I stopped short in the archway leading into the living room.

It was just like in Cole's vision.

The lamp and the walls and the wood floor and the junk. Looking at it now, it reminded me of when Mama would take us on a last-minute trip to Hampton Beach in the summertime. It was always a mad rush to pack, leaving a mess for when we got back home. Did they leave? Why would they leave? I pulled out the flashlight and clicked it on again. I shined the beam around the furniture, muscles taut and ready to jump at the first sight of glowing eyes. But there was nothing. No kids. No old lady. No ghouls.

I moved through the house, up a second staircase, down a hall. I peeked into the first bedroom. It was a little girl's room. I moved the flashlight around the room. It was an explosion of books and clothes, but no creature scurrying among the mess. I tried the second bedroom. It was the same as the first, but instead of books, there were Barbie dolls strewn about the floor and propped up in various poses in a makeshift dollhouse constructed from old cardboard boxes. I almost smiled. It looked like the time Fawn had hoarded all the Christmas boxes and made a fort in the living room. I inhaled sharply at the memory and hurried from the room. The next bedroom was another child's bedroom, but this one was dramatically different from the other two. Different from the entire house.

It was perfectly in order. Clean. Not one thing was out of place or untidy. The bed was made with care, and the books and stuffed animals were put away neatly on the bookshelf. I took a small step inside the room. Then another. I stopped beside the bedside table. Before I could stop myself, I clicked on the little lamp. I felt silly poking through the bedroom. Like Phin sitting in Drew Graham's bedroom, leafing through her diary. Pointless. But, despite myself, my eyes shifted around the room.

A smiled eased onto my face at the sight of the little stuffed bunny, propped up sweetly on the bed, with a blankie folded neatly underneath it. Like the bunny and blanket were waiting together for their little girl to come home. I looked back at the nightstand. There was a picture of her parents, zoomed in close on their smiling faces, in a homemade popsicle stick frame, propped up against the lamp. Phin would say it meant she loved her parents. The only other thing on the bedside table was a book. I sighed begrudgingly as though Phin were in my ear ordering me to go through the little girl's things. I picked up the book. There was a thick film of dust coating the cover. I smeared it off with my thumb. *Ella Enchanted.*

My heart tightened uncomfortably, and my eyes burned. Phin and I loved that one. Our copy was tattered, dog-eared, and falling apart. But, aside from the dust, this one was new. She couldn't have read through it more than once. If that. I flipped through the pages. Dust puffed out into the air. The bookmark slipped out, but I caught it just in time to slide it back into place between the pages. She'd stopped at chapter thirteen. Ella had just run away from her stepsisters.

My eyes shifted around the room.

The little girl hadn't been here in weeks.

There's no way she could've stopped at that part. She would've taken the book with her. Unless, maybe, she wasn't allowed to? Or she didn't know she wouldn't be back? There hadn't been a third girl in Cole's vision. But clearly, the Wollstonecrafts had three girls. Weird.

With almost reverent respect, I moved to put the book back on the nightstand but stopped. I went toward the bed instead, and I propped the book up on the bunny's lap, nestling it sweetly between its little arms. Then I switched off the lamp. With one final glance around the room, I backed out into the hall and headed down the stairs.

I made my way back into the living room and frowned, a mixture of confusion and impatience itched underneath my skin. I was ready to finish this. Where were the freaks?

The flashlight beam caught on a picture frame on the mantel. I hesitated. Without thinking, nearly forgetting where I was and what Cole's vision had foretold, I moved across the room to the fireplace and set the flashlight up on the shelf. I picked up the photograph. I'd seen it before. It was the same one I'd taken from Justine's house. The same one in my backpack. Victor Wollstonecraft, his wife, and Justine Kilpatrick. And three little girls. I squinted close at the girls.

I recognized the one from the road...and the second one I'd seen in Cole's vision...the third. There she was...my heart rose with my breath, both caught in my throat. For the first time, I realized—I knew her, too. But I didn't. It was that itchy kind of recognition. The kind where you *know* something but can't remember *why* you know it. It's familiar, but you can't place it. *Where had I seen her before?*

My ears prickled.

Something skittered in the silence of the house.

There was a soft scurrying sound at my back.

I spun fast on my heel, machete ready.

But there was nothing there.

Eyes straight ahead, I tossed the picture to the ground and felt behind me for the flashlight. Fingers closed tight around it, I shined the light all over. Nothing. But I'd heard it.

The phone in my pocket vibrated. I ignored the rumble as I moved toward the archway. It vibrated again. Then there was a low chitter from the depths of the darkened hall ahead of me. Then I saw the glint of the eyes in the shadow as I swept the flashlight over it. And the thing dropped, collapsing like a corpse to the ground. Then it scurried across the floor on its hands and knees. Hyena teeth bared and hissing sounds that made my blood curdle, it scrambled toward me like a cockroach.

I sliced and hacked.

It lunged forward, tackling me like a lion. Gnarled hands grabbed me, sickle claws sliced me. The weight of it slammed me into the couch. Images of Drew's blood-soaked cushions flashed in my mind. The thing clenched its stubby teeth in a grotesque, gruesome grin that pulled and stretched its skin. But I recognized the black bob of shiny hair. It was Tiffany Crane.

But she didn't look human.

She wasn't.

She hissed; her thick, long tongue uncurled to lick the blood that trickled from my nose. I flinched away in disgust. I couldn't swing the blade at her neck. She knew it, too. Tiffany let out a low, barking kind of laugh. I struggled to gain a vantage point, then I gripped the machete tight and slammed my fist into her skull, cracking her hard with the machete handle. It didn't hurt her— just surprised her. But it was enough.

I pooled all my strength and shoved her off me, pushed her back, and swung. And I connected. With her shoulder. Her arm dropped to the floor, followed by a rush of blood. She hissed and gnashed her teeth. She swiped at me with her remaining arm. I hacked and chopped at it. And connected with the forearm, which dropped to the ground, spilling blood all over my pants as she swung the stump at me. She lunged forward. I hardly held her back with my free hand. She was going to bite my face off.

The head.

I had to take her head.

I struggled against the weight of her, the strength of her, barely keeping her back. She chomped her teeth, snapping like a rabid wolf, breath hot and rancid, inches from my cheek as I twisted my face away.

I couldn't swing the machete. I couldn't hold her off. I dropped the blade and grabbed her neck. With both hands I shoved her back again, but her torso kept lunging, her teeth kept gnashing.

Then, out of the corner of my eye, I saw something shine.

There was a whistle and a thud.

I blinked.

The machete split Tiffany's face in half.

# GET THE PARTY STARTED

Tiffany's body sagged, and I shoved her away from me. She dropped to the ground, blood oozing onto the floor from the stubs of her limbs and the back of her head. Billie stood feet from me, staring down at Tiffany in shock. The blade was still lodged in Tiffany's skull, but her head wasn't severed, and I wasn't taking any chances. I grabbed the handle of the machete and yanked it back. It came free with a squelching sound and another gush of blood. Then I swung and chopped Tiffany's head off.

Billie heaved and backed up several steps. She bent over the back of the armchair and retched over the side.

I winced at the splash of vomit on the floor, my eyes still on Tiffany. My breathing was ragged. My body ached all over. But we weren't done. We still had work to do. Kids to save. I glanced at Billie, who straightened and wiped the corners of her mouth with the back of her hand.

She made her way over to me. "How could I not have known? They...they were my friends. We grew up together. I don't get it." She stared at me wide-eyed, her face pale. "Annie and Tiffany? *Both of them?*"

I grimaced and shrugged. "There was no way to know...unless they invited you to dinner, and you pulled back their lips and checked their teeth."

Billie blinked back tears as they leaked down her cheeks. "I thought we might find him. Sidney. But...if they...these *things* took him...I doubt he's still alive, huh?"

I grabbed Billie's shoulder and squeezed hard. "Hey. They kept Justine alive for weeks. There's no reason to think they won't keep him just as long."

Billie took a shaky breath and nodded furiously. "Okay."

"Okay. Now we need to clear the rest of the rooms; Where is Cole—"

"Phoenix..." Billie hesitated. "Didn't you get my texts?"

I scoffed. "Sorry, Billie, I was a little busy—"

Billie rolled her eyes as she gripped my arm and gave me a shake. "No one was at the motel. Room eight was empty."

It was a blur, moving from the Wollstonecrafts' house to the car. I didn't remember much of it. It was robotic. Clear the house. Check for victims. (No victims.) Hunt for ghouls. (No ghouls.) Get out. Then—find Cole. Logan. Phin.

Luckily, the rest of the Wollstonecraft house was empty. I wouldn't have been able to handle anything more. My mind was overwhelmed with uncertainty. Fear. Did the ghouls know we were hunting them? Cole should've been in the motel room. What if a ghoul had gotten to him? Logan and Phin should've been in the motel room. What if that hunter, Frankie, had hacked off Phin's head? Cole's vision flashed behind my eyes. Seraphina's severed head slipping off her neck. Logan wouldn't let that happen. *I* wouldn't let that happen.

Bile bubbled up. It pooled hot and sour in my throat. I forced it down with a wet cough. Fingers shaking, I fumbled the buttons on the phone. Before I could manage to call the motel room, I noticed the voicemail alert. It was old. By a few hours. Probably missed it when Billie and I were at the cemetery.

I swallowed and gritted my teeth as I brought the phone up to my ear. The message was garbled and staticy. The reception that deep in the mountains of Saranac Lake was awful.

"Nix. Don't move. Frankie said…We're headed back now. The ghouls…sixteen years…stopped when Cole found their tunnel… Stay…motel."

I checked the radio clock. They should've been back an hour ago.

I called the motel room.

My heart lodged in my throat.

No one answered.

I tried Cole's phone. Nothing. I tried Phin. Then Logan. No one answered. Not on the second, or third calls, either.

I glanced at the clock again. It was nearly two in the morning. An overwhelming feeling of helplessness washed over me. Goose bumps pricked up and down my arms. I'd screwed everything up. Nothing I'd done had gone right. I'd only made everything worse. Every single decision I'd made had been the wrong one. And now, not only was *everyone* missing. But so was my magic. Ever since I'd gone down that ghoul hole. I couldn't reach it. And without my magic, I was as good as lost, too.

"Billie," I breathed as I blinked back tears. "Drive faster."

And she did.

We got to the motel in record time.

I hopped out before Billie could park the car. "Wait here!" I shouted over my shoulder as I slammed the door.

I ran down the shadowy hall to our room. The light glowed in the window. The door was ajar. Instinctively, I reached for my wand sticking out of my topknot, but then I dropped my hand back to my side. My heart throbbed with a dull ache. I couldn't rely on my magic. I gritted my teeth and unsheathed the machete. I prodded the door with my foot.

It swung open.

It was empty.

I moved silently across the room, eyes on the bathroom in the corner as I drew nearer. I peeked inside. Empty. I crossed the dingy, tile floor and slapped aside the shower curtain. No one was there.

Heart hammering loud in my head, I backed out of the bathroom and surveyed the room. Nothing was disturbed. Not like Justine's house. No sign of a struggle. I slid the blade back into the sheath. My eyes went to Cole's bed and rested on a crumpled piece of paper chucked in the middle of the tangled mess of covers.

I smoothed it out. It was my note. So, Cole had read it...

I glanced around the room. His backpack was gone. I pulled out the phone to call Logan, but hesitated, my finger rested on the send button. Doubt, sick and sour in my stomach, made me pause. Question myself. What if they were in trouble, and my call got them caught?

They would want me to call.

I closed my eyes, and I pushed it.

Logan's voicemail recording played in my ear.

I shut the phone and slipped it back into my pocket.

Massaging my temples, I tried to think. Okay. Where were they? Not here, obviously. Logan and Phin should've gotten back from Saranac Lake by now. I hadn't seen the van or the truck when—

The truck.

I hurried to Logan's laptop and fired it up. In just a few clicks, I had his GPS software loaded. And there he was. Or at least, the truck was there. I grabbed the notepad and pen and scribbled the coordinates.

When I got to the car, Billie had just gotten out. She shot me an impatient glare. "About time! You scared me half to death! I thought something happened! I was just about to head in after you!"

"Get in." I jumped in the car and started tapping away at the GPS. "There. Drive there."

Billie scowled as she whipped the car out of the parking space and punched it out of the motel parking lot. "And now the plan is?"

"Find my sister and the Sasquatch."

"And then?"

I shook my head as I pressed my fist into my chest. My heart was beating too fast. It was distracting. "Tiffany and Annie were ghouls. So, I'm betting Pamela and Amanda are ghouls, too…"

Billie's eyebrows shot up, her mouth agape as she struggled to process everything. "But there's no way to know for sure unless—"

I nodded with a grimace. "Unless we get up close and personal…" I covered my face with my hands. "It just doesn't make sense."

"What?"

"Ghouls don't act like this. They eat dead people…like corpses from coffins," I added impatiently, cutting off Billie's retort. "And they don't attack people…or kidnap kids…or keep them alive to drain their blood." I sighed low like a growl in my chest. "I'm missing something…and where were the Wollstonecrafts?" I glanced at Billie, my face scrunched-up in confusion. "They weren't in their house, but *Tiffany* was? And the ghoul tunnel leads from the cemetery—where Victor works—*to his house*? How could he *not* be one of them?"

Billie bit her lip. "There's something about Victor I should tell you—"

I waved an impatient hand. "I know, I know. He's your uncle."

Billie glanced at me sharply. "Did Keirian tell you?"

I nodded.

"Well, what he *doesn't* know is the reason my grandmother kicked Victor out of the family."

"Wasn't it because he found Justine and brought shame to the Godwin name or whatever…" My voice trailed off as I remembered the photograph. Cole had said it was a family…

Justine was a victim...Victor found her...where did he meet his wife?

"Heh. No. She kicked him out because he got married. He eloped and married that...*woman*. Grandma never figured out where she came from...she'd always mutter about him finding a 'sewer rat.' And he wasn't the same kid after he met that woman... it was like he'd changed completely overnight."

I rubbed a hand over my eyes. The wife? Was it the wife? Could ghouls marry humans? But then, how do the girls come into it? And what about the decades prior? My head ached. I couldn't think straight.

Billie flipped a blonde braid over her shoulder. "The thing that I don't understand is...if these girls have been ghouls the whole time I've known them—why were they waiting around for sixteen years to start attacking people? And they weren't alive when the other kids went missing, so...?"

I shrugged. "That's what my sister was working on..."

Billie snorted. "Definitely would be helpful to know...I mean, we don't even know what these things want, how many of them there are—"

I groaned. "One step at a time."

"Right. Step one...find the rest of the Scooby gang."

I almost smiled. "Exactly."

We both fell silent, and then Billie murmured softly, "The whole time...I was sure it was Keirian."

I scoffed and looked at her with a smirk. "Did you?"

Billie forced a smile and a one shouldered shrug. "He's just the type. You know?"

Several lights, and multiple turns later, we cut down Adelaide. We exchanged a glance. Billie checked the GPS, and then her eyes slid back to the road. "I think we're heading—"

I nodded grimly. "Toward the Gossamer House."

Billie bit her lip. "Why would your sister be there?"

I shook my head. Instead of feeling relieved to be closing in on their location, fear twisted in my stomach. We neared the Wollstonecrafts' house, and I couldn't help but stare. My eyes flickered to the general location of the ghoul hole, then shifted up toward the house. Still no cars in the driveway. Still dark.

After a moment, the headlights of Billie's car illuminated a long row of vehicles pulled over on the left side of the road.

Car after car after car. Then the trees thinned making way for the twisting gravel drive and the old, white colonial farmhouse. Every window glowed with light. I checked the clock. There were dozens of vehicles parked in the driveway, on the road, and some even dared to pull up onto the grass. I couldn't find Logan's truck. Or the van. But then as Billie drove past the house to make a U-turn in the road, I saw the truck—just a shadow in the darkness in the distance.

"There." I touched Billie's shoulder. "Keep going."

Billie didn't make the turn. She straightened out and then pulled over to the truck. She eyed it apprehensively. "I don't think anyone's inside."

I nodded and threw open the door. "Hang on."

"Wait, Phoenix!"

I didn't.

I hurried around to the passenger side. It was locked. Instinctively, I held my hand to the handle. Then an ache throbbed in my heart. My magic. I'd forgotten. I tightened my jaw as my eyes blurred. I couldn't think about it. I cleared my throat and pressed my nose against the glass. My fingers fumbled in my pocket for the flashlight. I clicked on the beam and held it against the window, sliding it along the length of it.

Logan's rucksack was open in the middle of the front seat. Seraphina's backpack was missing. I jogged back to the car.

Billie regarded me with raised eyebrows as I slipped inside the seat. "Well?"

"They've gotta be inside the house."

Billie nodded and whipped the car back around, heading for

the house. She turned down the driveway and drove all the way up and over onto the lawn. The lights from the house spilled onto the dark grass, giving off a cozy, homy glow in the night. And as Billie switched off the car, I could feel the low boom of bass from the music that blared inside the house. But there was something else. I grabbed my bag and hopped outside. My eyes lingered over the dark back lawn. The staggered, sentinel trees loomed over like giants guarding the witching well hidden in the shadows. The cold air pressed against me. I could feel the hum of the well. The vibration of the traces of magic left like a taint in the air. Seraphina would've felt it, too. Would they have gone to the well? Or were they headed inside for Annie and Tiffany? What had the witch hunter told them? How did they know to come here?

"Hey!"

I turned sharply to stare at Billie. She leaned over the top of the car, her face just barely visible. "Are we still on step one?"

I nodded curtly and headed around the car to meet her. I checked the machete sheath and then unhooked the blowtorch from my belt and pressed it into Billie's hands. "Okay. Judging by the number of kids here—"

Billie scoffed. "Like, the entire junior class?"

"—we don't have to worry about the ghouls lashing out. Just make sure you don't go off alone...or go off *with* any of them. Supposedly, they can shapeshift..."

Billie muttered under her breath as she unzipped her purse and slipped the blowtorch inside. Then she looped her arm through mine, and I let her lead the way as we walked along the stone pathway toward the front door of the Gossamer House.

There were kids everywhere, broken off into different groups all over the yard, some huddled around a bonfire, some taking turns with firecrackers, and some dragging each other in sleds across the cold grass.

Billie eyed the kids uneasily as we walked. "So, if they can shapeshift—they could look like anybody?"

I winced. "Right." And literally, anybody.

"So, how—"

We reached the front door, and I leaned forward and rang the bell. "We'll just have to improvise."

"Great," Billie muttered through clenched teeth.

I snickered and squeezed her close just as the door opened.

We both stiffened.

Amanda and Pamela grinned at the sight of us.

I stared at their teeth.

Billie barely stifled a gasp. I gripped her arm hard in warning.

They completely ignored me and went for Billie. Amanda slung an arm around her. Pamela wedged herself in between us, forcing our arms apart. Pamela's ponytail smacked me in the face. The two of them practically carried Billie inside the house and across the threshold. "You said you weren't coming!"

"Thank God you came!" Pamela groaned. Then she blew her bangs. "This party was dead without you, Wilhelmina!"

Amanda snickered. "Stuart's actually calling it a *search* party. Like, in Sidney's honor."

Pamela giggled as her ponytail swayed. "It's so tacky, it's brilliant."

Amanda nodded. "We were actually just heading out."

I eyed them coolly, my fingers rested on the hilt of the machete in the sheath. "Is that so? Where to?"

"Stuart knows how to gather the masses, but he doesn't know anything about catering." Pamela rolled her eyes, a sly smirk in the corner of her over-lined lips.

Amanda nodded. "We're heading out for, like—what'd you say, Pamela?"

"Like, *seven*." Pamela giggled.

Amanda grinned. "Seven pizzas. We just barely got our order in. They stop taking them at three."

Pamela put a hand on Billie's shoulder. "We'll be right back though, okay?"

"Sure..."

"Have either of you seen Annie? Or Tiffany?" I asked, my eyes on Pamela. If she knew what happened to either of them, she was an excellent liar.

Amanda's lip curled in disgust. "No." She scoffed and waved an arm wide at the sitting room stuffed full of kids. "Why don't you start looking?"

"We'll be back, Wilhelmina!" Pamela singsonged. And the two of them left, slamming the door sharply behind them.

Billie tugged me off to the side and pulled back the curtain to watch the two girls walk along the path toward the driveway around the side of the house. "Why did we just let them walk out of here?"

I watched them slip out of view, my jaw tight, torn between finding Phin and Logan and following the girls and finishing this. "Because we need to be sure they are actually ghouls before we start hacking into high school cheerleaders in front of the entire student body."

But I wanted to follow them. It took every nerve of self-control to keep my feet planted and focus on the task at hand: finding Phin and Logan.

Billie let out a nervous chuckle and swiped her hand across her forehead, wiping the blonde wisps out of her face. She tugged on a braid and nodded furiously. "Right."

Before I could think of where to start, a large group of kids, some carrying soda cans, some shoving their hands into snack bags of chips, swarmed us.

One of the girls grabbed Billie's hands and jumped up and down. "Wilhelmiiiinaaa! *You came!*"

Then a guy slung his arm around Billie's shoulders, knocking me in the teeth. I scowled and sidestepped them. He didn't seem to notice. He grinned down at Billie. "Yo, Bill—search party starts in, like...what is it—when is it, Randy?" He glanced back at another kid. Billie's jaw clenched, and her face reddened with her temper.

Her emerald eyes, like slits, slid to stare at him sideways. If she were a snake, she would've bitten him. But because she was Billie, I figured he was dangerously close to a black eye.

A short boy shoved his way forward. "Like, twenty!"

The guy pulled Billie in tighter. "Like, twenty minutes! I'm glad you're here for it. Sid would appreciate it."

Billie's eyes flashed as she untangled herself from the kid. "And where are you all going to look for him?"

"*The Blood Farm*!" The group cheered, holding their cans and chip bags up in salute.

Billie hissed darkly under her breath and grabbed me roughly by the arm. She yanked me away from the group. More and more kids were spilling into the room, like it was New Year's, and they were waiting for the countdown.

Billie and I weaved through the bodies, forced our way down several narrow hallways and into a large living room at the back of the house. Kids were all over the place, some dancing by the stereo, some lounging in the oversized plush couches shouting and tossing popcorn at a Ghostface on the gigantic TV.

Billie pulled me into the corner of the room and took out her phone. She tapped away on the screen and then held it to one ear while she plugged the other with her finger.

"Stuart? Where are you? No—what? *I can't hear you!*" Billie turned her back on me, facing the wall as she struggled to hear her cousin.

My impatience grated on me. We had to find them. Especially if a herd of hooligans was about to go storm the Blood Farm in the dark. But how could I find Logan and Phin in this mess?

I frowned thoughtfully as I watched a girl with a too-tight skirt eye a boy as he entered the room. She bit her lip on a hopeful smile, which vanished as soon as he cut through another doorway and disappeared. She frowned and stuck her gum out with her tongue and blew a bright-pink bubble. I pursed my lips on a smirk and hurried over to her. I touched her arm.

She turned and flashed me a too-friendly smile that slipped into a scowl when she saw who I was: a short, punk girl with chunky red streaks in her hair. Far from her type.

"Hey." I slapped on a cheesy grin, and I schmoozed with so much extra cheesy sarcasm on top, I felt sick. "I'm looking for a friend of mine; I think you've probably seen him. He's not from around here, like, super tall...looks kinda like James Dean? Blonde hair...shwoopy on top and buzzed on the sides? *So hot.*" I gritted my teeth on my grin, struggling not to burst out laughing.

The girl smiled slyly and twirled a strand of dark hair. Then she nodded knowingly. "Sure. He was here...took a girl upstairs."

My face hardened. "Tall, blonde?"

She popped her gum and twisted it into a ball with her tongue. She smacked her lips. "Yup. Tough night, huh?"

"You've no idea."

I glanced back for Billie, but I couldn't see her in the crowd. She wasn't where I'd left her. I scanned the bodies, and then my heart stalled in my chest. I swore I saw Cole. I shoved past shoulders and pushed through cliques to get to the back of the room. I cut in front of the giant TV screen and was met with a chorus of boos and assaulted with popcorn.

But before I could make it to him, someone cut the music and shouted, "Search party...time now! Everybody hit the road!"

There was a mass exodus just like in the lunchroom at the school, and I forced my way through the sea of kids flooding back the way I'd come. Then I saw him—Cole—disappear down the hallway off the side, followed by Seraphina.

I stopped short at the sight of her. Then Seraphina turned, her honey-blonde hair pulled high in a ponytail, fanning about her face as she vanished around the corner after Cole.

I couldn't move. Frozen by a feral, primal kind of fear. The kind of fear that keeps you alive in the face of fatal danger.

Whatever that girl was...she wasn't a witch.

That tall, blonde, beautiful girl wasn't my sister.

## TERRIBLE THINGS

"Phoenix! What are you doing here?"

I flinched as someone grabbed me by the shoulder. I blinked stupidly, stomach sloshing, vision spinning. It was Stuart. With his bobbing, loping gait, he stood back a bit to study me. He cocked his head to the side and gripped my shoulder tight. "Are you okay? You're looking a little green. Here, come with me."

In shock, I allowed him to pull me out of the living room and into the kitchen. He shoved me into one of the bar stools at the granite island and went to the refrigerator. He grabbed a bottle of water and twisted off the cap, chucking it onto the counter, before passing me the bottle. "Drink."

I shook my head and stood from the chair. "No, I can't. I have to—I have to find my friend." Cole. He was with the ghoul wearing Seraphina's face. I swayed slightly as I slid the bottle onto the counter. Stuart hurried around the granite island and held me steady.

"Hey. Dude. No. You need to drink something." One hand on my arm, Stuart snatched the bottle and forced it into my face.

I rolled my eyes and slapped it to the ground. The bottle

bounced and spilled all over the hardwood floor. I glared at Stuart. "I need to find my friend."

Stuart's eyebrows wrinkled his forehead, and he held up his hands in surrender and stepped back. I pushed past him, stalking out of the kitchen and back into the living room. It was empty. Everyone had left for the 'search party' at the Blood Farm. I hurried across the carpet, past the television that screamed loudly in my ears, and turned around the corner down the corridor. It was a crossway from the living room to another hallway running parallel to this one, short and tight with too many doors.

I started shoving them open, one by one, not bothering to close them again. Linen closet. Broom closet. Then a small rec room. As I backed out of the room, I bumped into someone. Hand on the machete hilt, I elbowed them back and spun on my foot.

It was Rory.

I shoved him so hard he stumbled back through the open broom closet and knocked into several mops and brooms before he dropped onto his butt into a bucket. He stared up at me through the mess of handles, wide-eyed and startled, his eyes on the sheath. He smoothed back his hair against the sides of his face.

"Phoenix, what—"

I didn't move to help him up.

Stuart appeared at the end of the hall. "Have you guys seen, Billie? She told me to meet her in the living room..." His voice trailed off as he took in the situation.

I tilted my chin up to look down my nose at Rory. "Did you tell Annie about the hole?"

"What hole?" Rory struggled unsteadily to his feet and brushed off his pants. "Are—are you talking about the old well? That's why I came to find *you*—"

At the opposite end of the hall, Keirian skidded into view. "Guys! Quick! I found—*Oh, my God*!"

Keirian wasn't looking at me.

He was staring at Rory like he was looking at a ghost. Keirian gripped the frame of the archway with one hand and shook a shaky finger at Rory with the other. "You—you—I just *saw* you, Rory. *What*—"

I unsheathed the blade and held it out, low at my side.

Stuart rushed forward then, his hands out. "Woah, woah, Phoenix. What are you—"

"Rory!" Keirian shook his head furiously, his pale face waxen and taut. "Rory. *I just saw Rory.*"

Rory looked from Keirian to me. Our eyes met. His gray eyes glowed. His jaw sunk inward on his delicate face. Then he grinned with teeth sharp and stumpy and too big for his face. He raised his hands, fingers curved into long, thick claws.

He lunged.

But so did I.

I swung the blade up and sliced down with all my strength. Rory's head slipped off his neck and dropped with a thud. His body fell to the floor, crumpled and broken.

Keirian swayed in the archway. "What—*what*!"

Stuart looked from the decapitated head back to me, his face hard and serious.

"That wasn't him. It was a ghoul." I looked at Keirian. "Where's Rory?"

Keirian, eyes wide and round, jutted his thumb to his right, back the way he'd come. I nodded curtly and hurried toward him. Stuart scrambled after me.

Keirian led us into a side room off the hall. It looked like a tiny home office, with an antique, mahogany desk in front of two angled armchairs. There was a closet off to the left, the door opened wide, blocking our view. Keirian ran around the desk and held the closet door even wider, pushing it against the wall as far as it would go.

I followed, trying to remain calm as my heart pounded hard against my chest. Keirian leaned against the door, waving a limp hand at the closet interior. My stomach lurched. Among the winter coats and pantsuits, Rory Meeks was hanging by his wrists, tied to a hook on the closet ceiling. His head lulled to his shoulder, his lanky hair dangling in his face. He was still wearing his leather jacket. His shirt ripped and shredded. His arm mangled just as it had been back in the Blood Farm.

I rushed forward. With one hand, I sawed at the rope with the machete and caught him with the other as his thin frame sagged into me. I held him to my side and backed slowly out of the closet. He moaned slightly. The breath I'd been holding escaped me with a sharp gasp. He was alive. *He was alive.*

The boys sprang into action. Stuart pulled the armchair around, so I could guide Rory into it. Keirian went to shut the office door and snapped the lock.

Rory slumped in the seat, his head lulling to the side once again. I smoothed his hair back from his face. "Rory? Rory...can you hear me?"

His eyelids fluttered.

I sheathed the machete. My hands moved over him, first checking for a pulse—which was so faint I wouldn't have believed it was there if not for the slow rise and fall of his chest.

I winced. He had more bites.

My fingers gently prodded his neck. He had bites all over, some still gooey and oozing. Chunks missing from his shoulder and his other arm. That's why he was so out of it. He'd lost too much blood.

Stuart mumbled something about Billie. He dug into his pocket for his phone and tried to call her. Keirian stood beside me muttering about the Blood Farm witch. I rolled my eyes. "Would you please stop that; Keirian, I'm trying to think!"

*"She's the Blood Farm witch!"* Keirian shrieked at me, his voice high and thin.

I looked at him sharply. "What are you talking about?"

Keirian flapped his arms wide, smacking them against his sides.

"Don't you see where we are?"

I looked around us at the dark wood furnishings and stuffy bookshelves and glanced back at Keirian. Great. He was losing it. "Keirian—"

He grabbed my shoulders and squeezed. *"It's Catherine Godwin."*

My heart slowed, and time stalled.

"Catherine Godwin—foster mom—runs the Gossamer House." Keirian gave me a hard shake. "This is her office!"

Stuart lowered the phone as his eyes shifted around the room. "Wait, Keirian...what are *you* doing in here, man?"

Keirian's arms fell to his sides, and he took a deep breath. He blinked a few times and met me with a steady, hazel gaze. "I was in here looking for files..."

"Files?" I demanded, my impatience and rising panic thinning my voice. *"Keirian, explain faster!"*

"Okay, okay, yeah." Keirian nodded rapidly. He inhaled deeply, his nostrils flaring. He closed his eyes, and then he fixed me with a hard, focused stare. "When I dropped Rory off, he'd said something about Amanda. *Her perfume.* He said that when the thing chomped on his arm, that's all he smelled. That was weird, right? And then when you called and couldn't find him...I started to get a bit freaked out. So, I did some digging. All four of those girls showed up at the Gossamer House at the same time. Same age. All babies. Then I realized Catherine Godwin was the one who brought them in. But from where? Where did she get them? Not a birth mom. Not the government. That led me here. I was looking for proof that Catherine Godwin isn't..."

"Human." I finished.

Keirian nodded. "Yeah."

Stuart held up his hands, his phone still dialing Billie's number. "Woah, woah. Wait a minute, you're trying to tell me my mom's cousin is some kind of—"

"Catherine Godwin probably isn't *actually* Catherine

Godwin. Ghouls can take the form of people they've bitten. That's why Rory wasn't Rory. The ghoul who bit him, turned into him—"

I glanced at Stuart, who was on his phone again. Then I looked at Rory. He was still unconscious, sagging in the seat. "Okay. Here's what we're going to do—"

Stuart shook his head and scowled. His fingers tapped furiously against his phone. "She's not answering!"

"We have to get Rory to the hospital...Stuart—call Heather Meeks and get her here." I slipped my hand into my pocket for her number. Nothing. I'd left it in my other pants. "Keirian, what's the Meekses' house number?"

"Uh..." Keirian pinched his forehead and held out his hand for Stuart's phone.

Stuart scoffed, his eyes wide and lip curled. "What am I supposed to say?"

"Figure it out!" I snapped. "Unless *you* want to drive him there!"

Stuart rolled his eyes as Keirian punched in the number. He snatched his phone and stepped away to make the call, his finger in one ear.

Keirian stared at Rory. "I always knew it'd end up at the Gossamer House. I told you, didn't I?"

I slapped Keirian hard on the shoulder. "Keirian! Enough. You need to get a grip and help me here!"

"Meeks isn't answering!" Stuart shouted over the both of us.

"Okay!" Keirian snapped. "What do we do? *Tell me what to do!*"

"First thing: man-up and stop freaking out, dude!" Stuart snapped back.

Before I could answer Keirian, someone pounded loudly on the door.

The three of us flinched. We looked toward the door. The doorknob rattled loudly against the lock.

"Stuart!" someone shouted, their voice muffled through the wood. "Stuart, are you in here?"

"It's Billie!" Stuart went for the door, but Keirian cut in front of him.

"Wait!" Keirian held him fast. "She could be one of them!"

I shook my head. My fingers closed around the hilt of the machete. "I don't think that's Billie—"

Stuart shoved Keirian hard. "Get off, geek." He grabbed the handle and untwisted the lock. "Hang on, Bill—"

Before Stuart had time to turn the knob, the door burst open with a bang and cracked him hard in the head. He stumbled back and fell over the side of the chair.

In the doorway stood Amanda Thompson, her perfume exuding from her like a poisonous gas. She bent her chin against her chest, her eyes glaring at me. Then her body started to convulse, every major vein in her body raised like thick ropes underneath her skin as her body flexed. My stomach lurched as I realized what was happening. Beside me, Keirian gagged, dry heaving.

And we watched Amanda shed her skin.

She stood there, flaying herself with her fingers. Peeling off layers of skin and hair, ripping and tearing it off her in sheets of meat that flopped ooey and gooey to the ground.

I swayed in the spot as Rory Meeks smiled back at me where Amanda had been.

The ghoul Rory grinned. "You know, Phoenix Grey, you really should do your homework before you go meddling in things you don't understand...lesson number one—if a ghoul has shed its skin, you can't just take its head...you need to burn it...otherwise... well..." The ghoul gestured down at Rory's form. "As long as I'm wearing whittle Rory Meeks, and as long as he's alive, the only way to kill me...is with fire. And *I* heard your freaky pyrokinetic powers have short-circuited...haven't they?" The ghoul chuckled, its teeth gnashing awkwardly in its giant jaws.

I held the machete out like a sword. "Are you sure about that?"

The ghoul inclined its head, smoothing Rory's limp, dark hair against the sides of his face. "Go ahead. Hack my head off...it won't stop me for long. And it's not like you'll kill the real Rory..." The ghoul laughed a low, barking growl.

I shifted my feet closer. Keep it talking. Cut its head off. "Why did you kill Annie?"

The ghoul's eyes glowed feral and bright. "Because she was sloppy. And if she hadn't let her emotions cloud her stupid head, we wouldn't be dealing with hunters trying to ruin our birthday party."

I shrugged with a downturned smirk as though I understood the reasoning. "Annie attacked Nathan and Drew. I guess that is pretty sloppy. Calling attention to your whole centuries-long operation."

The ghoul grinned, its lips curling far back against Rory's narrow face, so he was nothing but stubby, yellow teeth. "Exactly. She needed to be punished."

I needed to rattle her. This wasn't working. I slid my feet forward ever so slightly and tried again. "Where's the Mother?"

The ghoul grinned, its teeth bared. "What do you know about the Mother?"

"I know ghouls have a matriarchal society...I know Catherine Godwin is the Mother Ghoul—"

The ghoul snickered and licked its teeth with a long, fat tongue.

"—but what I haven't figured out yet is *why*."

"Why?" The ghoul belched.

I moved just a bit closer. "Ghouls eat dead people. Not alive people. You're all freaks of your own nature," I spat nastily. "What's *wrong* with you?"

The ghoul's smile faltered, and she sneered at the insult. Amanda bent her head (Rory's head?) forward and lifted her arms, her fingers curved into giant claws.

She was about to lunge.

But so was I.

In one quick movement, I slashed the machete through the air and lobbed off the ghoul's head. Rory's hair fluttered over his blank face as the severed head arched through the air and bounced on the ground.

From behind me, Keirian let out a strangled cry that sounded remarkably like a chicken. On the other side of the chair, Stuart groaned and slowly got on all fours. He peeked around the seat. Then he looked up at me. "What in the—"

"We need to move." I reached for Keirian and tugged him toward Rory, the real Rory, still unconscious in the chair. "You drive Rory to the emergency room. Now."

"But—"

My fingers crushed Keirian's arm. "You drive him there. You wait there with him. You don't leave him!"

Keirian's nostrils flared as he stared down at his buddy. He gave a curt nod. "Okay."

I looked back at Stuart, who struggled to his feet, fingering the gash in his forehead. "Stuart and I will get you to the car." Stuart made a face and my eyes narrowed. "Won't we, Stuart?"

Stuart rolled his eyes and gave a begrudging, bobbing nod. "All right."

Stuart lifted Rory up and over his shoulder like a ragdoll. Rory was so limp, flopping over Stuart's side, it scared me. What if he didn't make it? I gritted my teeth. Can't think about that. I nudged Stuart with my elbow. "Lead the way."

Stuart trudged forward into the hallway, his lanky, loping gait knocked Rory up and down against his back. The house was deserted. All the kids had left for the Blood Farm for Stuart's dumb 'search party'...and any that remained, I was pretty sure—weren't really kids.

At every corner, Stuart stopped and leaned his long neck out to make sure we wouldn't run into anyone. It took a few hallways and doorways before we finally made it to the front door.

Stuart held the door open, and we slipped out into the night. Fortunately, because Keirian had crashed the party early, his car was one of the ones snaking around the driveway. As we hurried across the cold grass, leaves sticking to our shoes, my muscles tensed, ready for an attack from the darkness. I kept remembering the ghouls leaping from the shadows of the Blood Farm and ripping into Rory, dragging Lizzie away. And even as we approached the car, wrenched open the doors, and Stuart dropped Rory unceremoniously into the passenger seat, it wasn't until Keirian's headlights disappeared through the trees and down the road that I felt they were finally going to be safe.

"Now what?" Stuart whispered harshly in the dark, his words clouded around him in the cold November air.

I looked back at the old house. Quiet in the night. Calm, radiating a cozy glow from the wide-open front door and the lights shining in every window as though there weren't ghouls skittering like roaches around the narrow halls. I stared wildly around the woods, the trees looming high above like skeletal giants, branches outstretched like they meant to grab us.

I put a hand to my head and tried to think. What to do? I didn't know what to do. Every choice, everything I'd done—it was all wrong. I kept getting it wrong. Stuart put a gentle hand on my shoulder. I looked up at him, slightly startled. "Hey...you got Rory out. You got Keirian out. Now what?"

"Uhm...Billie. We need to find Billie." I licked my lips and scrunched up my face as I tried to think straight. Then I remembered Cole. Cole was with the ghoul wearing Seraphina's face. But was it Cole? Or was it another ghoul? My stomach lurched. The only way the ghoul could be wearing their skin is if they'd been bitten. "We need to find my friends."

There was a low chitter from the darkness. My fingers tightened around the handle of the machete. Slowly, I turned from the driveway to face the front door. Amanda (no longer in Rory's form) stood hunched over at the top of the cement steps, her eyes shining like an animal in the dark. I raised the machete like a sword. I was ready. Amanda chittered, her oversized jaw vibrating in her thin face. Then she dropped to the ground, crumpled like a fallen corpse. Her arms and legs clawed furiously across the lawn as she scurried to meet me like a human spider.

I sliced and hacked.

She jumped to her feet. Her gnarled hands grabbed me. The force of impact slammed me into the hood of the nearest car. She clawed at my arms, swiped at my face, her teeth chopped at the air trying to reach my throat. She hissed and gnashed her teeth, leaning her head toward me as I held her back with my free hand. She was going to bite my face off. The head. I had to take her head. I struggled against the weight of her, the power of her. My muscles burned, and my bones ached. I couldn't keep her back much longer. She chomped her teeth, snapping like a vicious dog.

I couldn't swing it.

My strength was leaving me.

Then, out of the corner of my eye, I saw something bright shoot through the darkness like a comet in the sky. I leaped to the right, lunging as far away from the heat as I could get, just as glass smashed at Amanda's feet. And with a monstrous roar that sent tremors of terror throughout my body, Amanda was engulfed in fire.

I scrambled across the gravel drive and fell back against a car hood. I watched, frozen in a fog of relief and horror as Amanda writhed around the lawn.

Then someone rushed to my side from the dark. I gasped, nearly dropping my machete. But before I could raise it, hands shook my shoulders, hard. "Phoenix! Phoenix, we have to go. Now!"

Cole.

And just over his shoulder...the ghoul wearing my sister's skin.

## 24

## AND THE HEROINE WILL DROWN

She didn't know that I knew.

The ghoul didn't know I could see her. Witches can see witches. Recognize them. Seraphina was a witch. This girl wasn't. And she didn't know that I knew.

Cole held me fast, and I looked into his eyes. They *looked* like his eyes. But so did Phin's...in the ghoul's face. It could be him. But it might not be. My eyes blurred, overwhelmed. I'd seen a creature with Cole's soulful, dark eyes before...in the church on Bird Island. With the demon looking through them. My breathing came sharp and panicked. The night spun around me. The glow of the lights in the house blurred. Cole steadied me as I swayed, and the ghoul with Seraphina's face hurried forward.

"Nix, are you okay?" The ghoul looked at me with Seraphina's silver eyes, her face, calm and sweet. "Just breathe! You did good, Phoenix. Real good. It's okay, now. We got you."

Yes, they did.

They had me. And I had to play along. At least for now. How on Earth was I going to figure out if Cole was a ghoul or not without alerting the other one?

"Where did you guys come from?" I winced as my head pounded. I tried to slow my breathing.

Suddenly, someone came charging onto the driveway from the yard. We all turned, Cole moving in front of me.

"Phoenix!" Stuart. "What—Who are these guys?" He pulled out a pocketknife and snapped it open.

Cole shouted out in alarm. The ghoul with Phin's face shied back a bit.

I stepped in front of them. How could I warn him? "Stuart." I cleared my throat in an effort to strengthen my voice. "We have to go back into the house."

"Yeah, no kidding. Billie's still inside." Stuart eyed Cole as he towered over him easily.

I shook my head. "Stuart, I want you to take your car and follow Keirian—"

Stuart swore and shook his head.

"I can't focus on finding Billie if I'm worried about you—"

Stuart slapped his pocketknife shut and dropped it back in his jeans. "Are you serious?" He scoffed. "I just saved your butt back there. That thing was going to eat your face off!"

"Uh, guys!"

Stuart and I turned to look at the fake Seraphina.

"We don't have time to be arguing about this!" she snapped with all the self-righteousness of my sister.

"Yeah, we've been trying to tell you..." Cole started to pull me toward the house. "The ghouls have Logan. We need your help, Phoenix."

"You went off to find me...to save Logan?" I asked incredulously. That didn't make any sense.

"Nix, with your magic, we can burn them all to the ground." Fake Seraphina smiled in the darkness. I shivered. I couldn't look at her. My fingers tightened on the machete.

"Where?" Stuart asked quickly, falling into step with us. "Do they have Billie, too?"

"They have everyone," the ghoul murmured serenely.

My teeth gritted. I wanted to cut her down right then. The whole thing was creepy and made my skin itch. "What happened at Saranac Lake?"

The ghoul laughed. It sounded just like Phin when she was forcing a happy face. "Let's just say, it was a *huge* waste of time." She snickered slightly. "It totally bit us in the butt at the end."

I inhaled deeply. My nostrils flared. Funny. She was a funny ghoul. I wanted to hack her to pieces. But I had to be smart. Controlled. And as we neared the house, I tried to make a plan. It was detailed and specific: Chop off Seraphina's head. But as we ascended the handful of cement steps, a scream echoed from inside the doorway.

The four of us froze for a second, and then charged forward.

Stuart and I crossed the threshold together, just in time to see Billie tear into the sitting room, cradling her arm. It was ripped open and bleeding. She'd been bitten. Stuart shouted curses as I unsheathed the machete.

"Oh, my God, *Phoenix*!" Billie shoved Stuart off her, and she hurried forward to me. She dropped her mangled arm and grabbed my shoulder, squeezing hard, her nails cutting into my skin. "It's— it's back there! In the library! And it was fast! *I didn't even see it coming*!"

I nodded curtly and looked to Stuart. I smacked him hard on the shoulder. "You help her." I slid my bag off my shoulder, yanked open the zipper, and shoved a hand into the pocket. I slapped a bottle of bungleweed into his hand. "Use this."

"Where are you going?" Stuart eyed the bottle dubiously.

I stepped back and held the machete low. "To the library." I pointed the blade at the ghoul and 'Cole.' "And you two are coming with me."

They didn't argue. In fact, for a moment, I swore I saw a look pass between them. But I didn't have time to think about what it could mean. More than the ghoul in the library, I had to get the ghoul and 'Cole' away from Billie and Stuart. As soon as I got them alone, I could handle it. But then how would I find the real Phin? I'd have to make the ghoul talk...and I wasn't experienced in interrogation...at all.

I held the machete out and led the two of them down the hall. I wasn't worried about them attacking me from behind. If they'd wanted me dead, they would've killed me in the driveway. For some reason, they wanted me to follow them somewhere...but they'd have to wait. Library first.

It was quiet in the house. So still I could hear the wind pressing against the frames and hissing through the tiny cracks in the old farmhouse.

"That way," the ghoul breathed as though she were worried about being overheard. I looked back at her with an eyebrow raised.

She flashed Seraphina's gentlest smile. "I saw the library earlier. It's a left and then a right and then French doors."

I couldn't look at her teeth. It made me think of them sinking back into her gums replaced by stubby, yellow canines. Ew. I winced and pressed on. Our sneakers creaked on the loose floorboards and squeaked on the waxed wood.

Left. Another narrow, empty hallway. I tried to keep the machete at the ready, but the walls were too tightly compressed.

Then a right. Still empty. I couldn't tell if it was my own personal paranoia, or if the ghoul was steadily creeping closer to my shoulder.

French doors. It wasn't much of a library. More of a small study room that you'd find in a school. There were a few bookshelves and some long tables with a few clunky, old computer monitors dropped on top. I squinted into the room as we slowly passed through the double doors.

I'd seen this room before.

In Cole's vision. When I'd cut off my sister's head.

My eyes scanned the room for any place a ghoul might hide. Billie said she hadn't seen it coming. There was a closet door at the end of the room. The door was cracked ever so slightly, just enough to see the darkness inside the space. As I slowly inched toward the closet, I realized...if there was a ghoul inside the closet, I was outnumbered. By at least one...and if Cole wasn't Cole...it'd be three on one. And there's no way I could cut all three of them down before they ripped me apart.

I turned back to the fake Phin and jutted my head toward the closet. "Open it."

The ghoul hesitated. "But, Nix...you have the blade...you have your magic..."

Cole pushed forward between us and marched for the door. The ghoul smiled slightly as she watched him near the closet.

Something wasn't right.

"Cole, wait—!"

He stopped short and glanced back at me. The door slowly opened, and long curved fingers hooked around the doorframe, one after the other like a drumroll. Then two eyes glowed in the depths of the darkened closet and a ghoulish grin shined in the black.

I didn't have time to think. I lifted the machete and swung at Seraphina's head.

Cole cried out in horror as Phin's head slid to the ground and rolled underneath the table.

He hadn't seen the ghoul in the closet. His back was turned. He stared at me like *I* was the monster. I shoved him aside as the ghoul from the closet dropped to the ground, and in a furious skitter of limbs, it scurried across the hardwood to meet me. It launched itself through the air, like a wolf lunging for its prey.

But I was ready.

With a back handed slice, I swiped off the ghoul's head. It arched through the air and skidded across the length of the long table, rolling into a computer monitor. I blinked stupidly as my brain struggled to keep up with the action. Then my stomach lurched as I studied the face. It was Logan.

The dead, glassy, green eyes stared at me. The oversized jaw and stubby, yellow teeth jeered. I glanced at Cole, my chest heaving.

Cole's eyes shifted from Logan's head on the table down to Phin's decapitated corpse, leaking blood at our feet. My Converse were drenched in it. The white laces soaked a deep red. I shifted uncomfortably where I stood, giving Cole a chance to process, my socks squishing warm and slick in my shoes.

Then Cole looked at me. He smiled slightly. "You can't be sure...can you, Nix?"

My fingers tightened on the machete handle. My feet shifted a step back from him. He took a step forward.

He looked back down at the blood on his skate shoes. Then he tossed his dark hair out of his eyes, his thick black lashes slowly lifted as he met my hard, amber stare, a lopsided grin on his handsome, happy-go-lucky face. "You think I'm one of them...and you want to take my head...don't you, Phoenix?"

I took another step back, sneakers smearing blood. "Yes. I do."

He snorted softly and nodded almost sadly. Then his lip curled as he smirked. "But you won't...you can't. Not if you aren't *sure*."

I stepped back again. My fingers twisted tight on the handle. "You don't know that."

He grinned. "But I do..." He took another step forward. His eyes never left mine. "Just one bite, one shed, and I know *everything*. And I know what happened in that old, abandoned church on Bird Island."

I tried to back up again, but I bumped into the bookshelf. I gasped, startled by the impact. I gritted my teeth and held up the blade in front of me like a shield. I could sidestep and duck out through the French doors on my right. Run for it down the hall. Maybe. But ghouls were fast. Like roaches.

He moved closer, just far enough away from my blade. "When that demon was cutting into your stomach..."

My arm wavered; the machete lowered as the memories flashed in my head.

"...the shallowest of slices, slow and thin like a hundred tiny tears..."

My heart slammed against my ribcage. My breathing came fast. My head spun.

"...burning like paper cuts all over your belly..."

The machete was too heavy. It lowered to my side. I couldn't focus. I was back in the church with the demon.

And Cole's voice came like a distant echo as I sagged against the bookshelf.

"...you didn't even bother wiggling your nose...*you didn't do anything*." He gave me a rueful smile and shrugged. "Because it was Cole...and he's the one person you can't hurt. Even when you know...it isn't him behind those dark, dreamy eyes."

Tears spilled down my face as I gasped for breath. I tried to lift the blade. Remember where I was. What I had to do. But I could only feel the burning slices cutting into my stomach. Only see the molten gold of the demon's eyes.

But then ghoul's eyes shined. Like a dog in the dark. And his teeth sank back into his gums, and his jaw stretched impossibly wide. Sharp, stubby teeth popped out one by one.

And I pulled myself out of the church. Off Bird Island. Back in the fight.

I lifted the machete.

But I was too slow.

He grabbed me first. He pinned my arms at my sides and shoved me against the shelves. Bruises burst in my skin and bloomed along my back. He leaned in toward me, his tongue slack in his too-wide grin. I winced away from him, turning my head far, and struggled against his inhuman strength. I could feel his fingers stretching as they crushed against my skin, curving and hardening and sharpening into claws, they tore into my leather jacket, all the way down to my skin.

"You really oughta see somebody about that PTSD." The ghoul giggled as it crushed me harder against the shelves. "You're just a broken, damaged, little girl...useless without that magic."

I clenched my teeth to stop my lip from trembling. I sniffed and fought to keep myself together.

"And you'll never get to use your magic again..." The ghoul's breath clouded hot and rancid around my nose. "The Mother has plans for you, Phoenix Grey."

I continued to struggle as his claws cut deeper. My arms dampened as blood soaked the sleeves of my flannel shirt. I looked away. It was too hard to see Cole's face so grotesquely distorted. I had to keep it talking. "What happened to it? My magic?"

"It's all part of the plan." The ghoul breath fogged around my face. He nuzzled his lumpy cheek against mine. "I told you, the Mother has plans for you."

I was going to be sick. But I had to keep it talking. "So, you snatch little kids and drag them through the tunnel in the school basement...and let me guess, Victor is one of you, too?" I scoffed in disgust as it all seemed to come together. "He literally hasn't been Victor Godwin since he was sixteen, has he?"

The ghoul moved back from me, his hold loosening just a bit, so he could study my face. He let out a low, rumbling laugh that sounded more like a growl. "My, my, Phoenix Grey, you certainly think you've got it all figured out, huh?"

I forced a mean laugh in response. "Nah, I still can't figure out why you losers like to snack on live people. You're ghouls. You're supposed to eat dead meat. What's wrong with you freaks?"

The ghoul squeezed me harder, crushing my bones, cutting off the blood circulation and numbing my hands. I flexed my fingers and choked up a bit on the handle. If I could swing it just enough, I might be able to take his arm. And if I could take his arm, then maybe I could take his head.

"*Haven't you heard of evolution?* We're the most civilized of our kind!" The ghoul shoved me violently against the shelf, knocking my head into the hard spines. I blinked rapidly as black spots sprinkled across my vision. The ghoul continued to hiss through oversized jaws. *"You haven't even begun to understand what we—"*

I rolled my eyes to the side as though I were bored. Then I looked back at him and interrupted his impassioned speech. "What's with the witching well? And the Blood Farm witch? Just a story to tell the townspeople?"

The ghoul hesitated as though confused. Conflicted. "She was real...once." He paused again. Like he wasn't sure how much he should say. This was my moment.

I bent to the side and swung the blade upward and around with all my strength. Like a band geek twirls a baton. The machete hacked through the ghoul's forearm just enough to leave it hanging by muscle and tendon and splintered bone. His other hand released me as he howled more in outraged surprise than pain. Then, before he could lunge for me, I sidestepped and backed through the French doors, out into the hall, the machete raised and ready.

But he didn't come.

There was a moment, a breath of time in which I could catch mine, and then something emerged from the library. It wasn't a ghoul. It was Cole again. His jaw and teeth, human. No, it wasn't. It couldn't be him. But my shock and hesitation at his fresh, healed human appearance was just what the ghoul needed.

It went for me.

But something yanked me out of reach.

The ghoul slammed against the wall. Someone tall with a bouncy swagger, pulled me behind him and without a word, smashed another glass stuffed with a burning shred of cloth at the ghoul's feet. It exploded. The ghoul burst into flames. But he looked like Cole. And my stomach heaved at the sight of his skin melting from his body in thick strips of burning meat. And then, as Cole's face dripped away, it was the ghoul. The librarian.

Another Godwin. Stuart shoved me back farther down the hall. "Go back for Billie, I'll be right there!"

"But—"

"Go! She's by herself!" Stuart shoved me back again so hard my bones rattled. "I gotta put this out and torch the others!"

I nodded furiously, struggling to focus. "Okay!" I turned on my heel and backtracked through the maze of corridors. Amanda. Tiffany. Annie. The librarian. But who was wearing Phin? Was it Pamela? And who was wearing Logan's face? And how long would it take him to put himself back together? Would Stuart be able to burn him in time? And how many more ghouls were walking around wearing skin that didn't belong to them?

I burst into the sitting room, and my heart sank slowly down from the lump in my throat. She was okay. Billie was okay. Huddled in a ball on the couch, bundled up in an oversized hoodie to hide the hideous bite on her arm. She looked up, startled as I came into the room.

"Stuart?"

"He's fine. Come on, we gotta get you to the car—" I grabbed her good arm and pulled her roughly to her feet. "No arguing."

"Heard that," she mumbled weakly.

"You don't have to worry. We'll get you and Stuart out of here, and then I'll find everyone else, okay?" I hurried her toward the front door and motioned for her to wait in the doorway, so I could check outside to make sure it was safe.

And finally, I had a plan.

The witching well. It had something to do with the witch. The ghoul—the librarian—hadn't wanted to talk about her. So, it had to be the well. Maybe that's where they were keeping all the bitten...and maybe Mary, Agatha, Lizzie, and Scott Tyler were all still alive.

I stepped outside into the dark night and squinted through the inky shadows for signs of ghouls skittering among the dead leaves and trunks of trees. We were going to be okay. I finally had a handle on things. I was figuring it out. And Stuart and I had cut down all the ghouls that had come at us. *We were winning.* And God, it felt good to be in the fresh air, away from the heat and the stink of ghoul. I spun slightly underneath the light of the moon, and then smiled back at Billie. "All clear—"

But she wasn't there.

*Billie wasn't in the doorway.*

"Billie?" I called back, my voice thin and strained with rising fear. I ran back toward the house. "It's okay, let's go!"

My heart lodged back in my throat. I shouldn't have left her. Why had I thought that'd be safe? I hurried up the steps and into the house.

The room was empty.

I twisted around in a panicked circle, and then something hard knocked into my head.

I dropped to the ground.

# BITE ME

I flinched.

My eyes flew open.

Then I thrashed.

I was laying on a cold, dirt floor. In a rusty cage.

In a dirty, old hospital gown, stained and gritty against my skin.

No pants. No socks.

Exposed. Defenseless.

My backpack was gone. My machete.

I inhaled sharply, my breath coming out in a cloud.

And I wasn't alone.

I scrambled up onto my knees and curled my fingers through the bars. "Cole?"

He smiled weakly. "I was wondering when you'd come to...are you okay? Did they bite you?"

It was then that I noticed his arm, bloody and mangled, barely concealed by the sleeve of that dirty potato sack he was wearing. It didn't look good, but the bleeding seemed to have stopped.

"Nix, did they bite you?" Cole repeated gently.

"Uhh..." I tore my eyes away from his arm and checked myself, moving my hands all over myself. I grabbed the bars of the cage and pressed my face through the rusty, rectangular spaces. "No. I'm fine."

Cole nodded with a small smile. "That's good. At least we won't have to worry about a ghoul shedding into you."

"Where are we?" My eyes shifted around us. It was a dark, cellar-like space, with only a single yellow light giving off a low, ambient glow overhead. Like a lantern in a coal mine.

"I'm not sure...but wherever we are—" Cole nodded his head toward the ceiling above us. "They're watching."

I inclined my head and stared up at the camera. A small red light seemed to wink at me, and I swore I saw it zoom in closer. I looked back at Cole. "How long have you been here?" I shook my head. "*How* did you get here? What happened? And where's Phin!" My questions tumbled out faster and squeakier as they came to me.

Cole held up a finger to his lips and shushed me, eying the shadowy cellar surrounding us. I nodded my understanding and waved him on.

"I'd read your note and then one of those girls—the girls who were hazing Drew and Lizzie? She said you were in trouble."

"And you followed her?" I whispered harshly. "Of all the—"

Cole frowned darkly. "Nix, you didn't answer your phone. What was I supposed to think?"

"So, obviously, she jumped you." I rolled my eyes.

"Actually, no." Cole muttered back. "We took the van and were pulled over by the sheriff—"

"The sheriff?" I demanded. I couldn't have heard him correctly.

"She asked the girl to step out of the vehicle. And then, I watched them go around the front to stand beside the cruiser. They were talking. Arguing. Then Logan called."

"Logan?" I repeated. "What did he say? Did he find anything out?"

Cole winced. "It was more of the same as Syracuse...that slayer, Frankie, could've just told him over the phone. But at least her information was helpful. She said that there was a sect of ghouls from Germany that served under a dark witch in exchange for protection and prolonged life. These ghouls ate the living...which isn't natural. It's not healthy for them. And actually makes them sick."

I made a face. "Why would they eat something that made them sick?"

Cole shook his head. "No, no. I mean, like—sick in the mind. See, ghouls are humanoids, right? Not much different from us. They have emotions like us and feelings. They live in family groups and mind their own business, rooting around old gravesites and keeping to themselves. But these ghouls...eating fresh meat changes their brain chemistry and makes them homicidal and sadistic. Think *House of 1000 Corpses* kind of crazy."

"Great..." I rubbed my forehead trying to process what he was telling me. "So, the kids...Mary Tran...she's—"

"No, Nix." Cole smiled slightly and shook his head again, pressing his face close to the bars of his cage. "I think she's alive. I think all the kids are alive."

"But—"

"That's the other part of it. The sixteen-year cycle? That's their *breeding* cycle."

I scrunched up my nose in disgust. "I'm sorry...*what*?"

Cole snorted and waved a hand. "Okay, this part Logan put together. They are supposed to eat dead things, right? But this clan is so messed up, they think that's beneath them. It's unclean or whatever. But whatever they think of it, it goes against their nutritional needs. And if they want to spawn healthy offspring, the Mother needs to eat one dead body per ghoul pup."

"Ew. Ew. Too much information."

Cole snickered and shrugged.

I pinched my temples and held up a hand. "So, why was Justine found with her blood drained?"

"Because the Mother wants them as fresh as ghoulishly possible before she eats them. And Justine was found on Thanksgiving...so that's probably the day they 'harvest' the bodies."

The pieces were fitting in a nasty, disgusting way. But they were fitting. Like Frankenstein. "Okay, so that's why the victims changed...it's about being 'pure' and 'clean'. First it was young women. Then the times changed...so the victims got younger."

Cole nodded.

"So, wait, how did you get here?"

Before he could answer, there was a low groan from the cage beside Cole. I leaned up, stooped over, and pressed my head against the wired cage, struggling to see past Cole's enclosure. The cages were barely four feet high. It was impossible.

"Dude, you okay?" Cole whispered to the cage.

There was another groan in response and then a yell. "I torched you! I burned you black!"

Stuart.

"STUART! *He's not a ghoul*!" I shouted over his bellows.

There was a pause and then a scuffle of dirt and a rattle of the rusty bars. "Phoenix? Is that you?"

"Obviously. Who else would it be?" I quipped dryly.

"Have you seen Billie?"

My heart sank. "No."

There was a heavy silence.

"We have to get out of here," Stuart muttered. Bars rattled and clanged loudly.

Cole glanced at me expectantly.

My heart hurt. Instinctively, my hand went for my wand. It was there, still stuck in what remained of my topknot, extra messy. No one could unarm a witch of her wand, save for another witch. I swallowed the sour bitterness that formed in my mouth at the thought of their nasty ghoul claws touching my wand.

Cole's eyes searched my face.

I shrugged. "I can't." I held up my hands, palms up and fingers splayed. "My magic. Something happened when I went down that first ghoul tunnel. I can't reach my magic."

Cole's eyes widened as he searched my face. The pity in his face was too much. I shrugged it off. "So, what do we do?"

Cole hesitated. He bit back a question and cleared his throat. "Our best bet is to pick the padlock." Cole moved his hands around the dirt floor of his cage. "But I haven't found anything."

I followed his example and ran my hands along the dirt. It was soft and loose. Nothing. I rubbed a hand across my forehead, sliding it down the length of my face and rubbed my neck. The chain of Billie's good luck charm scratched against my skin. Then I scoffed. Talk about luck.

I tugged the chain over my head and fingered the charm. It curved like a candy cane. Perfect for lock picking. I leaned up on my knees and jammed the charm into the lock.

Cole pressed his face against the bars and tried to coach me through it. Left. Right. It took awhile. Unlike Cole, I hadn't paid too much attention to Logan's lock-picking lessons, and this was a lot harder than the knife in the window hinge. But eventually, the padlock popped open and dropped to the ground. I shoved open the cage and crawled out. I jumped to my feet and slapped the dirt from my hands and legs, not bothering with the grimy hospital gown. Then I hurried to Cole's cage, highly aware of the darkened corners and stretches of shadows surrounding the cellar. It was like I could feel eyes watching, and not just the camera overhead. I eyed the darkness beyond as my fingers worked the charm into the lock. This was a bit faster. As soon as the lock dropped, I slid over to Stuart's cage and started on the padlock. Cole moved beside me, standing watch as I worked.

Stuart's lock dropped, and I stepped back for him to crawl out. I slipped Billie's charm back over my head and tucked it safely beneath the gown. Then Cole grabbed me. I recoiled instinctively, backing up several steps. Cole's face, half in shadow, crinkled with hurt. "It's me, Nix." He crooked his finger and pulled back his upper lip. He pressed hard into his gums. "See?"

No ghoul teeth.

I jumped at him then and wrapped my arms around him in a hard hug. I clung to him for a moment, pressed my nose into the hollow of his throat and breathed in the smell of him, flooded with a rush of emotions I'd barely kept bottled up inside.

"Well, as touching as this all is—You think we could celebrate after we actually get out of here?" Stuart snapped.

"Sorry," I mumbled, mortified. My face burned. I released Cole hastily and scooted to the side, giving him much more space than was necessary.

Stuart scanned the cellar. It was impossible to see beyond the weak, yellow lantern glow. There was no way to know how large the space was, or what else lay beyond the depths of the darkness.

Cole nodded in the direction of the lantern. "They always came in from that way."

I glanced at him. "You mean when they locked us in the cages?"

Cole shook his head, his eyes narrowed. "Nah. For that they switched off the light. I couldn't see who—what—brought you both in...I mean they came from that way when they...you know... were messing with me."

My stomach lurched. Sour bile churned in the pit of my belly. "What do you mean?"

Stuart eyed Cole warily, his lip curled in disgust.

Cole shrugged dismissively, his pale face yellow underneath the weak lamplight. "They came in...I thought it was Phin. She was trying to help me escape...but then they had another one wearing my face...he brought in a puppy. And then Phin...the ghoul...well, she just wasn't Phin."

"Why would they—"

"I told you, Nix. Their brains are all warped. They like to make people suffer. Emotional torture. It's fun for them."

I shifted closer. I wanted to take his hand, but I held back.

Cole shook his head, tossing his hair out of his eyes. "They kept saying, 'The Mother likes to play with her food.'" He looked as sick as I felt.

The three of us were quiet for a moment. Our eyes all shifted up to stare at the camera.

Then Cole cleared his throat and nodded in the direction of the lantern. "They always came from that way."

We stared past the light into the black. I inhaled deeply, trying to find some strength. We'd literally be walking into the unknown. And it'd be so easy to fall apart. Logan and Phin were missing. Billie was gone, too. Mary. Agatha. Scott. Lizzie. Sidney.

And I was practically naked, both physically and magically.

I licked my lips and bit down on them. Hard. It was okay. I didn't need magic. Hunters didn't need magic.

I could do this.

And I didn't need pants to kick someone in the face.

I glanced back at the cages. They were like wired dog kennels. Nothing we could break to use as a weapon. I looked up at the lantern. It was electric. No fire. We had nothing. "Okay. Let's go."

We passed underneath the light and into the darkness. The scariest part, even more unsettling than moving forward into nothingness, was not knowing if the boys were still with me. I couldn't see them at all. I cleared my throat as my feet passed over the cold dirt, sliding like skis in the snow. "Where do you think we are?"

Cole's voice murmured beside my ear, "Somewhere underneath the Gossamer House."

"I thought you were taken after the sheriff pulled you over?"

Cole scoffed softly. "No. I didn't realize it then...I was such an idiot. The girl—ghoul—jumped back in the van and said we were good to go. I assumed, you know, small town, she'd talked her way out of whatever it was...but the ghoul told me later that she took her head. The sheriff."

I winced. Stuart. His mother. But he didn't say a word. Maybe he wasn't listening. Hadn't heard.

I took a shaky breath and asked quickly, "So, then how did you get down here?"

"I—"

Something moved in the black. I felt the air as it rushed past me. I reached out for Cole and snatched him tight to my side. "*Did you guys see that?*"

We stopped and pressed in closer. Then there was a pop. Light after light switched on, a whole string of lanterns dangling above us, illuminating more of the cellar with its earthen floor and low ceiling. And cameras. Positioned strategically along the wall. We'd reached the end of the cellar. Just feet from where we stood there was an archway like an underground hallway dug into the earth. And on either side of it, the dirt walls were lined with wooden shelves. Like the kind you'd see in a garage or a basement. I squinted at the things arranged all over them...giant mason jars. Like preserves.

My stomach lurched.

Not preserves.

Heads.

Jars of severed heads.

My eyes moved from jar to jar.

There were dozens of heads. All men. Some old with white hair and wrinkly pickled faces. But most were young...thirties like Mama...and a few even younger. Their eyes were wide and glassy in whatever goo they were soaking. But their jaws weren't right. They were too big for their faces, with sharp, stubby teeth. Like hyenas.

They were ghouls.

I turned to Cole, but before I met his sickened expression with one to match, I grabbed him and pulled him aside, looking frantically past him.

Nothing.

I spun in a circle, my heart sunken into my churning stomach.

The dirt cellar with weak, yellow light and soaked in shadows was empty.

Stuart was gone.

"Where—" Cole swore under his breath. "He was with us! How—"

My eyes shifted toward the darkened tunnel of a hallway, flanked by the pickled faces.

I gritted my teeth. "We have to keep going."

We moved slowly toward the archway. The both of us kept our eyes straight ahead, pointedly ignoring the severed ghoul heads as we passed. I held out a hand in front of Cole and motioned for him to wait. I stuck my hand into the hallway, sliding it along the wall. It was solid. Not dirt. My fingers found a switch.

The light snapped on. We both flinched underneath the bright, fluorescent slab in the middle of the hallway ceiling. It was like a glaring spotlight as it poured down on the center of the corridor and splashed shadows everywhere else. But it looked ordinary enough, with the left wall lined with several doors and a staircase at the far end of it. I was tempted to run for it. Charge for the stairs and hurdle up them as fast as I could manage. It wasn't until then that I realized how claustrophobic being in the cellar had been, like we'd been buried and forgotten, left to rot like the faces in the jars.

Cole sensed my desperate urge for freedom, and he held me back. He nodded silently toward the doors on each side. I nodded back in reply. We had to search each one. Check for more victims. And for Stuart. How could he have vanished? Where had they taken him?

Cole went for the first door. He held his hand on the knob and waited for my nod. I braced myself and waved him on. It's not like we had any kind of weapon if there *was* a ghoul behind the door. He shoved the door open, hard. As though he hoped to knock into anyone lurking behind it. I reached inside and slapped my hand around for the switch.

The light flashed on. My ears prickled at the whirr of a camera zoom. My breath caught.

It was like some kind of break room. Like the one in the sheriff's department. But instead of sugar packets and coffee on the table, there was a body. Ripped open like one of those pig roasts. Justine Kilpatrick. The state of her...it was worse than anything I could've imagined. I swayed where I stood. My feet slipped on the cold tile. Cole pulled me to him, holding me up while I regained my footing. They'd eaten her. *Alive.* And left...so much. Too much. Like they hadn't even been hungry. I hadn't ever expected... anything like this.

Cole gripped me tight and sidestepped around her. He snatched something from the little kitchenette and shoved me roughly out of the room.

I shook my head as I mumbled softly and incoherently. "But Victor Wollstonecraft is a ghoul. She was with him in the photo. Why would the ghouls eat Justine? After all this time?"

"You said she'd wanted to tell you something..." Cole muttered gently. He pressed a butterknife into my palm.

I barely noticed. I stammered, "Why would they eat her?"

Cole guided me toward the next door. He put his hand on the knob and held the knife up at the ready. He glanced at me. I nodded, still shaky and dazed. He shoved it open. I slapped up the light switch. I squinted into the room, scared of what I'd see.

It was small. Like the size of a janitor closet. In the center of the room was a huge cylinder filled with liquid and inside was an old woman, floating and asleep, connected to cords with an oxygen mask over her face, her silver hair fanning about her as she bobbed slightly in the water.

I stood there, mouth slightly agape as I tried to process what I was seeing. Cole guided me inside the room and quietly shut the door. The both of us stood before the tank, staring. Confused. Shocked.

Then I realized—

"It...it looks like the mayor..."

I looked back at Cole, who pushed forward to peek at the glass. "Mayor Godwin?"

I nodded slowly, eyes wide and unblinking as I stared at the old woman floating in the tank, her face wrinkled, gray and aged. I couldn't process it. It didn't make sense. "It...looks like what the mayor would look like if she hadn't had all the hair dye and plastic surgeries..."

"Mayor Godwin." Cole turned to face me, his face grim. "You think?"

"Do I think—" My stomach soured. "—that the mayor is wearing this woman? Keeping her alive...so she can wear her forever?"

Cole shook his head, his eyes on the old woman. "Well...ghouls can shed into dead people, too. It's part of their camouflage...but keeping them alive makes them immune to head chops...so maybe..."

I raked a hand through the tendrils spilling from my topknot. "Wait, so the mayor is a ghoul...wearing this old woman? Why?"

"Nix, think about it...how long has the Mother ghoul been alive? Ghouls have human-like lifespans. Shorter even. But the Blood Farm witch gave these ghouls some kind of longevity spell. Experimented on them, according to that Frankie slayer. Maybe the Mother ghoul has been behind this whole thing for decades. Literally running the town. And if she's running the town...don't you think the people would be a little suspicious of some mayor lady who never dies?"

I made a face. "So, she grabs some poor woman and switches identities? Keeping her comatose in a tank like a fish?" The knife hanging limply at my side, I covered my face with my free hand as I tried to think. I was missing something. Then my jaw sagged as my thoughts cleared.

Cole meanwhile studied the monitors on the side of the tank. "We need to get her out of here." He rubbed his chin as he considered what to do.

But I wasn't worried about the old woman. My brain was racing too fast. "The Godwins adopt. They adopt from the Gossamer House. That's how they pass off all the new blood. The new babies."

Cole stepped back from the tank scowling. He shook his head sadly. "There's no way we can get her out now. We'll have to come back for her..."

I grabbed Cole's shoulder and turned him toward me. "All of the mean girls were left at the Gossamer House as infants...at the same time. Sixteen years ago. Mayor Godwin spawned them and left them there to be raised by Catherine Godwin. Her daughter!"

"But what about the sheriff? She's the mayor's daughter, too. If the girl ate her—"

"They ripped off Annie's head, too." I waved a hand dismissively. "It's their morbid, cultural punishment."

Cole inclined his head as his dark eyes searched my face. "So, you're telling me that the Godwins are ghouls..."

"Not all of them...just the ones left to be raised at the orphanage. Agatha, Stuart, Billie, and Sidney? They were *actually* adopted. They had no idea about any of this!"

"*Actually* adopted?" Cole scoffed and scrunched up his face. "I don't know, Nix. That's all a bit too 'tinfoil hat' for me..."

I let out a little manic chuckle. "There are no 'maybes' required with this theory. It all fits, Cole!"

Everything started to make sense. I shook Cole's shoulder. "The Wollstonecrafts had the same photo at their house!"

Cole crinkled his forehead. He inclined his head like he must've misheard. "What?"

"Justine Kilpatrick!" I gasped and gave his arm another hard shake. "Like you said, it was a family photo!"

"Uhh…"

"Keirian said the guy Godwins go bad…their men go bad." I waved the knife back toward the door. "Those heads were all men!"

"So, you think that the dudes…what? I don't—"

"It was *her sister*, Cole! Justine's sister in the photo!"

"But I thought her sister—"

"That's just it!" I cried excitedly. "Billie told me her grandmother was mad because Victor left the family over some girl he met! What if he met Jillian Kilpatrick, Justine's sister? They went to school together! Margaret Meeks told me all about it! And when the sisters were both taken, he knew exactly how to find them! He saved them both! *From his own family*!"

"So…Victor Wollstonecraft, what? Doesn't want to eat people —er, *alive* people?"

I smiled. "Nope. He wanted to marry his girlfriend and have a freaky, half-breed family and eat old corpses like a proper ghoul family man should!"

Cole hesitated. "But what about the other little girl? There was a third girl in the photo. From what I heard, Victor only has two daughters…"

I grabbed Cole and hurried for the door. "We can figure that out later. We're finally making sense of this mess!"

We filed out into the hallway, and this time, I opened the next door. But I should've waited for Cole. We should've gotten ready. Because as soon as I shoved open the door, something slammed into me and sent me crashing into the opposite wall.

26

## LIVING GHOUL GIRL

Before I could fight, the thing ran toward the cellar, but didn't make it far. Cole yanked her back by the scruff of her dingy potato sack and held her to him, crushing her close. He leaned his face into her ear and whispered harshly, "*It's okay. We're here to help!*"

That's when I recognized the filthy hospital gown, the length of her long, dirty, black hair and slight frame: it was Lizzie Tran.

Cole turned with her still crushed against him as she continued to twitch and thrash. I hurried over to them. I grabbed her chin and forced her to face me. I pulled back my lip. My finger pressed into my gums. "See? Not ghouls."

Lizzie stopped fighting, but her chest bumped up and down so fast it lifted Cole's arms up and down along with it. Her eyes were wide as they shifted between Cole and me.

"Now it's your turn." I nodded toward her, not about to get any more surprises.

Lizzie lifted her finger and pushed her lip up, revealing her white teeth. She poked hard into her upper gum. Nothing. The three of us relaxed a little. But we were still in the hallway, literally in the spotlight. Cole released her, and she grabbed me, squeezing my arms. *Did you find Mary?*

"Not yet."

Lizzie gritted her teeth and nodded stiffly. She tucked her dark hair behind her ears and noticed the butterknife in my hand. She pointed at it. "Where do I get one of those?"

Cole headed back to the kitchenette to find her a knife. I, meanwhile, went to check out Lizzie's room.

"There's nothing in there—" Lizzie started, but I didn't listen. I had to clear every room. We needed to learn everything we could, and this was part of the puzzle. I stood in the doorway. My eyes scanned the scene.

It was like a patient room. With a slanted operating table and a little metal tray for medical tools...but the tray was empty. All the drawers and cabinets had been pulled open, revealing empty interiors. I glanced up into the corner as a camera whirred, zooming in on us.

"They're watching." Lizzie snickered. "Or, at least, they're trying to." Lizzie jutted her chin up toward the camera.

She'd covered the lens with her thick, green hair ribbon.

I glanced sideways at her and smiled.

She nudged me gently. "Sorry for—"

"Attacking me?"

We both forced laughs, broken and strained. She shrugged. "They kept coming in to...mess with my head. I'd had enough."

I studied the table. The leather straps were still buckled in place.

I looked down at her wrists. They were red and raw, blood-stained and burned from the friction of the leather. She must've spent hours tugging herself free. Awkwardly, she folded her arms across her chest and shrugged again. "I wasn't about to let them cut me up while I lay helpless and strapped to that thing."

I inhaled deeply. I got it. "They were cutting you?"

"Not yet." Lizzie's face tightened. "They said the Mother had plans for me." Then the strength in Lizzie's voice faltered. "What do they want from us?"

My eyes moved up to the camera. "They want to watch us suffer. Because they're monsters." And they were more monstrous than I'd ever anticipated. It was, like...okay, werewolves, vampires, they gotta eat to live. Just surviving. But this? This wasn't surviving. This was—

"What's the plan?" Lizzie blurted. "Do you have a plan?"

I scoffed. "No."

Lizzie stared at me, her face twitched as though torn between wanting to laugh and cry. "What are they? Some kind of werewolf-freaks?"

I put a hand on her shoulder. "They're ghouls. They can't turn people into them. But they can turn into us...if they bite us."

She took a shaky breath. "Well, that explains some of the insane stuff I've seen..."

"It's the Godwins."

She rolled her eyes. "Sidney didn't—"

I shook my head and held her fierce stare. "No. Not Sidney. The women. The mayor. The sheriff. The doctor. Even the librarian!"

"My foster mom, Catherine?"

I nodded grimly. "And Tiffany. And Amanda. And—"

"Annie."

A dark smirk twitched in the corner of my mouth. "Well, Annie *was* one. They killed her."

Lizzie held up a hand. "So, it was Annie, then. Who killed Nathan and Drew."

Cole came up behind us. "Who have you seen come in here?"

Startled, the both of us jumped and grabbed at each other.

"Sorry! Sorry. I couldn't find any more knives, but—" He held up a fork sheepishly.

Lizzie snorted and snatched the fork.

Then the three of us moved back into the hallway, standing

beneath the glare of the light. There were two more doors left to clear.

I stepped toward the nearest, this time cautious and careful.

Lizzie put a hand on my shoulder. "I wouldn't."

My forehead crinkled quizzically. "What do you mean?"

Lizzie jutted her fork back toward her room, the one they'd locked her inside. "I've been next door since they grabbed me...and the noises I've heard come out of that room..."

My eyes searched her pale face. She was terrified. I looked back at the door. Then I looked at Cole. "We have to clear it." I tried to say it forcefully, but the words came out weak and uncertain.

Cole nodded encouragingly. "We have to clear it."

I licked my lips and choked up on my knife. I reached for the doorknob.

Behind me, Lizzie backed up against the far wall. "The doors don't open from the inside...at least, mine didn't. The doorknob wouldn't turn. So, whatever's in there...it really wanted to come out."

Cole moved to my right, his butterknife up and ready to stab. He mouthed a countdown: three...two...one. I cranked the knob and thrust the door wide.

Cole smacked on the light.

And we froze.

It was empty.

And trashed.

The room matched Lizzie's exactly...except instead of opened drawers and cabinets—they were broken. The operating table was bent in half. The cabinets were smashed and splintered. My eyes moved up to the camera. But there wasn't one. It had been ripped off the ceiling. I stepped around the wreckage and stood over what remained of the camera. It was crushed. Literally crushed into a million pieces of plastic and glass.

Cole moved through the debris and picked through the mess. We looked for a weapon more useful than a butterknife. But there was nothing. Lizzie, meanwhile, appeared in the doorway, her eyes wide and horrified. "Who could've done all this?" She stepped inside the room and spun in a slow circle. Then she gasped. "The wall! And the door! Look at the wall and the door!"

I glanced at her. Lizzie's back was to me as she faced the way we'd entered, her shoulders sagged in shock. And my mouth gaped. The walls and door were steel plated...but that hadn't stopped whatever had been held here. There were deep gashes in the metal, so deep that the metal was peeling and curling back like splinters of wood. I crossed the room and stood before the wall, my nose inches from the marks. I looked up. They stretched all the way to the ceiling. Then I turned to stare at Cole as he approached warily. "Cole, these are scratches."

His nostrils flared. His jaw tightened. "Claw marks."

I sidestepped into him and leaned my head close to keep Lizzie from hearing, "They locked a ghoul in here. Why?"

Cole shook his head.

Lizzie pulled on the sleeve of my gown. "Let's go..."

I nodded and led her out of the room, checking both ways before we stepped out into the corridor again. One more door.

"They're watching us." Lizzie mumbled to herself. The whole thing was finally starting to make her crack. "They're watching us. They're watching us."

Cole put a gentle hand on her shoulder and forced her to meet his eyes. "It's going to be okay, Lizzie, we're—"

She shook her head furiously and pointed her fork at the camera overhead. "*They're watching us!*"

I bit my lip and looked anxiously at Cole. "Yeah, Lizzie, they—"

She shook her head again, her long black hair swaying. She grabbed my arms and gave me a hard shake. "They're watching us! *So, why aren't they coming for us?!*"

My heart stuttered in my chest. My eyes darted toward Cole as Lizzie shoved me away from her. Why weren't they coming for us?

Cole shrugged, his face pained and sick. I looked back at Lizzie. "We can't worry about that. We have one more door."

Lizzie took several deep, shaky breaths. Cole gave her a one-armed hug as we stepped back out into the hall.

I moved toward the door. Last one. I put my hand on the knob and waited for Cole to get into position beside me. He mouthed the countdown. I thrust the door open wide.

Cole smacked on the light.

It was another patient room. And on the slanted operating table was a small little girl with dishwater-blonde hair.

"Agatha." I ran to her.

The camera whirred overhead and zoomed in on us.

Her thin face was drawn and pale. And unlike us, she was still dressed in a similar outfit to the one I'd first seen her in—stuffy, old lady clothes. I smoothed the hair back from her face. She didn't move. I traced my fingers to the hollow of her throat and felt her pulse. She was alive. I slid a finger down her temple. Her brow furrowed. She shook her head ever so slightly. Like Fawn when she didn't want to wake up in the morning.

I smiled and stroked her cheek again. Cole and Lizzie came up beside me, but I didn't bother to look up. The sight of her small, peaceful, sleeping face filled me with so much calm. I needed to hold onto the moment, however fleeting, before the terror started all over again. My eyes moved from her thick sweep of lashes to the soft rosebud of her lips, drinking in her sweetness.

"You found her, Nix," Cole whispered. "The third girl from the photo."

My fingers curled inward away from her hair. My hand fell to my side. I looked up at him sharply. "What?"

Cole smiled down at Agatha and jutted his chin toward the little girl. "Don't you remember? She was in the photo with Justine and Victor."

Lizzie wasn't listening. Instead, she hurried to unstrap the little girl from the table. My thoughts seemed to slow as I looked back down at the little girl. She was clean and dressed like an old lady. But she was the third girl...which meant...Cole and I locked eyes as we both realized the same thing.

"Wait!" Cole snatched Lizzie's wrist and tugged her way from the last strap.

Lizzie shoved him off her. "What?"

I held up a hand. Then with the other, I reached for Agatha's face. Gingerly, I slid back her lip and pressed her gums. Her teeth sank back into her skull. My heart dropped as my finger fell away, hanging limply at my side. Agatha's human teeth and lip moved back into place.

"Oh my God," Lizzie murmured. "She's one of them?"

"A ghoul," Cole muttered grimly. "What do you think, Nix?"

"*Agatha is one of them*?" Lizzie repeated frantically. "But she's Mary's best friend! They were best friends! She can't be one of them! She just moved here!"

"Wait, what? She couldn't have just moved here..." Cole raised an eyebrow at Lizzie. "She's Victor Wollstonecraft's daughter."

Lizzie made a face and shook her head, her whole body bristling with impatience. "What?! The undertaker?!"

I pinched my temples and held up a hand. "Wait a minute. Wait a minute!"

They stared at me expectantly.

I looked to Lizzie first. "What do you know about her?"

Lizzie flipped her dark hair over her shoulder and shrugged. "Dr. Godwin adopted her over the summer. Her name is Agatha Godwin. She moved into their house just in time for school to start. Sidney used to bring her over to Gossamer House all the time. Agatha and Mary are, like, best friends." Her voice broke and tears leaked down her face. She sniffed. "How can she be a ghoul?"

I looked at Cole. "If Agatha was Victor's daughter...why would his sister, Dr. Godwin, adopt her?"

Cole shrugged.

Lizzie scowled and rolled her eyes. Then she elbowed Cole out of the way and finished unfastening Agatha's restraints. "She's a child and hasn't done anything wrong. We're taking her with us."

Lizzie went to lift her up off the table. Agatha's eyes flew open. They darted around between us, round and frightened. I reached for her, but she flinched away from me.

"Hey, hey. It's okay. We're here to help," Lizzie smiled brightly through her tears.

"Can you tell us who you are?" I murmured gently.

Agatha glanced at me as she nibbled nervously on her lower lip. "My—my name is Agatha."

"This is Phoenix...that's—"

"Cole." He flashed a warm, lopsided grin.

"And I'm Lizzie, Mary's sister, you remember me?" Lizzie smoothed Agatha's hair back. The little girl whimpered and nodded. Her eyes blurred with tears. Then her lower lip trembled.

"They took her," Agatha whispered. "They took Mary, and I couldn't stop them. I'm so sorry."

Lizzie tried to take a breath, but it came as a sharp gasp. She scooped up the little girl and hugged her tight.

I glanced over them at Cole. He watched them with a sad smile. Then he tossed his hair out of his eyes which shined dark with emotion. I had to look away. I couldn't manage to swallow the lump in my throat.

The camera whirred overhead.

We had to hurry.

"Agatha, what can you tell us about the Godwins?"

Lizzie loosened her hold on the girl, but just barely. Lizzie kept her hands on Agatha's shoulders and pulled her into her as Agatha stared up at me. "The Godwins took me away from home...they wanted to make sure my daddy did what they told him to." Agatha kept her chin high as her voice wavered and her eyes continued to spill. "We're not like them. I promise you...we are...but we *aren't*."

"I believe you." I nodded earnestly. "That's why we're here to rescue you. You and Mary and all the others."

Agatha glanced over her shoulder at Lizzie. "If you bring me back, my daddy will help you. I know he will."

Lizzie's hold on Agatha tightened. "Does he know where Mary is?"

Yes." Agatha smiled slightly. "And so do I."

We stared at her.

Agatha's smile broadened. Her eyes shifted between us. "They keep them in the ghoul hole beneath the Blood Farm."

My heart sputtered in my chest. "There's a ghoul hole beneath—?"

Agatha chuckled softly at my shock. "Yup. It's connected to the old well behind the Gossamer House."

Finally. We had them. I put a hand on Agatha's shoulder. "Do you know where we are right now?"

Agatha crinkled her nose and thought for a moment. "I'm pretty sure we're underneath the Gossamer House."

I nodded excitedly and looked at Cole. "I bet you anything those stairs lead up to the main house. We get to the van; you take them to Agatha's house and find Victor. I'll head to the witching well and—"

Both Lizzie and Cole exploded with outraged objections so forceful I flinched in the face of them.

"Uhm, no. I'm coming with you to get my sister back, thanks—"

"If you think I'm going to let you go off by yourself—"

Agatha eyed them nervously.

I rolled my eyes. "Whatever. Let's just get to the van, and we'll draw straws then."

But we wouldn't. Because I was heading down that well no matter what Cole said.

We slipped out into the corridor. The camera whirred. Agatha reached for my hand. "They're watching us, aren't they?"

I nodded and pressed forward ahead of her, scooting her

behind me. Lizzie took up the rear, sandwiching Agatha between us.

Cole was at my side, butterknife raised. I held up mine with a sheepish smirk.

We neared the staircase.

The light went out with a pop.

Lizzie inhaled sharply, and we all instinctively moved closer together.

"It's okay," Agatha murmured. "There's nothing there."

I moved forward slowly, hands out and searching for the staircase. "Can you see?"

"Yes," Agatha whispered at my back. "They're just trying to scare you...I'd smell them before they could sneak up on us."

I relaxed, and Agatha's hand found mine. She guided me and put my hand on the railing. "There."

We moved up the stairs quickly with a new sense of confidence. With Agatha's keen senses, we'd know they were there before they could grab us. At the top of the stairs, I felt for the doorknob and pushed open the door. I squinted into the darkened room and recognized it instantly. It was the Gossamer House kitchen. I knew the way out now. The house was dark and quiet as we moved through the narrow halls, our feet cold on the hardwood.

We were almost to the sitting room, almost to the front door. Then Agatha snatched at the back of my hospital gown. "I can smell them. But I can't hear them."

I didn't stop. We were too close. By the time we reached the door, we were all running. I ripped open the door, and we charged full-speed into the night. I led the way across the lawn and onto the road. The gravel cut into the bottoms of our feet as we ran.

Cole took charge; he knew where he'd parked. "This way!"

We made it to the van. Each of us slammed against it, leaning into it, anchoring ourselves to the frame. I couldn't believe it. We made it out.

Lizzie couldn't believe it either. She pressed her back against the van, her chest rising and falling fast. "Why...did...they...let us...go?"

I winced and cradled the stitch in my side. "I don't..." I gasped for breath I couldn't seem to catch. "...know."

"Okay." Cole heaved a shaky breath. "We're all...going to... Agatha's house..."

I shook my head ready to argue, but Agatha beat me to it.

"Not my house." She shook her head, her blonde hair white in the moonlight. "They'll be at the funeral home. There's a false wall in the viewing room."

I pushed off the van and took Cole by the hand. I led him away from Lizzie and Agatha.

Cole groaned with impatience. "Nix, I'm not going—"

"Listen to me." I looked hard in his eyes, black in the shine of the moon. "I get it, okay. I understand how much I screwed up this hunt. But you all did, too."

"Nix—"

"Cole...I need you to trust me to handle this. To believe in me."

Cole sighed heavily. Before he could say anything else, I added, "And I'm not going alone. Lizzie's coming with me."

Cole's eyes widened. "What?"

Lizzie, who'd clearly been eavesdropping, pushed between us with Agatha at her side. "Of course, I'm coming. You take Agatha and bring her dad back here."

I nodded firmly. "Cole, you need to trust me to be smarter." I smirked with a lazily shrug. "And I'll trust you to come back to save the day."

Cole looked off to the side, staring hard into the darkness. His nostrils flared as his jaw flexed. He looked back at me. "Fine."

He wrapped an arm around Agatha and led her into the van. I wrenched open the door and dug in the back for spare blades, lighters, and bottles of lighter fluid, cursing the fact that we had no change of clothes. I stuffed everything in an empty backpack and slung it over one shoulder.

I wrapped a sheath around my waist, looking ridiculously like some kind of medieval peasant. I held one out for Lizzie. Before she could take it, Agatha flew at her and wrapped her thin arms around her in a tight hug. "Give this to Mary when you find her."

Lizzie squeezed her back. She rubbed her hands furiously up and down her back.

Then Agatha pulled away. Lizzie released her reluctantly. Agatha rushed into me with another hard hug. "Thank you for saving me," the little girl breathed into the scratchy fabric of the hospital gown.

"What—?"

"You could've taken my head." Agatha crushed me tighter. "But you saved me instead. Thank you."

She released me abruptly, almost anxiously, as though she were afraid I might change my mind. I wanted to say something to her, but I couldn't think of anything to say. And then she was gone, disappearing around the van.

Cole helped her into the passenger seat before he climbed into the driver's seat. And then he drove away without a word.

Lizzie and I exchanged hard glances in the dark.

"Let's go get your sister."

But we never made it to the witching well.

As soon as the van taillights disappeared down the road, and we turned onto the gravel drive, the ghouls attacked.

# HALF MAN, HALF MONSTER; EQUALS ONE COMPLETE GENTLEMAN

We heard them before we saw them.

As our bare feet crunched the cold, gravel stones of the driveway, our blades low at our sides, a sound chittered from behind us. We turned, foot pads spinning in the dirt. Their eyes glowed glassy, yellow and green, like wolves leering at us from the road. Their teeth bared in ghoulish grins shiny in the blue twilight with backs hunched like giant rats cloaked in shadow. Only two of them. Maybe that's all that was left? Doubtful.

"What do we do?" Lizzie whispered.

"Aim for the head," I breathed back. "Hard."

Then they leaped forward and scurried across the ground like roaches at an unbelievable speed. Their claws ripped up the road, casting a cloud of dirt in their wake. Before we could even take a swing, they grabbed our ankles, and we slammed into the gravel. My head smacked against the stones. Black stars burst in my vision as I stared up at the sky, stunned.

They were so fast. The strap of the backpack yanked against me as the bag trailed behind me at my side. The hospital gown pulled up around my thighs as it filled with rocks and driveway dirt that tore and burnt my back as the ghoul gripped my feet and dragged me down the road to the house. I kept my hand clenched around the blade and arched forward, trying to swing at any limbs I could manage, but it was impossible. It was too fast. And the road rash was unbearable. I had to do something. I dropped the blade. Then I twisted for the backpack, pulling it onto my chest. I fumbled with the zipper and drenched the bag in lighter fluid. I gripped the lighter tight, held up the strap, and I set the backpack ablaze. Then I arched to the side and swung the bag at the ghoul.

The effect was immediate. The ghoul dropped me. My ankles cracked against the road. It hissed and skittered into the shadows away from the backpack, still burning in the center of the drive-way. I forced myself to stand, my whole body aching and back stinging with road rash. I grabbed the strap of the burning bag and whipped it at the ghoul still dragging Lizzie.

The ghoul howled and dropped her to the ground. I ran for her. I snatched at her hands and yanked her to her feet. "RUN!"

We scrambled off the driveway and headed for the closest refuge: Gossamer House. Limping and ducking between the remaining cars at the end of the driveway, Lizzie fell upon the black back door of the house. She pulled me with her inside. To the left, it opened up into the oversized kitchen and dining room, but directly ahead, it faced a small archway with a staircase. Without hesitation, Lizzie dragged me up the steep, twisting staircase, and we stumbled out into a hallway. I recognized it. The girls' bedrooms. Lizzie shoved open her door, and we crashed inside. She slammed the door behind us and went for her dresser, a giant shadow in the darkness. I could barely see, but I fumbled my way through the mess of things all over the floor and rushed to her side. Together, we shoved the dresser up against the door.

Lizzie went for the light switch, but I grabbed her hand. "No lights," I breathed.

"Right." Lizzie nodded, a black figure beside me in the dark. Then she pushed past me and tugged open a dresser drawer. She dug around inside for a moment, feeling each individual garment. Then she passed me some pajama pants and a shirt. I scoffed in disbelief. I grinned and ripped off the potato sack, wincing as the fabric stuck to the raw skin of my back, and I pulled on the fuzzy flannel pants and slipped on the shirt. It hurt. But it felt good to finally have pants again.

"What else do you have in here?" I whispered with a smirk.

Lizzie finished changing and passed me her sheathed machete. I strapped it around my waist as she rummaged through her top drawer. She shook her head. "Nothing."

I nodded and gritted my teeth. "Okay." I moved between the two twin beds to the window between them and peeked through her shade. The witching well was like a black hole in the backyard. A sinkhole ready to swallow up all the surrounding trees.

"We need to get down that well." My breath fogged up the glass.

Lizzie came up next to me and stared down at the backyard, blue-black in the aging twilight. "How many ghouls do you think are out there?"

I inhaled deeply and gave a one-shouldered shrug. "No idea." I snorted and quipped. "At least two...unfortunately that fire only freaked them out."

Lizzie scoffed weakly. Then she took a shaky breath and asked in a voice barely above a whisper, "And how many are missing?"

"Mary, probably Scott Tyler, my sister, our friend, Logan, Stuart, and Billie."

"Stuart?" Lizzie stiffened beside me. "Did you say Stuart?"

My eyes shifted from the witching well to Lizzie. An uneasy shiver swept up my arms.

Before either of us could speak, the doorknob rattled softly, the sound muffled behind the dresser. We flinched at the noise, heads snapped in the direction of the door. The doorknob rattled louder and louder, angry and violent. Then it stopped. Silence deafening my ears, slowly I stepped forward toward the door. I moved in front of Lizzie, unsheathed the blade, and held it out to my side. I crossed past the twin beds and stood ready before the dresser, mind reeling with wild thoughts of how to escape.

Lizzie shrieked.

I turned just in time to see her jerk violently sideways, her whole body yanked downwards. Her head cracked against a bed frame. And with one final jerk, she disappeared underneath the bed.

I dropped to the floor. There was a hole. A ghoul tunnel hidden beneath the bed.

The door burst open.

The dresser slammed into the wall.

I scrambled to my feet. I raised the machete.

And the ghoul grinned, its eyes shining fluorescent in the darkness.

"Come on, Phoenix. It's time to go."

I blinked stupidly as the light switched on.

Stuart bobbed into the room.

One hand yanking hard on Billie's hair, the other hand curled around her throat.

"Let her go," I murmured in a voice low and threatening.

Billie's eyes fluttered, and she moaned slightly. Then her eyes lifted, and she found my face. "It's him, Phoenix. It's Stuart...he—"

His hand squeezed her throat, cutting off her words as well as her oxygen. "Shhh. Shhh." He bent his head low to nuzzle his cheek against hers.

"But..." I had no words. I couldn't catch my breath. The air was trapped in my chest. I couldn't breathe. Nothing made sense. I blinked furiously. Tears leaked from my eyes. Billie's lip was bleeding, and her sweatshirt was soaked dark with blood. Her honey hair was sticking out of her braids at odd angles like straw from a haystack as she sagged in Stuart's hard grip.

Stuart's ghoul teeth disappeared, replaced by his human teeth.

"All right…it's time to go. The Mother has plans for you, Phoenix. Big plans." He chuckled and bobbed up and down on the balls of his feet.

"You…" I couldn't finish. My brain wasn't connecting.

"I know. I get it." Stuart rolled his eyes and shook his head. "You're confused. I'll explain it all once we get downstairs. Okay?"

"No," I mumbled weakly. My fingers tightened on the handle. There was no way to hit him without hitting Billie.

"Now, I'm only going to tell you this one time…you drop that blade and follow me…or I'm going to rip out my sweet cousin's throat. Got it?"

I dropped the blade.

Stuart smiled.

Then there was a skittering sound behind me from beneath the bed. Then hard, bony hands, curled into sickle-like claws, grabbed my arms. And a ghoul wearing Seraphina's face and a too-tall ponytail, pressed her nose into my cheek. "Let's go, Sissy."


They brought us downstairs into the oversized kitchen and forced us into chairs at the long table in the dining area, binding us down with thick coils of rope. Billie's head lulled to the side. She was having a hard time staying conscious. I winced underneath the glare of the kitchen lights.

On the table were heads.

Ghoul heads.

On plates.

Dr. Godwin. Catherine Godwin. Sheriff Godwin. And both deputies from the school. Their eyes were glassy and clouded like taxidermy dogs, their teeth stubby and bared.

I looked over at Stuart as he bobbed around the dining table, surveying the scene. He nodded excitedly. Then he snapped his fingers and pointed at me. "Oh, Phoenix, you'll love this—one more thing…"

Stuart hurried around the counter to the door of the walk-in pantry just out of sight. As soon as he opened the door, the room filled with muffled grunts and hisses. Feral fear, the deep-rooted poisonous kind that keeps you alive, flooded my veins like a blood curse. My eyes darted toward the ghoul with Seraphina's skin. She smirked nastily and wiggled her fingers in a sly wave. Then her eyes slid back toward the kitchen, and she bounced up and down like a little kid waiting for the ice cream truck.

I craned my neck to see, but Stuart was still hidden behind the cabinets and refrigerator. It wasn't until Stuart came back around the corner, wheeling one of those upright slanted operating tables, that I could see. Stuart guided the table over to our perverse little dinner party and then spun it around, revealing who he'd brought as his surprise guest.

I recoiled at the sight of him.

Billie let out a low, slurred moan.

Sidney Godwin.

But instead of the laughing, happy-go-lucky, golden athlete I'd known...or even the rageful, hotheaded hero racing after his girl-friend...he was broken and bound.

Sidney Godwin, bloody and bruised, still wearing his letterman jacket from this morning, was strapped to the table with several leather buckles staggered up and down his arms and legs.

But the worst part of it was the mask.

Stuart had slapped a leather mask across Sidney's face, covering everything except for his eyes and forehead. There were holes for his nostrils. Nothing else.

Sid's eyes burned bright as he saw us. He began to thrash against the buckles binding him in place. Hissing noises came from the depths of his mask. Like he was gagged underneath. Or his jaw was wired shut. He couldn't speak. Much less scream.

Stuart leaned around the table and grinned wickedly at Sidney. "Don't worry, Sid. I've got a surprise for you, too." Stuart bit his lip on his widening grin. He clapped a hand over Sidney's chest.

"Might even make you scream." Stuart giggled, doubled over with his amusement. Then his head snapped up toward the other ghoul, his laughter completely gone. He sneered at her in disgust. "*Anytime now, Pamela!*" he bellowed.

My eyes narrowed. I should've known. Seraphina never wore ponytails that high. Dead giveaway. Pamela let out a little squeak and then hurried from the room. Blonde ponytail swaying, she ran into the living room that had only hours before shown the big screen viewing of *Scream* to a house full of kids.

I glanced over at Billie. The sight of Sidney had woken her from whatever broken state she'd been in, and she'd started to pull against the ropes at her wrists.

Stuart watched Billie, licking his lips with his giant tongue. He pushed off Sidney's operating table and loped over toward Billie, swaying like a slinky cat. He stopped behind her chair and smoothed her hair straighter and fluffed her braids. She flinched away from him and tugged hard at her binds.

Stuart snickered as he eyed her hungrily. "Everything's going according to plan." He pinched the end of her braid in two fingers and then dropped it back down. He met my eye with a smirk. "Mother knows best, after all."

"I don't understand." I spoke through gritted teeth, words silted and harsh. "You helped me. You burned those ghouls. *Why!*"

Stuart cocked his head to the side, his eyes glittering as he grinned. "It's all part of the plan, Phoenix. Haven't you heard? We Godwins like to play with our food before we eat it."

"But—"

"Nothing can compare to the taste. It tenderizes the meat. See you get a person all worked up—their meat gets marinated in all kinds of delicious chemicals. So juicy. Dopamine. Serotonin. Oxytocin. Endorphins. Cortisol. Adrenaline."

I stared.

Stuart nodded knowingly and pushed off Billie's chair. He loped over to the center of the table and scooped up his mother's head by the black, pin-straight ponytail. The sheriff's head dangled in the air, swaying slightly, her thin face stretched bizarrely with a mouthful of gruesome ghoul teeth. "See, my mommy..." He dropped her head back onto the plate with a thud. He grabbed the doctor by the blonde hair and tossed her into Billie's lap. "Auntie Penny."

Billie shrieked, her voice breaking into stifled, choking sobs. She thrashed in the chair and kicked her knees, knocking the head off her and to the floor.

Stuart grinned at Billie as she continued to cry. He cocked his head to the side and watched her with amused interest for a moment. Then he turned his attention back to the table. He smacked Catherine Godwin across the table, and then each of the deputies' severed heads in turn. The heads skidded off the table, smearing a trail of blood behind them. "All the little, old bitties." Stuart shook his head with a lazily smirk. "They had their time. They had their fun. But their ways..." Stuart shook his head again with a downturned smile and a boyish shrug. "They're *old* ways. It's time for a new era. New Mother. New rules."

With that, he took one of the plates and chucked it across the room. One after another, he sent them sailing into the wall. They smashed to pieces. And I flinched every time. He was insane. My heart thundered loudly in my ears as I struggled to remain in control. All I could do was pray that Cole brought Victor here in time before things got really bad. And with the way Stuart kept eying Billie...we didn't have long.

Once Stuart ran out of plates to smash, he wandered over to the doorway and leaned on the doorframe. "Pamela! Let's go! It's not like she's conscious!"

A moment later, Stuart pushed off the doorframe and hurried back to stand behind Sidney, his arm draped around the table, and his face by Sidney's ear. "Get ready, buddy boy."

My eyes flew to the doorway as Pamela dragged a limp Lizzie into the room. The ghoul had her by the ankles, hauling her into the dining area. Lizzie wasn't moving. My heart sank into the pit of my stomach, dropping fast like a stone. Lizzie had a huge, purple bruise on her forehead, but other than that, she could've been sleeping.

My pain at seeing her was nothing compared to the sounds that hummed out of Sidney's chest, muffled by his mask that sealed his mouth shut. It was tortured and heartbroken and rageful all at the same time. A long, low moan of the purest pain: love.

It hurt me to hear it. I couldn't imagine how it was to feel it. Tears blurred my eyes and leaked down my face. My lip trembled as I looked from Lizzie to Sidney and back.

Stuart thought it was hilarious.

He dissolved into giggles and stumbled backwards. He grabbed the operating table and used it for support as, breathless with laughter, he waved the ghoul toward the table. He jumped up and down eagerly as Pamela lifted Lizzie and tossed her cruelly onto the dining table.

I let out the breath stuck in my chest. A scoff of tortured disbelief.

Lizzie's dark hair splayed across the tabletop, fanning around her like she was underwater. Her face was turned toward me. She looked dead. I averted my eyes as my heart throbbed with the ache.

What were they going to do with her? Would they eat her in front of us?

I had to distract them.

Keep them talking.

It's all I had.

Cole would show up soon.

I inhaled a sharp, shallow breath and forced another dismissive scoff. I crinkled my nose in disgust. "So, you and your...what are they? Sisters? You're all having a little coup, is that it?"

Stuart grinned, his teeth big and wet in his mouth. "Exactly."

I rolled my eyes with a downturned smile. "But Annie is dead. You all killed her and tossed her over the willow tree—"

Stuart giggled. "Where do you think the phrase 'don't bite my head off' came from?"

"—I cut down Tiffany...but then *you* set Amanda on fire. And you burnt up the librarian. Who's left for your little clan of fan girls?" I glanced at Pamela with a mean smirk. "Pamela? *She's* your final girl?" I snickered darkly with a pitying shake of my head. "Awesome."

Pamela's eyes narrowed, and her teeth sank into her gums. Her ghoul jaws popped out, stretching Seraphina's face grotesquely wide.

Stuart smiled wider, his mouth open and thick tongue sticking out. "Pamela, go check on the tunnel. It's almost time to finish this. We've got a birthday party to attend!"

My eyes shifted to Stuart. My nostrils flared. The kids. Mary. Scott. And Phin and Logan. They were going to drain them. And the Mother was going to eat them before their bodies grew cold.

Pamela didn't move. Her eyes bored into me, and her fingers curled around the chair in front of her; long, thick claws pierced through her fingertips, extending out like a cat.

"Pamela!" Stuart barked.

"Yeah, Pamela. Run along like a good doggie." I grinned my cheesiest grin. Then I paused and cocked my head to the side. "Don't tell me you're going to be the new Mother! Ha!" I forced out a stream of riotous laughter. "Ew."

Pamela opened her mouth, but before she could fire a retort, a young woman with brilliant hair streaked like a pink sunset burst through the back door of the kitchen. Lenore. The girl from the morgue. I scoffed and rolled my eyes to the ceiling. Of course, it'd be her, too. They probably put her at the funeral home to keep an eye on Victor. But she didn't care about me. Her eyes were on Stuart. "There's a problem."

Stuart's entire demeanor changed. And for once, I could truly see the monster inside him, buried beneath the goofy swagger. His face darkened. His expression was murderous. He didn't speak. He only stared at her with slowly narrowing eyes.

Lenore cleared her throat and tried again. "In the tunnel. With the hunter."

Stuart let out a loud growl like the roar of a lion.

I flinched. Goose bumps burst up and down my arms.

Lenore swallowed hard and winced. "It—it wasn't my fault. It was the blonde. She tricked me and..."

Stuart roared again, silencing her mid-excuse. He ripped aside the chair in front of him. It smashed against the wall and broke into pieces. Then he stomped toward her. She backed up quickly and led the way through the back door.

The camera in the corner of the room whirred.

"Pamela! Watch them!" Stuart bellowed. *"And no snacking!"* The back door slammed so hard the house shuddered.

Pamela hissed at the back door and then stuck her obnoxiously long, thick tongue out.

A small smirk twitched in the corner of my mouth.

Two down.

One to go.

"So...Pamela. What's your angle? Let the Mother munch on the blood drained bodies, give her one final birthing round, and then rip her head off, too?"

Pamela's ghoul teeth shined wet and spitty in her oversized smile. "Something like that..."

"But if Stuart's so keen on a coup...what makes you think he would hesitate to hack off *your* head and burn *you* alive?"

Pamela puffed up her chest and tilted her chin high. "Because that's not the plan...*I'm* going to be the Mother."

I nodded with mock understanding. "Sure. You definitely are final girl material. Alpha written all over you. Makes sense. Stuart did all this just for you..." I rolled my eyes. It *didn't* make sense. The Mother would be leading the Father. But Stuart was clearly dominating Pamela. He was in charge. So, she wouldn't be his pick. And if Stuart really was running things, how?

He didn't ever come off as particularly smart. Much less smart enough to assassinate his elders and betray his siblings (ew) one by one. And he certainly had never shown any interest in Pamela. Maybe Lenore? I couldn't think. It all made my head hurt. Political dramas were not my thing.

The only thing that actually made sense in this—was Stuart torturing Sidney. It was obvious Stuart hated Sidney with a deeply rooted jealousy that bordered on biblical. Caine and Abel I could understand. But nothing else about this fit. "But tell me, if Stuart's really going to put *you* in charge...which, somehow, I highly doubt...what are your plans for me? You all keep saying the Mother has something planned—what is it?"

Pamela's nose wrinkled as her lip curled back in a monstrous sneer. "You think you're so perfect. So *special*. Look at you. All tied up with nowhere to go while your sister and the hunter are primed for slaughter."

"At least I'm not stuck on babysitting duty while the cavalry sneaks inside..."

Pamela's face fell as she considered this. "What does that mean?"

I raised my chin with a confident smirk. "It means, more hunters are going to swarm this place within minutes. And when they make it down that tunnel and burn it all down, it'll be all your fault." I scoffed with a nasty smile. "Well, at least Stuart will see it that way..."

Pamela glanced at the darkened windows. "You're lying."

I grinned. "You're right. I am."

She scowled, her confusion creasing her forehead.

I glanced sideways at Billie. She was staring at Lizzie. I looked at Sidney. His bloodshot eyes, still shining with emotion, stared at Lizzie, too.

Pamela turned toward the windows. She dropped to the

ground and scurried across the room to peer out the curtains. Watching her move, her limbs crooked bent and crawling...it turned my stomach.

Then without a word, she dropped back down and scurried straight for me. She clawed her way up my legs to sneer in my face. "If you try to run, I will personally peel the skin from your meat and make you taste your own intestines," she hissed.

I flinched away from the spray of her spit. "Whatever. At least it'll taste better than your breath. Bleh." I made a face.

Pamela let out a low, grumbling growl and skittered back down me and toward the back door. She opened and shut it quietly behind her as she disappeared into the night.

Billie's eyes shifted to the side in the direction of the back door. "Where do you think she went?"

"She must've heard a car or something." I had to move. Now.

"Is there really help coming?" Billie whispered.

"No." I pushed back in the chair and stood up on my feet, my back bent with the curve of the chair. Then I ran backwards as fast as I could and slammed the chair into the corner of the counter. I heard it splinter. Again. I rushed forward, stooped and bent like an old woman. Then charged backward. The chair cracked. One more. I ran and backed up and smashed the chair to pieces. I wiggled my wrists free of the ropes and ran around the counter for the knife block. I yanked out a butcher knife and hurried over to free Billie.

I sawed the ropes that bound her and then pulled her roughly to her feet. "Come on, Billie. We need to move!"

She moaned and swayed where she stood. "We...we have to help Sidney."

"I'm going to get you somewhere safe first!"

She shook her head as she struggled to stand in place. She blinked rapidly and forced her eyes open. She met my gaze with hard eyes. "No. We need to get Sidney."

"Billie, you can't even stand."

Billie swallowed hard and nodded furiously. She leaned forward, her hands on the table. "Yes. I can." She inhaled deeply as though she might breathe in clarity and strength. Then she pushed herself up and ran to him.

He flinched away from her, his fingers clenched and scratching. He looked wild and crazed.

"What did they do to him?" I eyed him warily. "It's like he doesn't recognize us."

Billie brushed his golden hair from his forehead. He lurched his head away from her. Billie didn't seem to notice. She smiled back at me. Hope shined in her eyes. Then she pressed her lips to his temple. "Shush, it's okay. Sidney, I'm here. And we're going to help Lizzie. Everything will be the way it was, I promise."

Sidney thrashed violently against the restraints. He grunted and groaned behind the mask.

I winced. "Billie, we don't know what he's been through—are you sure it's safe to—"

Sidney launched himself at her with such force the table rattled. She backed away from him and walked backward into me. I rested my hand on her shoulder, the butcher knife limp at my side.

"You're right," Billie breathed. "What are we going to do, Phoenix?"

Sidney's eyes pierced into Billie. It was like he couldn't even see me. Only his sister.

"We can at least take the mask off him..." I chewed my lower lip as I hesitated. He was freaking me out. The way he was acting... he was either messed up so bad he couldn't comprehend reality, or he was trying to warn us about something. "...that way he can talk to us instead of..." My words trailed off as Sidney continued to jerk against the straps.

Billie shook her head, taking another step back into me. Her words stumbled over themselves. "No...no. No. I can't, uhm...I want to leave it on him until he...calms down. I couldn't bear it if he..." She glanced over her shoulder at me, her brow furrowed and emerald eyes fearful. "If he wasn't himself."

I looked from Billie to her brother, my heart heavy. The last thing we needed was for him to make so much noise that Pamela came scurrying back through the door.

Sidney's eyes burned as they met mine. He groaned and hissed and his whole body convulsed like he was seizing. I had to look away. He was like a wounded beast, caged and tormented. It was inhumane. Evil.

I squeezed Billie's shoulder and inclined my head toward the kitchen. "Go grab the biggest knife you can find."

Billie nodded obediently and hurried away from her brother. She slipped around the counter to search the kitchen.

I turned and focused my attention on Lizzie. Gingerly, I pressed my fingers into the curve of her neck. Her pulse was there. I expected Sidney to freak out the moment I touched her, but he didn't thrash or hiss. I glanced over my shoulder at him. He watched me, his green eyes following me.

"She's okay," I breathed.

Sidney moaned softly at my back. I turned and approached him cautiously. I locked my amber eyes with his. "Sid...I'll take your mask off...but you need to be *quiet*. Do you understand? We'll need your help if we're going to get Lizzie out of here. And you're the only one who can carry her."

Sidney nodded stiffly. I stared for a moment, stunned he'd actually responded. "Okay, then." I put the butcher knife down beside Lizzie and went for Sidney's mask.

But before I could unfasten it, he jerked away and let out a feral, muffled groan.

I stepped back, stumbling into the dining table. "Sid—"

Then I saw it. His eyes. His eyes were looking behind me, toward the back door, narrowed and blazing as he thrashed. I snatched the blade and snapped around. Pamela scurried through the back door and straight for me.

I backed up, knife raised. I swung as she attacked, ghoul teeth bared and hands out like claws. The knife connected with her neck, cutting into her like a butcher block, but nowhere near all the way through. She clawed at me, rabid and frenzied. I held her back but couldn't swing again. The force of her impact sent us both slamming into the floor.

I turned my head, inching away from Pamela's snapping, growling jaws, just in time to see Billie. She didn't hesitate. She didn't even flinch. Knife raised, she rushed forward with all the speed of a track star. She snatched a fistful of Pamela's ponytail and executed her in one powerful swing. Then she flung the head as far from her as she could and shoved the body off me. She scooped me up by my armpits and pulled me into a tight, crushing hug. "Oh, my God, Phoenix! Are you okay?"

"How—" A delirious laugh escaped me like a cough. "How did you do that?" I blinked stupidly, still recovering from the adrenaline rush of a near-death experience. "You just swiped off her head...*with a butcher knife*? Just...wow."

She gripped my shoulders and held me at arm's length. "We need to go. You get Lizzie up, while I—"

Someone giggled.

We both twisted toward the living room. Stuart stood in the archway, his face streaked with blood, his nose swollen, hands on his hips, and his nasty ghoul teeth grinning. "Oh, look. My two best ladies. This must be the final girl moment."

I lunged for the knife.

But Stuart was on me first. He was too fast, dashing across the floor on all fours like a spider. He collided into me, knocking me to the ground. His weight crushed me into the hardwood. He grabbed me around the waist and yanked me up with him. He pinned my back to his chest, an arm around my stomach and a hand at my throat, holding my head back, so he could nuzzle his bloody, broken nose into my neck.

"Billie, get Sidney!" I flinched away from Stuart, but he jerked me back, his nails digging into me.

Billie ran for her brother.

Her hands found the buckles of his restraints.

But she hesitated.

She took a step back.

Then Billie looked at me, her eyes wide and fearful.

And she smiled.

"You know...I don't think I will just yet."

I blinked stupidly. My body went limp as I tried to understand what she was saying.

Stuart giggled and snuggled me tight.

Then Billie grinned, and her teeth slipped into her gums and ugly ghoul teeth emerged.

# BURN IT DOWN

"Put her over there."

Stuart crushed me to him, and stepped sideways until we were beside the dining table, facing Sidney. Eyes wide, body lank, I stared, unseeing, as Billie grinned up at her brother, still strapped to the tilted table.

What was happening?

Nothing made sense.

Billie didn't bother to explain.

Her attention was all on her brother. She reached up and unhooked his mask. Sidney's eyes blazed with hatred, his handsome face marred with it, as he spoke through bared teeth. "*You were supposed to be on my side.*"

Billie's brow crinkled as she stepped back and scoffed in sarcastic amusement. "You were supposed to be *at* my side, Sidney. Mine. Not hers." Billie pointed back at Lizzie. Her finger jabbed Lizzie cruelly in the cheek. "Now...I'm going to kill your girlfriend, nice and slow—" Billie chuckled and held up a hand. "No, I'm sorry, *you're* going to kill her. Or, at least, she'll think you are..."

Stuart couldn't keep quiet anymore. He shook with eagerness and giggled. "I'm going to shed into you, Sid!"

Billie glanced sideways at Stuart and gave him an indulgent grin. Then she looked back at Sidney with an odd, loving expression as her fingers trailed up and down his arms. "So, while Stuart is chopping Lizzie up into fine little cutlets for me, flaying her down to the bone like a stinky little fish…"

Sidney's eyes burned a bright emerald. "NO!"

Billie's ghoul-toothed smile parted like a laughing hyena. "—you and I are going to talk for a bit…"

Sidney jerked against the leather straps. His eyes pierced Stuart with the full force of his rage. "*If you touch her—*"

"Oh, I already did." Stuart licked his lips with a nasty smirk. "It was me that dragged her down the Blood Farm tunnel." He cocked his head to the side. "But you guessed that part already, didn't you, Sid?"

Sidney's face darkened burgundy as he let out a monstrous roar that made me flinch.

Stuart giggled manically. "You should've seen Lizzie's face when she saw me."

Billie's eyes glittered. "—and then when Stuart's done, I'll gobble up all the pieces of your girlfriend just in time for the ceremony." She beamed brightly and peeked around him at the clock on the stove. "It's almost time." She reached up to stroke his cheek. Sidney snapped his head around and bit down, catching her thumb and ripping it off.

Blood gushed down Billie's hand and streaked down her arm. Sidney crunched down and swallowed, his face murderous and mouth smeared red.

Billie laughed in delight as she stepped back from her brother. She sucked the stump where her thumb had been. Then she pursed her lips and in an amused smirk. Billie shook her head and held up her hand. Before I could blink, it healed itself. Her thumb regrew, whole again. The only trace of injury was the blood, sticky and shiny, all over her hand and arm.

"Wait, wait…" I stuttered and cleared my throat, finally finding a few words. "I don't—Billie?"

Billie stiffened as though she'd forgotten I was there. Her ghoul teeth sank back into her gums, replaced by her perfect human ones. She reached over to Lizzie and wiped the blood off her arm onto Lizzie's white tank top and smeared it on Lizzie's jeans.

Billie glanced sideways at me. "Pretty cool, isn't it, Phoenix?" She turned toward me and tugged on her oversized sweatshirt still black with dried blood. "All this blood? It wasn't ever mine." She pulled up the sleeve, revealing a completely healed arm where her bite should've been. "Ghouls have a pretty high tolerance for pain. It wasn't hard to take a bite out of myself and put on a pouty face." She shrugged almost sympathetically. "Don't feel too bad, Phoenix. I'm an incredible actress. Aren't I, Sidney?" Her gaze slid slyly toward her brother.

He spat at her face.

Billie rolled her eyes and sauntered over to me, her expression patient and kind.

She smoothed the sweaty, fallen tendrils of black and cherry hair from my forehead. "I'm sorry it had to be this way, Phoenix. But—"

I flinched away from her. "This whole thing…the rescue and all that…you were just messing with me? Letting me find Cole…and save Agatha and Lizzie…all that just so you could take it away again?"

"Nothing pounds the meat harder than the black moment." Billie grinned, her lips parted, and she licked her lips. "And we're not even to the good part, yet. I do have plans for you, after all."

I blinked rapidly. Tears leaked from my eyes. I shook my head. I hadn't heard her. She didn't say that. It didn't make sense because…

"*You helped me*," I stammered again. "You went to get Cole and—"

Billie nodded encouragingly.

I inclined my head as the tears rolled down my nose. "You were the one who brought him here. And you ate the sheriff. This whole thing...was your idea of a game?"

"More like a scary movie." Billie bit her lip on a radiant smile that lit up her whole face with glee. Her emerald eyes sparkled. "We had fun, didn't we? The whole 'she saves herself' trope and all that?"

My mouth sagged as my heart sank into a cloud of darkened despair. My voice broke as I repeated, "Fun."

Billie reached for my cheek.

I recoiled in disgust.

Stuart nuzzled the back of my head. I thrashed in his arms. He held me fast.

Billie's eyes lifted sweetly to meet mine. "I love your heart, Phoenix. I keep telling everyone, there isn't one better anywhere in the world. You're a rarity, Phoenix Grey. But don't worry." Her smile warmed, and her eyes blurred with emotion. "You'll understand everything soon enough."

Stuart giggled and squeezed me tight, swaying side to side. "Let me tell her, Billie, let me tell her!"

Billie's eyes slid up from mine to Stuart. Her smile twitched slightly. "Go ahead, Stuart."

"We like to play with our food, Phoenix." Stuart leaned his cheek against the top of my head. One arm clamped around me like a vise, he stroked the back of my hair like a dog. My lip curled in annoyance. My hurt at Billie's betrayal was hardening fast into furious rage.

Billie winced. Again, her mouth twitched with barely concealed impatience. "Stuart...I think she'll need a bit more of an explanation..." Billie cocked her eyebrow, and her eyes found mine again. "Phoenix, what do you know about ghouls?"

I groaned with exaggerated annoyance. "God, you science experiments love to hear yourselves talk, don't you?" I rolled my eyes. "Ghouls are fine. Keep to themselves. Don't bother anybody...I *love* ghouls, all right? But you mutts? You're on a whole other level of messed up—freaks." I spat the words.

Billie's eyes flashed, but her smile broadened. "Ghouls have a matriarchal society...but our family takes it a bit further—"

I snorted in disgust. "You know, I'm not really interested in hearing—"

Billie continued to grin with a suffocating air of superiority. "The Mother is the only one with a mate. She is the literal mother of us all. And in our family...we like to keep it in the family."

Stuart giggled. "Like the Pharaohs. Or Targaryens."

My stomach lurched as my brain began to catch up to their crazy. I raised my eyebrows and flashed a sarcastically sympathetic smile. "Like the Habsburgs...that explains the jaw."

Stuart frowned stupidly and looked from me to Billie as though trying to determine whether he'd been insulted. He had. Billie continued her lofty explanation, patiently arrogant. "Male Godwins...they aren't the strongest. Most of the time they die before adulthood..."

I scoffed. "Maybe it's because they should be eating *dead* meat, ever think of that?"

Stuart stiffened. He glanced down at me and then back up at Billie. Obviously, he'd never considered that before. Billie shook her head with a smile.

"So, the Mother arranges the next mated pair to follow her. The pair that will inherit the family, mother the next generation. Victor was promised to his sister—my mother, the pathetic, wilting, Dr. Penelope Godwin—"

"Don't you mean your *sister*?" I quipped nastily.

"But another problem with male Godwins? Not only are they weak, but they tend to go rogue. Abandon the family. Revert to our primitive ways—"

"How despicable," I muttered dryly.

"And when that happens, usually we memorialize them. You saw them in the basement..."

"The heads floating in the jars—"

"Memorialized. Enshrined."

I snorted and shook my head. Nuts. All of them. "Then why let Victor live?"

"Because Dr. Penelope Godwin was weak. Just like my aunt, Sheriff Alexandra Godwin..." Billie glanced back at the heads scattered around the floor. "There's nothing more irritating than weakness disguised as wit. *God, she was annoying.*" Billie rolled her eyes. She looked back at me and smiled sweetly. "As Stuart explained, we're doing massive management moves..." She snickered darkly. "Anyway—Victor...Dr. Penelope begged for his life. She *loved* her brother, you see." Billie pouted. Then she laughed. "The Mother agreed to let him live, on the condition that he kept his nose out of our business, turned a blind eye to the operation, and did as he was told."

I stifled a yawn. "Oh, is that it, then? Are you finally finished telling your disgusting, pathetic, life story?"

Billie's smile slipped.

I nodded toward her brother. "So, what about Sidney? He went rogue, too?"

Billie's gloating happiness fell from her face like a shadow. "Sidney and I were promised to each other. We were supposed to replace the Mother and her mate when we came of age. We aren't just brother and sister. *We're twins.* There's power in that. The children we'd have would be stronger than any ghoul generation before us!"

My stomach churned. I gagged. "You seriously don't hear how freaking *nasty* that sounds?" I scrunched up my nose. "Ugh. Can you blame him for seeing sense and running as far away from you freaks as inhumanly possible?"

Billie's face darkened. "Funny little Phoenix, always making jokes to mask all that pain. But you understand me better than anyone, don't you?"

I made a face.

Billie's eyes glittered. "Seraphina left you. *Again*. And she will keep leaving you. Over and over. Whenever she gets the chance, she prefers someone else over you...someone else's advice, someone else's company. *Anyone else but you*."

I shook my head, eyes shifting to the side.

"Seraphina left you in that motel room. She left you behind to run off with the hunter. And Sidney was the same. *Sidney was trying to leave me*—" she hissed through clenched teeth. Her eyes shined with emotion. "What did you say before? 'Everybody leaves?' Well, unlike you—the spineless, *powerless*, little witch—I'm not letting him get away with it. When Sidney 'fell in love' with stupid Elizabeth Tran, I arranged for her little sister to be taken. As a warning. To be kind. Generous. But he still wouldn't leave Lizzie. And he didn't think I'd do it. Didn't think I *could* do it...not right out from underneath his nose." Billie's eyes widened eagerly, her pupils dilated. "But I did. I had her taken. Ripped right from his fingers." Billie grinned like a Cheshire cat. "Now *that* was fun. Stuart scrambling out of the tunnel, snatching Lizzie in the dark, dragging her away as Sidney fought so hard to keep her." Billie sighed dreamily, her eyes drooping. "If I close my eyes, I can still hear her screams." Her eyes flashed open as she snapped, "But then, he *still* wouldn't give her up. He ran off to Victor to beg for his help...I knew he'd always fantasized about it—dreamed of 'overthrowing the establishment.' Longing to live in squalor just like Victor with his half-breed children." She made a face. "So, I made the call. Had Stuart beat him to the Wollstonecrafts' house."

"Yup. I did." Stuart giggled. "I bit him. Sidney. *Me*."

My eyes widened. "The little girls—"

"The feral little mutts? Oh, they'd already gone into hiding." Billie waved away my words. "Anyways, I need Victor. He has a very important part to play. Once the clan is dead, and I take my place as Mother, I'll need Victor to take the fall. I'll raid his house with all the bravado and idiocy of a human hunter, and I'll hack them all to bits. That way, we won't have any more 'Logan DeVarneys' poking around Watertown."

My stomach heaved at the mention of Logan. I thought of Phin. Locked away in cages awaiting the sacrificial slaughter. I swallowed thickly but couldn't rid my mouth of the sour taste.

Billie read my face easily. She gave me a pretty pout and twirled one of her braids around her finger. "Are you thinking about Cole? I've gotta ask: why do you think I let him drive off with sweet, little Agatha?"

I met her eyes.

Billie smiled. "I had a present waiting for them."

I swallowed hard. I gritted my teeth, struggling to maintain control. "So, what about Sidney?" I asked quietly. "His head goes in a jar?"

Billie scoffed. "That depends on how well our talk goes."

Stuart stiffened. Then his body sagged against my back. "Wait, Billie, you said *I* was going to be your mate...you said—"

Billie's expression flickered. "Of course, Stuart. I need you."

Pacified so easily, Stuart squeezed me hard.

"Well, that's a lie," I quipped dryly.

Billie tugged at a tendril of my hair. "And Phoenix, you're special. We are so much alike. And your heart is so strong. I have to have it. That's why you're still here. That's why we played for so long. And when I take it, you'll replace the old witch. And you'll live forever in a calm, comfortable unconsciousness until—"

"Woah, where's..." Stuart turned side to side, jerking me tight in his arms. "*Bill, where's Sid?*"

Billie's human teeth sunk into her gums and her ghoulish ones descended as she whirled around. Sidney was gone. The leather straps were still in place, still buckled, but slack with no body to hold down. On the floor, there was a pile of meat, ribbons of ripped flesh. Shedded. Ghoul shed.

Billie hissed and collapsed to the floor. On all fours, limbs bent like a spider, she scurried over to the gooey pile of meat.

Stuart clutched me to him like a kid with a teddy bear as he spun around in a panicked circle. "Where is he? *Where is he?*"

I blinked as the room spun. I snickered. "You know, they say 'may the best man win.' And I have a feeling he will. Really soon."

Billie tossed back her head and roared so ferociously I flinched.

Then she jumped to her feet and stalked over to us. She yanked me from Stuart's arms, sending me knocking into the dining table. But in the split second before she pulled me back into her, my fingers closed around the butcher knife forgotten at Lizzie's side. "Shed," she hissed at Stuart in a low growl. "*Now*. No more games. Time to start cutting."

Stuart glanced warily around the kitchen and dining area. "But Billie, what if—"

"NOW!"

Stuart's body started convulsing, tiny trembling jerks, until his skin had molted, dropping to the floor in thick, goopy chunks of flesh. His bones cracked as they stretched and Stuart's body was replaced by a loping, giggling version of Sidney.

Billie dragged me toward the empty, tilted table and unbuckled the straps. She shoved me against the table and slapped the buckles across me, tightening them around my torso and legs like thick ropes. I tucked the knife carefully behind my thigh. Billie was too distracted to notice. Too frightened by the idea of her brother skittering around the house out for revenge.

As soon as I was secured to the table, Billie stomped over to Stuart and pushed him hard into the dining table. The force of it doubled him over a bit. "Wake her up and get to work. I'll be back."

Stuart winced. "Wait..." His words trailed off as he looked at her with whimpering, puppy dog eyes.

"*What?*" Billie swung around, her braids flying, her eyes hard as emeralds. Her jaw jutted to the side, her ghoulish teeth sticking out at an angle. "What, Stuart! *You're scared?*" Billie's voice pitched high as she mocked him. "Of Sidney?" She held her arms out wide.

"Stuart, you've replaced him! You're Father Godwin, now. *Act like it*. Or I'll put your head in a jar beside our Father." Billie turned back around and muttered under her breath as she stalked out of the room. "*For the love of...*"

I wiggled the knife into position and flicked the buckle free.

And then my hand came free.

Stuart, wearing Sidney's skin, held out his hand and flexed his fingers. His claws extended like a cat. My stomach lurched. I stuck the knife handle in my mouth and using both hands, unbuckled the rest of the straps. I dropped to the ground.

Meanwhile, Stuart traced the tip of his index claw along Lizzie's arm. He dug deeper until she gasped awake. Her eyes flew open, wide and horrified. Then she saw Stuart, but she could only see Sidney, and dissolved into silent tears. "Sid...Sid...you're one of them, too?" She gasped again, choking on her emotion. "Pl-please, please don't do this. Just let me go."

Stuart smiled—Sidney's handsome face, scrunched-up in a goofy grin.

Lizzie moaned sorrowfully and continued to cry.

For a moment, it was like I was watching myself. Back in the church on Bird Island. With the demon in Cole.

I could feel myself losing it, slipping into that dark place, like I had back in the Gossamer House library.

No.

Not again.

It was Lizzie. Not me.

And I couldn't keep quiet. "Lizzie, that's not Sidney. It's a trick."

Stuart looked up, eyes narrowed. He pointed a claw at me. "Don't make me start on you first."

That's when he finally realized—I wasn't tied up anymore.

"How did you—" His eyes went to the knife in my hand. He snorted. "You think that scares me? I'd bite your head off before you even nicked my neck."

"Even if I can't manage to kill you...you're not getting out of here alive, Stuart." A sharp, barking laugh burst from my chest. "What are you going to do when Sidney finds you cutting into his girlfriend? What do you think he's going to do to you, huh?"

"I'm not afraid of Sidney," Stuart hissed through clenched teeth, spit spraying all over the floor. "I'm the Father! I replaced him! She picked me! *I'm better than him!*"

I laughed, breathless and hysterical. "Billie didn't pick you, Stuart. Not as her first, not even second choice—she's *stuck* with you. She has no other option. No one, not even a ghoul, would pick you over Sidney. Billie didn't. Lizzie didn't." I paused for a moment and pointed the knife at him. "And Drew didn't, either, did she?"

His anger exploded out of him. He shoved the dining table over and charged for me. Lizzie shrieked as she flipped over along with the table, crashing to the ground. Stuart crushed his fingers around my neck, collapsing my throat on my stifled breath. He held a claw up to my eye.

I flinched away.

He pressed his cheek up against mine. "You know, Phoenix, Billie can say what she wants about your heart...but your eyes... *They're* your best feature..." He licked his lips as he nuzzled my jaw. "They're like the color of...molten bronze...amber...caramel candy...and I think, when I'm done cutting them out of your pretty face, I'll keep them in my bedroom in a pretty glass case, so I can look into your eyes every day and remember this moment. Remember how much you screamed. How much you begged me to stop. And how—"

I wiggled just enough. In the blink of my pretty, amber eye, I stabbed the knife through his.

Stuart howled and staggered backward.

I scooped up Billie's discarded butcher knife, abandoned beside Pamela's stiff corpse. Stuart recovered as I ran for Lizzie.

"STUART!" Billie's shriek ripped through the room.

We all froze and turned to watch her enter from the hallway. Billie carried Lenore's head by the pink, sunset-streaked hair as she stomped into the room.

"*What are you doing?*" She tossed Lenore's head to the side as she glared at Stuart.

I stared wide-eyed as it rolled behind the overturned dining table, out of sight.

Billie crossed her arms, her face furious. "Can't you ever do one simple thing?"

Stuart, panting and knife handle still sticking out of his head, turned to face her, his shoulders slumped. He ripped the knife out of his eye with a loud squish. Then he pointed the blade at me as I slowly helped Lizzie to her feet, one arm around her waist, my other arm extended, holding the butcher knife out like a sword. Lizzie and I looked from Stuart to Billie, frozen. Trapped.

Billie ignored us. She marched over to Stuart and grabbed him by the throat. He gasped and clutched at her hand, but his claws retracted inside his fingers. He didn't dare fight her.

Billie's eyes slid to me.

Then she tossed me a lighter.

It clattered to the ground and skidded toward my feet, knocking into my toe.

Billie held my gaze with hard eyes. "The tunnel at the bottom of the well leads to the Blood Farm. The Mother will be there with the kids. And Billie. Go left. You have until sunrise. Just enough time to finish this. Light her up. And watch out for the Father."

I didn't move. I was too stunned to process.

Then I saw it.

The glance at Lizzie.

The flicker of love behind the emerald eyes.

I released Lizzie and snatched up the lighter.

Stuart continued to struggle. He hadn't seen it.

Then Billie's body began to twitch and jerk as ribbons of flesh peeled off, curling as they flopped to the ground.

And it was Sidney.

Lizzie whimpered, sinking to her knees in shock. I grabbed her again and pulled her toward the back door.

"You...can't...kill...me...*I'm wearing you*." Stuart wheezed. "I'll just come back."

"You won't. Because I won't, either." Sidney tugged a lighter out of his pocket. "I turned on the burner before I left. The whole time Billie was running her mouth? So was the gas. It's over. No more shedding. No more snatching little kids. No more spawning. No more munching on hitchhikers off the highway." Sidney pulled Stuart close and gave him a hard shake. "This whole Hell hole and every ghoul in it is going to *burn*."

"Sidney?" Lizzie pulled against me, desperate to reach him. "SIDNEY!"

Sidney didn't look at her. His eyes, shining with emotion, bored into mine. "Get her out. *Now!*"

"Come on, Lizzie." I gripped her arm and squeezed hard.

She wouldn't move.

I tried again. "*Mary*, Lizzie. We have to save Mary."

That did it.

With a shriek of tortured heartbreak, Lizzie allowed me to pull her toward the back door and shove her out into the dark.

As soon as I'd disappeared through the doorway after her, but before I'd kicked the door shut behind us, my ears twitched as the lighter flicked.

Fire roared, hot and raging.

And we both blasted forward into the dirt as the explosion ripped through Gossamer House.

29

BEATING HEART BABY

It was loud.

The single, ringing tone stretched out for several seconds. I blinked slowly, stunned and confounded. My cheek pressed into the gravel. Rocks and stones, blue and black in the twilight, were all I could see. My eyelashes swept against dirt. Then I saw the dark curve of a tire. And another.

I was in the driveway of Gossamer House.

My nostrils flared at the acrid stench of smoke. And the heat warmed my skin in the cold, biting November air. I was hot and cold all at once.

Then I remembered.

I pushed up onto my stinging hands and knees. Every muscle and bone ached. My body was torn on all sides. Old and new burns from the driveway. The ringing dulled. I swallowed hard, popping my ears.

And everything went quiet.

Gingerly, I forced myself up and onto my feet. My eyes found Lizzie a few feet away. Then she stirred, her back hunched as she struggled to all fours. She glanced over at me as I limped my way to her and pulled her up. She leaned into me and stared at the

397

Gossamer House. I turned to look over my shoulder at the building as the fire blazed. Black smoke billowed up to the tree branches leaning overhead.

"Come on." I gritted my teeth and swallowed the lump that'd formed in my throat at the thought of Sidney. "We aren't done yet."

Lizzie's trembling lip stiffened, and she sniffed. A single tear slid down the wide bridge of her nose. Her dark eyes fluttered furiously as she nodded. "Let's go."

Arm wrapped around her, I guided her through the parked cars toward the backyard. As soon as our feet touched the soft, cold grass, we both let out sighs of relief. We moved faster, then, each of us eying the shadows and the staggered trees, ready for the worst. But there was no one left to grab us. Sidney had seen to that.

As we neared the well, I felt the hum underneath my skin, static in the air like electricity. Lizzie rested her hands on the weathered stone of the well and peered down into the depths. I edged closer, almost reverent in my approach. The power it'd taken to create this...unimaginably impressive.

"How do we get down there?" She glanced over at me. "It goes on forever. At best, we only break our legs with the fall. At worst, we smash ourselves to pieces."

I shook my head, my eyes on the well. I placed my hands gently on the stone and felt a chill race up my arms. "No. It's a witching well. I can feel the magic."

"What?" Lizzie's eyes shifted from me to the well and back again.

I licked my lips. "And smashing apart on impact wouldn't be the worst thing that could happen."

Lizzie scoffed. "No?"

I shook my head, eyes wide and staring into the darkness below. "The worst thing that could happen is we get trapped in another realm."

"You're crazy. *This* is crazy." Lizzie slapped her hands over her face and moaned. Then she raked her fingers through her long, dark hair muttering to herself. "This cannot be happening. *Why is this happening?*"

I tore my eyes from the well. I took a deep breath and put a hard hand on Lizzie. "Have you seen *Alice in Wonderland*?"

Lizzie rolled her eyes as they leaked down her cheeks. "Yes."

"Okay. Well, this should work just like that...except the well is dead. So, it won't send us to another realm, it should just slow our fall before we hit the bottom."

"Oh, my God. We're going to die." Lizzie stared wildly at the witching well. "You're crazy, and we're going to die. *And I'm never going to see my sister again.*"

I squeezed down on her shoulder. "Sidney wouldn't have sent us to this well just to have you squashed like a bug!"

Lizzie's lip curled nastily. "Well, he was a monster, wasn't he?"

I flinched at the coldness in her words. He'd saved us. And in my eyes, that made him a better human than most people. I turned back to the well. "I'll call you when I get to the bottom."

I scooted my legs over the side and sat like a little kid on the edge of a bridge, ready to jump into the water. I inhaled deeply, but before I could push off into nothingness, Lizzie covered my hand with hers.

"I didn't mean it—"

I glanced back at her.

She took a deep breath, her eyes shining in the twilight. "I love him. I loved him. And I never told him. So, I need to say it out loud to someone...make it real...in case it's the last time I can. I love him."

I gave her a rueful smile. "He loved you, too."

And before I could back down, I pushed off into nothing.

And fell.

The cold air rushed past me as I dropped like a stone into a pond. I was sinking into the earth. And I wasn't slowing. My heart slammed against my chest. I gasped for breath I couldn't catch. Was I wrong again? Using magic as a crutch. I was going to die. Smash against the bottom of the well. Tears leaked from my eyes, sliding backwards into my hair as I fell.

And then, as though a hook snagged into my belly button, I jerked to a stop. My feet dropped to the dirt floor with all the impact of a small jump.

I stood still for a moment. Too scared. Too stunned to move. My eyes wide, I stared ahead stupidly, blinking blindly. I opened my mouth to call up to Lizzie, but nothing came out. I looked up. There was the smallest circle of blue-black sky overhead, but Lizzie's shadow cut into it, forming a crescent moon as she bent over the well, waiting.

I cleared my throat and tried again. "Lizzie! It's safe!"

I stepped into the tunnel ahead, giving her room to land at the bottom of the well, and waited for her to hit the ground. It took awhile. It took so long my stomach began to churn, and my mind began to question. What if it wouldn't work on an ordinary human? I heard the whistle of Lizzie falling fast. Had I fallen that fast? My eyes were round and unblinking as I watched the bottom of the well. I saw her feet. She wasn't stopping. I squeezed my eyes shut. But no bones cracked. No body splattered against the stones. Just a sharp gasp.

I peeked one eye open. And then the other.

Lizzie stared at me, eyes huge in her head. Her face petrified, frozen in her fear.

I gave her a minute to recover.

But only a minute.

We had work to do.

I squeezed her hand and then let it drop. I turned to face the opening of the ghoul tunnel. This one was different from the one connecting the cemetery to the Wollstonecrafts'. This one was old. Worn and well-traveled. The Wollstonecrafts' ghoul hole had probably been dug by Victor himself for his own personal use. But this one had been used by the Godwins for centuries. It was more like a cave than a dirt tunnel. There were little lights strung along the ceiling reminding me strongly of the Gossamer House basement. But unlike the basement, it wasn't wide or straight. It was narrow and curved. Weaving like a coiling snake, constantly turning and twisting toward the left. So much so, my stomach was getting sour, and my head started to spin.

There was something else.

Magic.

Dark and ancient and perverse.

It buzzed softly in the air like an insect I couldn't seem to swat.

We continued to move along the tunnel. The earthy smell of the dirt permeated the air and made it almost suffocating to breathe. But with every twist to the left, the magical hum grew stronger. Until the buzz tingled my bones and itched beneath my skin.

Then there was a fork in the tunnel. A left. And a right.

I looked right. Just as before, the tunnel curved all the way around. It was impossible to see what was around the corner. I looked left. It was the same.

I looked back toward the right. I felt the pull of the darkness. The magic drew me to it like a magnet. Instinctively, I flexed my fingers. My own magic was still beyond my reach. There was a dull ache in my heart over the loss of it. How would I ever find it again? When would I stretch my fingers and feel the soft hum of my own magic? The dark magic, unnatural and strange, called out to me. I took a step toward the right.

Lizzie's hand clamped down on my shoulder. *"Sidney said left,"* she breathed hot in my ear.

I closed my eyes.

I remembered.

But there was something down this way. Something I needed to see. I turned to Lizzie and pressed the lighter in both of her hands. I was going to tell her I'd be right back, but when I met her eyes in the low, yellow light of the lanterns, I finally understood what Logan had been hammering into my head. I flashed her an encouraging smile and nodded sharply. "You're right. Let's go."

We turned down the left path, but before we got around the bend, we ran straight into Billie.

"I've been waiting for you..." Her eyes glowed bright. "Ladies, I'd like you to meet my Father."

We turned and saw him.

He was so hideous, so monstrously distorted in his makeup, Lizzie swayed and nearly fainted. It was the creepy old man from the backyard, but with his oversized ghoul jaws protruding out of his skeletal face, his fluorescent eyes shining feral in his sockets, and his claws bursting from his gnarled hands—the sight of him made my skin twitch.

They dragged us backwards and down the right turning path which led to a giant wooden door, rotten and decayed. They shoved us through it.

My stomach lurched, soured with dread. It was a dank, dirty workshop, like some old man's toolshed with various shelves and worktables lining the walls. There was a large hole in a corner, and, based on the pile of loose dirt spread out around the opening, it was the Father ghoul's burrow...for sleeping when he wasn't 'working.' But instead of tinkering with wood carving or working on old cars...he was pulling people apart, judging from the bloody mess on the rusty, old table in the center of the earthen floor and the rotting limbs hanging from hooks anchored to the ceiling.

There was a stained sheet draped over half of what looked like a Frankenstein monster strapped to a tilted operating table, wearing the same filthy, hospital gowns we'd all been forced into. The thing...abomination...was a collection of different body parts, stitched together. And if that wasn't disturbing enough, the large sack hanging from a chain in a corner of the room twitched as though something big—and alive—was trapped inside it.

But even in the face of all the abhorrent evil, it was a cabinet, centered against the far back wall, that drew my eyes.

And, of course, Billie noticed.

She flashed a wicked smile as her fingers tightened on my arms, and she marched me over to the cabinet. "You can feel her, can't you, Phoenix?"

My eyes slid to meet Billie's.

I didn't speak.

The Father ghoul, meanwhile, was circling Lizzie as she stood stiffly, trembling slightly whenever he got too close. Her fists were clenched tight to her sides, and I could only pray she still had the lighter pressed hard in her palm.

"Daddy!" Billie snapped. "*No biting*!"

I flinched, and my eyes darted to Lizzie.

The old ghoul had his jaw wide, and his thick tongue dangled like a dopey dog. He hunched his shoulders and backed away from Lizzie a few paces. He looked at Billie, wounded and whimpering.

She rolled her eyes to the ceiling. "You chain her to that wall and go wait in your den!" Then she smiled sweetly at Lizzie. "Don't worry, Lizzie; I'll get to you in a moment." She turned her attention back to me, her emerald eyes shining yellow in the low lantern lights. "This is it, Phoenix. The moment I've been waiting for since I first met you."

I snorted with a downturned smile. "I'd say bite me, but you would."

Billie grinned. "You're smart, Phoenix. Crafty. But I'm smarter."

"Well, looks to me like you've pretty much lost. I mean, Sidney burned *everything*. The only ones left are you, that crazy old creature you've got horse whipped over there, and then the mayor..." I snickered. "Not much to work with, is it?"

"This wasn't about anything other than you. I told you, Phoenix. I love your heart. And I *want* your heart." Billie pressed her hand to hers. "And I will have your heart."

My stomach twisted uncomfortably. I forced a smirk. "Thanks, but I don't like you like that."

Billie giggled. "I'm going to cut out your heart and stitch it safely inside my chest."

I recoiled.

She giggled again. "You see, the secret to our longevity has been more dark *science* than magic. The dark witch, Adelaide the Pale, showed Gloria Godwin how to replace parts of herself with spares from others. But don't worry, you'll survive. Let me show you..." She pulled me to the side and with one hand clamped around my arm, she opened the cabinet.

It was cursed. The cabinet.

It glowed with a strange, sour, sickly-yellow magic that clouded around the cabinet like smoke rather than sparkled like glitter.

And the cabinet wasn't empty.

Inside, nailed to the backboard, was a witch.

The witch stared out at us with a dead, glassy look in her ice-blue eyes. Her pale skin was sallow and ashen, drawn against her bones. Then she blinked. Her head turned toward me. She inhaled a short little gasp. It was like witnessing a corpse take a breath—freaky. Then her eyelids fluttered. A single tear slipped down her cheek.

Billie gave me a little nudge, her hand on my arm never weakening. "This is Persephone Thomas. Now, she may not look a day over twenty, but she's actually over a hundred. And after I eat her, you'll take her place." Billie's eyes glittered hungrily as they moved over my face, but I couldn't look away from Persephone.

I blinked back tears as they blurred my vision. "*What have you done to her?*"

"Aww, Phoenix, I thought you were over story time!" Billie laughed and shrugged. "Well, the Mother knew she needed to give the Father *something* to play with...to keep his mind from devolving too far beyond her reach..." Billie shook her head in disgust. "It's the men. They just don't have the mental capacity to keep up with us." Billie shrugged. "But anyways—what better being for him to play with than a witch that won't die no matter how much you cut into her?"

My eyes moved from Persephone to Billie. My lip curled in disgust. "He *tortures* her?"

Billie bit her lip on a smile. "Think of it as an endless game of Operation. How do you think the Mother has been able to live for centuries?" Billie shook her head at me as though I were a silly little girl.

I stood, staring at the witch nailed to the cabinet, stunned stupid at the horror of it all. Then Billie tugged me toward a work-table off to the side. It was covered with bottles of herbs and jars of spell ingredients and in the center was an old Book of Shadows. A dark tome. Thick as three Bibles. I flinched away from it, averting my eyes from the evil emanating off the pages, leaking into the air like a poisonous gas.

"A long, long time ago...the witch, Adelaide the Pale, sailed across the ocean and settled here with Mother, Gloria Godwin. Adelaide's most trusted servant. Together, they controlled the town, luring unsuspecting young women to the Blood Farm. You see, Adelaide the Pale was a powerful, dark witch who had developed an immortality spell for herself...but, of course, it came at a price. The blood of the innocent."

I scoffed. "Well, that's not a cliche or anything, is it?"

Billie smiled. "Aw, Phoenix, you know I love a good cliche." She licked her lips hungrily before she continued, "Now, long before this, back when they'd lived in Germany, Adelaide had experimented on Gloria to prolong Gloria's lifespan to ensure Adelaide'd never be without her. But, no matter what she did, her spell wouldn't work on a ghoul...then after years of failed experiments, she discovered something else that would. Something as simple as science, laced with a little dark magic. Black magic organ transplants." Billie snickered. "The Mother always said that

Adelaide the Pale was the inspiration for Mary Shelley's *Franken-stein*. But then...Adelaide grew tired of Gloria rooting around graves and eating the dead. It was behavior far beneath a servant of hers. So, Adelaide encouraged Gloria to eat fresh meat. Alive meat. And Gloria thrived. So, Gloria tried to teach this new way of thinking to her beloved sister, Brunhilde. With Brunhilde, Gloria wanted to create a new clan of ghoul, a clan to be proud of. But Brunhilde couldn't stomach it. And she decided to leave shortly after Adelaide and Gloria settled Watertown. Brunhilde separated from the clan, and Gloria gifted her a bit of property with the promise that she'd leave her alone—and she did—until the towns-people were out for blood of their own. They needed *someone* to blame for all the missing townsfolk..."

I snorted. "So, Phin was right. You freaks needed a scapegoat, so you had the town turn on Brunhilde. Burn her to death for your crimes." I shook my head in disgust. "Yeah, Gloria sure loved her sister."

Billie smiled. "It wasn't just Brunhilde that proved to be a problem for the new clan—the male ghouls...weren't taking well to the new dietary changes. The fresh meat was giving the *females* strength and power, but—"

"Don't you mean psychopathy?"

"Well," Billie smirked. "You've seen the state of my Father... Gloria realized the need for an outlet for the males...something they could play with that would be dead enough to sate their primal urges but living enough to be *civilized*."

"Dead *enough*?" I blinked. They were nuts. Bonkers. Completely.

"Fortunately, in 1916, a pair of hunters came to Watertown to investigate the missing girls. And they hunted down Adelaide the Pale, but before the hunters could take her head, she sealed one of them in that cabinet. And what a pleasant surprise it was for us to find that the hunter she'd caught was a witch in disguise."

Billie pulled me back to the cabinet. She forced my hand

against the inside of the door. The sickly-yellow magic wisped around my skin as my hand passed through it.

"You stay here...I've got one more surprise for you." Billie hurried over to the body bag dangling from a chain in the nearest corner. I tried to move, but the curse held me fast to the cabinet door.

My eyes shifted to the witch.

Her lips trembled into a twitch of a smile. She blinked slowly in greeting.

"Can't you cast your way out of here?" I whispered softly so only she could hear. "Is the curse that strong?"

Her eyes spilled down her cheeks, and she smiled weakly. "No. It isn't strong. A child could break through this spell. It's merely traces left from Adelaide the Pale. Not strong at all.

"Then why—"

"It's the visterium." The witch looked down at her chest, at the chain hanging low between her collarbones. There was a thin, metal charm, curving like half of a heart. Mine stopped at the sight of it.

I'd seen that charm before.

I was wearing it.

# HERE'S TO NEVER GROWING UP

"The visterium acts like a magic blocker."

My brain blurred. I could barely hear her whispers. The metal blocked magic.

"And these—"

My eyes moved from the hooked metal charm at her neck to her hands nailed to the back of the cabinet. She wiggled her fingers around the nine-inch nails hammered through her palms. "—make taking it off impossible."

I shifted my gaze to Billie. While we'd been whispering, Billie had dragged the body bag across the dirt effortlessly. She didn't even bother to hide her inhuman strength any longer. "I was going to eat him myself..." Billie tugged the giant sack like it was an empty sleeping bag and shook out the contents. "But when I realized his blood is unclean...I had to come up with a different plan." She tossed the bag aside as Cole crumpled to the ground.

I stiffened.

His whole body was limp.

His eyes were closed.

"Don't worry. He's not dead yet." Billie smiled sweetly as she ruffled his thick, dark hair. "He's a gift for the Father. You know, considering you stole the boy *I* loved, I figured I might as well return the favor."

"What?" I mumbled stupidly as my fingers found the hook of metal at my neck.

"*Sidney*!" Billie screamed, so suddenly, so violently, I flinched.

My fingers slipped on the charm.

Billie snatched Cole up by the throat and lifted him like a limp marionette up to her face. She pressed a kiss into his cheek.

From the opposite wall, Lizzie scoffed in disgust. "Sidney died because of *you*, Billie!" Lizzie shouted. "His blood is on your freaky, cat-clawed hands!"

Billie sighed heavily. Her eyes rolled to the ceiling, and she dropped Cole, who crumpled in a pile at her feet. Her eyes slid sideways to look at Lizzie. "You always have to have all the attention, don't you, Elizabeth Tran?" Then Billie grinned. "That's fine." She shrugged and turned to face Lizzie from across the room. "I'll deal with you first."

Lizzie's dark eyes glittered wickedly. A snarky smirk pierced her cheek. "*Eat me, you freak.*"

Billie roared; her human teeth sank into her gums. Stubby, yellow canines popped out one by one. Her jaw stretched, distorting her features into the hideous monster she was, and she dropped to the ground. With impossible speed, she scurried across the dirt. Her limbs bent at crude angles like a spider, she skittered up to meet Lizzie. She lunged for her. Her claws ripped into Lizzie's legs as she crawled up to her torso, jaws wide.

But Lizzie was ready for her.

As Billie leaned in to bite off her face, Lizzie flicked the lighter and set her ablaze.

In the same moment, I yanked the chain over my head and flung it to the other end of the room.

Billie skittered backwards, away from Lizzie, clutching her burning face in her curved, clawed hands. She hissed and yipped as she scratched at her face.

I didn't even hesitate. I felt it. My magic. There. Just as it always had been.

A tickle of a smile twitched at my lips.

I heated my magic in my hand, separating myself from the cabinet easily.

I stood with the cabinet at my back, feet planted firmly in the dirt floor. I clenched my fingers, one hand over the other, and pooled the orange glitter into a magic fire that burned bright in my palm.

As though she sensed more heat, Billie sprang to her feet and whirled around. Her face was charred and blackened, completely unrecognizable as the blonde, athletic beauty I'd known.

But her ghoulish teeth were unmistakable.

She opened her mouth in a broad grin.

Then she lunged, her claws spread wide, curved like blades.

I twisted my wrist and blasted the fire in her face like a flamethrower.

By the time I dropped my hands and the fire disappeared, Wilhelmina Godwin was nothing but a pile of ash on the earthen floor. My chest rose and fell with quickened breath. Then I remember the Father. I glanced toward his hole. His eyes burned like yellow lights in the darkened burrow. He'd seen everything.

I pulled my wand out of my hair, pointed it at his eyes, and I sent a shot of fire into his face. The entire burrow went up in flames, burning a blackened hole in the corner of the room. As the flames died and disappeared, I slipped my wand back into my hair as I exhaled the breath I'd been holding and closed my eyes.

Almost done.

I dropped down to check on Cole. He seemed okay. He was breathing, at least. And his heartbeat was steady.

"They might've given him something," Persephone murmured from the depths of the cabinet. I laid him out on his back, so his body wasn't so uncomfortably crumpled. I went to Lizzie next and broke her chains with a simple magic touch. The lighter still crushed in her palm, she grasped her wrist with the other. "You couldn't have done all that earlier?"

I snorted and shook my head, slightly dazed. I went back to the cabinet for Persephone. I reached for the charm at her neck, but she flinched away from me. Then she met my eyes with a strong, steady gaze. Her lips trembling on her forced smile. "As soon as I leave this cabinet, I will start to age..." Tears streamed down her face and spilled onto her mouth. She licked her lips and continued, her words trembling, "And I will die."

"But—"

She took a breath, and a warmth strengthened her smile. "I don't expect you to understand...but my mother and I—and her mother before her—were Visteri. Witches in service of the Visteri Valkyrie. That means we took a sacred vow to sacrifice our magic in service of the Visteri Valkyrie. And I'd appreciate it if I could die as I lived."

I narrowed my eyes, brow crinkled in confusion. I didn't have time for this. I opened my mouth to argue, but Persephone tried again. "That charm you tossed off your neck? It is the other half of mine. Together they make a Visteri Heart. One for mother. One for daughter. When my mother died, I had both pieces. Adelaide recognized the visterium at once. Visterium is a rare metal, forged by angelic fire and tempered in angel tears. It is known to many practiced in the dark arts for it is capable of destroying all evil. And if you would return it to me, before you take me out of here, I would be at peace."

"I can't just let you die!" I blurted out angrily.

"My dear girl, I'm old. My husband is long dead by now. I've been in this cabinet for decades. Bathed in dark magic. Dissected, over and over." She blinked rapidly, overcome by the memories. "And I want nothing more than to rest. Please let me do it in peace."

Lizzie came up behind me with the necklace in hand. I shifted away from the wretched thing. Lizzie reached into the cabinet and slipped it over Persephone's head. The two pieces clinked together over her thin chest like magnets, forming a heart.

Persephone closed her eyes and smiled. *"Thank you."*

I gritted my teeth. Holding my palm flat against one nail, I drew it out with the force of my magic. Then the other. Before I released her from the cursed cabinet, Persephone met my eyes. "Wait. There's something you should know about the Dark One..."

I paused, uncertain I'd heard her correctly. "The Dark One?" I repeated stupidly.

Persephone blinked in answer. "She came here—"

"She came *here*? When?" I looked around wildly as though a supreme leader of darkness might jump at us from the shadows.

"She came here for Adelaide the Pale's spellbook..."

I glanced over at the worktable on which sat the wicked tome. "It's there—I can see it, Persephone, it's—"

She shook her head. "I heard her speaking with the Mother. The Dark One has chosen her next apprentice. She came here for the spellbook Adelaide had drafted during her apprenticeship centuries ago. And now that the Dark One has it, she has begun her search for the key to unleashing the Devil from Hell."

"But—"

Persephone winced. "I don't know any more than that. But you must remember...the Mother is a ghoul...a shapeshifter...a master of deception...do not trust anything you see...or anything you hear..."

I bit my tongue on frustrated questions, nodded my understanding, and waited for her consent to lift her from the cabinet.

Then Persephone smiled and jutted her chin forward; her whole body, her whole being, unburdened, radiating a calmness I couldn't begin to understand.

Obediently, I waved my hands, and Persephone was surrounded by bright, shimmering, orange light. My magic lifted her from the cabinet and floated her through the air. I wouldn't let her touch the dirty ground. I kept her in the warm aura of magic, bright and sparkling, as her soft skin wrinkled and her hair paled and thinned. And I held her safe in my magic until I saw the life leave her in a small sigh of relief. Then I laid her down gently beside Cole. I slapped at the tears streaking my face and muttered, "Let's go."

And Lizzie and I ran down the left tunnel to find the Mother.

She was waiting for me.

Wearing my sister's face.

My fingers clenched at my sides as the anger raged through my body. Orange magic burned around my hands, glittering in sparkles of bright flame. How many of the ghouls had bitten off a piece of her?

I stepped slowly into the circular cavern. My eyes flickered around the earthen room. It could've been a cozy little den, if not for all the half-dead bodies hanging from chains like meat on hooks. I saw Seraphina first. With Logan beside her. They were hanging suspended by their wrists, IVs connected to their necks, draining them dry. How much longer did they have? I'd wasted so much time.

But I'd found them. All of them.

Victor. His wife. Agatha and her two sisters. Seraphina. Logan. Scott Tyler. And Mary Tran.

The Mother smiled Seraphina's gentlest smile as I drew closer. I slowed and stopped only yards from where the Mother stood in the center of the room. My eyes shifted upwards as I felt the familiar hum of magic in my bones.

We were standing beneath the opening of another witching well.

Beneath the Blood Farm.

Lizzie came up behind me. She let out a little gasp at the sight of her sister. She grabbed my shoulder and squeezed tight. Lizzie wanted to run for her, but she was waiting for my direction. Then she whispered, "This is where Stuart dragged me down. Through a hidden hole in the Blood Farm floor."

Eyes on the Mother, I snapped my fingers. One by one, each IV needle sparkled with orange magic dust and slipped from each neck, dangling uselessly in the air. It was over. And the Mother knew it. So why was she smiling?

As though she could hear my thoughts, the Mother bowed her head ever so slightly. "The Dark One said you'd be the end of things, Phoenix Grey. I just didn't realize the end would come so soon."

I hesitated. I wanted to laugh it off. But after what Persephone had said, my interest was piqued. "What would a ghoul know about the Dark One?" I gave an unimpressed smirk. "Aside from what you've seen in Seraphina's memories."

"Much more than your mother ever dared to tell the two of you." The Mother smiled. "Adelaide the Pale was a disciple of the Dark One. And I was Adelaide's pet. People tend to confide in their pets, don't they? Especially lonely women like Adelaide." She nodded almost sadly and held out her arms wide. "Go ahead, Phoenix Grey. Burn your sister alive. You'll have to kill her in the end. This will be good practice."

I closed my hands into fists. The fire vanished. "What are you talking about?"

"My beloved Wilhelmina was wrong about many things...but she was right about one thing: there is something special about you, Phoenix Grey." The Mother pursed her lips into a thoughtful smirk. "Perhaps I can spill a few secrets...but I must warn you, Phoenix, secrets are like blood. Once spilt, they leave a stain that is hard to remove..."

I scowled darkly and put my hands out, one over the other. Magic pooled in my palm.

"Very well. I see you've run out of patience. I will speak fast." A small smile twitched in the corner of her mouth. "There's a reason Seraphina Grey is a witch without magic. There is a reason why Seraphina Grey has influence over grims. And there is a reason why the St. Claire boy has cursed blood. And it all has to do with the prophecy."

"The prophecy?"

The Mother smiled slyly. "What kind of end of times would it be if there wasn't a prophecy? It has become a requirement, hasn't it?"

I inclined my head ever so slightly. The magic flame burning in my palm flickered. I couldn't keep my face straight. She'd surprised me.

And she knew it.

The Mother grinned broadly. "Seraphina didn't tell you about that, did she? About the grim at the lake house that she ordered away. She doesn't know why the grim listened to her...but I do. I could see it in her memories. And I knew what it meant." The Mother ran her fingers through the honey-blonde hair that wasn't hers. "The boy with cursed blood and horrific visions unaffected by somnum. The witch without magic who can control a grim. *I understood everything*." She scoffed. Her lip curled nastily. "After all, I hadn't groveled like a dog at the feet of Adelaide the Pale for centuries for nothing. I'd picked up enough knowledge; I'd heard enough of the whispers. And as soon as you stormed Gossamer House this evening, I sent word to the Dark One. *And told her everything*." She ran her tongue across her teeth and bit her lip on a smirk.

Fear trickled up and down my arms. The magic fire in my hand died. I swallowed, my tongue dry in my mouth. "What did you tell her? Why doesn't Seraphina have magic? What's wrong with Cole's blood? *What did you tell her?*"

The Mother smiled, a wicked, greedy smile. Then she bowed her head. "You may have destroyed my family, Phoenix Grey. My legacy. But believe me when I tell you...I will burn in peace knowing that you will burn in torture in the end."

I inhaled sharply at the ominous words.

"What's wrong with Cole?" I demanded again before I could think of a clearer question.

The Mother smiled again, this time almost kindly, and she shook her head. Then she took a step forward, and another, closing the distance between us until she was so close I could reach out and touch her. Then slowly, she lifted her hands to her face, which was my sister's. Her claws extended and peeled off the flesh from her bones, chunks of wet meat ripping and slapping to the ground in red ribbons. I had to look away. I couldn't stomach seeing Seraphina—real or not—torn to pieces in front of my face. When she was done shedding, I looked back. It wasn't the mayor I'd known, the one who was wearing an old lady's face held up with plastic surgery.

It was the *real* Mother. The old woman from Cole's vision.

Leathery and clumpy. Darkened, sunken eyes. Swollen lips. White, stringy hair. Glassy eyes, blinking blind, her teeth sunk into her gums. Then a second set descended. Stained. Stubby. Sharp.

Then her face scrunched into a snarl.

And I was ready.

Magic fire licked my fingers, and I put my hand to her cheek. Her head erupted in flames that rushed down the length of her, setting her ablaze like a bonfire. Her teeth bared, and her hands reached for me, clawing and scratching as she shrieked and howled.

Lizzie and I stepped back, and we stared blankly at the Mother. She sank to her knees, her ghoulish teeth still biting at the flames as she slowly melted into a puddle of meat, oozing into the dirt at our feet.

It was over.

There was a groan from the edge of the cavern. My heart leapt into my throat. The kids. I went to Mary first. I touched her little cheek and smoothed back her light, golden hair as I unlocked her chains. Her eyelids fluttered, opening slightly as she sank to the ground. I bent down with her and hugged her tight for a moment, breathing in the sweet smell of her honey-blonde hair.

I found her.

I had her.

Finally.

I waved Lizzie over. Dazed from shock, she stumbled forward. Her shoulders caved underneath the weight of her emotion as she made her way over to us, her eyes flooded with tears. I pulled Lizzie down and pressed Mary safely into her arms.

I smiled, my eyes blurred, and I pushed up to my feet to help the others.

3 1

GRAND THEFT AUTO / WHERE'S
YOUR BOY

Once we made it out of the ghoul tunnels, I called Keirian, who convinced Heather Meeks to get ready for some house guests. We raided Phin's bag of all her potions. The girl came prepared. In turns, we slapped the bungle-weed on the road rash and torn feet and forced Phin's bloodroot potion down every throat to replenish the blood lost. Then we took everyone home. Well, I did. I was the only one safe to drive because I hadn't had to take any bloodroot. Phin's bloodroot mixture was a powerful blood cure, but with a strong side effect of drowsiness. The lot of them would sleep for the next 24 hours, at least. And no one managed to wait until we got back into bed.

By the time we'd helped the Wollstonecrafts into their house, and then drove to the Meekses' and walked Lizzie and Mary and little Scott Tyler up into the spare bedroom, and finally headed toward the motel, the three of them were all asleep. Phin slumped over in the passenger seat, her cheek smushed against the window, her shallow breath fogging up the glass. The boys flopped over each other sideways in the back like little kids passed out on the final trek of a long road trip. And somebody was snoring...and it very well could've been Phin.

I smiled to myself as I drove down the road, the soft morning light shimmering like glitter on the fog.

There was a lightness in my heart.

I'd done it.

I'd brought Mary Tran home to her sister.

And saved Scott Tyler.

And Agatha and her family.

But I didn't want to think about Sidney.

Or Justine.

Or Persephone.

It was too hard. Too depressing to think of the losses in the face of so much good. No. This morning, I was going to count my blessings because there were so many. Enough to keep me busy for the day, anyway. And as I pulled into a motel parking space, I switched off the van, rested my hands on the wheel and breathed in.

With a little magic, I managed to haul the three of them one by one into the motel room, tucking them in not nearly as neatly as Phin would've managed, but nice enough. Then I curled up next to my sister in the bed in the midmorning of early afternoon and clicked on the TV. And I spent the whole day snuggled against my sleeping sister, watching reruns of the old show about the witch and her uptight husband. But when it started to get dark, and my eyes started to droop, instinctively, I reached for Icarus.

But Icarus hadn't come back yet.

And, in the cold absence he'd left at my side, I remembered what the Mother had said as I drifted off into a restless sleep. She'd told the Dark One about Seraphina and Cole. And the Dark One had told her I was 'the end of things.' What did that mean? And what was wrong with Cole? Something so 'unclean,' Billie didn't dare to eat him. What darkness did he have inside him? And how could we get it out? What curse stained his blood? And how could I break it?


I woke up early the next morning to the smell of vinegar drenched french fries. They had snuck out and brought me back a gift of snack-bar-style, salty, fatty goodness. And I was happy to accept it with a wide smile and an empty stomach.

"You did good, Grey."

I grinned broadly at Logan as I stuck out my chin and shoveled more fries into my face. "Well, I didn't want to brag—it's nice to hear you finally admit it." I munched my mouthful and dunked another handful of fries into the mayonnaise cup. "I totally saved your butt."

Logan glanced at me sideways as his jaw tightened begrudgingly in tight-lipped tolerance. "Don't push it."

I chuckled happily and dropped onto the bed beside Phin. I leaned my head into the hollow of her neck and smiled up at her. "And what do you have to say, hmmm?"

Seraphina's eyes slid from the laptop screen propped up by her knees to meet mine. She arched an eyebrow. The corner of her mouth twitched as she struggled to hide her smirk. "I have to say: I hope you learned something from this."

I sat back, sinking into my pillow, and crossed my arms as I nodded. "Sure did."

"Something *aside* from the fact that you're awesome..." Seraphina grinned despite herself and continued clicking through her internet tabs.

I scrunched up my face as I considered this. I clucked my tongue against the roof of my mouth and shrugged. "Got nothing."

Seraphina groaned and elbowed me in the side. "Phoenix!"

Logan watched us, his stony disapproval hardening the angles of his face.

I laughed. "Okay, fine. I learned not to use my magic as a crutch." I recited robotically as I ticked it off my fingers. "And I learned not to go off without backup and to always ask for help."

Logan scowled. "I hope you did—"

"I learned to never accept someone else's lucky charm." I dug out more fries from my carton and tossed them in my mouth. Around the salty, soft potatoes, I added sincerely, "And I learned that monsters don't always behave in the ways they're supposed to…"

Seraphina frowned thoughtfully as she eyed me. "What do you mean?"

"I mean, the Godwins were like completely batty, straight-jacket crazy, even by ghoul standards. But Victor didn't want any part of it. He left, started a family, and kept his nose clean…or as clean as you can keep it, digging graves and caring for your mentally scarred, traumatized wife. And Sidney—" I trailed off. I couldn't finish. I shoveled more fries into my mouth and chewed. I hadn't thought about Sidney since yesterday. And I hadn't planned on thinking of him again for a while…not until I could without my eyes burning.

Seraphina slapped her hand to mine and squeezed. "Nix, I'm sorry you went through that alone."

I shrugged and dug for more fries.

The door of the motel room opened. Cole popped his head inside. He nodded toward Logan. "Ready?"

Logan smacked his knees and stood with a quick, "Yup." He reached for his bag and slung it over his shoulder before trudging toward the door.

My eyes narrowed. "Where are you guys going?"

Logan paused, his hand on the door. He looked back over his shoulder. "Nowhere."

I sat up straight on the bed. "Seriously?"

Logan flashed a sarcastic smile. "Seriously."

I looked at Phin. She frowned. "Cole?"

He exchanged a grim glance with Logan. He pushed his hand through his dark hair. "We're going to finish the job."

My heart sputtered as I choked on a fry. I pressed my fist into my chest and swallowed. Then I coughed. "Excuse me —*what?*"

Logan sighed heavily. He glanced at Cole and inclined his head toward the room. Cole rolled his eyes, trudged obediently back inside the room, and dropped into a chair. Logan shut the door and turned to face us girls, his jaw tight and his eyes hard.

"You heard him." Logan didn't flinch. He didn't even look sorry. "We're finishing the job."

I stood slowly from the bed, my hands held up. "Wait, wait, wait. Finishing the job?"

Logan snorted. "Repeating it over and over won't change the words, Grey."

I glared at him and gritted my teeth. "The job *is* finished. Every last Godwin ghoul was burned. I set the entire tunnel network ablaze. Sealed up the hole in the school. Case closed."

"Not every Godwin."

The cold look on his face made me shiver. Before I could speak, Phin inclined her head. "Are you talking about Victor? He tried to help us, Logan."

Logan's tan cheeks darkened ever so slightly. He shifted uncomfortably under the weight of Seraphina's words. He shoved a hand through his sandy hair as he tried to explain. "He's a ghoul."

I scrunched up my face, stricken by his callousness. I stared at him, eyes wide.

"That's the job." Logan shrugged. "We hunt monsters. We kill monsters."

"So, what about his daughters, then?" I challenged. "You're going to let them go...it's the same—"

"Never said I was." Logan smiled coolly.

Cole had the decency to look uncomfortable.

"No." I shook my head, frowning as I looked at each of them in turn. "No. You aren't 'finishing' any of them."

The boys exchanged another glance as though they'd talked about this. As though they knew this would happen. Expected me to throw a temper tantrum, like I was too immature to understand the reality of the job. My blood boiled hot. My stomach clenched tight.

Logan bent his head and looked at me with a stupid, patient smile on his stupid face. "Listen, no one said this job would be easy, but—"

I grinded my teeth against the hateful words rising inside me. My face burned, and my fists tightened. I opened my mouth, but before I could start shouting, Seraphina interrupted Logan. "But, Logan, that's *not* the job."

All of us looked at her, the boys in surprise, me in gratitude. She stood from the bed, her arms across her chest and her chin high as she shook her head, her blonde hair shimmering as it swayed.

Logan shifted where he stood. He tilted his head back slightly as he studied her. "What do you mean?"

The two of them stood there like some sort of Greek legend where Bigfoot faces off with an Amazonian warrior. Although Phin was tall, Logan still had a good couple inches on her, and he stood up straight to illustrate that fact.

She didn't care. She lifted her chin higher and met his gaze, silver to gold-speckled green. "You always say the job is killing monsters, saving people—"

Logan scoffed with an indulgent smile. "Yeah, Sam, *people.* They aren't—"

Phin didn't flinch. "They aren't monsters, Logan. Monsters *hurt* people. Living people. Or do you agree with your friend, Frankie?"

Logan's face burned dark red. "She's not my—"

"Anything that has a hint of magic blood, anything other than strictly human, isn't 'natural' and needs to be—what was it she said? How'd she put it so articulately? '*Snuffed out?*' No matter how they live their life, what *choices* they make, what they do—"

Logan held up a hand, clearly flustered. "Sam, I—"

"Well?" Seraphina prompted icily.

In the corner, Cole snorted. Logan's eyes slid to his left to glare at him sideways. Cole hid his smirk in the palm of his hand.

Seraphina wasn't amused. "Because according to that...that *girl*, I'm not human—"

My brow furrowed. "Wait, what girl?" I whispered loudly, eyes darting curiously between the two of them. "The witch hunter?"

Phin ignored me and kept going, "—and I know you like to pretend that I'm 'normal,' but I am a *witch*, Logan. So, do you agree with Frankie? Do you think I should be 'snuffed out,' too?"

Logan's jaw flexed. He exhaled deeply, his nostrils flaring. "You know I don't think that."

"Then leave that family alone!" I snapped, angrily. All the fury bottled up came steaming out of me. "It's no different."

Logan glared at me. "It is different."

I glared right back. "No, it's not!"

"How?" Phin challenged, her hands on her hips. "How is it different?"

Logan turned back to her, his whole demeanor shifted from impatient annoyance at me, to flustered embarrassment underneath the silver doe-eyes of my sister.

"Seraphina, you haven't killed anyone," Cole murmured softly from his spectator seat.

I scoffed and cocked an eyebrow at Cole. "And Agatha has? From what I can recall, Cole, she helped us escape from the Gossamer House basement."

Logan rolled his eyes and rounded on me. "The Godwins ate fresh meat. They *killed people* to eat. Are you trying to tell me that the whole time Agatha was with them she wasn't eating? Ghouls eat people to live. She looks alive to me."

"Agatha wasn't with them that long. They kidnapped her because her father was trying to stop them! And Victor eats dead people. *Already* dead," I added hastily.

"He didn't always, though. Did he?" Logan snapped.

I threw my arms up in the air. "He hasn't for thirty years, at least!" I turned to Cole. "How can you not get the difference?"

Cole covered his face in his hands.

I scoffed in disbelief. "Victor tried to help us! All of us and all those kids!"

Logan's jaw pulsed as he gritted his teeth. "You don't understand because you're new to this...but what happens if we walk away?"

"Happily ever after," I quipped with a smirk.

Logan rolled his eyes, his face hard and his eyes haunted. "And then in a year...maybe two...maybe ten—" Logan shrugged, his mouth downturned. "Agatha decides Grandma Godwin didn't have such a bad idea...fresh meat tastes a lot better than rotting, decayed scraps off a dead guy—God knows, even I get that. So, she grabs some baby out of its crib and eats its face off. Or she decides, you know what? She'd like to see better, so she grabs some little kid and scoops out their eyeballs. Or, shoot, she'd like to live forever just like Grandma Godwin. Why not snag a new heart?"

I scowled. "That's a lot of maybes to fit your theory, Logan."

"No. Forget the maybes. I want you to tell me!" Logan shook his head, his voice rising with his temper. "How are you going to feel, Phoenix, tell me?" He stepped forward, his chin high as he jutted his thumb at the door behind him. "How are you going to feel if Victor starts snatching little kids on their way home from school?"

I looked away.

The edges of Logan's face softened slightly as did his voice. "I *know* how you'd feel, Phoenix, because like it or not, you and me? Just give me a box of cheap hair dye, and we're pretty much the same person. Give or take a few inches."

I snorted angrily and crossed my arms over my chest. I glared daggers into the dingy carpet.

Phin cleared her throat and murmured gently, "But, Logan, don't you think it's possible that they could choose to be different from their family? That they will *continue* to choose to be different? Ghouls naturally have no inclination to eat fresh meat…"

Logan sighed and massaged his temples. My eyes flickered between the two of them. If anyone could change Logan's mind, it'd be Seraphina. I chewed my cheek as I watched her bite her lip.

Logan winced in the face of her sweet, doe-eyed stare. "Listen, Sam—"

"You haven't ever let something live?" she continued in her soft, gentle way. "Decided, maybe things aren't always black and white." She smiled slightly. "That if you looked closer, things might just be silver?"

Logan's nostrils flared. His eyes searched her face.

I held my breath.

"Sure…once." Logan licked his lips and pursed them as he nodded his head. "One time I let something live, and you know what, Phoenix?" His eyes found me. "I went back six months later to a dead baby. A two-year-old kid, ripped apart by her own mother. *Because I didn't finish the job.*"

I flinched. His eyes shined, but he didn't break. I tossed up my hands. "But—"

"No." Logan held up a hand, his lip curled as he gave a final, hard shake of his head. "It sucks. But this is the job. Keeping people safe. Finishing what needs to be finished. If you can't handle it, you both can go back to Nile." He smacked Cole's shoulder. "Let's go."

I stared, mouth agape, stunned speechless in the face of his dismissive anger. Silently, I watched Cole push off the table. Without a word or backwards glance, he headed out the door. And Logan slammed it behind him so hard the little window above the table rattled in its frame.

My shoulders slumped as I blinked at the door.

Seraphina sighed and made her way around the bed to squeeze my shoulders. "I'm sorry, Nix. I tried."

My eyes blurred, and I sniffed. "You did." I gritted my teeth. "But I didn't. Come on."

I snatched my wand off the table, stabbed it through my topknot, and yanked open the door.

"What are you going to—"

"No idea. All I know is, I'll hex his face to his butt before I'll let him kill anybody that doesn't deserve it." I shook the door as I held it open for her. "You with me?"

Phin grinned. "Always."


The boys took both of them.

The truck and the van.

They were both gone.

I stood stunned and staring stupidly into the empty parking spaces. Seraphina came up behind me and bumped into my shoulder.

"They took both of them." My fists clenched at my sides. "*They took both of them!*" I stomped my sneaker into the sidewalk and kicked the curb stop. Bad idea. I cried out in pain, hopping up and down, muttering and cursing under my breath.

Phin gripped my shoulder. "Nix, Nix, calm down. You're hissing and spitting worse than Icarus!"

I snapped my head around to glare at her.

She didn't flinch. She squeezed my shoulder and looked deep into my eyes. "It's going to be okay!"

I stopped bouncing and slapped my hands at my sides. "How? How is it going to be okay? When Mr. MopeyPants and that— that overgrown Wookiee are going to murder those little girls! That whole family!" I gritted my teeth. "He drives like a maniac...probably there by now...I swear I'll hex his..."

Seraphina's mouth twitched as she struggled not to smile. Her steady, silver eyes held my gaze, and she spoke slowly, "Phoenix... you're a witch, aren't you?"

"So?" I snapped, shrugging in defeat. "I can't fly without a broomstick, and I can't vanish like Mama—"

Seraphina smirked and pushed me in front of her to survey the parking lot. She waved her arm at the handful of cars in front of us. "Take your pick."

I blinked. Then I burst out laughing. I elbowed Phin hard in the ribs. "Mustang."

We ran across the parking lot, and while Phin kept a lookout, I pressed a hand on the car door. The locks clicked open, and we hopped inside.

Phin cranked up the radio as I jammed my foot down on the accelerator. The car screeched and roared out of the parking lot, down the backroads, skidding into the turns, and slamming into every pothole until we jerked to a stop in front of the Wollstonecrafts' patchwork farmhouse.

Logan's truck was in the driveway. So was the van. My heart stalled. Were we too late? I tried to catch my breath as I kicked open the Mustang door and stalked up the weathered porch steps. I ripped my wand out of my hair and held it out low at my side like a knight with her sword. Seraphina ran after me, but she stopped short of the front door. I didn't hesitate. I held out my palm, blasted the door open from the frame, and marched inside the house.

I stopped.

Phin slammed into my back.

I lowered my wand.

Through the archway, I could see into the living room. The two Wollstonecraft girls were scrubbing the floors, while Agatha washed the walls. They turned as one, craning their necks to see out into the hall.

Slowly, I walked through the doorway. My eyes moved over the room. It was clean...or rather...cleaner. They must've been working since they'd woken up from the bloodroot potion.

Agatha dropped her sponge into the bucket. It sloshed soapy water over the sides. She wiped her brow with the back of her small hand. She smiled at me. "You came."

Her sisters stood up.

The taller of the two put her fists on her hips and the shorter folded her arms across her chest. "She's friends with the bad girl." Faster than I could blink, she whipped out a pocketknife and fingered it, her eyes on me.

"I'm not friends with the bad girl." I frowned as I looked between them. "She tricked me."

The smaller girl scoffed, but before she could comment, Cole came through the opposite doorway with his arms full of cleaning supplies. He grinned at the sight of us.

He set the stuff down and waved us over. I eyed the girls with an impatient frown as I moved past them. The bigger one looked like she might jump me the second my back was turned. I glanced over my shoulder, keeping an eye on her and walking slower than Phin liked. Phin prodded me sharply in the back. Repeatedly, until we crossed into the kitchen.

I froze. The kitchen was clean, too. No trash piles. No rotten food or dirty dishes. No bugs or grime.

"I'll be in the living room." Cole clapped me on the back, the force of which sent me stumbling forward.

My eyes moved to the people seated at the table.

I snorted despite myself.

It was Logan.

Logan DeVarney, covered in flour, rolling out a pie, seated beside a short, sturdy woman whose dishwater-blonde hair spilled out of a topknot as she busied about measuring ingredients and dumping them into a big bowl, all the while instructing Logan on how to properly operate the pin.

The woman...

I had to bite my lip to keep my mouth from sagging. It was Mrs. Wollstonecraft. Jillian. Justine's sister.

I studied Logan, trying to decide whether this was some kind of Trojan horse thing...but the look on his face: embarrassment, twinged with genuine curiosity. My nerves were calmed. And I had to wonder if he'd ever—

"Since when do *you* bake?" Phin laughed with delighted disbelief as she stepped out from behind me, her hands on her hips. I snickered. My thoughts exactly.

Logan scowled. His golden cheeks burned a deep burgundy as he muttered something that sounded suspiciously like something about women's work.

Mrs. Wollstonecraft smacked him on the back of the head. "You're almost as bad as my girls. Feral. Wildling. No more. I'm setting things right. Right now." She smiled up at Phin and me. "Logan told me you'd both show up...come, sit, please."

Seraphina's smile lit up the room like new sunshine, and she nearly skipped around the table to help Logan with the pie crust.

I yanked out a chair and plopped down. I couldn't help but stare at Mrs. Wollstonecraft. It was like she'd woken up from a cursed state. She caught my eye and slapped her wooden spoon around the sides of the bowl. "You're wondering what in the world is going on...aren't you?"

I snorted. "A little."

Mrs. Wollstonecraft nodded, her mouth downturned. "I have not been the best mother to my girls. Not the best wife to my husband. And that's on me. But the weight of them watching us. Carrying the burden of knowing and no way to stop the horrors from happening, over and over." She sighed heavily. "I've made so many mistakes." She waved her hand around the freshly scrubbed kitchen. "But they're gone...and that's a start."

I considered this for a moment as I reached my finger into the bowl and scooped out a bit of batter before Mrs. Wollstonecraft had time to crack me with the spoon. I stuck my finger into my mouth and sucked off the apple cinnamon goodness while she watched. She scrunched up her face in amused disapproval and continued to slap at the batter.

I hesitated. Then I reached out to gently touch her arm. "I'm so sorry about your sister, Mrs. Wollstonecraft."

She stiffened and took a sharp breath. Her eyelashes fluttered furiously as she folded her lips together. Then she glanced at me with a sad smile. "She spent her last moments trying to save my little Agatha. To the very end. You know, like Victor, she'd had enough. She started being difficult. Too much trouble for what she was worth. So, Wilhelmina Godwin made sure she knew Agatha was one of the missing to punish her. And, in the end, they took her anyway."

I nodded sadly. "She tried to warn me. She was unbelievably brave. And she loved you so much."

Mrs. Wollstonecraft grinned at that. "She wanted nothing more than to know we were safe. Now we are. And I thank you for that."

*Were* they safe? I glanced across the table at Logan.

There wasn't any sign of aggression or homicidal urges. And he was too preoccupied with crimping the dough and the close proximity of my sister leaning over his shoulder to notice my stare. I smiled slightly at the sight of them.

Then I peeked at Mrs. Wollstonecraft. "Where's Victor?"

She nodded toward the back door. "He's with Deputy Meeks now. They're figuring out how soon he can knock that wretched place down."

"The Blood Farm?" I looked at her in surprise.

Mrs. Wollstonecraft nodded. Her face struggled to find a smile, her eyes haunted. "Once it's gone...Victor says he'll build me a stable, and we can raise horses. But I think maybe just a sea of irises...an ocean of purple in the middle of the forest. For the girls to stumble upon one day when they're running wild in the woods." Mrs. Wollstonecraft's smile crinkled the creases in the corners of her eyes. A couple of tears trickled down her cheeks. "Justine's favorite flowers were irises."

I leaned over the table and put a hand on her shoulder and squeezed. "I think a field of irises would be magical."

Mrs. Wollstonecraft nodded again. Her lip trembled. She shoved the bowl in front of me. "Go on. Get this batter done. Dinner's in a few hours."

I started beating the batter. "You eat early." I grinned. "I like that."

Mrs. Wollstonecraft stood from her chair and pressed a hand on my head. "Most people eat early on Thanksgiving, sweetheart."

I lowered the spoon. I'd forgotten all about Thanksgiving.

"How do you like your potatoes, girls?"

I looked over at Phin, and we exchanged bemused glances. Seraphina bit her lip. Logan's fingers clumsily crimped the dough into the tin as he muttered, "Cheesy, bacon mash are the best."

I turned in my seat. "Potatoes?"

Mrs. Wollstonecraft plucked up a notepad and pencil, and she scribbled a note, her back to me. "Yes, dear. Potatoes. The boys each want them done up in different ways." She turned and leaned against the counter. She glanced up briefly from her notepad. "How do you both take them?"

Seraphina glanced at me with a mischievous glint in her silver eyes. I grinned. Then we said together, "Baked parmesan mashed potatoes, please."

Logan snorted. "Grey, I'm surprised at you...I thought you'd prefer them chipped or fried French."

"Ha. Ha. Ha." I stuck my tongue out at him.

Mrs. Wollstonecraft smiled with a shake of her head. "All right...You take Cole to the store and grab everything on this list. You tell them to put it on Victor Wollstonecraft's tab. Yes?" She tore off the page and slapped the paper onto the table. Then she took the bowl and passed it over to Phin. "Here you are, Seraphina, sweetheart."

Seraphina blushed prettily, tucking her golden hair behind her ears before taking the bowl and giving it a stir.

I stood slowly, hesitating with my hand on the back of my chair. I cast one last glance at Logan. He was completely wrapped up in pie dough and batter...and Phin. His gold-speckled green eyes kept flicking up to her face, a hint of a smile in the corner of his mouth.

Yup. No question. Happily ever after.

I grinned, grabbed the paper, and bounced off to find Cole.

But I'd forgotten about the Mustang.

Cole raked a hand through his hair as we stood on the porch, staring at the car I'd stolen.

I glanced sideways at him with a guilty grin. I shrugged. "It was Phin's idea."

Cole snorted. "Seraphina Grey told you to steal a car?"

I scoffed, eyes wide. "She did! It wasn't *my* idea!"

Cole laughed, a real, belly laugh, bursting from the gut. He nudged my arm. "Come on. Let's bring it back before they notice it's gone." He peeked back at me as he headed for the van, a small smirk on his sweet face. "You wouldn't want to be arrested and have to miss a Thanksgiving dinner."

"Pfft." I waved a dismissive hand and yanked open the driver's side door. "I just saved the children of Watertown. You think they'll arrest me? I bet they'd *give* me the car if I asked. Plus, the only Watertown deputy left alive loves me."

Cole chuckled and shook his head. "I'll see you at the motel."

Luckily, no one had noticed their car was missing. I parked the Mustang in the same spot I found it—roughly. And hopped into the van with a satisfied sigh.

Cole cocked an eyebrow as he shifted the van into reverse.

I grinned. "What?"

Cole shook his head and pulled out of the motel parking lot, headed for the grocery store. We drove in noisy Nirvana silence for a while. But I couldn't keep my mouth shut. I had to ask. I looked over at Cole. "What happened?"

Cole snorted and bit his lip on a smirk. "Phin."

"Phin." I snickered. "Explain?"

Cole sighed heavily. "We got halfway there. Down that long stretch of backroad. And suddenly, he cranks the truck off the road, onto the shoulder, and slams it in park. I pull over behind him and jump out." Cole shrugged. "I thought something was wrong."

I nodded encouragingly as I rifled through the bottom of the van for a snack. I popped a mini bag of chips. "And?"

Cole glanced at me. "You know we're eating dinner in just a few hours..."

I tipped the bag. Chips skidded into my mouth. I spoke through my munching, "Yeah, exactly. *Hours.*" I waved a hand. "Go on."

Cole chuckled. An indulgent smirk crinkled the dimple in his cheek. "Okay, so Logan—he's pacing along the side of the road. His hands on the back of his head like he does. Back and forth. Back and forth. Muttering, cursing under his breath. And I wait. Lean against the truck. Give him a minute. Then he just stops dead, mid-step, and looks at me. *Furious.*" Cole chuckled at the memory. "He is so mad I can almost see the steam coming off his hot head."

I grinned at the thought. "Was his temple throbbing?"

Cole laughed and nodded eagerly. He licked his lips and bit his smile. "So, he's seething, right? Actually *seething*, and he says—he goes, 'Did you see the way she looked at me?'"

My forehead wrinkled as I half smirked, half pouted. "Baww!"

Cole snickered.

"So, what'd you say?" I shook more chips into my mouth.

Cole's dark eyes slid sideways. "Nix..."

I licked the salt of my mouth and pursed my lips into a puppy dog pout. "Aw, come on, Cole! I know you said something..." I grinned wickedly. "It was girlie, wasn't it? All mushy and mopey." I giggled.

"Hey!" Cole held up a finger. "I prefer broody. Much more manly. Dark and mysterious."

I snorted. "Keep telling yourself that." I tossed a pinch of chip crumbs into my mouth. I licked my fingers. "Well?"

Cole sighed heavily. "I told him...that face he saw? That look in her eyes?" Cole cocked an eyebrow at me. "It'd never go away if he killed those little ghoul girls."

I wobbled my lower lip and smacked his arm. "Awww. You *are* Guitar Hero, aren't you?"

Cole's pale cheeks twinged pink. He made a face as he pulled into the store. "What's that supposed to mean?"

I grinned. "It was you, Cole. Not Phin. *You* changed his mind. You made him see that all that glitters is Grey." I scrunched up my face on my smile and studied him for a moment. My eyes blurred, but I blinked it away.

Cole rolled his eyes and shoved the van into park. "You're nuts, Nix."

"And you're a Cry Baby." I snickered. "*Guitar Hero, to the rescue!*" I punched out my fist and did a wicked rendition of 'Free Bird' on an air guitar.


Back at the Wollstonecrafts', we had the best Thanksgiving I could've hoped for on the road so far from home. Logan and Cole argued over which was better, basketball or football, in between shouts at the Patriots to run faster, while Phin read Ella Enchanted aloud to the girls in front of the fireplace, and I cast the book scenes in magic glitter over the flames crackling in the fireplace. And in the background, soft Christmas music played as Victor and Mrs. Wollstonecraft slow danced in the kitchen.

But later that night, back at the motel, everything went wrong.

After we'd all crashed on full stomachs, stuffed with three different kinds of potatoes and way too much turkey—that Logan had politely confirmed was in fact dead *bird* meat—

Cole woke up in the middle of the night.

And he was screaming.

**Thank you so much for reading.**

This story is a lot different from how it began. Originally—it was a vampire story. But then I wanted to make it not so obvious… because you hear 'Blood Farm' and you immediately think vampire. And then I wanted a *Frankenstein* element but with monsters. The first draft even had everyone running around an abandoned hospital instead of the Gossamer House! That didn't work. Hah. But a lot of the names in *Blood Farm* are inspired by *Frankenstein* and Mary Shelley herself. But the biggest *wink*wink*s are nods to *Scream*. And without spoiling the movie, if you saw the references in the book—email me and let me know!

I had so much fun with this story, and I hope you enjoyed reading it!

If you did, let everyone know when you leave a review!

Share your thoughts on Goodreads and/or your preferred book seller.

And don't forget to post a picture!

# WELCOME TO THE NILE UNIVERSE

Sign up for the Courcy Camp newsletter for exclusive (free) early release access to *The First Hunt of Phoenix Grey* at

**cristinecourcy.com/newsletter**

But if newsletters (or eBooks) aren't your thing, pre-order *The First Hunt of Phoenix Grey* at **www.cristinecourcy.com/exclusive-releases** or your preferred book seller!

*Seraphina Grey Summons a Demon*

Book One of the Grey Sisters Saga

### AVAILABLE NOW

A witch without magic. A demon out for blood. A dark family secret. How can teenage witch, Seraphina, solve the mystery and hunt down the demon when she can't even do magic?

*Seraphina Grey and the Carnival of Nightmares*

Book Three of the Grey Sisters Saga

### COMING NOVEMBER 2024

Subscribe to the Courcy Camp newsletter for updates:

**cristinecourcy.com/newsletter**

# ABOUT THE AUTHOR

Hi, I'm Cristine!
I love old sitcoms and slasher films.
When I'm not writing, I'm playing Animal Crossing or Harvest
Moon 64.
When I am writing, I like to write dark fantasy with a light heart.
This means I want to disturb you without leaving you feeling
yucky at the end of the story. In short, I'm inventing a new genre I
like to call 'cozy dark fantasy.'
My books are heavily influenced by my experiences growing up
wild on an island in the middle of the lake.
Almost all the things I write about are inspired by real life...but for
legal purposes— that's a lie.
To read more lies and see photos of the things that *did not* inspire
my writing, sign up for my newsletter at
cristinecourcy.com/newsletter.

Connect with me online:
WWW.CRISTINECOURCY.COM

goodreads.com/cristinecourcy

facebook.com/cristinecourcy

instagram.com/cristinecourcy

threads.net/@cristinecourcy

youtube.com/@cristinecourcy

x.com/cristinecourcy

tiktok.com/@cristinecourcy

amazon.com/author/cristinecourcy

* 9 7 8 1 9 6 2 7 5 3 0 3 6 *